PORTIONS

FROM A

WINE-STAINED

NOTEBOOK

Charles Bukowski

PORTIONS

FROM A

WINE-STAINED

NOTEBOOK

UNCOLLECTED STORIES

AND

ESSAYS, 1944–1990

EDITED AND WITH AN INTRODUCTION BY

David Stephen Calonne

CITY LIGHTS : SAN FRANCISCO

Library of Congress Cataloging-in-Publication Data

Bukowski, Charles.

Charles Bukowski : portions from a wine-stained notebook :
uncollected stories and essays, 1944–1990 /
edited and with an introduction by David Stephen Calonne.

p. cm.

Includes bibliographical references.

ISBN 978-0-87286-496-2 (hardback)

ISBN 978-0-87286-492-4 (paperback)

I. Calonne, David Stephen, 1953– II. Title.

PS3552.U4A6 2008

811´.54—dc22

2008020485

Design and composition by Quemadura

Cover photograph by Linda Lee Bukowski

Visit our website: www.citylights.com

City Lights Books are published
at the City Lights Bookstore
261 Columbus Avenue
San Francisco, CA 94133

CONTENTS

ACKNOWLEDGMENTS

Many people have helped me in the making of this book over the past eight years. Thanks to Ed Fields, University of California at Santa Barbara, Department of Special Collections, Davidson Library for permission to include the unpublished manuscript "Foreword to William Wantling's *7 on Style*" as well as sections from the manuscript of "The L.A. Scene"; Roger Myers, University of Arizona Library, Special Collections; the Interlibrary Loan staff at Eastern Michigan University; and Julie Herrada, Head of the Labadie Collection, Special Collections, University of Michigan, Ann Arbor. Jamie Boran was immensely helpful to me as I began this project back in 2000. Thanks to Abel Debritto of Spain, Bukowski scholar extraordinaire, who brought to my attention several superb and undiscovered stories and essays. Michael Montfort kindly spent time with me in Freiburg, Germany. Many thanks as always to Maria Beye. Elaine Katzenberger at City Lights guided the project with great aplomb. Special thanks to my very smart, very literary, and very professional editor at City Lights Garrett Caples, who made the challenging process of creating this book a very pleasurable experience. Deepest gratitude to Ludwig Wittgenstein, who keeps me clear and high. Finally, special thanks to John Martin for his support and to Linda Lee Bukowski, who gave generously of her time and patiently encouraged me to find just the right home for Hank's work.

INTRODUCTION

Only now, fourteen years after Charles Bukowski (1920–1994) typed his final words, has it become possible to fully fathom his protean creativity. Although primarily known as a poet, he composed a wide variety of prose: short stories, autobiographical essays, introductions to other poets' works, book reviews, literary essays, the famous "Notes of a Dirty Old Man" series, as well as a sequence of "manifestos" on his evolving poetics and aesthetics. He was also a superb letter writer (now partially collected in five volumes) and published six novels: *Post Office* (1971), *Factotum* (1975), *Women* (1978), *Ham On Rye* (1982), *Hollywood* (1989), and *Pulp* (1994). Because Bukowski was so prolific, scholars have been unable to keep up with his pace and there is still no adequate or complete bibliography of his works. This volume demonstrates the richness and variety of his unknown *oeuvre* and contains uncollected as well as previously unpublished stories and essays.[1]

Bukowski's earliest stories—"Aftermath of a Lengthy Rejection Slip" (1944) and "20 Tanks from Kasseldown" (1946)—represent the opposing yet complementary styles which would mark his entire career. "Aftermath" is an imaginative portrait of the quixotic young artist as outsider and clown, while in "20 Tanks" Bukowski is dark and brooding in the tradition of his masters Nietzsche and Dostoyevsky, at the furthest reaches of spiritual solitude, scrawling anguished notes from underground. Yet his originality would be to ultimately combine existential hardness with comic verve into an inimitable "Bukowskian" fusion. Like his nihilistic, philosophizing character, Bukowski was himself a sensitive, tortured, vulnerable person of genius trapped in a small room, but he also possessed a wry sense of humor and was a charming cartoonist in the tradition of another of his literary heroes, James Thurber.

Bukowski made his literary debut at age twenty-four, publishing "Aftermath" in the prestigious *Story*, edited by Whit Burnett and Martha Foley, followed two years later by "20 Tanks" in Caresse Crosby's avant-garde *Port-*

folio, where he appeared alongside Jean Genet, Federico Garcia Lorca, Henry Miller, and Jean Paul Sartre. Yet Bukowski, contrary to myth, not only wrote prose during this period but was also composing poetry. For example, in the Summer 1946 issue of *Matrix*, his first published poem "Hello" appears, as well as the story "The Reason Behind Reason." And in the Fall-Winter 1947 issue of *Matrix*, both the poem "Voice in a New York Subway" and the story "Cacoethes Scribendi" were published. Thus his practice from the beginning was to alternate between poetry, story, and essay, establishing his twin identity as poet and prose writer. This "doubleness" can be discerned in a work written in 1959 but published in 1961, "Portions from a Wine-Stained Notebook," in which Bukowski composes in a hybrid genre outside the categories of prose, poetry, or prose-poetry.

Many of his subsequent writings would appear in an immense variety of "little magazines."[2] Just as the famous birthplaces of Modernism—*Blast, Criterion, Little Review, The Dial, transition*—were central to the promulgation of the masterworks of Ezra Pound, T. S. Eliot, and James Joyce, so too did the literary journals and alternative press—*Trace, Ole, Harlequin, Quixote, Wormwood Review, Spectroscope, Simbolica, Klactoveedsedsteen*—provide outlets for Bukowski's unconventional work. And in the tradition of the great modernists, Bukowski became a militant manifesto writer. In his essay on poetry accompanied by jazz for *Trace* (edited by James Boyer May and published in London), he began to develop aesthetic theories which he would continually refine and expand. Bukowski's style and approach were essentially experimental and as he once declared, "there are not enough readers to understand, enjoy, digest advanced writing."[3]

In one of his strongest manifestos, "In Defense of a Certain Type of Poetry, a Certain Type of Life, a Certain Type of Blood-Filled Creature Who Will Someday Die," he begins to evolve a poetics of the heart, a poetics of tenderness and openness: *it catches my heart in its hands*. Bukowski chose this variation on a line from Robinson Jeffers' poem "Hellenistics" as the title for one of his early books of poetry and it precisely describes his own romantic and spiritual yearnings in our "broken world."[4] Throughout his childhood, Bukowski had been brutally beaten and emotionally abused by his father. Thus the "blood-filled creature" here bears multiple significance: D. H. Lawrence's "blood" or instinct/intuition, primal feeling being wiser than intellect, but also literal blood spilled during Bukowski's agonized sessions of corporal punishment, and finally the blood which would erupt from his body in 1955 when, at age 35, he was taken to the charity ward of the Los Angeles County Hospital and nearly died from a massive alcoholic hemorrhage of his stomach.[5] Thus he would understandably wonder why the official, safe, Establishment literature of the ages had so often been silent about those in the most pain: the victimized, the poor, the mad, the unemployed, the skid row bums, the alcoholics, the misfits, the abused children, the working class. His poetic world, like Samuel Beckett's, is the world of the dispossessed, "the proud thin dying," and he defines himself as a "poetic outlaw"; there can be no safety in a life lived *in extremis* at the edges of madness and death. Bukowski's most intense ire was reserved for the elitist "University boys" who betrayed poetry by playing a safe, neat, clever, professorial game of words devoid of inspiration, who tried to domesticate the sacred barbaric Muse: the disruptive, primal, archaic, violent, inchoate forces of the creative unconscious. Bukowski's art is dedicated to revealing his own bloody stigmata, to dramatizing himself (often humorously) as sacrificial victim in simple, direct, raw, hammered language free of pretense and affectation. As he writes in his unpublished foreword to William Wantling's 7 *On Style*: "Style means no shield at all. Style means no front at all. Style means ultimate naturalness. Style means one man alone with billions of men about."[6]

In several of these manifestos with their at once outrageous and lyrical titles such as "A Rambling Essay on Poetics and the Bleeding Life Written While Drinking a Six-Pack (Tall)" and "Upon the Mathematics of the Breath and the Way," Bukowski explores the relation of writing to the quest for authentic being. He goes to the racetrack to examine Life so he can come home to his "typer" and turn it into Art. Like Henry David Thoreau, he wants to drive life into a corner and find out what is there: no ivory tower aestheticism here. Bukowski sees the making of art as directly related to his own interior evolution and there is as serious a discipline involved in being an artist as there is in becoming a Zen monk. He combines a precise "mathematics" of accurate perception with the Breath and Way of Taoist practice: the writer is on the road and he should observe exactly everything he sees on his path through the actual, quotidian world. There at the racetrack, in the bar, listening to Sibelius in his small room on his small radio, in the beaten empty streets, he will find the way he seeks. Bukowski, as he tells us in "The Dirty Old Man Confesses," was beat before the Beats and it is no accident that he felt a great affinity for the poetry of Allen Ginsberg, correctly perceiving the connection between *Howl* and the gifted young poet's early work, later collected as *Empty Mirror*.

The underground publications—little magazines, newspapers, chapbooks, mimeographs—to which Bukowski contributed his stories and essays began to proliferate during the Sixties and it was then that his creativity detonated in multiple directions. One should remember that Bukowski studied journalism at Los Angeles City College and originally hoped to work for a newspaper. Perhaps the model of Hemingway inspired this desire, but he tells us in an autobiographical note at the conclusion of *Longshot Pomes for Broke Players* (1962) that "the closest I ever got to being a reporter was as an errand boy in the composing room of the *New Orleans Item*. Used to have nickel beers in a place out back and the nights passed quickly."[7] But that was to change when the Summer of Love arrived in 1967, for now we have the curious synchronicity of the 47-year-old Bukowski arriving at full middle age and taking up his long-deferred career as a journalist, just as the hippie/youth/sexual revolution began to reach its apogee. He now began to compose his "Notes of A Dirty Old Man" series: the first installment, concerning proper protocol for law enforcement to follow when dealing with driving under the influence, appeared in John Bryan's *Open City* in the May 12–18, 1967 issue. Two years later, in November 1969, with the financial assistance of his publisher John Martin of Black Sparrow Press, Bukowski finally exited his long years of servitude at the Post Office and began his new life as a professional writer.

"Notes of A Dirty Old Man" would appear variously in the *Los Angeles Free Press, Berkeley Tribe, Nola Express, The New York Review of Sex and Politics, National Underground Review,* and later, in the Eighties, in *High Times.* The series covered a wide range of topics including the student rebellion, the war in Vietnam, the war of the sexes, racism, and the misadventures of Henry ("Hank") Chinaski (we meet the first incarnation of Bukowski's literary alter ego in the early story "The Reason Behind Reason" (1946), in which he is named "Chelaski"). The columns, as they appeared in the *L.A. Free Press,* were artistically composed, for they were decorated with Bukowski's own humorous cartoons placed at appropriate moments in the narrative. After a selection from the series was published in book form in 1969 by Essex House, Bukowski's fame began to spread and Los Angeles, San Francisco/Berkeley, and New Orleans became the triple centers of his literary activity. Bukowski had established links to San Francisco in the early Sixties when he submitted his anti-war essay "Peace, Baby, Is Hard Sell" to John Bryant's *Renaissance* magazine. And he had appeared in New Orleans' *The Outsider,* edited by Jon Edgar Webb and his wife Gypsy Lou, whose Loujon Press also published his first major books of poetry, *It Catches My Heart in Its Hands: New and Selected Poems 1955-1963* (1963) and *Crucifix in a Deathhand* (1965). The New Orleans-based *Nola Express* also was significant in expanding Bukowski's reputation beyond Los Angeles.[8]

Bukowski now began to refine his image/mask as a rambunctious, wily, lusty survivor who shamelessly drinks, fights, pursues sexual intercourse, and writes poems and stories while listening to Mozart, Bach, Stravinsky, Mahler, and Beethoven. He invents a new genre midway between fiction and autobiography: a blend of topical references, literary and cultural allusions, and imaginative elaboration of personal experiences. All the years of letter writing and constant devotion to his craft began to pay off, for Bukowski's prose now exhibited a remarkable degree of self-assurance and control; it is sharp, lively, funny, quirky, steely, constantly on the move. He hews to Hemingway's simple vocabulary and rapid dialogue, but moves beyond his model in his tremendous energy, humor, and gifts for caricature and exaggeration. His mastery of rhythm, timing, and comic surprise is evident in "The Night Nobody Believed I Was Allen Ginsberg," in which his driven, breathless, zany narrative moves swiftly from one improbable scene to the next. The story also illustrates the ways Bukowski combines fantasy with autobiography. The appearance of Harold Norse at the finale and the wild reported phone discussion concerning *Penguin Modern Poets 13* (in which Bukowski had actually just been published along with Norse and Philip Lamantia) allows Bukowski to send up a important turning point in his own poetic career in an off-the-cuff and hilarious way. After the ribald sexual play, Keystone Cops slapstick violence, and literary in-jokes, the story concludes in a perfectly pitched mood of resigned calm as surrealistic images surface perhaps from the narrator's submerged childhood memories ("The Abraham Lincoln Battalion and eleven dead pollywogs under a clothesline in 1932") as he speaks tenderly by telephone with his young daughter.

Bukowski's breaking of taboos has a certain ferocious (and ironic/humorous) intentionality about it. He is violent and sexually manic in ways that his two American masters — William Saroyan and John Fante — are not, although this aggressive pose should be understood as the tough carapace he adopts to protect himself from violation.[9] Yet there is nothing in his "obscenity" which is not in a long classical literary tradition: in Petronius' *Satyricon*, in Apuleius' *The Golden Ass*, in Catullus' anguished, angry, fevered love/hate poems to Lesbia, or in Boccaccio's *The Decameron*, on which Bukowski modeled his novel *Women*.[10]

However Bukowski *is* a literary rebel in the manner of Céline and Artaud. Bukowski adored Céline's *Voyage au Bout de la Nuit* and he pays homage to the great French misanthrope in several poems and interviews, while he sees Antonin Artaud as an artist who hated the hypocrisy of the society which both misunderstood and rejected him.[11] And Bukowski was transgressive in the tradition of a third French author he did not know—Georges Bataille. Bataille theorized about the connection between taboo, obscenity, violence, madness, and the sacred, remarking that "the words in various languages that designate the sacred signify both 'pure' and 'filthy.' The meaning of the sacred can be seen as lost to the extent that the awareness of the secret horrors at the basis of religions is lost."[12] Thus Bukowski's alter ego is a "dirty" old man, capturing in English the double valence of sexuality throughout his work. A story such as "The Silver Christ of Santa Fe" exemplifies several Batailleian strands: the play around psychiatry and madness, the "primitive" Indians encroaching on the "civilized" Anglo's bathroom, the "illicit" sexual encounter when the main character beholds a terrifying silver crucifix, *la nostalgie pour la boue*. Yet in Bukowski there is virtually always an element of dark—or black—humor to leaven his absurd existential vision.

Indeed, part of the failure of American critics to properly take Bukowski's measure is their ignorance of his essentially European cultural sensibility. This explains as well his success in Germany and France, where both intellectuals and "common readers" were quick to comprehend his originality and his place in the European philosophical tradition. One might imagine Charles Bukowski at a bistro in Paris with Bataille or trading sardonic, astringent aphorisms with the great Romanian writer E. M. Cioran, more readily than one can picture him in the company of his American contemporaries Saul Bellow or John Updike. The "fuzzy blackness, impractical meditations, and repressed desires of an Eastern European"—qualities he mentions humorously in "Aftermath of a Lengthy Rejection Slip"—aptly describe significant aspects of his own character.

The "obscenity" in Bukowski's writings ultimately placed him at the center of the American debates over censorship, which were hardly a new thing: James Joyce's *Ulysses*, D. H. Lawrence's *Lady Chatterly's Lover*, Henry Miller's *Tropic of Cancer*, Vladimir Nabokov's *Lolita*, William Burroughs' *Naked Lunch*, and Allen Ginsberg's *Howl* had all elicited official outrage and such battles were not over as the Sixties progressed. Bukowski wrote two essays in support of d.a. levy, a Cleveland poet who had been charged with "obscenity," while a raid on Jim Lowell's Asphodel Bookshop in the same city inspired another essay by Bukowski in *A Tribute to Jim Lowell*, along with contributions by a roster of distinguished American writers including Robert Lowell, Lawrence Ferlinghetti, Guy Davenport, and Charles Olson. Bukowski's own "provocative" writing for the underground periodicals as well as his advocacy of freedom of speech ultimately made him the target of an FBI probe, one of the factors which led to his separation from employment at the Post Office.[13]

Had the FBI taken the trouble to read a thoughtful essay such as "Should We Burn Uncle Sam's Ass," they would have discovered that Bukowski was far from believing that the Age of Aquarius had arrived quite yet. Writing following the burning of the Bank of America by students in Isla Vista, Santa Barbara, and the Chicago Seven Trial, Bukowski declares that "romantic slogans won't do." After an informed survey of the Leftist writers of the Thirties—John Dos Passos, Arthur Koestler, John Steinbeck, and their shifting political allegiances—Bukowski tells the student revolutionaries: "The whole accent of your thinking must not be how to destroy a government but how to create a better one. Don't be trapped and fooled again." And he counseled the hippies preparing for the Revolution with a slogan that would have made both Gandhi and Thoreau happy: "Everything you own must be able to fit inside one suitcase; then your mind might be free." Bukowski was sympathetic to the ideals of the Californian counterculture but he was essentially apolitical and anarchistic and, like many artists, was a dreamer rather than a man of action. Poets, as Shelley remarked, may well be the "unacknowledged legislators of the world," but when they put their toes into the hot water of politics (Left or Right), they often get burned, as Bukowski points out in his essay on Ezra Pound, "Looking Back at a Big One."

In the late Fifties, the Southern Californian counterculture had been documented in Lawrence Lipton's *The Holy Barbarians* (1959) and Bukowski similarly describes some of the contemporary bohemian characters he encountered in the city in his essay "The L.A. Scene." Bukowski's best work is set against a group of recurring precincts: East Hollywood, MacArthur Park, Lincoln Heights, Bunker Hill, Venice Beach, the Terminal Annex Post Office; Melrose Avenue, Alvarado Street, Carlton Way, Hollywood Boulevard, Western Avenue, DeLongpre Avenue.[14] The race tracks at Santa Anita, Hollywood Park, and Los Alamitos, the boxing matches at the Olympic Auditorium, the smog, the endless freeways, the endless automobiles, the infinitely silent Pacific Ocean, the orange groves, and the palm trees form the familiar signposts of his beautifully terrible poetic universe.[15] Furthermore, his admiration for John Fante has its roots in the fact that, in books such as *Ask the Dust*, Fante was making the City of Angels worthy of attention as a place where great literature could be written. Bukowski saw himself as following in Fante's footsteps in his effort to claim for Los Angeles equal or greater literary importance as any other American literary center; late in his career he would render homage to Fante in his story "I Meet the Master."

Los Angeles was Bukowski's journalistic "beat" and his reportage included a visit to a Rolling Stones concert at the Forum. In "Jaggernaut," he places himself at the center of an actual event as both participant and observer, blurring the lines between fact and fiction in very much the same fashion as Norman Mailer and Hunter S. Thompson in their forays into "New Journalism." It is perhaps also noteworthy that during this time the prominent cultural theorist Hayden White published *Metahistory* (1975), which caused historians to look afresh at the fictional structure of the narratives they composed to describe purportedly "objective" events, while simultaneously writers such as Bukowski were exploring the intersection between the supposed "facts" of autobiography and the imaginative remaking of experience.[16]

In the Seventies and Eighties, interviews with Bukowski appeared in magazines such as *Rolling Stone* and Andy Warhol's *Interview*, while the film *Barfly* with Mickey Rourke in 1987 brought international recognition. During this period, in order to supplement his income, he began to contribute to adult magazines including *Fling, Rogue, Pix, Adam, Oui, Knight, Penthouse,* and *Hustler,* as well as to magazines of the drug/rock and roll counterculture, *High Times* and *Creem.*[17] As noted above, Bukowski's practice throughout his career was to alternate rather methodically between the composition of poems, essays, and stories. His last period was no exception and from the 1980s to his death in 1994 he continued to create prolifically and masterfully in each genre.

Among the late stories, "The Way It Happened" is a Gnostic parable of the reversal and violation of the natural order in which Bukowski returns to the apocalyptic themes which are evident in many of his earlier poems and stories, while "Just Passing Time" recalls the Philadelphia bar memorialized in "Portions from a Wine-Stained Notebook." This story also introduces characters and situations which Bukowski would soon reshape in *Barfly*: the bartenders Jim and Eddy, and the mood of mystical unity and transcendence which unfortunately cannot be sustained: "And we all felt good, you could feel it reaching all around: we were there, finally, everybody was beautiful and grand and entertaining, and each moment glowed, bright and unwasted."

Bukowski's Zen-like ability to render an intense sense of complete reality during each moment's experience is demonstrated in "Distractions of the Literary Life." The opening sentences of each paragraph are all in the present tense, giving a vivid immediacy to the narration and placing the reader at the center of the action: "It's a hot summer night"; "the phone rings in the other room"; "Anyway, Sandra hands me the phone"; "It's my dealer who lives in one of the courts up front." We also encounter here a typical Bukowski trope: a writer who writes about the story he is writing, erasing the boundaries between art and life, and mentioning along the way other writers: Updike, Cheever, Ginsberg, Mailer, Tolstoy, Céline. Bukowski had been "postmodern" and "metafictional" all along: his writers write as frequently about writing and being a writer as about anything else.[18]

His last story "The Other" is a tightly fashioned *doppelganger* tale which anticipates some of the themes in his final novel *Pulp*: a mystery story in which the Other/Death/Self becomes one's most intimate twin and enemy. And in "Basic Training," his valedictory essay on writing, Bukowski declares: "I hurled myself toward my personal god: SIMPLICITY. The tighter and smaller you got it the less chance there was of error and the lie. Genius could be the ability to say a profound thing in a simple way. Words were bullets, words were sunbeams, words cracked through doom and damnation." In my end is my beginning and Charles Bukowski's long literary journey describes a perfect circle as he invokes a final time the magical fires of *poiesis*: typer, wine bottle, and Mozart on the radio.

NOTES

1. Sanford Dorbin, *A Bibliography of Charles Bukowski*, Los Angeles: Black Sparrow Press, 1969; Hugh Fox, *Charles Bukowski: A Critical and Bibliographical Study*, E. Lansing, MI: Abyss Publications, 1969; Aaron Krumhansl, *A Descriptive Bibliography of the Primary Publications of Charles Bukowski*, Santa Rosa, CA: Black Sparrow Press, 1999; Al Fogel, *Charles Bukowski: A Comprehensive Price Guide and Checklist: 1944–1999*, Surfside, FL: The Sole Proprietor Press, 2000. The immense Bukowski archives were bequeathed by his widow Linda Lee Bukowski to the Huntington Library in San Marino, California in September 2006. There are also major collections of both published and unpublished works, including manuscripts at the University of California at Santa Barbara and the University of Arizona, Tucson.

2. See Elliott Anderson and Mary Kinzie, *The Little Magazine in America: A Modern Documentary History*, Yonkers, NY: The Pushcart Press, 1978; Loss Pequeno Glazier, *Small Press: An Annotated Guide*, Westport, CT: Greenwood Press, 1992; Robert J. Gleesing, *The Underground Press in America*, Bloomington and London: Indiana University Press, 1970; Abe Peck, *Uncovering the Sixties: The Life and Times of the Underground Press*, New York: Pantheon, 1985; Jerome Rothenberg, with contributions by Steven Clay and Rodney Phillips, *A Secret Location on the Lower East Side: Adventures in Writing 1969–1980*, New York: Granary Books; Sanford Dorbin, "Charles Bukowski and the Little Mag/Small Press Movement," in *Soundings: Collections of the University Library, University of California, Santa Barbara*, May 1970, pp. 17–32.

3. Untitled essay in *A Tribute to Jim Lowell*, Cleveland: Ghost Press, 1967, n.p.

4. "Hellenistics" in *The Collected Poetry of Robinson Jeffers*, volume two, 1928–1938, ed. Tim Hunt, Stanford, CA: Stanford University Press, 1989, p. 526. "I am past childhood, I look at this ocean and the fishing birds, the / screaming skerries, the shining water, / The foam-heads, the exultant dawn-light going west, the pelicans, their / huge wings half folded, plunging like stones. / Whatever it is catches my heart in its hands, whatever it is makes me shudder with love/And painful joy . . ." And Bukowski's Gnostic sense of alienation and high romanticism recall Hart Crane: "And so it was I entered the broken world / To trace the visionary company of love, its voice/An instant in the wind (I know not whither hurled)/But not for long to hold each desperate choice." "The Broken Tower" in *The Complete Poems and Selected Letters and Prose of Hart Crane*, ed. and with an Introduction and Notes by Brom Weber, New York: Anchor Books, 1966, p. 193.

5. Bukowski's brutalized childhood provided the traumata which set in motion his lifelong alcoholism and frequent bouts of suicidal depression as well as the inner strength which powered his genius. On artistic creativity and woundedness, see Edmund Wilson, "Philoctetes: The Wound and the Bow," in *The Wound and the Bow: Seven Studies in Literature*, Athens, OH: Ohio University Press, 1997. On writers and drug use, see the excellent survey, Marcus Boon, *The Road of Excess: A History of Writers on Drugs*, Cambridge: Harvard University Press, 2005. For biographical information, see Barry Miles, *Charles Bukowski*, London: Virgin Books, 2005; Howard Sounes, *Charles Bukowski: Locked in the Arms of a Crazy Life*, New York: Grove, 2000; David Stephen Calonne, ed., *Charles Bukowski: Sunlight Here I Am/Interviews & Encounters 1963-1993*, Northville, MI: Sundog Press, 2003.

6. Unpublished Foreword to William Wantling's *7 On Style*.

7. Charles Bukowski, *Longshot Pomes for Broke Players*, New York: 7 Poets Press, 1962.

8. See Jeff Weedle, *Bohemian New Orleans: The Story of the Outsider and Loujon Press*, Jackson, MS: University Press of Missisippi, 2007. Chapter 6, "Focusing on Bukowski"; Chapter 7, "Meeting Bukowski." The *Nola Express* was edited by Darlene Fife and Robert Head. Its name is an acronym: New Orleans, LouisianA and was based on the title of the William Burroughs novel *Nova Express*.

9. On the influence of Saroyan and Fante on Bukowski, see David Stephen Calonne, "Two on the Trapeze: Charles Bukowski and William Saroyan," in *Sure: The Charles Bukowski Newsletter*, 5/6, 1992, pp. 26–35.

10. Bukowski's poem "To the Whore Who Took My Poems," is an homage to Cat-

ullus 42, "*Adeste, hendecasyllabi, quot estis / omnes.*" See *Burning in Water Drowning in Flame: Selected Poems, 1955–1973*, Santa Barbara: Black Sparrow Press, 1978, p. 16; Peter Green, trans., *The Poems of Catullus: A Bilingual Edition*, Berkeley: University of California Press, 2005, pp. 88–91. Bukowski's references to Hamsun, Turgenev, Li Po, Boccaccio, Tu Fu, Vallejo, Catullus, Pound, Céline, Dostoyevsky, Nietzsche, and Schopenhauer illustrate the wide range of his reading. He also possessed a great knowledge of and love for classical music. For example, Bukowski's first story, "Aftermath of a Lengthy Rejection Slip" (1944), refers to Tchaikovsky's Sixth Symphony. "Hard Without Music" (1948) also includes references to a number of classical composers and the main character delivers an impassioned speech on the ecstatic, transcendent, ineffable power of great music. Similar ideas appear in Bukowski's poetry, such as the tremendous uncollected late poem on Shostakovich's *Tenth Symphony*, "2 a.m.": "so now / Shostakovich's Tenth, / 2 a.m. closing / time / but not here / tonight, / Dmitri spins / it out / and I borrow from his / immense psyche, / I feel better and better / and better / listening to him, / he cures me onward, / each drink / finer, / my stupid wounds / closing, / the Tenth goes on / circling these / walls, / I owe this bastard . . ." in *The New Censorship*, Vol. 2, no. 3, 1991. And in "Classical Music and Me," Bukowski gets high on Mahler: "now Mahler is in the room / with me / and the chills run up my / arms, reach the back / of my neck . . . / it's all so unbelievably / splendid . . ." in *The Last Night of the Earth Poems*, Santa Rosa, CA: Black Sparrow Press, 1992, p. 374. Bukowski composed a wide array of poems which either are direct homages to great composers or make references to their lives and works, including Bach, Beethoven, Brahms, Bruckner, Chopin, Handel, Haydn, Mozart, Schumann, Sibelius, Stravinsky, Vivaldi, and Wagner.

11. On Céline, see *Sunlight Here I Am*, pp. 41, 69, 129, 134, 160, 163, 168, 198, 215, 242, 246, 267, 273 and "Céline with cane and basket" in *The Last Night of the Earth Poems*, Santa Rosa, CA: Black Sparrow Press, 1992, p. 242. Céline is also a major character in Bukowski's final novel, *Pulp.*

12. Georges Bataille, *Visions of Excess: Selected Writings, 1927–1939*, ed. and with an Introduction by Allan Stoekl, Minneapolis: University of Minnesota Press, 1985. Bataille comments elsewhere: "*sacred* has two contradictory meanings. Whatever is the subject of a prohibition is basically sacred. The taboo gives a negative definition of the sacred object and inspires us with awe on the religious plane . . . Men are swayed by two simultaneous emotions: they are driven away by terror and drawn by an awed fascination. Taboo and transgression reflect these contradictory urges."

Bataille, *Erotism: Death & Sensuality*, San Francisco: City Lights, 1986, p. 68. The author of *Story of the Eye* would find the subject matter of many of Bukowski's poems and stories congenial: voyeurism, fetishism, etc. See also Mary Douglas, *Purity and Danger: An Analysis of the Concept of Pollution and Taboo*, London and New York: Routledge Classics, 2002.

13. See the recently published *Federal Bureau of Investigation File #140-35907, 1957–1970. Henry Charles Bukowski, Jr. (a.k.a."Charles Bukowski")*.

14. Lawrence Lipton, *The Holy Barbarians*, New York: Julian Messner, Inc., 1959. See also Herbert Gold, *Bohemia: Digging the Roots of Cool*, New York: Simon and Schuster, 1993.

15. On Los Angeles' literary tradition, see also Lionel Rolfe, *Literary L.A.*, San Francisco: Chronicle Books, 1981; John Miller, ed. *Los Angeles Stories: Great Writers on the City*, San Francisco: Chronicle Books, 1991; David M. Fine, *Imagining Los Angeles: A City in Fiction*, Albuquerque, NM: University of New Mexico Press, 2000; David L. Ulin, *Writing Los Angeles: A Literary Anthology*, New York: Library of America, 2002.

16. Hayden White, *Metahistory: The Historical Imagination in Nineteenth Century Europe*, Baltimore: Johns Hopkins, 1975.

17. In an interview with Silvia Bizio, Bukowski remarked: "The reason sex got into so much of my stories is because when I quit the post office, at the age of fifty, I had to make money. What I really wanted to do was write about something that interested me. But there were all those pornographic magazines on Melrose Avenue, and they had read my stuff in the *Free Press*, and started asking me to send them something. So what I would do was write a good story, and then in the middle I had to throw in some gross act of sex. And so I would write a story, and at a certain point I would say: 'Well it's time to throw some sex into it.' And I would throw some sex in it and kept writing the story. It was okay: I would mail the story and immediately get a three-hundred-dollar check." *Sunlight Here I Am: Interviews & Encounters, 1963–1993*, p. 181.

18. See Patricia Waugh, *Metafiction: The Theory and Practice of Self-Consuming Fiction*, London: Routledge, 1990; Robert Scholes, *Fabulation and Metafiction*, Urbana, IL: University of Illinois Press, 1979; Jules Smith, "Charles Bukowski and the Avant-Garde," in *The Review of Contemporary Fiction: Charles Bukowski and Michel Butor*, Vol. 5, Number 3, Fall 1985, pp. 56–59.

PORTIONS

FROM A

WINE-STAINED
NOTEBOOK

AFTERMATH OF A LENGTHY
REJECTION SLIP

I walked around outside and thought about it. It was the longest one I ever got. Usually they only said, "Sorry, this did not quite make the grade" or "Sorry, this didn't quite work in." Or more often, the regular printed rejection form.

But this was the longest, the longest ever. It was from my story "My Adventures in Half a Hundred Rooming Houses." I walked under a lamppost, took the slip out of my pocket, and reread it—

Dear Mr. Bukowski:

Again, this is a conglomeration of extremely good stuff and other stuff so full of idolized prostitutes, morning-after vomiting scenes, misanthropy, praise for suicide etc. that it is not quite for a magazine of any circulation at all. This is, however, pretty much a saga of a certain type of person and in it I think you've done an honest job. Possibly we will print you sometime, but I don't know exactly when. That depends on you.

Sincerely yours,
Whit Burnett

Oh, I knew the signature: the long "h" that twisted into the end of the "W," and the beginning of the "B" which dropped halfway down the page.

I put the slip back in my pocket and walked on down the street. I felt pretty good.

Here I had only been writing two years. Two short years. It took Hemingway ten years. And Sherwood Anderson, he was forty before he was published.

I guess I would have to give up drinking and women of ill-fame, though. Whiskey was hard to get anyhow and wine was ruining my stomach. Millie though—Millie, that would be harder, much harder.

... But Millie, Millie, we must remember art. Dostoevsky, Gorki, for Russia, and now America wants an Eastern European. America is tired of Browns and Smiths. The Browns and Smiths are good writers but there are too many of them and they all write alike. America wants the fuzzy blackness, impractical meditations, and repressed desires of an Eastern European.

Millie, Millie, your figure is just right: it all pours down tight to the hips and loving you is as easy as putting on a pair of gloves in zero weather. Your room is always warm and cheerful and you have record albums and cheese sandwiches that I like. And, Millie, your cat, remember? Remember when he was a kitten? I tried to teach him to shake hands and to roll over, and you said a cat wasn't a dog and it couldn't be done. Well, I did it, didn't I, Millie? The cat's big now and he's been a mother and had kittens. But it's going to have to go now, Millie: cats and figures and Tchaikovsky's 6th Symphony. America needs an Eastern European. . . .

I found I was in front of my rooming house by then and I started to go in. Then I saw a light on in my window. I looked in: Carson and Shipkey were at the table with somebody I didn't know. They were playing cards and in the center sat a huge jug of wine. Carson and Shipkey were painters who couldn't make up their minds whether to paint like Salvador Dali or Rockwell Kent, and they worked at the shipyards while trying to decide.

Then I saw a man sitting very quietly on the edge of my bed. He had a mustache and a goatee and looked familiar. I seemed to remember his face. I had seen it in a book, a newspaper, a movie, maybe. I wondered.

Then I remembered.

When I remembered, I didn't know whether to go in or not. After all, what did one say? How did one act? With a man like that it was hard. You had to be careful not to say the wrong words, you had to be careful about everything.

I decided to walk around the block once first. I read someplace that that helped when you were nervous. I heard Shipkey swearing as I left and I heard somebody drop a glass. That wouldn't help me any.

I decided to make up my speech ahead of time. "Really, I'm not a very good speaker at all. I'm very withdrawn and tense. I save it all and put it in words on paper. I'm sure you'll be disappointed in me, but it's the way I've always been."

I thought that would do it and when I finished my block's walk I went right into my room.

I could see that Carson and Shipkey were rather drunk, and I knew they wouldn't help me any. The little card player they had brought with them was also bad off, except he had all the money on his side of the table.

The man with the goatee got up off the bed. "How do you do, sir?" he asked.

"Fine, and you?" I shook hands with him. "I hope you haven't been waiting too long?" I said.

"Oh no."

"Really," I said, "I'm not a very good speaker at all —"

"Except when he's drunk, then he yells his head off. Sometimes he goes to the square and lectures and if nobody listens to him he talks to the birds," said Shipkey.

The man with the goatee grinned. He had a marvelous grin. Evidently a man of understanding.

The other two went on playing cards, but Shipkey turned his chair around and watched us.

"I'm very withdrawn and tense," I continued, "and —"

"Past tense or circus tents?" yelled Shipkey.

That was very bad, but the man with the goatee smiled again and I felt better.

"I save it all and put it in words on paper and —"

"Nine-tenths or pretense?" yelled Shipkey.

" — and I'm sure you'll be disappointed in me, but it's the way I've always been."

"Listen, mister!" yelled Shipkey wobbling back and forth in his chair. "Listen, you with the goatee!"

"Yes?"

"Listen, I'm six feet tall with wavy hair, a glass eye, and a pair of red dice."

The man laughed.

"You don't believe me then? You don't believe I have a pair of red dice?"

Shipkey, when intoxicated, always wanted, for some reason, to make people believe he had a glass eye. He would point to one eye or the other and maintain it was a glass eye. He claimed the glass eye was made for him by his father, the greatest specialist in the world, who had, unfortunately, been killed by a tiger in China.

Suddenly Carson began yelling, "I saw you take that card! Where did you get it? Give it here, *here*! Marked, *marked*! I thought so! No wonder you've been winning! So! *So!*"

Carson rose up and grabbed the little card player by the tie and pulled up on it. Carson was blue in the face with anger and the little card player began to turn red as Carson pulled up on the tie.

"What's up, ha! Ha! What's up! What's goin' on?" yelled Shipkey. "Lemme see, ha? Gimme tha dope!"

Carson was all blue and could hardly speak. He hissed the words out of his lips with a great effort and held up on the tie. The little card player began to flop his arms about like a great octopus brought to the surface.

"He crossed us!" hissed Carson. "Crossed us! Pulled one from under his sleeve, sure as the Lord! Crossed us, I tell you!"

Shipkey walked behind the little card player and grabbed him by the hair and yanked his head back and forth. Carson remained at the tie.

"Did you cross us, huh? Did you! Speak! Speak!" yelled Shipkey pulling at the hair.

The little card player didn't speak. He just flopped his arms and began to sweat.

"I'll take you someplace where we can get a beer and something to eat," I said to the man with the goatee.

"Come on! Talk! Give out! You can't cross us!"

"Oh, that won't be necessary," said the man with the goatee.

"Rat! Louse! Fish-faced pig!"

"I insist," I said.

"Rob a man with a glass eye, will you? *I'll* show you, fish-faced pig!"

"That's very kind of you, and I am a little hungry, thanks," said the man with the goatee.

"Speak! Speak, fish-faced pig! If you don't speak in two minutes, in just two minutes, I'll cut your heart out for a doorknob!"

"Let's leave right away," I said.

"All right," said the man with the goatee.

■

All the eating places were closed at that time of night and it was a long ride into town. I couldn't take him back to my room, so I had to take a chance on Millie. She always had plenty of food. At any rate, she *always* had cheese.

I was right. She made us cheese sandwiches with coffee. The cat knew me and leaped into my lap.

I put the cat on the floor.

"Watch, Mr. Burnett," I said.

"Shake hands!" I said to the cat. "Shake hands!"

The cat just sat there.

"That's funny, it always used to do it," I said. "Shake hands!"

I remembered Shipkey had told Mr. Burnett that I talked to birds.

"Come on now! Shake hands!"

I began to feel foolish.

"Come *on*! Shake hands!"

I put my head right down by the cat's head and put everything I had into it.

"Shake hands!"

The cat just sat there.

I went back to my chair and picked up my cheese sandwich.

"Cats are funny animals, Mr. Burnett. You can never tell. Millie, put on Tchaikovsky's 6th for Mr. Burnett."

We listened to the music. Millie came over and sat in my lap. She just had on a negligee. She dropped down against me. I put my sandwich to one side.

"I want you to notice," I said to Mr. Burnett, "the section which brings forth the marching movement in this symphony. I think it's one of the most beautiful movements in all music. And besides its beauty and force, its structure is perfect. You can feel intelligence at work."

The cat jumped up into the lap of the man with the goatee. Millie laid her cheek against mine, put a hand on my chest. "Where ya been, baby boy? Millie's missed ya, ya know."

The record ended and the man with the goatee took the cat off his lap, got up, and turned the record over. He should have found record #2 in the album. By turning it over we would get the climax rather early. I didn't say anything, though, and we listened to it end.

"How did you like it?" I asked.

"Fine! Just fine!"

He had the cat on the floor.

"Shake hands! Shake hands!" he said to the cat.

The cat shook hands.

"Look," he said, "I can make the cat shake hands."

"Shake hands!"

The cat rolled over.

"No, shake *hands*! Shake *hands*!"

The cat just sat there.

He put his head down by the cat's head and talked into its ear. "Shake hands!"

The cat stuck its paw right into his goatee.

"Did you see? I made him shake hands!" Mr. Burnett seemed pleased.

Millie pressed tight against me. "Kiss me, baby boy," she said, "kiss me."

"No."

"Good Lord, ya gone off ya nut, baby boy? What's eatin' at ya? Sompin's botherin' ya tonight, I can tell! Tell Millie all about ut! Millie'd go ta hell for ya, baby boy, ya know that. Whats'a matter, huh? Ha?"

"Now I'll get the cat to roll over," said Mr. Burnett.

Millie wrapped her arms tight around me and peered down into my upward eye. She looked very sad and motherish and smelled like cheese. "Tell Millie what's eatin' ya up, baby boy."

"Roll over!" said Mr. Burnett to the cat.

The cat just sat there.

"Listen," I said to Millie, "see that man over there?"

"Yeah, I see him."

"Well, that's Whit Burnett."

"Who's that?"

"The magazine editor. The one I send my stories to."

"Ya mean the one who sends you those little tiny notes?"

"Rejection slips, Millie."

"Well, he's mean. I don't like him."

"Roll over!" said Mr. Burnett to the cat. The cat rolled over. "Look!" he yelled. "I made the cat roll over! I'd like to buy this cat! It's marvelous!"

Millie tightened her grip about me and peered down into my eye. I was quite helpless. I felt like a still-live fish on ice in a butcher's counter on Friday morning.

"Listen," she said, "I can get him ta print one a ya stories. I can get him to print *alla* them!"

"Watch me make the cat roll over!" said Mr. Burnett.

"No, no, Millie, you don't understand. Editors aren't like tired business men. Editors have *scruples*!"

"Scruples?"

"Scruples."

"Roll over!" said Mr. Burnett.

The cat just sat there.

"I know all about ya *scruples*! Don't ya worry about scruples! Baby boy, I'll get him to print *alla* ya stories!"

"Roll over!" said Mr. Burnett to the cat. Nothing happened.

"No, Millie, I won't have it."

She was all wound around me. It was hard to breathe and she was rather heavy. I felt my feet going to sleep. Millie pressed her cheek against mine and rubbed a hand up and down my chest. "Baby boy, ya got nothin' to say!"

Mr. Burnett put his head down by the cat's head and talked into its ear. "Roll over!"

The cat stuck its paw right into his goatee.

"I think this cat wants something to eat," he said.

With that, he got back into his chair. Millie went over and sat on his knee.

"Where'd ya get tha cute little goaty?" she asked.

"Pardon me," I said, "I'm going to get a drink of water."

I went in and sat in the breakfast nook and looked down at the flower designs on the table. I tried to scratch them off with a fingernail.

It was hard enough to share Millie's love with the cheese salesman and the welder. Millie with the figure right down to the hips. Damn, damn.

I kept sitting there and after a while I took my rejection slip out of my pocket and read it again. The places where the slip was folded were beginning to get brown with dirt and torn. I would have to stop looking at it and put it between book pages like a pressed rose.

I began to think about what it said. I always had that trouble. In college, even, I was drawn to the fuzzy blackness. The short story instructress took me to dinner and a show one night and lectured to me on the beauties of life. I had given her a story I had written in which I, as the main character, had gone down to the beach at night on the sand and began meditating on the meaning in Christ, on the meaning in death, on the meaning and fullness and rhythm in all things. Then in the middle of my meditations, along walks a bleary-eyed tramp kicking sand in my face. I talk to him, buy him a bottle and we drink. We get sick. Afterward we go to a house of ill-fame.

After the dinner, the short story instructress opened her purse and brought forth my story of the beach. She opened it up about halfway down, to the entrance of the bleary-eyed tramp and the exit of the meaning in Christ.

"Up to here," she said, "up to here, this was very good, in fact, beautiful."

Then she glared up at me with that glare that only the artistically intelligent who have somehow fallen into money and position can have. "But pardon me, pardon me very much," she tapped at the bottom half of my story," just what the *hell* is *this* stuff doing in here?"

■

I couldn't stay away any longer. I got up and walked into the front room.

Millie was all wrapped around him and peering down into his upward eye. He looked like a fish on ice.

Millie must have thought I wanted to talk to him about publishing procedures.

"Pardon me, I have to comb my hair," she said and left the room.

"Nice girl, isn't she, Mr. Burnett?" I asked.

He pulled himself back into shape and straightened his tie. "Pardon me," he said, "why do you keep calling me 'Mr. Burnett'?"

"Well, aren't you?"

"I'm Hoffman. Joseph Hoffman. I'm from the Curtis Life Insurance Company. I came in response to your postcard."

"But I didn't send a postcard."

"We received one from you."

"I never sent any."

"Aren't you Andrew Spickwich?"

"Who?"

"Spickwich. Andrew Spickwich, 3631 Taylor Street."

Millie came back and wound herself around Joseph Hoffman. I didn't have the heart to tell her.

I closed the door very softly and went down the steps and out into the street. I walked part way down the block and then I saw the lights go out.

I ran like hell toward my room hoping that there would be some wine left in that huge jug on the table. I didn't think I'd be that lucky, though, because I am too much a saga of a certain type of person: fuzzy blackness, impractical meditations, and repressed desires.

20 TANKS FROM KASSELDOWN

He sat in his cell tapping his fingers on the bottle, thinking, it's very sporting of them to give me this bottle. When he tapped at the glass it felt good on his fingers, spreading them a bit so, and getting the cool, clean touch. He had used whiskey before, found it made life bearable; took off the edge; was a good wash for minds that turned too fast: culling it, slowing it, settling it to a visible mark.

A roach moved across the floor, click-fast, then click-stopped before one of his shoes. It stood there and he stopped tapping, and watched. From the still fingers on the bottle to the very shape of the shoe by the roach, his lines were slim, pliable, womanish without being feminine; and there was a dignity that made you think of kings, of princes, of sheltered and spoiled things, and if you hadn't known, you'd think he had been untouched by life. (He stepped out and crushed the roach.) He was about thirty and the face, like a thinker's face, looked at the same time younger and older. His movements were restrained and quiet, always subservient to the mind, and sometimes when in crowds, falsified and churned up bluntly so as not to attract attention. During the trial, when he was news, the cell was piqued with reporters. He smiled continually when they questioned him, yet they could see he wasn't the least happy—as if he *should* be! And yet it wasn't a mocking smile. It was pleasant in a sense. There didn't seem much hatred in him; just a vagueness, an inconsistency. He hadn't bothered to shave and had a fine-grained beard, thin, like the hair under the armpits. It *did* give him that martyred look, that beard, the ghost eyes, and he would lean back against the wall, light his cigarette in soft-handed movements, looking down. Then he would smile at the reporters: "Well, friends, what can I do for you?"

"Just keep the priests away . . ." he said . . .

He sat in the cell and the fingers began tapping again, tapping the bottle. Still, it was the second time, and it wasn't as good because he expected it. He began to smile.

Had time to write a book. Should have written a book. Print on pages, you know. The first letter of each chapter very fancy. Done up with a rose or a leaf or a maiden's knee. Should have written a book. They all do it. "Treason ... is only being on the losing side of revolution." This is a small country, but I could have written a large book ... This is a small country, but with 20 more tanks, just 20, I would be at Kasseldown and Curtwright would be here—writing a book. Hell, even with 100 horses ...

But now you are the peculiar target to make the glory of country more armorous in the history textbooks. You see, you have killed a roach and they have too—that is, they will today when the sun goes down ... See the little ones reading, reading, and there the teacher with her long wooden stick and her blackboard, pointing to a colored map. The notebooks, the fat ink in desks ... memorize, memorize this. A whole movement, a whole flow of word and thought and idea ... hours of talk and counter-talk, examination, tradition bent in hard on soft minds, and forever unchanged. And now they sing, sing, and march out of classrooms and bounce balls and believe ... and grow and read the newspapers, and believe ... all this, on the difference of 100 horses, 100 chunks of beast flesh, fed and dunged; dumb, dumb mass of beast flesh that made the notes of song ... *Curtwright's* horses.

He sucked at the bottle again, feeling very lonely but not because of four wet and arenaceous walls.

But *still* ... you tried it. And if you had won, it would have been the same thing at the other end ... Why did you bother with it? Didn't you know that beyond the numbered few, even slight meaning ends?...No, it wasn't am-bition—in that sense ... It was just the people, all lives running, all lives running so weak, plunged through with fear. Everything was a ritual of no-do, no-hurt, no-chance. He had just gotten a hunger, a hunger for *doing* ... doing anything at all to break the suffocating shell.

He sat in the cell and held the bottle before his eyes. The light was poor but still he could make out the branded words in the glass: FEDERAL LAW FORBIDS SALE OR REUSE OF THIS BOTTLE ...

He stood up and found he was looking at the walls. Walls funny grey, sweating cold, thick—yet bunched through with a drama of their own—and so old ... Old. Funny about women, too ... How they got old. Sad, really sad. You saw the young ones walking all tight and high ... and you hated their proudness, for proudness had no right in things mechanical and momentary. Proudness only belonged to those who created new forms, and won ... He smiled again and stood looking at the walls. They seemed pleasant and meaningful and he touched a finger to the rough edge, grey and wet.

His throat felt dry and he went over to the tap and filled his tin cup. The water came hard and made a swirling, white rising of foam in the cup. He shut the tap, but too late, and there was a splash of overflow making a blotch of clean, porous leather on one shoe. Something turned slowly in his forehead and he thought, it is too quiet. He drank the water but it tasted badly of tin, and all of a sudden he felt sick, very sick. He sat down again on his cot, the room all shadow and cement, and he was conscious that he was breathing, and through each inhale came the taste of tin. He drank what was left of the whiskey bottle, then set it very quietly on the floor. The setting down of a bottle was one of the few independent actions he had left. He leaned back against the wall, closed his eyes, opened them, and knew he was just perhaps really frightened, the mind trying to work up some apology for the death of the flesh.

As the thought set in, a chill began in the fingers and went up both arms, making him jerk his shoulders spasmodically to shake it out of his back. It is very quiet, he thought again, and all of a sudden his mind found an outlet, a base, and he hated the swirl, the meaning-drenched swirl, the vast mass and computation, the weight of numbers and chance; mass and press of unchanneled and baseless things that could kill without a glisten, a sigh, a tick.

But here, he thought, never let passion deform the frame. Passion, unmoulded, is a sign of inferiority! Listen. Take this, all this, and for *them*— make numerals, symbols, hard and fought-out, well-balanced formulas.

Then he, at last, began laughing—not laughing but sniggering, womanish, only half-understood, semi-mad.

"Guard!"

"Guard!" he yelled.

The guard came and stood there, outside the bars. "Do you want the priest?" he asked.

The guard was bald and fat, and looking at him he thought: bald and fat, his face is crossed between brutality and humor and can't make up its mind, and the eyes are so small, so small.

"You mustn't accuse me of crassness or bitterness, guard, but a man like you—makes no difference when he lives: now, or two thousand years hence, or some place in between. You make no marks, no sounds, no new entrances ... Still, it's grand to be alive, grand even as you. Grand to stand there and ask me if I want a priest, grand to play your little safe game and watch the larger clash going on. After all, you do absorb something, even standing aside ... but I'm sick of hearing my voice. You say something. What do you think, guard?"

"What do I think?"

"Yes."

"Do you want the priest?"

"No. Go away."

He sat in his cell, sick.

I try, I try ... I *try* to see. But the whole goddamn world seems fake, *fake* ... Oh, I should have stayed at the hospital, tinkering with people, painting at night. I could have made my own world at night. But I wanted to stir the whole pond, shake the base. Oh hunger—hunger.

He looked down at the floor, at the spot that had once been a roach, and smiled again.

HARD WITHOUT MUSIC

Larry was stopped by his landlady in the hall as he came in from the street.

"Somebody's up in your room. They saw your ad about the phonograph and records. I thought it'd be all right to let 'em up there. I talked with 'em quite awhile, and besides . . ."

"It's all right." He walked past.

She caught his elbow. "Larry."

"What?" He turned.

"They're nuns."

He didn't answer.

"Are you all right, Larry?"

"I'm all right."

"Are you sure, Larry? They're Sisters. It wouldn't be bad if they weren't Sisters."

He went on up the stairs, then into the bathroom. He closed the door and looked into the mirror. He drank a glass of water, then lit a cigarette. He drew on it quickly in heavy inhales. The smoke rose in the bathroom and the cigarette developed a thin, hard red ash. He took a last draw, walked over to the toilet and dropped it in. Then he walked back to the mirror and looked again . . .

The door to his room was open and he went in. One nun was sitting in the straight-backed chair and the other was walking toward the phonograph with a record in her hands.

The other one in the chair saw him first. "Oh, they're lovely, *lovely!*"

Larry walked over to the stuffed chair and sat down. It was near the window. He could see the trees and the backyard. Was it true what Paul said? That they shaved their heads?

The nun with the record in her hands put it down next to the phonograph and stood facing him.

"Listen," he said, "go ahead and play it. Play all you want."

15

"Oh, I'm sure they're *all* lovely," said the one in the chair.

"Sister Celia knows them all," said the one standing.

The one in the chair smiled. Her teeth were very white. "You have such good taste. Almost all of Beethoven, and Brahms, and Bach and . . ."

"Yes," said Larry. "Yes, thank you." He turned to the other nun. "Won't you sit down?" he asked. But she didn't move.

The sweat was coming out on his forehead, the palms of his hands, the hollow of his throat. He wiped his hands on his knees. Why was it he had a feeling that he was going to do something dreadful? How black they were dressed; and the white: such a contrast. And the faces. "My favorite," he said, "is Beethoven's Ninth." It wasn't. He didn't have any favorites.

"I'd like to use these to teach in the classes," said Sister Celia, the one in the chair. "It's so hard . . . without music."

"Yes," said Larry. "For all of us." His voice had sounded dramatic. He felt as if he didn't belong in the room. It was hot summer. His eyes filmed, his throat felt dry. A thin string of breeze passed for a moment across his brow. He thought of hospitals, of disinfectant.

"It's a shame to sell them. I mean . . . for you," said Sister Celia. She was evidently the buyer, he thought; the other was just along.

Larry waited a moment and then he answered, "I have to move. To another city. They'd break, you know."

"I'm sure these would be lovely for my class, for the older girls."

"Older girls," said Larry. Then his eyes opened and he stared straight at Sister Celia, at her smooth face and pale nun's eyes. "That's wise," he said. "Extremely wise." His voice had become harsh and metallic. The sweat formed on his legs and the wool of his trousers pointed into the skin. His hands moved about his knees. He looked down, then back up at Sister Celia. The other nun seemed to hang suspended, way off.

Then he began. "Modern elementary education, for reasons unknown, at least to myself, finds it plausible to introduce Beethoven into the souls of eight-year-olds. Somebody once asked the question, 'Are composers human?' Well, I don't know, but I do know that the sounds that came out of my teacher's phonograph in the third grade were not, to me, human sounds, sounds in any way relative to real life and real living, the sea or the baseball diamond. And the teacher steeped with her ethereally ponderous and magnificent, her rimless glasses, her white wig and Fifth Symphony, were no more a real part of life than the rest of it . . . Mozart, Chopin, Handel . . . The others learned the meaning of the little black dots with tails, and without tails, that climbed up and down the chalk-marked ladders on the blackboard. But I—through fear and revulsion—turtle fashion, withdrew my mind into the dark shell. And today, when I slip my program notes from my record albums . . . it is still dark . . ."

He laughed. He felt suddenly old and worldly. He waited for the nuns to speak but they didn't speak.

"Good music crept up on me. I don't know how. But suddenly, there it was, and I was a young man in San Francisco spending whatever money I could get feeding symphonies to the hungry insides of my landlady's wooden, man-high victrola. I think those were the best days of them all, being very young and seeing the Golden Gate Bridge from my window. Almost every day I discovered a new symphony . . . I selected my albums pretty much by chance, being too nervous and uncomfortable to understand them in the glass partitions of the somehow clinical music shops . . . There are moments, I have found, when a piece, after previous listenings that were sterile and dry . . . I have found that a moment comes when the piece at last unfolds itself fully to the mind . . ."

"Yes, how true," said Sister Celia.

"You are listening haphazardly, carelessly. And then, through the lazy sheen you have effected, almost *upon* the sheen, climbing upon it, through it, centering lithely upon the unguarded brain . . . in comes the melody, curling, singing, dancing . . . All the full potency of the variations, the counter notes, gliding cool and utterly unbelievable in the mind. In the kindness it is . . . like the buzzing of countless little steel bees whirling in ever-heightened beauty and knowing . . . A sudden movement of the body, an *effort* to follow, will often kill it, and after awhile you learn this. You learn not to kill music. But I guess that's what I'm doing now, isn't it?"

The nuns didn't answer. The one standing moved a little.

"Isn't it?" Larry repeated.

"How much do you want? How much is it?" asked Sister Celia.

He looked out of the window. Now he felt disgusted. It was the time for jazz and oranges, shaking buttocks. He had waited too long. Outside he saw a woman hanging up a bedsheet. "The ad," he said quietly, steadily, "asked forty dollars."

There was a circle of silence. The woman was finished with her bedsheet. Somebody stumbled up the rooming house stairs.

"However," he looked at Sister Celia and smiled, "I ask thirty-five . . ."

■

They left in a taxi after he carried the things down and put them in the back seat between them. They felt very bad about taking the taxi, but said it was the only way. He agreed. They felt bad about the thirty-five dollars too, but they didn't say anything . . .

Larry met the landlady as he came back up the steps. "It's a good thing," she said.

"What?"

"For the school, the girls."

"Oh, yes," he said, "I feel fine about it."

He went up the stairs and back into his room. He sat on the edge of his bed and pulled out his wallet. He ran his fingers along the edges of the bills. Then he took them out and spread them on the bed. The bills were neither old nor new; just middle-aged. There were three tens and a five.

It seemed very little.

. . . In this rifacimento are we deliberately manufacturing a lozenge that the public will swallow? Who is the poet that will dance before the serried mob? Jazz should not hold hands with poetry. Jazz can be vital, stimulating. It may be folklore and it may be ingested — at times — into art, but jazz is not a proper art. Jazz is beat, jazz is surface, jazz is suggestive of sexual rhythms and the act: jazz is congo, jazz is good, jazz is bad; but jazz, for all its claims is thin and confined and tenuous — it borrows tricks from the classics, but it never learns. Poetry? Poetry is good and bad and great — most of it bad — and going to bed with jazz is not going to produce strong children.

All right, you get an audience. But is it an intellectual audience or a gang out "for kicks"? And who is getting kicked? What eremite, what Ivory-Tower personage is going to sing their tune as the very nereids drown? It would seem to me that a poet who would put himself into this position must be somewhat the actor and extrovert, and more or less hungry for immediate acclaim: the applause of those close enough to give him the warmth of being recognized as at least alive, whether or not they perceive any of the concepts he may still retain after leveling his work to suit their genre.

I am not reading-down poetry audiences — I am reading-*up* poetry. When poetry becomes popular enough to fill cabarets and music halls, then something is wrong with that poetry or with that audience. Either the audience looks upon that poet as a freak, a clown jiggling to jazz, a moment to be remembered as something-odd-between-drinks, or that poet is deliberately reading down to that audience in order to captivate it. We deserve the bearded vulture for sitting with the croupier, and two or five or ten years from now, when we look back upon ourselves for taking the bait, those who are now in most lucifugous crowing, I'm sure will then be most inarticulate in phrasing their contribution to prostitutions and the gelding of the muse.

PORTIONS FROM A

WINE-STAINED NOTEBOOK

no corrections on the falcon or the shimmy of your behind, my dear—correction on the destiny of man.... death, god death is unbelievable... I have seen the green walls and the rosary and death before Christmas, a locked door, turned away ... watered lawns; and always sunshine, sunshine ... why?

I have come through a hell far greater than any personal surmising can ever evaluate, and I should think there would be others, I should think the laughter would be at ever breathing, but the books say no, the books speak of monotonous things, very monotonous things in monotonous ways—there is no one with a knife on the leprosy of screaming; let us not leave life to the idiots to spill like some poor porridge, or the girls on gin. I think today I will break a window and listen to E. Power Biggs. What's your excuse?

I have chased the whores out of here and mopped the kitchen floor. The next problem is the rent. I'll be 39 in & near 7 days and I still live like a gypsy. I do think poetry is important though, if you don't strive at it, if you don't fill it full of stars and falseness. Poetry, paint, sand, whores ... food, fire, death, bullshit ... the turning of a fan ... the bottle.

... well, who do *you* consider the greatest writer of all time?

I do not consider the greatest writer of all time. I consider a few moderns, then forget them. This is not conceit but a defense against intrusion.

do you believe in God?

Not if God is invented and only if He will allow me to. God must invent us without knowledge of Him, and if there is One, He probably has. An impossible question.

Why do you write?

I write as a function. Without it I would fall ill and die. It's as much a part of one as the liver or intestine, and just about as glamorous.

Does pain make a writer?

Pain doesn't make anything, nor does poverty. The artist is there first. What becomes of him depends upon his luck. If his luck is good (worldly-speaking) he becomes a bad artist. If his luck is bad, he becomes a good one. In relation to the substance involved.

death is victory.
        I am dead
        I am dead
        DEAD

a trigger before the distant
        eyes of China
and three old men smoking in
        the fog;
nearly, nearly, says the heater
and the dog springs past the
        golden bough.
before the mast of God
swabbed steep in cotton and
        olive oil,

the waves leap high like
            celluloid films
showing the beautiful face of
            Satan.

perhaps, of course, the delicate
            reasoning of the piano
            keys:
perhaps, even the running of
            horses
mounted by small men in bean
            and green and red and
            blue silks
whipping their mounts through
            the brush
calling names across the lake,
and here with the heavy-breasted
            blond,
the prize, I wait the winning
            horse,
the spreading
of the legs for champions,
but how simple and unreasonable
she is
waiting for a number
to prove my fertility across
one mile of dirt
when
any stallion
would do the same.

There are not enough lives in one man to conquer Art, let alone enough men in one world to criticize it. it was the paint; it was not my fault; the scenery was bad. I am dying without illness, I am dying with an existence too cold for striving. I stare out of a window into the bright and horrible day that wrenches at my stomach. Does no one else feel this way? Am I truly mad?

ah, to be a dresser holding bits
        of clothing,
a warm-gutted sanctuary as
        immortal as a Rodin,
and free
because
it's dead.

Dear E.T.: Regarding your letter, I sense an undercurrent, a feeling for humanity, a sense of sanity and science and politics, a striving for forwardness in the Arts, or at least a hope for these things. I do (at weak moments) admire the intellectual broad warm outlook and wish (at weak moments) that I had it. But actually I find this age as dull, indecent, and castrated as the slaughter of an old steer for blue steak. Man is rotted and rooted in an amphigen pit and doesn't wish to come out. Very well, I probably would have been malcontent in any other age, probably more so than I am now. Yet anything is pardonable if you believe in God, and I believe in the God of Myself: the one who finds as much color in a brick as in a rose, superable yet adamant. Trappo! Smolzando sognado solenne.

I would still like to say that your friend who fits glasses somewhere (he fitted mine, remember?) so revolted and still so revolts me with his sophisticated assuredness of his bald handsomeness, the very deadness of his pink scrubbed skin, that I could not look him in the eye or the face or any portion of that thin but dead surface self-victory. I wasn't gambling (for once), I was merrily eating an olive and thinking of the Ballet Russe de Monte Carlo group when these guys came in with straw hats on and started throwing knuckles and clubs, and there was nothing to do but duck and I landed in a hyacinth bush and tried to look like a blossom dream-dancing but this guy flushed me out with a flashlight the size of a Pantages searchlight, and I crossed with a right and he crossed with a pellet beholden in leather stropping, and coming to I awakened in a cell no larger that a midget's clothes closet, no place to read Rimbaud or try on a top hat. . . . Ah, *Mexico*!

and the trick is to stay propped up for 50 or 60 or 70 or 80 or 90 years yes eyes open while the flies get stuck in the paper and the great paintings are stolen and the faithful wives run off with unfaithful lovers, all to die in the morning, unclasped and cold and kissless.

There was the day at the corner of Haggerty and 8th when God tumbled from the sky like a broken kite falling, falling, the string of power broken . . . wound about His throat, and a piston-powered spear riven in His heart.

I ran to the vacant lot where He sprawled like a harpooned whale, golden beads of sweat upon His brow and He winked at me, He winked a magnificent eye upon me and spoke: "Old man, it's all been a waste of time. Hasn't it?"

all that I know is that I believe in the sound of music and the running of a horse. all else is squabble.

perhaps the greatest achievement of Man is his ability to die, and his ability to disregard it. certainly poetry and paint are no deterrent, nor the high hurdles of the mind over the skulls of realism. let us say, finally, that truth is not all that matters—often, it is the putting aside of a truth.

You cross me you bastard he said reaching under the mattress for the tire iron, and you've had it. listen, Lou, I said, all I do is write poetry and drink and listen to music and fuck, I have no other choice . . . I don't trust no book-readers, he said. You guys are all pansies who couldn't hit a baseball. You've got me all wrong, Lou: I wasn't *interested* in hitting a baseball, and if I *had* gotten interested and thought it meant something I would have hit it further than a Baltimore orphan, and I could probably whip your ass if I figured it was worthwhile. He laughed through his stupid face and never realized how close to death he came . . .

what we need is a single hero to uphold the defeated, a Quijote of the windmills, here and now, and after we've thought we've found him, only later to see him breaking bread with the enemy, and smiling and tipping his hat as though he thought we were damn fools for believing in him, and we were.

drunk again in a crackerbox room, dreaming of Shelley and youth, bearded, jobless bastard with a walletful of win tickets un-cashable as Shakespeare's bones. we all hate poems of pity or cries of the wailing poor—a good man can climb any flag and salute prosperity (we're told) but how many good men can you get in an air-tight jar? and how many good poets can you find at IBM or snoring under the sheets of a fifty-dollar whore? more good men have died for poetry than all your crooked battlefields were worth; so if I fall drunk in a four-dollar room: you messed up your history—let me dawdle in mine.

slowly they came by, all the faces like the faces of fishermen in a passing boat, and fisherwomen too with their hooks and baits and golden barbed nets, with their taunts and calls and accusations. yes, like fish themselves hung upright from their strings, their button eyes launching wicked points of light beneath the stiffled covering of fear.

When I was 24 or 5 I ran errands for sandwiches and cleaned venetian blinds and answered questions on the classics in a bar in Philly straight East of the Eastern pen. Most days were memory-less but not meaningless: I was feeling toward the classic of self, almost found it one day when I failed my errand and fell in an alley like a great wounded bird, white belly up to sun, and children came up and poked at me, and I heard a woman's voice: "Now you leave that man alone!" and I laughed quietly inside myself, on such a fine Spring day to be a castratedly inept, a young man printed on both sides of the Atlantic, and somebody's fine sandwich in the dirt.

past the desk with a face, past coffins filled with love, past the sparrow sick with dreams.

they move the dead at night on soft wheels as the living sleep. life becomes less and less as moment falls on moment like dry leaves.

Caprice elevates doom to the stature of knowledge.

Once in Paris I saw a hog as great as any of your mothers and the sprig of my indecent soul wretched and I offered her a cigarette and a blossom of wine, and we sat among the young and the fertile and she knew I was quite insane, and I said mother I love you, I love the youth that was you; I can still see it, death will not rob us for I see beneath the waters. And we drank and she, the fool believed, which was all that was necessary and she took me to her little cupboard of a room and through the stink of her age I made a love that killed the tiny love that was left in me, and when Barbara wrote from New York I stared at the ink, and I tore its eagerness and turned and turned to my hog and said, a child, nothing but a child.

could I but wash away meaning like a sore, and would that the animal in my wisdom eat and disgorge my tender brain.

"Poets are faced with the tremendous task of regaining public confidence."
Warren G. French, EPOS, Winter 1959.

If I ever gained public confidence I would most surely examine myself and wonder whereupon and how I had failed. I cannot see poetry as a public vehicle, nor even, as an extant, a private vehicle of the few. It is less that that—when I have a poem accepted by a magazine that prints so-called quality poetry, I ask myself where I have failed. Poetry must continually move out of itself, away from shadows and reflections. The reason so much bad poetry is written is that it is written as poetry instead of concept. And the reason the public doesn't understand poetry is that there is nothing to understand, and the reason most poets write it is that they think they understand. Nothing is to be understood or "regained." It is simply to be written. By someone. Sometime. And not too often.

a good violin braced with agony, piano players drunk in stale bars; lights, lights, cats in alleys; priests asleep, men shining bombers.

and so, I apologize to death for living so with casket toes and books of skulls and histories of the vultures; I should have painted like a cloud into the rim of outwardness, but I paused to look upon a final nylon kneecap, the idle clatter of the cats, the blasphemy of food and wine. I read of Napoleon and Cicero and planted things that bloomed. Ah well, how many have paused upon the crevice. . . . looking back, and making signs of flight, or obeisance, or treason? I stare into the pit, into the god-faces, the fiery masks of hallucination and ask . . . how can I worry about a dead battery or the future of Spain? need I close the door tonight?

our Art is our agony turned to reason. We are the prize of a twisted mind, dirty bits of clay that sit and wait on some imbecile table in some imbecile darkness. our world turns on a violated wheel held up by the thin spokes of poetry . . .

I've lost 5 ballpoint pens in 2 months and just cracked 3 of my toenails across the foot of my bed. If you think Christ was crucified, come again; the phone hasn't rung for 7 weeks and I am lying here with a 4-day beard, lifting the shades up and down, up and down, trying to figure whether it is noon or midnight, and they keep sending me circulars in the mail advertising tombstones, tombstones whetted across the paper like a moth on a lampshade while I am busy listening to some opera in Italian which is also advertising tombstones.

. . . to be swallowed by a whale would be better than being hacked and nibbled by the barracuda. it is not death, but the manner of dying. perhaps that is why we bank them with flowers, to slacken the sting, evolve and distort the ending as a commencing, a controlled and reckoned thing. that is civilization, and, of course, it fails.

I am sitting here drunk wondering how and where I'll live tomorrow. The row is no place for a man who desires the privacy of his thoughts. they say I am a fair poet and wield a nice brush, and I get perfumed letters from distant ladies, but I am ready for the crows against the sun of my reason, as I listen to Rachmaninoff on a radio I must hock tomorrow, I tell you we are all mad and misfits and the university officials who teach poesy from dusty quiet campus windows know nothing of these walls or the landladies of South Hollywood or the torn faces on the row where the words Rimbaud or Rilke mean less than a nickel, where all the love of man and life are less than rolls of paper that flap as our sheets, are less than the rats that know us and share our alleys, our small unheard defeats.

I don't force the hand to write the lie for the sake of creating another poem.

death batters at my mind like a wild bat enclosed in my skull.

like a yellow dresser in an old rooming house in New Orleans or Atlanta or Savannah, or Temple Street in Los Angeles, standing with a cigarette and gambling with insanity and death. You can tell me about rivers and rain and I can tell you about dead thin bodies on dope and agony, dreaming a greater life than given without woman or job or country, fallen across bars blooming with homosexuals playing untuned pianos, and dull-faced cashier-owners whistling in dead coins.

The police ask, what are you doing here down by the water? as I spit out a rotten tooth and hold the bleeding of my side. the police ask, why aren't you asleep at this time of night? as fish attacks fish and the bones of Caesar are so very still, the police ask, where do you live? not, why do you live? but where? and they take me to their jail, a thing of wood and steel. what is your name? they ask. they ask all the easy questions and I suppose that is why they are so fat and fearless and clean.

My young friend is *very* young and asks young questions. I doubt that he has even yet had sexual intercourse. But that doesn't matter. Some whore will find him. There is no escape.

Do you believe in the price of life? he asks. I don't quite understand your question. I do not believe in the price of anything. I am a dreamer. I believe in possession without pain. I am not a realist. I lack backbone, I hate boredom and striving. I'd rather listen to the overture to *Samson* by Handel.

Do you believe in God?

Anything is possible . . .

could I only blow off my head with a .45 without thinking, the grass is so very green.

cool is the wind in my old man's
heart.

the bones of my love are down amongst my ladies, down amongst my ladies,
and my languor is so precious now.

the dead are so very old and the
living so very practical.

bestial rhymes assault my heart, congregate there, stamp their flabby feet
amongst the plague and wreckage.

your love is Cuba with a beard, a ten-penny press breathing rum; your love
is baseball in a bow-tie playing mandolins to Brahms; your love is 14 cats
kicking in my brain; your love is gin-rummy and sanctimonious freaks selling pamphlets on East First; your love is a tailor-made in a lonely jail; your
love is the sinking of the ships, the torpedo of doubt; your love is wine and
the painting and painting of Picasso; your love is a sleeping bear in the cellar of the *Moulin Rouge*; your love is a broken tower struck by the lightning
of Eiffel; your love walks the hills and climbs the mountains and shoots Rus-
sians to the moon.
    why do you
    walk
    away?

death, at last, is a bore—no more than pulling a shade. we do not die all at
once, generally, but piece by piece, little by little. the young die hardest and
live hardest and understand nothing. but they are the most generous and
the truest and better fit to lead than the cautious wise. who survives out of
candor? not even a spider. show me those who are left and I will show you
nothing. the young have yet to surrender to fact. and fact is nothing but the

grime of centuries. the young bud is the hardest. I am old, so you cannot censure me with prejudice.

we have all been drinking and picked up off the streets. the cell is filled with drunks who do not sing or who have never heard Beethoven's marvelous symphony #9. It is like a monastery, only God is very far away. the guards pass by, see me standing. "Go to sleep," they say. "Go to sleep." They remind me of my wife.

why do they always want sleep? why must I close my eyes on this beastly universe? I am dreaming a song . . . how these men snore as the moon paints their faces with death . . . in the morning they will awaken and scratch and curse as the gulls whirl down to peck out their dimming eyes.

you're just playing around, pally, he said, and I clubbed him across the eye with a platinum pipe, gouged out the eye, and flipped it to a passing vulture. I know you can do better than that, he said, as I cut up his belly like a checkerboard. you're the greatest, he said, when you sit down to a typewriter the mountains move. never mind that crap, I said. I want the winner of the 6th. write me a sonnet, he laughed, write me a *beautiful* sonnet! I sliced him again and he fell forward, and then he lifted his ugly dripping head one last time: I started as a hot-walker when I was 12 years old, he laughed, knowing I was trapped, and I'll tell you this: you'll never beat the ponies.

I switched out the light and left him in his own blood. outside the lamplights were going and the fog was going and I was sick of everything, especially poetry.

especially poetry. poetry. My head aches like a cocoanut rolling over the rocks. poetry. their damned artillery has been blasting wince and since the Christ of Easter, and the dirt falls in my ears. my teeth ache, my liver's black (no racial discrimination here), I'm constipated (also no racial discrimination here—I have to be very careful since this is a democracy and I am white) but for Christ's sake, do you think it's worth living? do you? this is not it—my teeth ache and my liver's white. there's nothing but shrapnel and confusion and nobody knows what the hell he's fighting for. Yet, they all go on. and on. and on.

do you want an ending?

write it yourself. me?

I'm going to open another vottle. not a vottle, but a bottle. you open it and I'll drink it. and you try writing as much as I did without falling off of your chair. Meanwhile go to hell until you can understand the desperateness of living art without a false mustache. I know, I know, this is not it, this is certainly not it: my head aches like a coconut rolling over rocks and all the blondes are old, and the leaves crack under my feet.

A RAMBLING ESSAY ON POETICS AND THE BLEEDING LIFE WRITTEN WHILE DRINKING A SIX-PACK (TALL)

In the days when I thought I was a genius and starved and nobody published me I used to waste much more time in the libraries than I do now. It was best to get an empty table where the sun came through a window and get the sun on my neck and the back of my head and my hands and then I did not feel so bad that all the books were dull in their red and orange and green and blue covers sitting there like mockeries. It was best to get the sun on my neck and then dream and doze and try not to think of rent and food and America and responsibility. Whether I was a genius or not did not so much concern me as the fact that I simply did not want a part of anything. The animal-drive and energy of my fellow man amazed me: that a man could change tires all day long or drive an ice cream truck or run for Congress or cut into a man's guts in surgery or murder, this was all beyond me. I did not want to begin. I still don't. Any day that I could cheat away from this system of living seemed a good victory for me. I drank wine and slept in the parks and starved. Suicide was my biggest weapon. The thought of it gave me some peace; the thought that the cage was not entirely closed actually gave me some small strength to linger within the cage. Religion seemed a con-game, a trick of mirrors, and I felt that if there was to be Faith, the faith should begin within me without the easiness of ready-made aids, ready-made gods. . . . Women seemed a part of everything else: they put a value on themselves and extracted a price, but from the sensibility of my eye and what soul I possessed it seemed that they all made demands beyond their worth. And having watched my father, that brutalized monster who bastardized me upon this sad earth, I realized that a man could work a lifetime and still remain poor; his wages were taken in buying things he needed, small things, like automobiles and beds and radios and food and clothing, which, like women, demanded a price far beyond their worth and kept him poor, and even his casket was the final outrage of decency: all that fine varnished beautiful wood for the blind worms of hell.

Then too, you could become rich and it wouldn't mean anything. Laugh if you wish. I will take all the money you will send me but I will really know that I have essentially nothing. If the rich are our superior race I want to get out fast. I've seen the skulls of the dead hog's heads biting into dead apples that were less ugly; that in comparison were not ugly at all. Sitting there at that library table, starving, sitting in the sun. I felt it all: the shit war, the dullness, the death, the buzzing of the flies . . .

Then I was lost and young; now I am lost and old. There I sat in that library, the knowledge of generations there and not worth a damn to me, and not a living voice in the world that had spoken anything. There I sat among all those books and I was thinking, the way they kill people they ought to use the screwdriver and pliers and pour acid in their eyes; they ought to break their legs right off; they ought to put them in cages with tigers. The way they kill people not one or 2 come out alive in a million, and who's doing it, and why?

And if I left the library I would have to walk the streets and pass doors with locks, windows that were bolted at night. Women who tilted their heads up at me because I was dressed in rags but women who would sleep with any fat swine who owned a string of race horses and pawnshops. I would walk through streets of dead men that moved and spoke and had names and pride and possessions but who were really dead. Any avenue of faces would be a dream of horror—the vicious & bone-dry & shit-bowl faces . . . I would reel dizzy after viewing such a parade, not from hunger but from knowing that I lived and would live forever in this life, in a world of the dead.

Finally, the library being my room for the day, walls at last!! No green steel or wooden slab of bench. I began to look around some more. I had begun my reading early, at 14, having to hide the bed lamp under the covers to shut out the light because my father demanded lights out at 8 p.m., so he could gather strength for the next day of being a contemporary imp of toil without meaning.

Well, I began in the Philosophy and Religion Room and by the time I got to the Current Affairs Room with its copies of the *New York Times*, I was still a poor bet for life, and the razors and the gas pipes and the bridges and Thomas Chatterton's rat poison were still arguing for first shot. Again, it was the old problem: dead affairs of dead men with a dead viewpoint, wasted, wasted pages! The old con game, the old joke of a knowledge that didn't really exist, dressed up in a pretty & painted terminology. Actually almost all the time they were talking about things that had nothing to do with ME; and ego be damned, what was more important (I almost said impotent) than me? I was actually bouncing up and down the teeter-totter of death and they were talking about cupcakes in the window! Or worse, they would go through pages of fancy drivel, almost then finally TOUCH SOMETHING!, and then, LEAVE OFF! At the time I thought they might be holding back; now I know better: they simply had nothing to say. Yet even then, I was suspect of them. I was aware of the glass-prison terminology: that fancy, long, and twisted words were evasions, crutches, weaknesses. And so I used to think of it as "bullshit padding": talking about useless things in useless terminology.

Yet I was drawn into an area: what answers there were and what force there was (feeble as it might seem) appeared to be in the creative art of writing—novel, short story, poetry. And I guess more through love than reason (and what can be a better reason?) I have long since decided that POETRY is the shortest, sweetest, bangingest way. Why write a novel when you can say it in ten lines? Why write ten novels when you can write 10,000? CRIME AND

PUNISHMENT, of course, could not have been written in ten lines, and although I do not agree with the ending which was forced by pressurized formula of our society's cant, it was a beautiful act still, and I give grace to the few novelists, but they are certainly no excuse for those 1/10th wits who follow. The 3/4s of C. and P. are one of the few things to keep a young starving madman alive in the dullness of our public libraries. Sherwood Anderson was good until he learned he could fool them with a pose: something first pointed out to Faulkner (one of the greatest lousiest fakes of this age, accepted grandly) and then later to Hemingway and a pose which he later fell heir to himself. Yet poetry is the big good horse in the stretch: you can't deny him; they're going to hang up his number. Get on.

So I laid around there on the park benches and I went into the library, the librarians sniffing at my clothes, and I came across the critical articles in the *Kenyon* and *Sewanee Reviews*, and for some vague reason this stuff looks pretty good when you haven't eaten for a couple of days. I guess it's the feeling of stolidity, and I like the smell of the unread pages and that soft-hard language intermixed as if they really knew what was going on and could talk about it from a sort of façade of gentleness and learning. Such musical and efficient language! And such nice ways of knifing! I read these most officious and learned magazines, they gave me tiny moments of pleasure—3 minutes or 5 minutes and then I was done, CHEATED AGAIN: the magazines really said nothing real, nothing about the streets outside, the park benches, the faces, the almost uselessness of living. They were talking about dead men who had become safe and staid enough to talk about.

I wrote short stories and printed them out in longhand because I had no typewriter and often no address, and I imagine many a fat warm editor had his laugh and threw them away, except Whit Burnett of the old *Story* magazine who seemed interested in a kind of amused off-hand fashion, and I threw them away too when they came back—and he finally took one. Yet I had been thinking of poetry for some time. It was back there in my skull somewhere. I guess I thought of it while riding west to Sacramento with the track gangs. I guess I thought of it while celling with public enemy #1 Court-ney Taylor; I guess I thought of it while using a borrowed portable type-writer on the top of a Filipino's head while escaping from a smashed and drunken room in L.A. But hell, you know America. Somewhere along the line, somewhere from the schoolyard on up they get *to* you. They tell you, essentially, that the poet is a sissy. And they are not always wrong. One time, in my madness, I happened to take a course in Creative Writing at L.A. City College. They were sissies, baby! Simpering, pretty, gutless wonders. Writ-ing about the lovely spiders and flowers and stars and family picnics. The women were larger and stronger than the men but they wrote just as badly. They were lonely-hearts and they enjoyed being together; they enjoyed the tight little chatter; they enjoyed their angers and their stale dead unoriginal opinions. The instructor sat on a hand-knitted rug in the center of the floor, his eyes glazed with stupidity and lifelessness, and they gathered around him, smiling upward at their god, the women with their large skirts flounced and the men with their tight little male buttocks reamed out with joy. They read to each other and giggled and simmered and drank tea with their cookies.

Laugh! — I sat alone against a wall, hollow-eyed and pissed and tried to listen and I realized that even when they argued with each other it was still some kind of truce between limited minds.

"Bukowski," the instructor asked me one day, "why don't you ever say anything? What do you think?"

"It's all crap," I said, "everything that has been said in this room is crap."

And that was the best poem of the semester. Three weeks later, after some luck with the dice in the urinal in the local bar, I was sleeping on the sands of Miami Beach and working as a part-time stockboy for Di Prima's.

It's like the old weather gag: everybody talks about poetry but nobody can do anything about it. Well, generally, and more so than in the other Arts, we ball and jack with traditions too much. I don't see why the written word cannot be made as paint or sound. Certainly we have no excuse to linger in the rut and let the other Arts take the play away from us. But tradition has worked and the apes are working their way toward *hurrah! hurrah!* carefully. Tradition is tough, sweetheart—if you've got a hangover you take a seltzer. If you want to write a poem you reread your Keats and Shelley, or if you want to appear modern you reread your Auden, Spender, Eliot, Jeffers, Pound and W. C. Williams and your E.E.C. The whole game stinks. There aren't 5 men in the land who can lay down 4 real lines. The game still belongs to the sissies, the stargazers, the lesbians, and the English teachers.

Call me a hardhead if you wish, uncultured, drunken, whatever. The world has shaped me and I have shaped what I can. I have carried the bleeding 1/2 steer on my shoulder that was alive a minute ago and swung him to the dull hook on the truck-roof through gristle; I've entered the women's can with a mop while you slept; I've rolled and been rolled; I've prayed to a toteboard; I've been blackjacked in a pisser for making a play for a gangster's moll; I was married to a woman with a million dollars and left her; I have crawled drunken in alleys from coast to coast; I've pumped gas, worked in a dog biscuit factory, sold Xmas trees, even been a foreman; I've been a truck driver, I've guarded door, looking for boots in a Texas whorehouse; I lived a year on a yacht by learning how to start the auxiliary engine and by making love to the woman of a rich madman with one arm who thought he was a genius at playing the organ and I had to write the words for his damned operas, and I was drunk most of the time and he was drunk most of the time and it worked until he died, but why go on with the rest? The subject is poetry.

The subject is dull.

Poetry must become, must right itself. Whitman had it backwards: I'd say that to have great audiences we must *first* have great poetry. I've never said this before but I am now high enough as I write this to perhaps say that Ginsberg has been the most awakening force in American poetry since Walt. It's a goddamn shame he's a homo. It's a goddamn shame Genet is a homo. Not that it is a shame to be a homo but that we have to wait around and let the homos teach us how to write. Whitman, I understand, used to chase the sailors. That manly man with those nice white, white, whiskers of contemplation, with that beautiful face! — chasing sailors!

Can you blame the schoolyard boys for saying that poets are sissies? Can't you see Whitman pinching a dull sailor's leg and grinning? Can't you see the rest?

The rest of you, the one or 2 of you must come around. I figure I am writing pretty good stuff but not nearly good enough. But I'm getting old, drink too much, talk too much, and it's time for some surly hardhead to come on through—

> make at last
> those tough-faced schoolboys
> put down their fists and their bats and
> their rocks
> and listen to the real
> strong
> . . . E. E. Cummings in bronze.
> out front, in front of whorehouse and
> high school . . .
>   old Ezra coming home at age
>   of 100
>   tattooed with Chinese hieroglyphics and
> being elected governor of New Hampshire.

And now I hear the old woman in the next room rocking my child in the rocker: squeeeee! squeeee! squeeee!

It's good, and yet it's a shame what they do to men, and it's a shame what they've done to me, as careful and careless and I have been. I would say that a poet must be careful with his occupation and with his cock and with his ego if he is to survive more than just a moment. But first of all cancel your subscription to the *Kenyon Review* and come here to *Ole* where you have to squint at what you read and laugh because we can't spell or punctuate. You'll still feel better. You'll gain 15 pounds and begin sleeping with your sister or your best friend's wife. There's a chance for almost anything.

Even ending this article.

See?

IN DEFENSE OF A CERTAIN TYPE

OF POETRY, A CERTAIN TYPE

OF LIFE, A CERTAIN TYPE

OF BLOOD-FILLED CREATURE

WHO WILL SOMEDAY DIE

For some of us the game is certainly not easy for we know the mockery of most funerals and most lives and most ways. We are surrounded by the dead who are in positions of power because in order to obtain this power it is necessary for them to die. The dead are easy to find—they are all about us; the difficulty is in finding the living. Notice the first person you pass upon the sidewalk outside—the color has gone from the eye; the walk is crude, awkward, ugly; even the hair on the head seems to grow in a diseased fashion. There are many more signs of death—one is a feeling of *radiation*, the dead actually throw off rays, stink from the dead soul, that can make you lose your lunch if you remain about too long.

> Finding Life and keeping it until death
> that
> in our cowardly and cruel and paper-faced society
> is the problem, said the cat,
> jumping backward over its
> ass.

We have had some good teachers in the Arts. And some bad ones. But within the history of nations all the leaders of the centuries behind us, our political leaders, have been bad teachers and have now led us into an almost dead-end alley. Our leaders of State have necessarily been vicious, narrow, and stupid men . . . because to lead the dead mass our so-called leaders have had to speak dead words and preach dead ways (and war is one of their ways) in order to be heard by dead minds. History, because it is built in this bee-hive fashion, has left us nothing but blood and torture and waste—even now after almost 2,000 years of semi-Christian culture the streets are full of drunks and poor and starving, and murderers and police and the crippled lonely, and the newly-born shoved right into the center of the remaining shit—Society.

I don't know if the world can ever be saved; it would take a tremendous and almost impossible turnabout. But if we cannot save the world, then at least let us know what it is, where we are.

You can find many many world-savers. Almost as many world-savers as you can dead. And, unfortunately, most world-savers are already dead. Having forgotten, somewhere, to save themselves.

Which brings us right about now up to that dirty word POETRY. All right:

The writers of poetry, being members of a surviving society, are necessarily a turning wheel of that society to the *exact* extent to which they have become involved with it, within it. In actuality, if they survive well, $$$-wise, within that society they must necessarily support that society with their poesy, or if they do not agree with history or society they are vicious enough or clever enough to dearly mention it not. Most often this leaves their poetry talking about useless things with great subtlety. A dirty dull little game. Most of our bad and acceptable poetry is written by English profs of state-supported, rich-supported, industry-supported universities. These are careful teachers picked to breed careful men to keep the upper-game going while the lower-game, the lower echelon of men and nations, gets the going over. This game is played with *complete* cooperation among the upper culture dummies . . . except with certain minor and bitter and chickenshit power disputes among themselves.

A man with any sense in his head or feeling in his heart would never go to a university even if he could afford to. There is nothing for him to learn there except what has happened in the history of things and he already knows what has happened in the history of things by walking around any city block one time. Let us say then, that a man is born into the world with a certain manner of given sense and that he retains a portion of this as he grows in inches, in feet, in years. The university won't do because it is an extension of the natural history of death. Yet society says that a man without a university education, because he refuses to carry the game forward, must act as a lower or end-agent of the game: newsboy, busboy, dishwasher, car-washer, janitor, whatever.

So you think it over and spit it out. Given 2 choices, being a professor of English or a dishwasher, you take the dishwasher. Perhaps not to save the world but to harm it less. But, saying you have the inclination, you reserve yourself the right to write poetry, not as it is *taught* but as the force or lack of force of it enters and exits within you as you live your small choice. If you are lucky you may even choose to starve for even washing dishes holds its own death.

Yesterday a literary bit of a magazine, with some reputation, landed in my mailbox. And within it was this long evaluation of an English teacher and lecturer and poet who everybody seems to fear, and who, obviously, writes very badly and without heart. He writes about nothing with great tenacity and follows most of his poesy up with "organic matter" theories and much dead and stilted terminology, which like his art almost seems to say something if you scratch long enough. But even crickets seem to say something, if you scratch long enough, and you can mouth a lot of bullshit about that too. I gave this literary bit of a magazine away to somebody passing through here (the paper was too hard to wipe my ass with) or I would have more exact quotes. Forgive me. But in this long love-fear piece for this English teacher and poet and scholar, it was mentioned that this dear and very real man said at one of his lectures, something like:

> "Now, perhaps, maybe, my troubles, are
> your
> troubles, too."

This was evaluated as a very profound and subtle statement, saturated with wisdom, but of course it was only a stolen statement said on many streetcorners long ago, and, in this case, a damned two-bit hoax. His troubles are *not* my troubles. He has chosen against trouble and to die. I have chosen trouble and to live.

Yet the situation is standard and continuing. All through this article this poet was given credit for tremendous insights while writing insipid and flat and lifeless statements . . . statements of yawn and impurity. And he has his followers and the whole boatload write in the same fashion — missing the point: LIFE — and adding more dead history to already dead history, more lousy tricks to more lousy tricks, more lousy lies to more lousy lies . . . more yawns and dead-dog dirt to the poor and already-mashed soul.

And then come the standard fatheads of the outer ring wanting to get *in*, and the inner ring meanwhile conning everybody, until you get a fathead dead poetry which is speaking always of nothing, nothing, NOTHING . . .

i & meeley////

chopsticks/ 7 --- *

&

it was there

i was there   i   &

gwatammurrrra mass #9/ .

1/4///. . ./ .

A poem like this can be given tremendous insight for saying almost anything you care for it to say, for who can prove that it doesn't? Listen to your cricket. I am not against exploration in the Arts but I am against being taken for a sucker by men who lack the ability to create. We are interested only in the pure crap and scream of Art.

Our days in the jails and madhouses and flophouses have let us know more where the sun comes from than any workable knowledge of Shakespeare, Keats, Shelley . . . We've been hired and fired and quit, and shot at and slugged; we've been rolled while drunk; we've been spat upon because we did not play the role of *their* history and were waiting for a moment enough in a small room with a typewriter or even without a typewriter, just the paper of our skin, sure, and what was under it, and so, of course, when we sat down to write—being slugged and weary but still alive—we did not write *exactly* as some thought POETRY should be written or as some thought *anything* should be written. We did not, of course, fit the pleasant and numbing form of their death. There is nothing that the dead hate worse than to see something alive. So, somehow, we were printed in the very few places that dared to print us. And then came the cries of the dead:

FILTH! STINK! THIS IS NOT *POETRY*! We are turning you over to the postal authorities.

To many, poetry should only say safe things or nothing because poetry is a safe world and a safe way to them. The delicacy of their poetry is that it talks about everything that does not count. Poetry in their world is like a bank account. Poetry is *Poetry Chicago* which has been dead for so god-damned long that it is hardly worthwhile to attack them: it would be like hitting an old grandmother of 80 in church while she was praying.

But I guess that the little, insidious, snot-filled, death-filled people will always be there. And while we say, let them live, let them be, let them have their way, just let *us* breathe . . . *they* come down upon *us*, brothers, history wrankling their crooked dwarfed university brains, their little housewives' brains piddling with plants and ancient and unreal 17th century verse while their neurotic husbands blandly rob some poor sons of bitches in the mighty names of Progress and Profit, they, all of them, damn them, damn our works as unreal, filthy, distraught, merciless, unseeing . . .

My god my god, if I could only rip my fucking heart out tonight and let them see it! But even then they would only take it as an apricot, a dried lemon, an old melon seed.

The most ordinary and real things are inconceivable to them. Say that it is even possible that a janitor who cleans out the ladies' shithouse could be equal or superior to the president of the United States of America, in non-destructive worthwhileness, or that he could be a better man than the head of any seeming nation that has existed through its terrible and shameful history of death. This they could never see for their eyes are taught only to recognize and see and acclaim death.

We, who write the poetry of Life, many of us are getting very tired and sad and sick and almost beaten (but not quite). Yet we still know that we do not need God to be Divine, that we do not need garden verses to be Saved, that we do not need War to be Free, that we do not need Creeleys to admire, that we do not need Ginsbergs who crumble into ranting freaks, but maybe we do need small tears for all the lovely girls grown old, the spilled beer, the fights on the front lawn over nothing but the drunkness of our sad love. I verily defend our poetry, we live ones of the Stockpile Generation, I verily defend our poetry and our right to say it, our right to write it. Without suit. Without a magazine raided by the police as "obscene." Without loss of chickenshit job. Please understand that I am not defending anything I write as immortal; I ask no special preciousness — yet all is precious enough: when I put on my shoes I only see 2 feet down there. But let us say this: some few such men as I have made a choice, whether talented or no, we are sick of the continual game of death, we are trying to import through broken arms and noses and brains and bones and lives that small touch of sanity and big prick sun: LIVING? Yeah, living, that which touches us all, you living dead and we living living.

The world of poetry drags in some terrible asses. Mostly terrible ones. Often the Arts are hiding places for people who would have *preferred* to make it elsewhere. Their shirttails and dirty panties will show. But Art, more so than the history and ways of nations, takes its time. But usually police raids indicate that some decent creation is going on. And the most beautiful thing of all is that most very good creators have little or no politics. Hence raids are left up to city instead of national police, who, hell, are kept busy enough elsewhere. The main trouble being, that in our courts of today, being innocent is not enough. It takes money to fight the tricks of injustice and the mind-state of our judges and juries. Hell, you can tell a lawyer what *you* are thinking but he must re-level and revise your thinking to fit the procedures of dead laws written by dead men to protect the dead. Nobody really understands; they have been drowned through the long steam-like and unreal years.

I often think of the Arts when fairly sober and I guess time will burn down most of it even if those STOCKPILES don't get jumping. I look ahead and see that Van Gogh will be eliminated as a wonderful jackass boy whose final failure will be proclaimed as lack of innocence, heart, and flair—just the things he is recognized for now. But this is the way Time works. Matisse, on the other hand, will last because he will not weary us. Dostoevsky will last, although portions of his work will be laughed at as the works of a crank and a fidget. O'Hara, our modern novelist will go very fast, followed quickly by Norman Mailer. Kafka, although real enough, will not last when the new dimensions are found. D. H. Lawrence will last, although why, I cannot tell you now. My brain does not have it; only the senses. Some of the early short stories of William Saroyan will last. Conrad Aiken will last a very long time and then wilt against the tide. Dylan Thomas, no, and Bob Dylan, certainly no. I don't know, I certainly don't know, ah Christ it all seems *wasted*, doesn't it? Camus, of course. Artaud, of course. Then I have to go back to Walt Whitman, that fairy who ached to and probably did suck sailor's cocks, and there's your *culture*, what?

But if you think Time and the fuzz is rough around here, listen to this letter from J. Bennett, Dec. 2, 1965, editor of *Vagabond*, Munich in the Deutschland: "... they're not printing all your old poems here—poems like yours they burn. That's a compliment. They just got through setting the match to a pile of Günter Grass', Heinrich Böll's, & Nabokov's books in Dusseldorf—some god fearing christian organization. They really got into the swing of things in Berlin—they set old Günter Grass' house on fire. Grass just smiles wryly and keeps on writing ..."

They have been after us forever (see Lorca) or we have been after ourselves with our own knives. We are the butterflies of a bad summer. And so, fuck, this article *still* remains a defense for poetry as against certain so-called poetries and lives. Many us do not make it, but through luck and o my god love, much will still somehow make it, which does not mean driving a Cadillac but which means *not* driving one, and many other things. I wrote this article because so few of us poetic outlaws have formulated any ground or reason to stand upon. The muddle-heads and English teachers talk continually from a rather absent and disabled platform of life. Yet, their drivel, like a continuing rain, drowns almost everybody. I hope that these few words from the corner barstool have gotten through to some — that our seemingly unsuccessful lives and ways and poesy are *chosen* ways. We are, most of us, neither killers or fakes. But someday we will write down the word so beautifully, o, so perfect and real, that all you monkeys will come out of your gardens and *begin to be* enough for me to look

upon
　　　that which makes the
　　　face and body and love of you
and
　　　I will not twitch in my damned
　　　rented cot
　　　for hours of
　　　spasm and pain and horror

　　　I die and pray for you and
　　　myself

　　　if I could wish all you
　　　bent dead bastards
　　　the tiny inch of my life left
　　　I would plunge it into you
　　　and
　　　sleep forever.

ARTAUD ANTHOLOGY

Antonin Artaud Anthology, EDITED BY JACK HIRSCHMAN.
CITY LIGHTS BOOKS, SAN FRANCISCO; 255 PP; $3.

It has been within the grace and genius of City Lights to publish our im-
mortals while they breathe. This beats blowing up Chinese firecrackers or
egging them to toss us a few. Among the almost four dozen titles they have
published are the almost and possibly durable classics: *Gasoline* (Corso);
Bottom Dogs (Dahlberg); *Human Songs* (Kay Johnson — kaja); *Selected Poems* (Lowry); *Meat Science Essays* (McClure); *Poems of Humor and Protest*
(Patchen); *Poem from Jail* (Sanders) and *Korea in Hell: Improvisations*
(W. C. Williams). The Ginsberg *Howl*, although historical (and which
came at the right time to loosen our neckties) contains a sad and straight
life-energy, but its possible artistic durability is suspect just as much as the
musical "Guys and Dolls"—which also helped to save my life. A little time
and print was also wasted on the "B's"—Bowles, Buckley and Burns—but
many comes the time when there is nothing to print and the machine just
stands there. Let it go—why not?

However, the latest, the Artaud, edited by Jack Hirschman, is the goddamned bell-ringer and what is to happen after this one—a topper? or an
apology? It's your guess, or mine, or anybody's. The last time Jack Hirschman and I met, it did not work out too well. It was my fault. No, it was HIS:
he was not as drunk as I. Nonetheless, the bastard has done a beautiful job
of assembly, and with the exception of one or two of his translators, Artaud
comes upon us—straight shot, no chaser. The only way to take him.

The Artistic public is always indecent. It will admire a man for his way
of life rather than for what he produces. They especially prefer madmen,
killers, addicts, suicides, starvation cases ... yet the same Artistic public
which later reveres one of these is the SAME public which drove him drink-
mad, mind-mad, dope-mad because he could not stand the sight of their

mugs or their ways. Artaud might come a little easier to them now . . . he's been dead since March 4, 1948.

I am not a student of literature. All I know is what I g.d. feel. The book is broken into two parts—"Before Rodez" and "Rodez and After." We don't divide a man by madhouses. Or breaks with surrealism. We follow a man's soul like a rotting string. And begin anywhere . . .

"To Adolph Hitler," page 105, is followed by an excuse (apology) for Artaud having produced such a thing. This is an old Artaud game: proving that he was NOT anti-semitic. It is an old parlor game and grows tiring. Artaud wrote and he wrote what he pleased to write. He wrote the black blood and the arrow. That a Jew or a dictator sometimes climbed aboard or had his nuts sliced off did not concern Artaud. Tedious points can be linked up by dull scholars that praise or blame a man for everything or anything. Artaud was not bothered by the game of historical pressures or even fanciful ejaculations of his own soul-ego. Artaud said what he had to say, not what he should say. This, of course, is what distinguishes madmen from motorcycle policemen.

"All Writing is Pigshit," page 38, defines for me (at least) something that I have always thought—that (along with the world) the artists, the writers are also intolerable, more weight to an already-anchor, more pain to an already-pain, more weight of shit to already so much shit that it is almost impossible to awaken alive, urinate, whatever, put clothes on and go out into the streets. The imbecility and horror and greediness and ego present in our so-called best minds . . . this dominant swill, this accepted glory, this eyetooth breaking into the top plank of our already manacled souls . . . it's obvious, or would be, only all eyes are closed, the damnation is as ordinary as winding a Thrifty Drug Store special wristwatch and hoping all the tenuous and snake-feeler guts don't pop out, give up. Almost without exception our writers—any writers—are the weakest creatures of our existence posing as martyrs, seers, directors, gods. Their weakness is so great that their practiced lie becomes literature.

Artaud, of course, being a madman, knew all of this:

"All those who have vantage points in their spirit . . ."

". . . all those who are masters of the language . . ."

". . . all those for whom words have a meaning . . ."

". . . all those who are the spirit of the times, and have named these currents of thought . . ."

What Artaud means is those who quickly take ANY bait in order to make more sublime their ends through weakness and death. Their thought-cells quickly going to bed with anything near instead of anything real. I can't blame the average mortal for failing because they are edgy and lose heart; but I can blame them for failing and trying to spread their lovely slime upon me.

"those who are fussy . . ."

"those who brandish whatever ideologies belong to the hierarchy of the times . . ."

"those about whom women talk so well, who talk of contemporary currents of thought . . ."

"you beard-asses, you pertinent pigs, you masters of fake verbiage, confectioners of portraits, pamphleteers, ground-floor lace-curtain herb collectors, entomologists, plague of my tongue."

■

In "Van Gogh: The Man Suicided by Society" Artaud tells us: "Indeed there is not a psychiatrist who is not a notorious erotomaniac."

When Artaud's headshrinker objected to this charge, Artaud answered:

"All I need to do, Dr. L_____, is to point you out as proof."

"You bear the stigma on your mug, you dirty bastard." Then Artaud went on to explain in detail. Poor Dr. L_____ had drawn a lion.

Artaud's sight-in on Van Gogh—one nut speaking of another—is a decry against society AND life, a life which Artaud felt Van Gogh released in his paintings, truly: a shuddering, somewhat horrible brooding thing, whirling with bats and black blood and gruff, mashed and stinking energy, searing and crawling landscapes, candles, chairs . . .

"I think that he died at 37 because, alas, he had reached the end of the dismal and revolting story of a man garroted by an evil spirit," says Artaud.

Dr. Gachet, under whom Van Gogh was treated, is given much of the responsibility for Van Gogh's suicide. Artaud has it in for the good Doctors and Medicine, as would any intelligent man who has spent any time in hospitals and institutions. It becomes more and more clear that Medicine's first impulse is to make money. Its second? To torture the patient, kill him if at all possible. If the patient dies there is another empty bed and more profit—for the undertaking profession (and, at times, for the clergy).

Artaud says, "I, myself, spent nine years in an insane asylum and never had any suicidal tendencies, but I know that every conversation I had with a psychiatrist during the morning visit made me long to hang myself because I was aware that I could not slit his throat."

Artaud speaks strongly because he is one of those rare Artists who did not bother to fool himself or anybody else. His clarity, his hard brittle lines, his disgust with the Lie, are nothing but the results of a man squeezed to pieces by Life, by the massive horror of the realization that his fellow men, his fellow Artists were, in a sense, only "pigshit."

When a truly great man comes along there is nobody to understand his simplest statement—the masses are a nightmare of Life, Artists and intellectuals are a worse nightmare than the masses (for here in the last chance to understand he sees that the so-called best brains and spirits understand nothing—understand LESS, actually, than the masses). Love is impossible. Women, by nature, are attracted to the Lie. So much so that they eventually marry the Lie forever. This is Nature's way of keeping this horrendous cream of floating going, to keep the cysts open, to arrange that nitwits clutch each other in order that future nitwits clutch each other in order that—The stronger a man is the more alone he will be—it is mathematic. And whether they spend their lives in madhouses or aircraft plants will not alter their pain ... or their greatness.

This thick book, 255 pages, is damn well worth the $3 asked. Also enclosed are many photos of Artaud, and also some of his drawings. The drawings have charm—yes, love—and the juice of live stirring in them. I would suggest a purchase. Certainly when you get the blues, when the old going gets rough, a reading of some of these lines will gather your blood together for another try. Artaud was one of the world's most beautiful madmen. Just try to find anything comparable in the streets or even in the room with you or in the room next to you. You won't. City Lights Books and Jack Hirschman have done it. The honor is everywhere. All you need do is touch it.

AN OLD DRUNK WHO

RAN OUT OF LUCK

Papa Hemingway BY A. E. HOTCHNER, A BANTAM BOOK,
335 PAGES WITH 16 PAGES OF PHOTOS, $1.25.

If there aren't, there soon will be more books on about above below inside
and outside of Hemingway than there were—are—about D. H. Lawrence.
Certain men whet the scandal curiosity of the crowd, most of the crowd
hardly caring what the man created, only what he did, how he did it, with
hair on chest, ear cut off for whore, suicide from back of boat ground into
propeller, homosexual; no damn matter *what* they created, the crowd wants
to look at their arse-hairs, their sex bed, their medicine cabinets, their dirty
laundry. It is a vulture and inane crowd but it is a crowd that will BUY these
things, as I myself have bought one, this Bantam edition. And first, of
course, you look at the photos. And, yes, of course, the old man didn't look
so good. Is this what happens when you write books like that? He could have
as well been a pawnshop broker. Real stuff for the scandal boys. Especially
those who can't write worth a crap and need a buffer, a sustainer, an excuse.
Look at them—walking down the steps of the Roman coliseum at Nimes,
1949. Hemingway looks like an arthritic rabbi and Mary like a chorus girl
gone blind. But there are worse photos, plenty for the vultures. Let's get into
the story, the biography . . .

Hotchner met Hemingway in Cuba, 1948, Havana to be precise, on an
assignment for *Cosmopolitan*, to get, or rather try to get, E.H. to write an article on "The Future of Literature"—the article was never written but
Hotchner managed to hang around, off and on, until Hem's suicide, and
what we have here are the bits, tied together, as Hotch trailed his Papa
throughout Spain, Paris, Cuba, Key West, Ketchum, so forth. There is conversation, description, so forth. Hotchner is not a great writer, of course, but

his style is enough to move you through without too much roughness or too much involuteness. Hotchner adapted some of Hem's work for television and the movies. In other words, Hotch made it off of Ernie and Ernie made it too. Hotchner often acted as middle-man in dickering for rights. Hem had an aptitude for picking the proper friends; he learned it early and stayed with it late. On the other hand he picked up some sycophants, suckbutts who drained him with hardly a return either in character or reverence. The world is cancer-ridden with these suckerfish who attach and ride with the winner, the champ, and Hemingway was no exception—they leeched upon him and had a boatride. Sometimes he would shake one loose but there was always another replacement. Hem's name, his image had been blown all out of proportion to his talent. Once at Cuneo the mob recognized him and he would have been crushed except for the intervention of an army squadron. This wild adulation is a sickness caused by the fact that the crowd has no marrow, no soul, no nothing, and they are looking for something to hang within the gap. Hem was their guy. A man's man. Good with fist and gun and drink and woman and war, and he also wrote on the side, wrote something?, and went to bullfights and caught very large fish. When he went the way of suicide it was over for them. For a while. There is always another. Another man's man. Or another Van Gogh. Or another Artaud. Or another Céline. Or even a Genet. One drink calls for another— let the good times roll!

In this portion of Hemingway's life Hotchner met a man who could no longer write as the early Hemingway had done. (My opinion.) *Across the River and into the Trees* and *The Moveable Feast* lacked the Hemingway sparseness of style. And along with the style the content too seemed ineffectual, flabby, drab. Both books were hard to read because we expected more. In *The Old Man and the Sea*, which fooled the Nobel people and many other people that I know, Hemingway, taking note of his failures (my opinion), attempted to return to the Atlantic cable style of his earlier writings. He got the style back, that is, the structure, but the *content* again failed. For most of those who *read* writing, it seemed like quite a comeback, but for those who *wrote* writing as well as read it—the signs were in: Hem was finished. Buddies with Ava Gardner, Gary Cooper; admired in America, loved in Spain in Paris in Cuba; sitting with nights of wine at a tableful of pickups he talked talked talked, just an old drunk talking about the past, and running out of luck too with a couple of plane crashes and the death of his buddy Cooper. What a fix! He knew Toots Shor, Leonard Lyons, Jimmy Cannon, *all* the winners. He spoke of a champ stepping down when ready. He spoke of Ted Williams, DiMag. He had a list. The rest was fast come-down. First thinking he was going blind. The haggles for money. The dirty laundry bit. His mind going, imagining things. Sneaking into institutions under another name; or rather, almost being taken there. Electric shocks. The world knows the story. The shotgun. Ketchum, 1961, at the age of 61. Not too long ago. It seems Hemingway had been dead longer than that. Maybe it's true.

The tragedy is the American situation where a man has to be a winner. Nothing else is acceptable. And when the winner comes down he saves nothing. Winner take nothing. Hotchner finishes the book: "Ernest had had it right: Man is not made for defeat. Man can be destroyed but not de-feated."

No, Ernest had it wrong: Man is made for defeat. Man *can* be destroyed *and* defeated. So long as Man will only settle for top rung and no come-down, Man will be defeated, destroyed and defeated and defeated and de-feated and destroyed. It will only be when *Man learns to save what he can* that he will be defeated less and destroyed less. Our lesson with Heming-way is that of a man who lived well but badly, seeing victory as the only course. He lived on war and combat and when he forgot how to fight he quit. But he left us some early work that is perhaps immortal? But something with the cape movements there. Some flaw. Ah, who the hell cares? Let's have a drink for him!

NOTES OF A DIRTY OLD MAN

Open City, MAY 12–18, 1967

Well, you see what happens when a couple of cops stop me when I go out for cigars? I want to change the whole social penal structure. Don't misunderstand me—I am not saying that the drunk driver is a superior citizen. I was once run over by a drunk driver. And the auto insurance companies don't like them either. But I am saying that there are too many near cases where a man can make it *home* without harming a fly's butt and he is interrupted and thrown into jail because when jails are there, jails will be used. And when officers ride about the streets they feel almost OBLIGATED TO MAKE ARRESTS.

I always feel guilty when approached by an officer because he is TAUGHT to sense that I AM guilty. So it is the guilt and father complex standing there: the badge, the helmet, the gun, the radio squawking, the red lights, the well-fed immovable face. It is really a scene of horror. And we are just not that BAD. There must be a better way than the voice that will not understand, does not care to understand anything that one says.

My advice to *Open City* readers is to stay inside a while. Stay clean, bolt the doors, and let them ride up and down the empty boulevards flashing their red lights at the moon. There's nothing out there anyhow. And we can enjoy the drinks just as well while re-reading Tolstoy or listening to Mozart's 41st symphony. Amen.

Was stopped on the streets about a week ago. Pulled over by 2 motorcycle patrolmen who said that my brake lights were not working. Since I had had a few beers I was asked to go through various tests of balance. I was neither man-handled or prodded into statements except—where had I come from and where was I going?

Having one drunk driving rap behind me, it was a rather nervous situation. I am not quite sure whether we can survive either *with* or *without* the police. It is a question for stronger minds than mine. The French used to have a saying. "Who is to guard the guards themselves?" For me, it is closer to, "Who are the guards working for?" Or I think of a line from a comedian I heard once: "THE CROOKS? WHERE ARE THE CROOKS? IT'S THE PO-LICE WHO GIVE ME ALL MY TROUBLE!"

■

The last part of the tests is the flashlight bit. They shine a flashlight into your eyes. I suppose to check out the pupils for being on a dope trip. But the strange thing was—after shining the flashlight into my eyes, the officer walked over and shined his flashlight into his fellow officer's eyes. And it *appeared* to me that the officer being flashed seemed quite frightened. Suppose this guy had had 3 or 4 joints before mounting his bike? What a spot, eh? I could see it:

"O.K., buddy, you're on the stuff! I gotta run you in!"

"But, Marty, we're *tight*, baby! We've blown together many a night! Leave off! I only had a couple!"

"That's what they *all* say!"

"But don't be a *shit*, Marty!"

"It sticks, baby. I'm a police officer first, your friend later . . ."

But it didn't happen. The officer lowered his flash and told me, "O.K. you can go on. You passed the tests. But you better go straight home."

I did. After a stop at the corner liquor store.

■

All right, you ask. So what? What's it all about? What's the angelic solution of police vs. drunk drivers? You know, these police are a little different under a shower or playing ball with their kids or mowing the lawn. They are troubled with constipation, insomnia, divorce, fear, love, toothache, so forth, just like the rest of us.

The difference between a man who does harm and a man who doesn't do harm is very little.

I would guess that one of the theories of Crime Prevention is to prevent the crime before it happens. In other words, a man can be punished as a drunk driver not because he *has* inflicted damage upon person and/or property but because he *possibly might*. And I would also presume that the line between being drunk and not being drunk can be a very *thin* line and oftentimes closer to sober than justifiably fair. And even if a man can prove, against their standards, that he was not intoxicated, he is still harmed, for he must post bail, lawyer's costs, and there is the havoc upon his nerves; and the depression, the worry, the wonder, the loss of time cannot be discounted either.

In other words, on the theory that the drunk driver *might* possibly inflict damage and/or pain, he himself is jailed and fined heavily upon this theory of what he *might* have done. Now extend this same theory to other areas of life activity and you will then see that *every living human being* must be jailed because any one of them *might* be capable of committing some crime, either minor or major, against society.

Now let's take a drunk driver who has inflicted no pain/damage—yet he himself *is* inflicted with pain and damage by law under the name of justice. In other words, THE LAW INFLICTS PAIN WHERE HERETOFORE THERE HAD BEEN NO PAIN. Besides fine and jail, there is often loss of driver's license or loss of a man's employment, and often difficulty in finding new employment because of his "record."

If we are to have a better world (and who is sophisticated enough not to want one?) the elimination of unnecessary pain is a good beginner. You want some laughs? You know what I think officers ought to do with drunks? They ought to take them to their homes instead of to jail. Tuck the mother drunks under the covers, get them a drink if necessary, and tell them to stay in the rest of the night. Ridiculous? Why? *What the hell is ridiculous about a little understanding?* I pay taxes to be served, not molested.

If necessary, if the drunk is raving and belligerent, find a way to lock him in his own home, wherein he can still use bathroom facilities or phone his aunt in New Haven. It beats jail. And forget court. We can turn judges loose to fill the holes in the streets or something. I can see the day, the Bomb be-ing willing, of no jails at all. I can see the day when almost every man, out of common sense, would reject deliberately harming/paining/killing his fellow man. Of course, there are always some swine in the woodpile. But the swine would become less and less as understanding took the place of punishment.

UNTITLED ESSAY IN

A TRIBUTE TO JIM LOWELL

Good Art, Creation, is generally 2 decades to 2 centuries ahead of its time in relationship to the establishment and the police state. Good Art is not only not understood but also feared because to make the future better it must state that the present is bad, very bad, and this is hardly an endearment to those in control—it threatens their jobs, their souls, their children, their wives, their new cars, and their rosebushes, at least. "Obscenity" is the word they use to excuse their own rot in order to raid the works and outposts of creative men. Jim Lowell's bookstore was raided about the same time as Steve Richmond's here on the West Coast, so the cancer is nationwide and as somebody said to me, "It's just *Howl* all over again." Which shows that we just haven't gotten anywhere very fast. The problem with these raids is that the judges themselves are only a little better attuned to the actuality and meaning of pure creation than the police themselves. The "little magazines" are not little in circulation because the writers write badly but because there are not enough readers to understand, enjoy, digest advanced writing. The creative artist has always been continually harassed by officialdom and the public itself—Van Gogh was hooted by children who threw stones against his window. He was lucky to have a window. He was lucky to have one ear. Hemingway was lucky to have a shotgun. I am lucky right now, to have this typewriter, this room, to type this thing, to tell you about it. I do not ask mercy for the artist, I do not ask public funds, I do not even ask understanding; I only ask that they leave us alone in the joy and horror and mystery of our work, and if they sell our work for millions of dollars after we are dead, after we are carried from our roach-filled, rat-filled, ghost-filled, bottle-filled rooms, that is their business. But I ask that they leave us alone— we have let you have the fine ladies, the castles, the new cars, the tv's, the war, the steaks, the $45 shoes, the 5 thousand dollar funerals, the mile-wide cactus gardens, the original Van Goghs — just leave us alone with your "obscenity" and raid the newsstands with their titty and ass photos, page after page after page, naked dull stupid meat, blank-faced meat for high school boys to jackoff to, for mud-caked madmen to rape young children from, raid these, raid this million dollar industry IF YOU MUST RAID SOME DAMN THING but leave us alone LEAVE US ALONE. A hundred years from now those books that you are confiscating will be taught in your universities if your leaders are not silly enough to get us blown to hell. I think that when you raid that you raid your own fear, you raid your own conscience (what little there is), and you raid, in anger, the lostness of your souls. I do not ask you to understand too much. Please do not force me to make you understand. I am busy with something else.

NOTES OF A DIRTY OLD MAN

National Underground Review, MAY 15, 1968

"YOWWWWWWW!"

I was having visions in those days. They came mostly when I was drying out, not drinking, waiting around for money or something to arrive, and the visions were very real—technicolor and with music—mostly they flashed across the top of the ceiling while I was on the bed in a half-slumberous state. I had worked in too many factories, had seen too many jails, had drunk too many bottles of cheap wine to maintain any sort of cool and intelligent state toward my visions—

"OH, GO AWAY YOU BASTARDS! I BEG YOU! GET THE HELL OUT! YOU'RE GOING TO FLAKE ME FOR SURE! OH MY GOD, OH MY JESUS, MERCY!"

It was San Francisco. Then I'd hear a knock on the door. It was the old woman who ran the place, Mama Fazzio.

"Mr. Bukowski?" she said through the door.

"AAAAAAAAKKKKK!"

"What?"

"Ulll. Ummph. . . ."

"Are you all right?"

"Oh, sure."

"Can I come in?"

I'd get up and open the door. Sweat now cold behind my ears.

"Say . . ."

"What?"

"You need something to keep your wine and beer cold, you don't have a refrigerator. Even a pan of water with ice in it would help. I'll get you a pan of water with ice in it."

"Thanks."

"And I remember when you were here two years ago you used to have a phonograph. You'd play symphony music all the time. Don't you miss your music?"

"Yeah."

Then she left. I was afraid to lay down on the bed or the visions would come again. They always came just the moment before sleep. Or the moment before one would have slept. Horrible things: spiders eating fat babies in webs, babies with milk-white skin and sea-blue eyes. Then came faces, 3 feet across with puss-holes circled with red, white, and blue circles. Things like that. I sat in a hard wooden chair and peered at the San Francisco Bay Bridge. Then I heard a rumbling sound on the stairway. Some giant beast crawling toward me? I opened the door. There was Mama Fazzio, 80 years old, pushing and twisting an ancient stand-up green wooden victrola, the wind-em-up kind, and the thing must have been twice her weight and clumsy up that narrow stairway and I stood there and said, "Jesus Christ, hold it, don't move!"

"I can get it!"

"You're going to kill yourself!"

I ran down and grabbed the thing but she insisted on helping me. We took it into my room. It looked good.

"There. Now you can have some music."

"Yes. Thanks very much. As soon as I get some records."

"You had breakfast?"

"Not hungry."

"Come on down to breakfast any day."

"Thanks."

"And if you don't have the rent, don't pay it."

"I'll try to have the rent."

"And excuse me, but my daughter was helping me clean your room when she found some papers with writing on them. She was very fascinated with your writing. She and her husband want you to come to dinner at their place."

"No."

"I told them that you were funny. I told them that you wouldn't come."

"Thanks."

After she left I walked around the block a few times and when I came back there was a huge pan of ice with 6 or 7 quarts of beer floating in it plus 2 bottles of good Italian wine. Mama came up 3 or 4 hours later and had a beer.

"You goin' to dinner at my daughter's?"

"You've bought my soul, Mama. Name the night."

She fooled me. She named the night.

The rest of that night I drank the stuff and wound up the old victrola and watched the empty felt-covered wheel run at different speeds, and I put my head down to the little wooden slits in the belly of the machine and listened to the humming sound. The whole machine smelled good, holy, and sad; the thing fascinated me like graveyards and pictures of the dead, and the night went well. Later in the night I even found a lone record in the belly of the machine and I put it on;

> *He's got the whole world*
> *in His hands*
>
> *He's got you and me, brother*
>
> *He's got the little babies*
> *in His hands*
>
> *He's got everybody*
> *in His hands....*

This scared me so much that the next day, hangover and all, I went out and got a job as a stockboy in a department store. I started the day after. Some old gal in cosmetics (she seemed at the bad age for women — 46 to 53) kept hollering that she had to have the stuff RIGHT AWAY. I think it was the insistent shrill insanity in her voice. I told her: "Keep your pants on, baby,

I'll be along soon to relieve you of your tensions. . . ." The manager fired me 5 minutes later. I could hear her screaming over the phone: "If that isn't the damndest SNOTTIEST STOCK BOY I ever heard!!! Who the hell does he think he is?"

"Now, Mrs. Jason, please calm yourself . . ."

At the dinner it was confusing also. The daughter looked real good and the husband was a big Italian. They were both communists. He had a fine fancy night job somewhere and she just layed around and read books and rubbed her lovely legs. They poured me Italian wine. But nothing made sense to me. I felt like an idiot. Communism didn't make any more sense to me than democracy. And the thought often did come to me as it came to me at the table that night: I am an idiot. Can't everybody see that? What's this wine? What's this talk? I'm not interested. It had no connection with me. Can't they see through my skin, can't they see that I am nothing?

"We like your writing. You remind us of Voltaire," she said.

"Who's Voltaire?" I asked.

"Oh Jesus," said the husband.

They mostly ate and talked and I mostly drank the Italian wine. I got the idea that they were disgusted with me but since I had expected that, it did-n't bother me. I mean, not too much. He had to go to work and I stayed on.

"I might rape your wife," I told him. He laughed all the way down the stairway.

She sat in front of the fireplace, showing her legs above the knees. I sat in a chair, watching. I hadn't had a piece of ass in two years. "There's this very sensitive boy," she said, "who goes with my girlfriend. They both sit around and talk communism for hours and he never touches her. It's very strange. She's confused and . . ."

"Lift your dress higher."

"What?"

"I said, lift your dress higher. I want to see more of your legs. Pretend I'm Voltaire."

She did show me a little more. I was surprised. But it was more than I could stand. I walked over and pulled her dress back to her hips. Then I pulled her to the floor and was on top of her like some sick thing. I got the panties off. It was hot in front of that fire, very hot. Then when it was over I became the idiot again:

"I'm sorry. I'm out of my mind. Do you want to call the police? How can you be so young when your mother is so old?"

"It's grandma. She just calls me 'daughter.' I'm going to the bathroom. Be right back."

"Sure."

I wiped off with my shorts and when she came out we had some small talk and then I opened the door to leave and walked into a closetful of overcoats and various things. We both laughed.

"Goddamn," I said, "I'm crazy."

"No, you're not."

I walked on down the stairway, back over the streets of San Francisco and back to my room. And there in the pan was more beer, more wine, floating in water and ice. I drank it all, sitting there in that wooden chair by the window, all the lights out in the room, looking out, drinking.

The luck was mine. A hundred dollar piece of ass and ten bucks worth of drink. It could go on and on. I could get luckier and luckier. More fine Italian wine, more fine Italian ass; free breakfast, free rent, the flowing and glowing of the goddamned soul overtaking everything. Each man was a name and a way but what a horrible waste most of them were. I was going to be different. I kept drinking and didn't quite remember going to bed.

In the morning it wasn't bad. I found a half empty and warm quart bottle of beer. Drank that. Then I laid down on the bed, started to sweat. I layed there quite a time, became sleepy.

This time it was a lampshade that turned into a very evil and large face and then back into a lampshade again. It went on and on, like a repeat movie, and I sweated sweated sweated, thinking that each time, that face would be the unbearable thing to me, whatever that unbearable thing was. There it came AGAIN!

"AAAAAAAAKKKKK! AKKKKK! JESUS! JESUS EAT PUSSY! SAVE ME, OH LORD JESUS!

The knock on the door.

"Mr. Bukowski?"

"Ummph?"

"Are you all right?"

"Yowp?"

"I said, 'Are you all right?'"

"Oh fine, just fine!"

"May I come in?"

In came old Mama Fazzio. "You drank all your stuff."

"Yes, it was a hot night last night."

"You got records yet?"

"Just 'He's got the little babies in His hands.'"

"My daughter wants you to come to dinner again."

"I can't. Got something going. Got to clear it up."

"What do you mean?"

"Sacramento, by the 26th of this month."

"Are you in trouble of some sort?"

"Oh no, Mama, no trouble at all."

"I like you. When you come back, you come live with us again."

"Sure, Mama."

I listened to the old woman going down the stairs. Then I threw myself down on the mattress. How the wind howls in the mouth of the brain; how sad it is to be alive with arms and legs and eyes and brain and cock and balls and bellybutton and all the else and waiting waiting waiting for the whole thing to die, so silly, but nothing else to do, nothing else to do, really. A Tom Mix life with a constipation flaw. I was almost asleep.

"AAAAHHHHHHHHKKKKK! WHEEEEE! MOTHER OF MARY!"

"Mr. Bukowski?"

"Glaglaa$$$"

"What's wrong?"

"Wha'?"

"Are you all right?"

"Oh, fine, jus' fine!"

■

I finally had to get out of San Francisco. They were driving me crazy. With their free wine and free everything. I'm in Los Angeles now where they don't give anything away, and I'm feeling a little bit better . . .

HEY! What was THAT??? . . .

THE NIGHT NOBODY BELIEVED

I WAS ALLEN GINSBERG

I drove all the way to Venice to see this guy and he wasn't in and I was a little drunk and at first I got the wrong door—"I'm looking for Hal. Hey, he got himself a bitch now! You're not bad, baby, not bad!"

I pushed on in. She put out an arm.

"Hey, stop!"

"Stop what? I wanna see Hal."

"What's wrong with you? There's no Hal here."

"Norse. Hal Norse."

"He's one floor up. You've got the wrong floor."

"Well, suppose I come in and make it with you now that I'm here? Whatya say, baby?"

"Hey, are you crazy? Get out!"

Bitches. They always think their pussy is something special. I ran up the stairway in the rain. And pushed the Norse button. And he wasn't in.

I always wanted to be a songwriter. Now that I had nothing to do I started to make up a song (about myself):

> *Oh, you ain't worth saving,*
> *de da da*
> *oh, you ain't worth saving*
> *da da da da . . .*

Oh hell. That was from *Carmen*, and I hated *Carmen*.

I forgot where I parked my car and just walked along. I walked along and walked along in the rain. I got to a bar. Went in. For a rainy night, the place was quite crowded. I could only find one seat. There was a young woman sitting there. Nothing special but I thought I'd try it.

"Hey, baby, I'm a writer. I'm a great writer!"

She turned her face full toward me. I could see her hatred shaping up beneath her flesh.

"HEY, BUDDY!" she screamed so the whole bar could hear: "WILL YOU PLEASE, WILL YOU PULLLEEEEZ STOP BUGGING ME?"

The bartender stood waiting for my order.

"Double scotch with water."

A little greasy-looking guy in a suit and necktie walked up behind her.

"Oh, Helen, darling!"

"Oh, Robbie! Robbie! It's been so long, so LONG!"

Robbie took a rose from his lapel and handed it to her. Then kissed her on the cheek. "Oh, Robbie!!"

Where the fuck was I? In a nest of actors? They all acted as if they were sitting in front of a camera. It was like sitting in at *Barney's*.

"Who's this guy?" he asked her. He was talking about me.

"I'm Allen Ginsberg," I said, "and she doesn't want to talk to me."

She turned that face upon me again. It was putty working into a lightning bolt.

"YOU DAMN FOOL! DON'T YOU THINK I KNOW WHAT ALLEN GINS-BERG LOOKS LIKE?"

"Listen, why do you shout like that? You make me feel very uncomfortable. It isn't fair."

"YOU'RE BUGGING ME! THAT'S WHY! YOU'RE BUGGING ME!"

"Listen," I leaned closer to her, "why don't you go fingerfuck yourself?"

"Robbie! Did you hear what he told me?"

"No, darling, what did he tell you?"

"HE TOLD ME TO GO FINGERFUCK MYSELF! THE BASTARD!"

I drained my scotch glass.

"Listen, Mister," said Robbie, "I don't know who you are, but I think you're looking for a fat lip!"

A fat lip? Lord, that was James Cagney. 1935?

So I gave him some Cagney back: "O.K., baby, if you care to dance I'll be waiting outside!"

I just figured I'd walk outside and keep on walking until I found my car, but I heard him walking behind me.

The whole damned bar was getting up and following him out.

"KILL THAT SON OF A BITCH, ROBBIE!"

"GIVE IT TO HIM GOOD, ROBBIE!"

"KILL HIM, ROBBIE! IF YOU DON'T, WE WILL!"

Oh Lord have mercy on my poor Soul, I thought. 50 years old. I have fainting spells. I can't even bend over to tie a shoelace, I blackout, the world spins. I'm fucked. Why wasn't Norse home? Why do I get into things like this? Any bar, any place, any time . . .

Robbie shoved me and I staggered a bit, hands still down at my sides. Then he hit me. Right on the nose. It was nice to be stoned. It didn't hurt at all. Then he banged one on my ratty goatee. I didn't feel it. I smiled.

Then I threw one. Very slow motion. A lousy punch. No power. Just threw it to be part of the show. Not a hard punch at all. A fat and stinking 230-lb. beer punch.

Robbie screamed as if he were having a tooth pulled without an anaesthetic.

Then he twisted, jack-knifed rather backwards, then dropped forward, landed on both knees. Then threw himself down like a man diving under a wave. And landed flat. On that wet and dirty cement. For a moment I felt like a young Jack Dempsey. But I knew it wasn't true. Robbie was crazy. There was something wrong with him. . . . Christ, oh mighty, he was a bigger coward than I was! The world was a splendid place after all!

When he got up he looked strangely twisted and done. One of the pantlegs was torn and I could see a blood-smear on the knee peeking through the tear.

"You want some more, mother?" I asked him like a tough guy does.

"Your shit stinks!" he hissed.

I thought that was a good answer. I landed again. He seemed to just wait for it. I didn't understand it. I had been in tougher fights with a barmaid.

Down he went again.

"He's trying to kill Robbie!"

Then:

"HE'S TRYING TO KILL ROBBIE!"

Then:

"GET HIM! GET HIM! KILL HIM!" screamed the bitch who knew what Allen Ginsberg looked like.

Still nobody moved. We watched Robbie roll over on his face as if he were dead. The rain rained on his back in that cheap-ass parking lot. I pushed between 2 or 3 people, ran through the parking lot, and started sprinting along the boardwalk. The bar was right on the shore.

5 or 6 of them were after me.

I doubled around a park-bench cove, feet sinking into sand then, and they were after me, yapping like hounds after the fox, and they kept gaining, and there was only one way out—I ran toward the water (Ginsberg. They wouldn't do it to Ginsberg.) I ran toward the waves, toward Death's sweet phony kiss, and I made it to the wet sand, looked around, and here they were:

4 or 5 guys and 2 or 3 insane women, including her:

"GET HIM! KILL HIS ASS! HE TRIED TO KILL ROBBIE!"

I backed into the sea, water already running into my shoes, lapping at my pantslegs.

"I'LL KILL THE FIRST COCKSUCKER WHO COMES NEAR ME!" I screamed.

They kept moving in. 7 or 8 of them. Men, women, intermixed. I backed further in. A wave hit me on the back, knocked me down.

"CHICKENSHIT!" somebody screamed.

"ONE AT A TIME!" I screamed back. "I'll take you ONE AT A TIME! THAT'S ALL I ASK! A DECENT CHANCE!"

"OK! COME ON OUT! LOUIE WILL TAKE YOU!"

(Louie? That didn't sound too bad.)

I came out cold, pants wet and heavy, legs and stockings and shoes chilled, full of sand and crap and death.

I walked up near them.

"Which one is Louie?" I asked.

"I'm Louie," a big fat guy said, stepping out, smoking a cigar and look-ing rather stupid. He was short—around 5 feet but around 179 pounds. He didn't look too hard.

"I'll kill you, you motherfucker!" I said.

I moved in. I gave him full leverage. Hemingway would have been proud of me. I landed full force right into the center of his big belly.

He tossed his cigar aside and then he . . .

FLIPPED me.

I flew through the air. Landed hard. First on my ass. Then backwards upon my back.

When I got up, I rushed him again.

FLIP!

Every time I got up and rushed him, back I'd flip.

The landings were upon my ass, my head, my back. He even lit a new ci-gar and waited. That pissed me off. But the more angry I got, the harder I charged—each time it seemed easier for fat Louise to toss me back into the sea.

I really gave him the Tijuana bull on the last one.

And the last flip was the greatest. My head seemed to hit some hidden rock in the sand. So then—the ocean and the stars and the agony seemed to mix it rather good.

Then I got up to run at Louie again. Only, at the last moment I cut, swung East and there I was running along the water . . .

"LOOK AT HIM FLY!"

"YA! YOU CHICKENSHIT!"

"AFTER HIM!"

Here they came again. Men, women, Fat Louie, and even the bartender in his dirty white apron.

Who was guarding the bar? Was my first thought.

Who cares? Was my second.

The trouble with running from 7 or 8 people is that there are usually 3 or 4 who can run faster than you.

"GET HIM!"

"KILL HIM!"

Venice, Calif. Who were these people? Where were the hippies? Where were the Flower Children? Where was LOVE? What the hell was this?

Then it started to rain, suddenly and hard. It was an icy and vicious downpour with no thought for Humanity.

"Jesus, IT'S RAINING!"

"LET HIM GO! TO HELL WITH HIM!"

The human race was insane—they'd rather stay dry than beat me. They were afraid of drops of water yet they got into bathtubs full of it.

I rather liked the rain, especially as I watched them turn and run back toward the bar. I ran up through the soft sand toward the boardwalk. But the rain was even too hard for me—almost a single sheet of water. My clothing sucked it up like a mop. I could feel my shorts hanging and sagging, soaked around my cock, slipping off my ass.

I ran down a side street, found an old house, stood on the porch.

A guy came to the door. A woman behind him. Inside was a tv. A heater going. Yellow warm light.

"HEY MAN! WHATCHA DOING ON MY PORCH?"

"Peace, brother," I said. "It's raining. I'm only standing here to get dry. I have no evil intent."

"You got no rights on our porch," the woman spoke over his shoulder.

"All right, as soon as it stops raining, I'll leave."

"We want you to leave now," the man said.

"Listen, I'm not hurting anything. . . ."

"Get off our porch!" the man said.

"Yes, get off our porch!" the woman said.

"Go to hell," I said quietly.

"You're looking for trouble, eh?"

"Yeah, I'm looking for trouble."

I waited for him to come out. But he went back inside and picked up the phone. He was calling the police. MERCY!

I leaped off the porch and jumped into the cold and inhuman rain. Ran to the end of the block, turned east, and walked along in the rain. When they got you down, they really kept you there. I felt lower than a flea near a dog's crotch.

So this was Venice? The new Village of L.A. but where were the writers, the painters, the hippies, the bums? When it rained they all had a place to go. It was a con. I was the only one out in the rain.

Then as I walked along I saw a car that looked like mine. Impossible. I got closer. It was . . . that chickenshit blue '62 Comet. It was mine! Well, 4 more payments. But MINE! I had something . . .

Did I have the keys after all that fighting? I'd found the car another night similar conditions. East L.A., a fight with 3 Mexican boys. I'd kept the wallet but lost the keys.

I reached—they were there. Wet, sandy miracle keys.

I opened the door and got in. The engine even started, though it was hesitant. I sat there warming the engine as the squad car went by. I watched it turn the corner and go down to the man with the very possessive front porch. I put it into gear and moved out.

When I got in, I took off my clothes, toweled myself, got into a Japanese kimono John Thomas had given me, then opened a beer.

The phone rang. I picked it up.

"Bukowski's whorehouse."

"Hank?"

"Yeah."

"It's Hal, where you been? Been trying to get you on the phone."

"Been to the races."

"How'd it go?"

"Tough card, real tough."

"How'd you make out?"

"Came out about even."

"I heard from Stangos. He mailed *Penguin* 13. Did you get a copy?"

"Yeah."

"Looks like a pussy on the cover. Rock section but looks like a pussy."

"A pussy in monthly. I only wish they'd printed a real one."

"It's coming out in the US June 29th. But it's already out in Eng—blah blah . . . Nikos says it's best of the series . . . blah blah . . . establishment blah university groups blah blah already after our blah blah asses . . . Beiles wrote a good review blah blah blah *London Magazine* refused to blah blah blah then blah blah blah blah blah to a paper in South Africa blah and they refused blah blah the fix is in blah they are after our asses blah."

"Yeah."

He talked a while and then we gave it up. I finished the beer and opened another one, and it began to rain HARD all over again . . . people's life-savings spilling into canyons, into cracks in the earth, uninsured, the insurance companies had known, the architects and contractors had known . . . in 15 minutes I'd walk up for 2 six-packs (tall) but first changing out of the Japanese kimono. 2 six-packs, 3 cigars, and the *L.A. Times*.

The phone rang.

"Where've you been, Hank? I've been trying to get you. Your little girl wants to talk to you."

The little girl was four and the woman put her on and I laughed and drank my beer as she talked very seriously to me. Good sense stuff too. The inside. Everything was very serious and very funny somehow as I heard her and the rain, and the continuous sound of sirens outside. Vaguely, I thought of strange things like the Abraham Lincoln Battalion and eleven dead pollywogs under a clothesline in 1932. Then she said goodbye. It took a long time to say goodbye.

When it was over I got out of the kimono and got ready to get the shit up the street.

SHOULD WE BURN

UNCLE SAM'S ASS?

Should we burn Uncle Sam's ass?

Or will he burn ours? I'll be 50 in August so don't trust me. That's 20 years over 30, and I wonder who the boys under 30 are going to trust when they are over 30? But maybe you ought to trust me a little—I am unemployed, even have a stubble of a goatee, drink each night until early morning, write my little poems and dirty stories, still trying to find the target, maybe missing, getting up at noon for alka seltzer, finding watercolor paintings on the floor along with empty beerbottles and last week's *Racing Form*. The *Berkeley Tribe* sends me a copy of their paper free each week, so they must know that I am here. Also I drink with anybody and listen. My door is open to Left and Right, black and white and yellow and red and various man, woman, dyke, homo. I do not teach; I learn. I was anti-war when pro-war was a popular fad. I believed that we could have remained out of World War II and the course of history would have been just about as it is now. This is a hell of a statement and, of course, can be disputed. I am still anti-war. Whether a war is against the Left or the Right, I still consider it a war. Among the American intellectuals a "good" war is one that is against the Right; a "bad" war is one against the Left. This is all too easy. The lesson is not to be tricked. If you are going to sacrifice human lives for a Cause, follow it up. Replace it with a new constitution or make the old one work. Say, "We have died. Now this is what we want." The moment an enemy is removed in a war, this creates a void of imbalance and a new enemy forms itself. If you destroy the Left you tend to become the Left; if you destroy the Right you tend to become the Right. It's all a quicksilver, a teeter-totter, and great men have been trapped and fooled by the switching of the balance. Politics, wars, causes — for thousands of years we have ended up with a sack of shit. It's time we learned to think.

Back in the '30s and running right up to World War II there was a strong revolutionary feeling in this country. Franco was about to take over Spain—writers were hooked on the "noble cause"—Hemingway, Koestler who turned around later—in fact, *Darkness at Noon* was one of the earlier turnings. Then there was Lillian Hellman, Irwin Shaw, the sweetheart of the intellectuals and the darling of the *New Yorker*—see the story, "Sailor Off the Bremen" . . . and, of course, there was Steinbeck and Dos Passos—who turned later. Even William Saroyan, who said he'd never go to war, got caught up, went, and wrote a very bad novel about it—*The Adventures of Wesley Jackson*. There were dozens, hundreds of others. You just weren't a writer worth shit if you weren't for the war. I was a writer who wasn't worth a shit. And, of course, before the war there was a depression. The people, young and old both, used to meet in dark garages and talk about revolution. The Abraham Lincoln Brigade was formed to go off to Spain to stop "the rising tide of fascism. Stop it now!" Well, the Brigade was poorly armed and they screamed at the crowds: "Join the Party! Join the Brigade! We must stop them now! Our lives are at stake!" Up in San Francisco it was the same. Communist Party dances, well attended. No man could stand aside, they said. Any man who wasn't involved at some level wasn't a thinking and feeling human being. Exciting times for some. But where did they go? What happened to the Left after Hitler was defeated? What happened to Irwin Shaw, Hemingway, Dos Passos, Steinbeck, Saroyan, the gang? Well, there was a stupid novel by Steinbeck, *The Moon is Down*, and a stupid novel by Hemingway, *Across the River and Into the Trees*, and I have no idea if these things were written after or during or just before the war—it was part of the process. Dos Passos gave up. The others found they couldn't write any more. Camus, who justified the war in "Letter to a German Friend," Camus ran around giving speeches at the Academies until the car crash saved him from that kind of life.

My point is that I have heard a similar screaming in the streets once before, and it was wasted. There were betrayals and turnings galore. The people had food in their bellies. The people had made money on the war. Russia the ally became Russia the enemy. Joe Stalin, now that the world was saved, was playing Hitler with his people. Once again—as always—the intellectuals had been fooled. Actuality overcame theory. Human greed, human smallness became history. So-called good men knifed good men. Treason. Documents. Tattle-tales. Irwin Shaw saw it and wrote it—his best book, although I no longer remember the title. Joe McCarthy showed up on time. The dirty stockings of Adolph. We had the big ten run out of the motion picture industry. The Right was back in again. But how? Hadn't they been destroyed in World War II? Every man was suspect. "Did you ever belong to the Communist Party? Weren't most of us?" But nobody ever said that. They had their orders from above and like good boys, they obeyed. And now the children of the Jews we saved from the ovens, they are on the Right. They run in their panzers and blitzkriegs and swift air power against the LEFT. It is confusing.

Now once again the intellectuals are crying "Revolution." A bank is burned, IBM bombed, a telephone co. bombed, others . . . Cops are stoned, their cars burned; cops are killed, cops kill—always have. Then we have the big 7 of Chicago and an incredibly senile old crotch of a man for a judge. (By the way, I don't mean the cops are "stoned," I mean that stones are thrown at them.) If Kunstler hadn't warned the kids to lay off in a recent speech, it might have happened. But Kunstler knew it would have been slaughter and would have ended the Revolution right there. He saved them for another day. Like, you say, what is my POINT? Well, I am a photographer of life, not an activist. But before you decide on a Revolution make sure that you have a good chance to win it—by this, I mean violent overthrow. Before this can be accomplished you must have some revolution within the ranks of the National Guard and the police force. This just isn't happening to any degree. Then you must do it at the polls. And your chances there were taken away with both Kennedys. At this time there are too many people afraid for their jobs, there are too many people buying cars, tv sets, homes, educations on credit. Credit and property and the 8-hour day are great friends of the Establishment. If you must buy things, pay cash, and only buy things of value—no trinkets, no gimmicks. Everything you own must be able to fit inside one suitcase; then your mind might be free. And before you face the troops in the street, DECIDE and KNOW what you are going to replace them with and why. Romantic slogans won't do. Have a definite program, clearly worded, so if you DO win you will have a suitable and decent form of government. For remember, in any movement there are opportunists, power-grabbers, wolves in Revolutionary clothing. These are the men who bring down a Cause. I am for a better world, for my child, for myself, for you, but be careful. A change of power is not a cure. Power to the people is not a cure. Power is not a cure. The whole accent of your thinking must not be how to destroy a government but how to create a better one. Don't be trapped and fooled again. And if you win, beware of a very Authoritarian government with rules that might bind you worse than ever before. I am not exactly a patriot but for all the hell of a lot of injustice, you are still able to express and protest and act within rather wide areas. Tell me, could I write an anti-government piece AFTER you take over? Could I stand in the parks and streets and tell you what I think? I should hope so. But be careful unless you even lose this in some name of Justice. I call for a program so that I may make a choice between you and them, between Revolution and the government that exists. Will you put me to work cutting down sugar cane? That would bore me. Would you build new factories? I've spent my life running away from factories. Would all my writings, my music, my paintings have to be for the good of the State? Could I lay around on park benches and in tiny rooms, drinking wine, dreaming, feeling good and easy? Let me know what you have for me before I burn down a bank. I need more than hippy beads, a beard, an Indian headband, legal grass. What is your program? I am tired of all the dead. Let's not waste them again. If I must face a State Trooper's bayonet I want to know what you will give me if I take it away from him.

Tell me.

Then I got a letter from Marx who had moved to Santa Fe. He said he'd pay trainfare and put me up if I came out for a while. He and his wife had a rent-free situation with this rich psychiatrist. The psychiatrist wanted them to move their printing press in there, but the press was too big to get into any of the doors, so the psychiatrist offered to have one of the walls smashed down to get the press in and then have the wall put back up. I think that's what worried Marx—having his beloved press locked in there like that. So Marx wanted me to come out and look at the psychiatrist and tell him if the psychiatrist was o.k. I don't know quite how it got to be that way but I had been corresponding with this rich psychiatrist, who was also a very bad poet, for some time, but had never met him. I had also been corresponding with a poetess, a not very good poetess, Mona, and the next thing I knew the psychiatrist had divorced his wife and Mona had divorced her husband and then Mona had married the psychiatrist and now Mona was down there and Marx and his wife were down there and the psychiatrist's ex-wife, Constance, was still on the grounds. And I was supposed to go down there and see if *everything* were all right. Marx thought I knew something. Well, I did. I could tell him that everything wasn't all right, you didn't have to be a sage to smell that one out but I guess Marx was so close to it, plus the rent-free situation, that he couldn't smell it. Jesus Christ. Well, I wasn't writing. I had written some dirty stories for the sex mags and had them accepted. I had a backlog of dirty stories accepted by the sex mags. So it was time for me to gather material for another dirty story and I felt sure there was a dirty story in Santa Fe. So I told Marx to wire the money . . .

■

The psychaitrist's name was Paul, if it matters.

I was sitting with Marx and his wife—Lorraine—and I was drinking a beer when Paul walked in with a highball. I don't know where he had come from. He had houses all over the hillside. There were 4 bathrooms with 4 bathtubs and 4 toilets to the door from the north. It simply appeared that Paul had walked out from the 4 bathrooms with 4 bathtubs and 4 toilets with the cocktail in his hand. Marx introduced us. There was a silent hostility between Marx and Paul because Marx had allowed some Indians to bathe in one or more of the bathtubs. Paul didn't like Indians.

"Look, Paul," I asked, sucking at my beer, "tell me something?"

"What?"

"Am I crazy?"

"It'll cost you to find out."

"Forget it. I already know."

Then Mona seemed to walk out of the bathrooms. She was holding a boy in her arms from the other marriage, a boy of about 3 or 4. They both had been crying. I was introduced to Mona and the boy. Then they walked away somewhere. Then Paul seemed to walk away with his cocktail glass.

"They hold poetry readings at Paul's place," said Marx. "Each Sunday. I saw the first one last Sunday. He makes them all line up single-file outside his door. Then he lets them in one by one and seats them and reads his own stuff first. He has all these bottles all over the place, everybody's tongue is hanging out for a drink, but he won't pour one. Whatcha think of a son of a bitch like that?"

"Well, now," I said, "let's not get too hasty. Deep underneath all that crud, Paul might be a very fine man."

Marx stared at me and didn't answer. Lorraine just laughed. I walked out and got another beer, opened it.

"No, no, you see," I said, "it might be his money. All that money is causing some kind of block; his goodness is locked in there, can't get out, you see? Now maybe if he got rid of some of his money he'd feel better, more human. Maybe everybody would feel better . . ."

"But what about the Indians?" Lorraine asked.

"We'll give them some too."

"No, I mean, I told Paul that I was going to let them keep coming up here and taking baths. And they can crap too."

"Of course they can."

"And I like to talk to the Indians. I like the Indians. But Paul says he doesn't want them around."

"How many Indians come around here everyday to bathe?"

"Oh, 8 or 9. The squaws come too."

"Any young squaws?"

"No."

"Well, let's not worry too much about the Indians . . ."

■

The next night Constance, the ex-wife came in. She had a cocktail glass in her hand and was a bit high. She was still living in one of Paul's houses. And Paul was still seeing her. In other words, Paul had 2 wives. Maybe more. She sat next to me and I felt her flank up against mine. She was around 23 and looked a hell of a lot better than Mona. She spoke with a mixed French-German accent.

"I just came from a party," she said. "Everybody bored me to death. Lee-tle turds of people, phonies, I *just* couldn't stand it!"

Then Constance turned to me. "Henry Chinaski, you look *just* like what you write!"

"Honey, I don't write *that* badly!"

She laughed and I kissed her. "You're a very beautiful lady," I told her. "You are one of those class bitches that I'll go to my grave without ever possessing. There's such a gap, educational, social, cultural, all that crap—like age. It's sad."

"I could be your granddaughter," she said.

I kissed her again, my hands around her hips.

"I don't need any granddaughters," I said.

"I have something to drink at my place," she said.

"To hell with these people," I said. "Let's go to your place."

"Very vell," she said.

I got up and followed her . . .

We sat in the kitchen drinking. Constance had on one of these, well, what could you call it? . . . one of these green peasant dresses . . . a necklace of white? pearls that wound around and around and around, and her hips came in at the right place and her ass came out at the right place and her breasts came out at the right places and her eyes were green and she was blonde and she danced to music coming over the intercom — classical music — and I sat there drinking, and she danced, whirled, with a drink in her hand and I got up and grabbed her and said, "Jesus Christ Jesus Christ, I CAN'T STAND IT!" I kissed her and felt her all over. Our tongues met. Those green eyes stayed open and looked into mine. She broke off.

"VAIT! I'll be back!"

I sat down and had another drink.

Then I heard her voice. "I'm in here!"

I walked into the other room and there was Constance, naked, stretched on a leather couch, her eyes closed. All the lights were on, which only made it better. She was milk-white and *all* there, only the hairs of her pussy had a rather golden-red tint instead of the blonde like the hair on her head. I began to work on her breasts and the nipples became hard immediately. I put my hand between her legs and worked a finger in. I kissed her all about the throat and ears and as I slipped it in, I found her mouth. I knew I was going to make it at last. It was good and she was responding, she was wiggling like a snake. At last, I had my manhood back. I was going to score. All those misses . . . so many of them . . . at the age of 50 . . . it *could* make a man doubt. And, after all, what was a man if he couldn't? What did poems mean? The ability to screw a lovely woman was Man's greatest Art. Everything else was tinfoil. Immortality was the ability to screw until you died . . .

Then I looked up as I was stroking. There on the wall opposite to my sight hung a life-sized silver Christ nailed to a life-sized silver cross. His eyes appeared to be open and He was watching me.

I missed a stroke.

"Vas?" she asked.

It's just something *manufactured,* I thought, it's just a bunch of silver hanging on the wall. That's all it is, just a bunch of silver. And you're not religious.

His eyes seemed to grow larger, pulsate. Those nails, the thorns. The poor Guy, they'd murdered Him, now He was just a hunk of silver on the wall, watching, watching . . .

My pecker went down and I pulled out.

"Vas iss it? Vas iss it?"

I got back into my clothes.

"I'm leaving!"

I walked out the back door. It clicked locked behind me. Jesus Christ! It was raining! An unbelievable burst of water. It was one of those rains you knew wouldn't stop for hours. *Ice cold!* I ran to Marx's place which was next door and beat on the door. I beat and I beat and I beat. They didn't answer. I ran back to Constance's place and I beat and I beat and I beat.

"Constance, it's raining! Constance, my LOVE, it's raining, I'm DYING OUT HERE IN THE COLD RAIN AND MARX WON'T LET ME IN! MARX IS MAD AT ME!"

I heard her voice through the door.

"Go away, you . . . you rotten sune of a bitcher!"

I ran back to Marx's door. I beat and beat. No answer. There were cars parked all around. I tried the doors. Locked. There was a garage but it was just made out of slats; the rain poured through. Paul knew how to save money. Paul would never be poor. Paul would never be locked out in the rain.

"MARX, MERCY! I'VE GOT A LITTLE GIRL! SHE'LL CRY IF I DIE!"

Finally the editor of *Overthrow* opened the door. I walked in. I got a bottle of beer and sat on my couch-bed after taking off my clothes.

"You said, 'To hell with these people!' when you left," said Marx. "You can talk to me that way but you can't talk to Lorraine that way!"

Marx kept on with the same thing, over and over—you can't talk to my wife that way, you can't talk to my wife that way, you can't—I drank 3 more bottles of beer and he went on and on.

"For Christ's sake," I said, "I'll leave in the morning. You've got my train-ticket. There aren't any trains running now."

Marx bitched a while longer and then he was asleep and I had a beer, a nightcap beer, and I thought, I wonder if Constance is asleep? . . . It rained.

DIRTY OLD MAN CONFESSES

I was born a bastard—that is, out of wedlock—in Andernach, Germany, August 16, 1920. My father was an American soldier with the army of occupation; my mother was a dumb German wench. I was brought to the United States at the age of two—Baltimore first, then Los Angeles, where most of my youth was wasted and where I live today.

My father was a brutal and cowardly man who continually whipped me with a razor strap for the slightest reasons, often invented. My mother was in sympathy with his treatment of me. "Children should be seen but not heard" was my father's favorite expression.

I was given continual duties about the house and yard, and unless these duties were done with 100% perfection, I was given a beating. The duties were *never*, it seemed, perfectly done. I received one beating a day. I was forced to mow the lawn twice on Saturday—one time in each direction—trim and edge the outer areas, then water both lawns and all the flowers. During this time, my mates were playing football and baseball in the streets, laughing and learning each other.

My father would inspect the lawns after I had finished. He would get down on his knees, put his head down along the grass and scan for what he called "hairs." If he found one "hair," one blade of grass longer than any of the others, I would get my beating. He always found a "hair."

I never spoke except to say yes or no. After the age of five or six, I stopped crying when I was beaten. I hated the man so much that my only revenge upon him was *not* to cry, which made him beat me harder. The tears would come but they were silent tears. The beatings were always in the bathroom —I guess because the razor strap was there. And when he was finished he would say, "Go to your room."

I was in the Underground early.

My ass and the backs of my legs were a continual mass of welts and bruises. When I was called to dinner—it was always difficult for me to eat—

they allowed me to sit upon one cushion, or if the beating had been exceptional I was sometimes allowed two cushions.

I had to sleep on my belly at night because of the pain. Although one fine night at the age of seventeen I knocked my father out with one punch, and many years later I buried him, the habit of sleeping upon my stomach still remains.

I don't *want* to make this confessional a tear-jerker; I like to laugh as well as anybody—now. Or maybe it is funny, looking back, me in bed on my belly, listening to them snore or fuck, and thinking, "What chance does a guy four feet tall have?" Now I am six feet tall and other monsters have replaced my father.

School wasn't much better. Not having had any practice in street sports, I hardly knew what a football or a baseball was. My first chance at it came at recess time. Baseball. They threw the thing up to me and I couldn't hit it. They threw the football at me and I couldn't catch it. I didn't understand half of their conversation. I was a "sissy." Gangs of them would follow me home after school and taunt me. I didn't fit.

Even in the classroom I was backed up. I was still fighting the father image, and the mother image as well. Whatever I didn't want to learn in class, I decided not to learn. Sometimes it was the face of the teacher; other times it was simply the dullness of learning. I refused to learn the notes of music, I refused to learn the rules of grammar, I refused to learn algebra. Just more damned jobs.

Most of the time I received a "4" or a "D," but sometimes I did receive an "F." I was always being found guilty of something—I was never quite told what it was—and I was kept after school much of the time.

I didn't have any friends but I didn't seem to miss this.

Then somewhere, as the years went along, a transition took place; it began somewhere between high school and my two years at L.A. City College. I became the toughest guy on the grounds. It must have been after coming out of the L.A. County Hospital. I had to take six months off. I had boils the size of apples all over my face and back—in my eyes, on my nose, behind my ears, in the hair of my head. The poisoned life had finally exploded out of me. There they were—all the withheld screams—spouting out in another form.

The doctors drilled me with a large drill. That's all they could think of to do, just drill me with this drill. I could smell the burning of oil as the drill got hot. They'd punch into those apple-sized boils while the blood spurted out.

"I never saw a case like this," said one of the docs. "Look at the *size* of those things! Acne Vulgaris Supreme!"

Then five or six of them would gather around to look at the size of them.

Idiots. That was when I put the medical profession on my shitlist. In fact, everything was on my shitlist. Actually, I didn't hate the doctors as I hated my father; I just felt that they were simply rather stupid.

"I never *saw* a guy go under the needle like that! He doesn't even flinch or show emotion of any sort. I don't understand it."

When I went back to school, something showed in my manner. I had passed through too many fires. Nothing mattered. Instead of fearing and not understanding the mob, I was finally the "tough boy." Other tough boys tried to make friends. I told them to fuck off.

I found that I could hit a baseball long and far. And football was sweet. Especially when we played tackle in the vacant lots and asphalt streets— and we did play in the streets in the mid and late '30s.

I went from sissy to superman overnight, then I lost interest. Sports were as idiotic as anything else, perhaps more so.

I found a small library near La Cienega and West Adams boulevards. I began finding books in this library without guidance. The way I found a good book was to open it and look at the shape of the print upon the paper. If the shape of the print looked good, I would read a paragraph. If the paragraph read well, I would read the book. In this way I found D. H. Lawrence, Thomas Wolfe, Turgenev—no, wait, Wolfe came a little later at the big downtown library—but at the little library I also found old Upton Sinclair, Sinclair Lewis, Gorky, and the mighty Feodor Mikhailovitch Dostoevsky.

All these, long before anybody ever told me they were more than the run-of-stock shit that gagged the public libraries. Of course, since then only Dostoevsky and some of the short stories of Turgenev have held up for me.

Well, if you are still with me, I left dear old mama and papa and moved to a place at Third and Flower, where I lived on my luck—which was then my ability to win drinking contests and be lucky with the dice. I was also lucky matching odd-man at ten bucks a flip.

I was evicted from Third and Flower by an old man who owned the place. He got up close to me and said, "Sonny, you're tearin' my place up." He had bad breath. And rats. "You're tearin' my place up and keeping folks awake all night. We got lots of good old folks here who just want to rest. Gotta ask ya to move,"

Shit. I knew the old folks. They only went two ways—to God or to wine. And those on God complained.

■

I found a place on Temple Street, which was then the Filipino district, drank heavily, continued to be lucky at gambling. My room again became the meeting place of the gamblers, but the landlady was tough, didn't seem to mind at all, owned a piece of the bar downstairs and, I do believe, sent some of the gamblers up to my place. I drank as I gambled and it kept me loose enough to be lucky. My plan was always the same—I got ahead at *some* time during the game at *some* time every night, and as soon as I got the sum that I wanted I would stagger around acting drunk and angry. "All right, everybody out! For Christ's sake, don't you guys have anyplace to *sleep*? This ain't the Mission and this ain't a French whorehouse! I *live* here!" Then I'd curse a good string and tell them, while breaking a waterglass full of whiskey against the wall, "I said '*everybody out!*'"

They'd start to file out the door.

"Next game starts at six tomorrow evening. Be here. On time."

They'd leave. I was still the tough boy. Or the bluff boy. I didn't know.

It went better and better until one night I got in a fight with a guy I thought was my friend. He was in the Marine Corps, but in spite of that he had a good mind, could almost stay up with me on the drinking, but he had this proclivity toward Thomas Wolfe and Teddy Dreiser. The trouble was that Wolfe was a good man who didn't know how to write and Dreiser was an intelligent man who couldn't write at *all*.

One night after the gamblers left, we sat down with the whiskey and tried to talk it out. I also told him that Faulkner was playing children's games. Chekhov, no—a playpiece of the comfortable masses. Steinbeck, a technician. Hemingway, only halfway. He liked them *all*. He was a damn fool. Then I said that Sherwood Anderson could outwrite the whole bloody gang. That started something.

It was a good fight. Finally, every mirror and bit of furniture in the room was flattened out.

Can you imagine a fight over the meaning of literature instead of a fight over some worthless pussy? We were as crazy as the rest.

I don't know who won the fight. He probably did. But when I awakened in the morning and looked around, I felt that it wouldn't be fair for me to pay the entire repair bill. I gathered my money, got out, made New Orleans by bus.

I disdained the French Quarter as fakery and stayed west of Canal Street, sleeping with the rats. Somehow, I decided to become a writer. I began writing short stories, hand printing them in ink and sending them to *Harper's*, the *Atlantic* or the *New Yorker*. When they came back, I tore them up.

I wrote six to ten stories a week, drank wine, and sat in the cheap bars.

I moved from city to city, having to work long and dull dime-and-nickle jobs—Houston, Los Angeles, St. Louis, Frisco twice, New York City, Miami Beach, Savannah, Atlanta, Fort Worth, Dallas, Kansas City, and probably some that I have forgotten.

I worked the slaughterhouses, railroad track gangs, shipping clerk gigs, receiving clerk gigs. I even worked for the American Red Cross (bravo!), was foreman in a book distributing house. Also, errand-boy wino on the end bar stool in Philly on Fairmount Avenue, running out for sandwiches for the big boys. A beer or a whiskey for a tip, usually a beer.

I met some canned-heat bums, sternos. The best part about them, besides their horrible breaths, was that in their inexact gaggle you could now and then find a jewel. But I decided not to join them.

I became just another drunk, thinking of suicide, sitting in little rooms for days with all the shades down, wondering what was out there and what was wrong with it—not knowing whether to blame it on my father or myself or *them*.

I was anti-war in a time of pro-war. I couldn't tell a good war from a bad one—I still can't. I was a hippie when there weren't any hippies; I was a beat before the beats.

I was a protest march, alone.

I was in some Underground like a blind mole and no other moles even existed.

This is why I couldn't adjust my sights, make sense of it. I had already done it all. And when Tim Leary advised "drop out" twenty-five years *after* I had already dropped out, I couldn't get excited. Leary's big "drop out" was a loss of a professorship somewhere (Harvard?).

I was the Underground when there wasn't any Underground. I was the dirty young man. I went from six feet tall and 215 pounds of good young muscle to 139 pounds of bone. I went to jail, celling with Courtney Taylor, the great swindler and then Public Enemy Number One. A bum rap, of course. Mine, not Taylor's

And getting out, going back to Philly, getting into those rooming houses again, and getting kicked out once a week.

Walking down the street at nine in the morning, I'd hear the old ladies hiss from their front-porch rockers: "See that young man? *Drunk* already! I got him out of *my* place! Lord, have mercy, I was so *glad* to get rid of him!"

Those old gals, their husbands long dead from overwork to keep them in lace panties. Those old gals, no longer looking good in lace panties, blaming everything on me because I didn't have my head and soul bent over some subnormal drill press.

"Do you have a job?" they'd always ask me when I knocked at their door.

"Sure," I'd say, meaning that my job was to stay alive, and it was a rotten job. And then they'd let you in there the first night with signs on the wall like "JESUS SAVES!"

■

Then it seemed I was in the Village in New York—the old Village, a chickenshit place full of phonies as I might guess the new Village is now. The artist must always move on, one step ahead of the jellymen.

While I was in the Village I passed a drugstore, and in the magazine rack was the then-famous *Story* mag edited by Whit Burnett and Martha Foley. When you made *Story* that meant that you were some type of real okay genius. I'd tried them now and then, along with the *Atlantic-Harper's-New Yorker* shots. I reached for the mag to look through it, then saw *my* name on the cover! They'd published me. At twenty-four. I'd been moving so fast the mail hadn't caught up or had been lost. I picked up the mag, went inside, and paid for it.

Meanwhile, I had found a job, reluctantly, as a stockboy or something for a distributing house of magazines and books. A couple of days later my foreman came over with this copy of *Story*. He said, "Hey, here's a funny thing. Look, here's a guy in this magazine whose last name is the same as yours!"

"No," I said, "that's me."

"Ah, bullshit! *You* wrote this story?"

"Yeah."

A couple of days later I was called into personnel. I'd missed two or three days because of drunkenness. There was a beautiful young bitch there.

"You're Charles Bukowski?"

"Yeah."

"You wrote that story in *Story*?"

"What does it matter?"

"We are promoting you to foreman of the outgoing book section."

"It's up to you," I told her.

I knew it was a stupid move. Being a writer had nothing to do with being anything else.

I wasn't a very good foreman. I'd come in drunk and goose the workers with hammer handles while they were nailing their crates shut. But they liked me. Which was wrong—a good foreman is a man you fear. The entire world functions on fear.

I was supposed to count the total books mailed in the coffin boxes, sign the invoice, drop it in there, say, "Nail it up!" I just pretended to count. It was so easy and such a bore. And they knew more about it than I did. I'd just close my eyes, pretend to count, sign the fucker and say, "Okay, nail it up."

I'd been around the world long enough to know that soon the word would get around that I was ball-and-jacking the job, so I quit before the Eye could finger me.

But before I left town a very strange thing happened. I met my idol! *I* met the great Whit Burnett, mighty editor of *Story*. But he didn't meet me. Because he didn't know what I looked like. But I knew him because of the many photographs I had seen of him. I was walking north, and he, south. I was passing the world's greatest editor. He had this look of pain in his eyes, but I caught it as a rather spoiled and sheltered pain, even though his eyes were beautiful. But I knew then that we were *very* different. I held my belly and doubled in laughter before him. My idol had broken. It was a true good laughter, without malice. He stared at me for a moment, then walked on.

Well, there was another hit in Caresse Crosby's *Portfolio*. I was in with Henry Miller, Genet, Sartre, Lorca, many others that I have forgotten because my two copies have since been stolen by friends.

I kicked it over then. Stopped writing. Gave it up. Got drunk for ten years. I settled back in Los Angeles. Worked enough to stay alive, barely. Drank enough to kill myself, almost. Became the great fucker of the whores on Alvarado Street.

Well, as my luck would have it, I had to meet the most beautiful untamed one of all—Jane, an old-fashioned name, but a wild half-Irish half-Indian. Nothing but temper and madness, but beautiful legs and ass, and a certain way about her—some soul—meaning that most of the things she said were fairly damned relevant, and there was *never* a finer piece of ass.

I don't know what it was about her on the lovebed. I believe it was this fine mixture of loving it and hating it at the same time—never conning you—and then finally giving way into a final and total submission. Besides all this, she had a very fine cunt.

I remember the first night I met her, left the bar with her. Big Johnny, the hotshot salesman, told me, "Nobody can tame her, Hank, but if anybody can, I think you can."

She was well-dressed in expensive clothing, especially the shoes, and she didn't *look* like trouble. I picked up two fifths of bourbon, plenty of cigarettes, and we took a taxi to my place which was fairly clean for a change. All went well for a while. I sat her on the couch and she crossed those fine legs and I talked to her, thought about how I was going to fuck her, gave her one of the fifths of bourbon, took the other for myself, and told her, "Drink right out of the bottle."

"You think you're Mr. Van Bilderass, don't you?"

"No, not really. The road has been quite rough for me."

"Bullshit! You think you're Mr. Van Bilderass!"

Jane's eyes became very wide. She picked up her fifth of bourbon, raised it above her head.

"Hold it!" I said.

"What?"

"You throw that son of a bitch—make *sure* to hit me and knock me out! Otherwise it's coming right back at you. And I ain't gonna miss! Now, go on, throw it!"

She looked at me and put the bottle down.

We made it a couple of times that night. It was very good.

And after that, we shacked from six to eight years in hell.

I am trying to be concise here, make a digest of it all, but how can you squeeze forty-nine years into four or five thousand words? So I must say various things about this Jane—like the first night I was riding her, I stopped in the middle of a stroke, asked, "Say, I don't know your name! What is your name?"

Her answer: "What the hell difference does it make?"

One night with my Jane, so drunk I had fallen off the couch beside her, looking up at those slim ankles in those high heels, those calves, perfect, those knees perfect, and her just sitting there. I'd been outdrinking her two to one and had just fallen off the couch. And looking up at those legs from my back, I said the immortal line: "Baby, I am a genius and nobody knows it but me."

And she answered with the immortal line: "Oh, get up off the floor and sit down, you damn fool!"

One day, I had to bury her too. Like my father. Like my mother. I buried her two years after we separated.

But before that, I went to the charity ward of the L.A. County General Hospital (my old home) and I was put down in a dark cellar, and my papers got lost. "The papers," the head nurse said, "went downstairs while I was upstairs." So I got lost somewhere down there in that Underground cellar, a body without papers, dying, hemorrhaging out of my mouth and ass continually. All that cheap wine and hard living coming through and out— fountains of blood. Then somebody found my papers and after three days in the cellar I was brought up to a more lighted area. But then it was found that I didn't have any blood credit. "Mr. Bukowski," the head nurse told me, "if you can't establish any blood credit you can't get any blood." Which meant I was going to die.

It appeared that all they did for the dying or the sick was let them lay there until they died. I saw them pull the dead out from all about me. Then they had room for new bodies. Room was the problem. And no nurses, no doctors. The sight of an intern was even a miracle.

Then they found that my father had established blood credit while working his job. Besides, I was messing up the whole ward with my blood, and failing to die. A nurse arrived like an angel from the sky and inserted a needle into my vein, hung up the bottle. I took thirteen pints of blood and thirteen of glucose without stop.

I found a place on Kingsley Drive, got a job driving a truck, and bought an old typewriter. And each night after work I'd get drunk. I wouldn't eat, just knock out eight or ten poems. I don't know *how* I got off the short story. I was writing poems but I didn't know why. Somehow I'd learned about J.B. May and his *Trace* magazine, which was then the only gathering force of the new emergence of the little magazines, listing them. And the "littles" were then a much finer stomping ground for the little bit of good and realistic writing that was being done. Now the littles have changed, materialized into a bunch of operators with cheap mimeo setups that have become a dumping ground of very poor literature and poetry. The littles and the bigs are all on the same ground now—they both print garbage and their main purpose is publicity and group power and money, any damned way they can get it. The horse's ass has finally met the horse's mouth and is eating its own shit.

I wrote more poems, changed jobs and women, buried Jane, and then they began to pick up on me. Little chapbooks of poems appeared: *Flower, Fist and Bestial Wail. Run With the Hunted. Longshot Pomes for Broke Players.* My style was very simple and I said anything I wanted to. The books sold out right away. I was understood by Kansas City whores and Harvard professors. Who knows more?

Things moved fast. Whit Burnett had laid it down. *Story* was finished. The new great editor of our time was Jon Edgar Webb of *Loujon Press Books* and the publisher of the magazine *The Outsider*. Next my photo was on the cover of *The Outsider*—the battered and torn mug, and the poems and letters inside. I was the new poetic concept—far away from the educated and careful poesy—I laid it down raw. Some hated it, others loved it. I couldn't be bothered. I just drank more and wrote more poems. My typewriter was my machine gun and it was loaded.

The new great editor, old Jon Webb, had this flair for finely printed books. Both of my books, *It Catches My Heart in Its Hands* and *Crucifix in a Deathhand*, are printed on paper warranted to last 2,000 years. That's frightening, you know. The books were bought up early by collectors, who now ask $25 to $75 a copy while Webb and I sit with our fingers up our assholes wondering where our next dime will come from. Webb finally got desperate and wise and published some Henry Miller letters to a painter, a French painter if I have it right. Miller has done some great writing but the letters weren't much good, as writing. Anyhow, Webb charged $25 a copy right off. Now let the collectors worry about that one.

But going back a bit. Are you still awake? *It Catches* only came out in 500 signed copies. Webb wanted to go to 2500 on *Crucifix*. I didn't have any poems on hand, so I wrote them right from the typer into the press—all the poems in *Crucifix*, except one, were never sent to the magazines. They were written right into the book. In a sense it was hell.

Webb: "I need more poems, Bukowski."

"Damn! Give me a little more time!"

It was hell but it was action, and I've always been for action.

It was New Orleans this time, and the last poem was written, and the book was coming off the press, and then came the blow—I had to *sign* 2500 motherfucking pages! The pages were purple and when I stacked them up they stood seven feet high. It looked like I could never do it. And Webb wanted each page signed with a silver felt tip special pen, and it took each page five minutes to dry. I got tired of signing name and date, so I began to add drawings, say things. It was either that or go crazy, but the drawings and words only slowed the process, and all I did was drink drink drink and insult the woman they had moved me in with.

A couple of days later I was still living there, drunk all the time, signing these 2500 pages in silver ink. I got plenty tired of the name Charles Bukowski. I began to hate the son of a bitch.

Meanwhile, a woman and a young child, my own daughter, waited upon me in Los Angeles. After all the pages were signed I flipped a coin. It said: go back to woman and child. I did.

But there was always Jon Webb, the great editor, and if it wasn't a book of mine, it was something else. He liked me around. He liked to argue with me. I didn't like to argue. One time they got me set up as poet-in-residence at the cottage at the University of Arizona, which took some doing because I refuse to read my shit in public, feeling that is only a sucking at public adulation and weakened whatever was left of my soul. (When I get down to my last penny I'll want to read and then they won't want to hear me.)

The cottage wasn't bad. Air-conditioned, and it was over 100 degrees every day. I never knew Tucson was such an oven.

The cottage had been set a little back from the campus walk, but still some of the students always managed to see this strange-looking, badly dressed, unpoetic-looking man, around noon, coming out the doorway with this huge sack of empties, and dumping the bottles into a trashcan marked "Univ. of Ariz." and after dumping the bottles, without fail, vomiting into the can. I was told that some great writers had lived in that shack. I won't name their names but some of their books were there and I tried to read them and that was part of the vomiting in the morning. Also, there was a radio, but Tucson plays no symphony music at night, so I had to listen to the latest rock hits, and between that and the books of "great writers" and the drinking, I think I was sicker in that cottage than I had been anyplace else. The word was out that they had a madman in there. Nobody ever came around, which was wonderful. Although the prof who had set up my residence phoned me from the hospital (where he had ulcers) (this sounds so cockeyed but it's true), and he said over the phone, "As soon as you leave, Bukowski, we are going to bust that shack down with a steel wrecking-ball."

"Thank you, sir," I said, "but first don't forget to save all the great books in here."

"We won't," he said.

The son of a bitch was crazy.

Well, I got out of there after an argument brought on by Webb about the "hippies." Hell, I had no particular love for the hippies. I was a loner. And some of the things they were finding out about, just finding out about—like war and the deadening effect of working forty or forty-eight hours a week at something you didn't want to do, and about marriage, the trap of it. But the hippies were set apart from me. Their discoveries of things were late, and they liked to gather in crowds, mill, and holler about it. And drugs? What was holy about that? That was just something somebody gave me, usually for free—meth, reds, yellows, LSD. It didn't matter. I just popped it down and came out the same way I entered.

Let's say, I was hardened. There wasn't any *real* particular thrill. Just a glow, or with LSD, a controlled sideshow.

Sniff the big c, smoke hash. It all passed and I had to enter the world again. The world was *always* there when you came down. That was the strange thing you found out. For all the up, there was always the comedown, and you had to *make* it somehow, and that was hard, because after coming down you were in sad shape to make it through ordinary channels—shipping clerk, busboy, dishwasher, carwash boy. And if you had a police record, all the worse.

Hell is everywhere bounding.

Everything was a trap: women, drugs, whiskey, wine, scotch, beer—even beer—cigars, and cigarettes. Traps: Work or no work. Traps: Artistry or no artistry; everything sucked you into some spiderweb. I disdained the use of the needle for the same reason that I disdained some so-called beautiful women—the price was far beyond the measure of the worth. I didn't want to hustle that hard.

So the hippies and their yell of LOVE LOVE LOVE meant very little to me. It seemed more of a command, and I don't like commands. I ignored it. Then Webb began banging against the hippies that night in his place in Tucson. His hair that had once been a wonderful white was now dyed red. And the old man, the great editor, kept hollering for his pills. "Lou, have I had my pill for today?" A hell of a lousy pill—some kind of vitamin pill or iron pill—and then the old man would start raving to me about the hippies.

"Bukowski, you *know* the hippies aren't any good!"

"I'm not crazy about them, Jon. They are weak. They have the herd instinct. They are jammed with phonies. They are mostly an unfeeling and false people yapping about something they are *told* to yap about. But then, I think of the little businessmen with their suits and neckties, making the eight to five grind, and the hippies are against *this*, and I feel that they are right about this. The hip is more alive than the stockbroker."

"Look, Bukowski, I want you to write an anti-hippie article for me."

"Well, I don't know."

"I mean, these kids don't assume any *responsibility*, they don't try, they don't do anything, they don't want to do anything—they won't support society!" The great editor Webb sounded like my father who I had buried. Look. Here you get kids born into a world and the first thing you learn is that there are things called hydrogen bombs being stockpiled by various nations, enough at this time to kill everybody thirty times over—except the rich buried deep enough or the boys getting their spaceships ready, the new Noah's Arks. There *would* be a second flood, as the old street criers in Pershing Square used to warn us, but this time it would be flame instead of water.

So who, at the age of eighteen, would want to go to work for a motor company, turning bolts while in thirty seconds his ass might be separated from his balls forever? There is only *one* human responsible for each demolition button. And someday, maybe tomorrow, that idiot would come along . . . by the sheer mathematics of the thing and do it?

Why not let your hair grow and smoke a bit of grass? Relax. Take each moment as a miracle gift.

I was that way before the invention of the Bomb. I was hip on the premise born before the hips—if a man is going to die, why stockpile useless human possessions?

So Webb said, "I want you to do an anti-hippie article."

Here was a man who had done two collector's items of my poems; a man who had read my poems over and over and still did not know who I was.

"I can't write an anti-hippie article, Jon. They've never hurt me. They've never thought of it. Others have. For instance, I've been in jail. So have you."

Webb had been a diamond thief before he had gained respectability as an editor. He'd made jail. Even though he had, long ago, written an earlier paperback on it, the whole thing wasn't supposed to be mentioned. Now he needed a credit rating with the paper-selling houses, and others. If you mentioned that Webb had done time you were blacklisted by Loujon Press forever. One poor guy, in a review of *Crucifix*, once made a mistake and mentioned that Webb had done time.

The great editor snapped his fingers at me. "That's it! He's finished, forever!"

Webb also knocked off Mike McClure because he showed up on television dressed like a pansy, dark shading under his eyes.

"That's all," Webb said, turning to me, "McClure's finished!"

Well, I went back to L.A. without writing the anti-hippie article before Webb finished me off too. I guess if he ever reads this, a bullet will come flying through my window some night.

More of my books came out. Most of the editions were in very limited quantity and only known in the Underground. But the college profs began to knock upon my door, bringing in their soft floppy limbs and white soft faces and little six packs of beer. They got high very quickly on a couple of cans of beer and I listened to their talk. I never did get along with English teachers when they were trying to teach me.

People keep coming through my door, talking to me; uninvited, they come and I listen, give them what I have to drink, and they leave. But those hours are not wasted—man learns from man, and if he doesn't, he has missed the first trumpeter and blown the bag of shit!

Both the profs and the bums were always very sincere—unloading all they had, which was not enough.

■

One day John Bryan decided to start an Underground newspaper called *Open City*. I was asked to contribute a column a week. I called the column "Notes of a Dirty Old Man." And I wrote short stories under that guise. Once a week for almost two years. After the horse races, win or lose, on a Friday or a Saturday I would pick up three or four six-packs and knock out the column say while listening to Mahler, who makes both Beethoven and Bach look like sissies.

Bryan printed everything I handed him. It was a very curious time in my life—everybody treated me like a genius, so I had to play the game and write the stuff. It wasn't hard to do—all it takes to be a genius is to be one. "You gonna buy one or *be* one?" they used to ask me in those dark Philadelphia bars. "I'm gonna buy one," I'd tell them.

Meanwhile, there were Underground meetings I was urged to attend. Usually, I arrived drunk or not at all. The crew did not seem very fiery. Strangely calm and dead and well-fed for their ages. Sitting around making little flip anti-war jokes, or jokes about pot. Everybody understood the jokes but me. Run a pig for president. What the fuck was that? It excited them. It bored me.

I felt that if there were going to be a time for ATTACK, we should arm ourselves properly with the latest weapons, train ourselves properly, kill the stooges, get the job done. I wasn't even a revolutionary, but I knew how a true revolutionary should think. The kids finally ended up playing the Great Romanticism and fingerfucking each other.

They clowned. They didn't have the guts. They fell almost willingly into the hands of the Establishment.

At one meeting everybody was excited about the Chicago thing. Everybody was talking at once. Chicago hadn't happened as yet. I finally held up my hand, drunk, was allowed to speak:

"The Establishment has much more intelligence than you allow it to have. They will only use whatever force is *necessary* to put you down. I doubt that there will be any machine gun fire or mass murder of you people in Chicago. Of course, there will be blood—lots of it—and Papa will spank. But don't you realize that they are worried about propaganda worldwide and that Chicago is finally Washington, D.C.? Don't you *realize* that they are *controlling* you and looking upon you as bad children? Be bad, and Papa spank! Be badder, Papa spank harder! You are under control, *their* control. You underestimate their intelligence. That's *your* mistake. They are playing with you, don't forget it! You've shown your whole hand and what have you got—just openers—and they sit with the royal flush, smiling. You might beat them, but you've got to change your game. You've been suckered in."

I was going on with more but some Mexican fellow, a young math teacher from an East L.A. high school, leaned over a banister and shouted:

"You don't know what you're talking about, Bukowski! Chicago is going to be mass MURDER! PEOPLE ARE GOING TO BE MURDERED BY THE HUNDREDS RIGHT IN FRONT OF YOUR EYES! MACHINE GUNNED, YES! YOU WILL SEE IT!"

Of course, it didn't happen—the revolution; and the pig wasn't elected president, he was put in jail, and the Underground paper folded, and God walked down the staircase spreading gladiolus to the wind.

The paper folded, Haight Ashbury became a myth. "When you go to San Francisco, wear a flower in your hair." The *Berkeley Barb* had inner haggles. The word went out: "The Underground is dead."

But I had some luck—Essex House picked up the columns from *Open City* and came out with a paperback *Notes of A Dirty Old Man*. The work that I had done as a joy and almost for nothing was coming back in hard coin. I felt like a junior Hemingway. What a joy it must be to be a truly great writer, even if it means the shotgun at the finish.

And that's why maybe I, Bukowski, am still sitting here no more holy than Gandhi, and, baby, maybe a little bit less dead, crashing out stories that maybe only people interested in sex understand. I drink; my head falls upon the typewriter; that is my pillow.

I am the Underground, alone. And I don't know what to do.

So I write this and get drunk again.

Concisely.

READING AND BREEDING

FOR KENNETH

It was another benefit for Kenneth Patchen, and I'd told F. I wasn't quite
that holy but he said there'd be a lot of girls with tight dresses up there, so I
said, "All right, write the address down here." Then he walked out through
the screen. My front door is stuck shut.

I couldn't understand F. It was a 2nd Patchen benefit; I'd been to his first
one over at West L.A. I'd told the people before reading that I didn't believe
a poet with a bad back deserved any more than anybody else with a bad
back, and here he was asking me again and here I was going again—this
time up in the Hollywood Hills. My car isn't much good on hills so I phoned
Cornelia and Cornelia put on her tight red pants outfit and we got in her
car and Cornelia drove.

"Marlon Brando lives up here," she told me. "I used to drive up here. I
stopped and looked at his garbage once. Marlon is my secret love."

"Shit," I said.

We kept watching the numbers and we drove higher and higher into the
hills and the houses got richer and richer and I got more nervous. It's true
that the richer people became the less human they became, and so I began
to get unhappy. Nervous and unhappy.

"I think we've made a mistake," I said.

She just drove along in her tight red outfit, probably thinking she might
find a rich one with a bit of soul, or maybe without that bit. We found it and
turned in. A long driveway and at the bottom, sitting on a ledge overlook-
ing the canyon sat a rather large-sized house. We entered at ground-level
and then descended a large marble stairway. The ceilings were high, white,
and decorated with bad paintings, all painted by the same artist, a cross
between a bad Orozco and a bad Picasso. People stood about in groups of
two and threes looking comfortable, as comfortable as tombstones. Most

of them were outside around the swimming pool, holding stale drinks and lighting cigarettes. I saw a poet I knew, George Dunning. George kept changing writing styles and he was not very good but he read loudly and pretended that he was a genius and some people believed him. His wife believed him. He wrote while she worked. George changed styles but kept the same wife. I introduced Cornelia and I laughed while Dunning insulted me, then Cornelia walked off to the swimming pool crowd to explore that territory. Her ass looked good in those tight red pants and she had fringes in the front that flopped about to show an open area of belly and bellybutton.

Then I saw the poetess Vanna Roget, she was in her 40's but had a very good figure. She had a large nose and large hands but also a nice large ass. She sat on the couch and I walked over and sat beside her. I gave her one of my beers. I had entered with 6 beers.

Vanna had just gotten off the black-lover kick; some of the white poets secretly disliked her for this but I didn't care, she had this large nice ass. Of course, I was with Cornelia but I figured if Cornelia ran off with the president of a brassiere house or a golfball manufacturing company then I could run off with that ass. Vanna wrote fair poetry but she didn't know how to talk. I was always trying to get her to talk, to bring her out of that silence, so I always tried to shock her.

"God," I said, "I have real hot nuts tonight. They feel like burning coals filled with cocoanut juice."

Vanna just looked at me with those wide blue eyes and lifted her beer-bottle and stuck the end of it into her mouth.

"Suction," I said, "suck. Suck. I feel like I'm gonna come in my shorts right now."

I watched the beer run into her mouth.

"I'd eat your shit out of a milk bottle just to get my drill into you."

"Bukowski, you just talk that way because you think you're a great poet."

"You just get that milk bottle."

Vanna just looked at me.

The people were coming up the steps from the swimming pool. Cornelia saw me and came on over. I introduced Cornelia and Vanna. They looked at each other the way women do, immediately knowing everything I had done to either of them or wanted to do or would do.

The poetry reading was beginning. Dunning began it, grinning humanely he took off his hat, put it on the floor, emptied his change into it. Then he began to read, LOUDLY. He screamed. Dunning was insane without being interesting. But he *believed* in himself, which is a common disease among writers good and bad. In fact, the bad writers usually have more belief than the good ones. Dunning raged on. It was embarrassing, somehow, like finding a monkey in bed with your wife; but you really couldn't get angry. There was simply the feeling that you were being taken and there wasn't much that could be done. The world is full of Dunnings and monkeys, more Dunnings than monkeys.

Then a very ineffectual one got up and he read what he called a piece of "whimsey." One must have supposed that his mother liked it, or a friend on ATD. It was so darling that it was nothing at all. The poet was quite sure that he was charming everybody but he was only charming himself. He finished and got on off.

Others tried and failed. Then the Jewish poetess who had lost her job for reading a dirty poem to her class got up and read 2 bad poems and one good one. The good one wasn't that good, it was simply that after the first 2 poems and Dunning and Whimsey and the others, it was like swallowing sand instead of shit.

I had my turn. F. introduced me. By then, I was in pain. I said, "Wait . . . I need a drink . . ." I ran to the bar but there wasn't a bottle in sight. An old blonde sat at the bar, drinkless, and stared at me as if all my wits had gone running into the night.

"Damned chippy," I hissed at her, "you suck dogs . . ."

I circled back to the podium and began reading. First I told them that the place reminded me of a Catholic church and that I had quit the

Catholic Church at age 12, then I read 3 poems, one about a stripteaser, one about a sex fiend, and one about a man who wanted to lick a woman's asshole. The poem about the stripteaser wasn't about me.

There were others. Nobody put any money in the hat for Patchen, all those rich bastards, they sat with their hands in their pockets. Then a guy who taught at a college in town got up. He was the worst of the night. His wife read with him. It was a play, a play for 2 people. It was unbelievably juvenile and it went on and on and on. I went back to the bar and discovered that the whiskey was underneath, the whiskey and the vodka and the gin and . . . I began to mix 2 good whiskeys and waters when this young brunette stepped behind the bar. She stood real close to me, putting 2 large brown eyes upon me. She wanted it, she didn't leave any doubt of that. I felt as if I were backed into a corner. I looked around and I was.

"Mr. Bukowski," she said, "your poems were really memorable. And funny. Those others can't write, you really shame them. I just *adore* you . . ."

"You're really nicely built," I said, "and you're young and I like your eyes . . ."

"I'm yours . . ." she said, "fuck me."

"What?" I asked.

"You heard it right."

"Now?" I asked.

"No, later . . ."

"Pardon me," I said. I took my 2 drinks and slid around her. She kept smiling at me. I walked back to Cornelia and handed her a drink. The professor and his wife were *still* reading his play. Then, it ended. The last to read was the lady who owned the house or the lady of the husband who owned the house. She wasn't quite as bad as the professor, but the cruelties people bestow in the name of Patchen I will never quite forget. The rich lady finished and people began leaving, most of them ignoring the hat for Patchen.

I walked behind the bar and began serving the 6 or 7 people sitting there. For each drink I mixed for somebody I mixed one for myself and drank it. Then I began ranting about the dirty rich and the bad poetry and selfish games played in the name of Kenneth P. Some of them thought it was funny. Well, they laughed. I looked around and Cornelia was back there with me, helping me serve drinks. Soon we just outdrank everybody and it was just Cornelia and I sitting there. It seemed as if we were alone in the house. I decided it might be a good idea if we took a bottle of whiskey and I handed Cornelia a 5th to put in her purse but then the husband of the house appeared running down the marble steps saying, "Oh no! Oh no! Oh no!" He had grey hair and a grey goatee and he grabbed the bottle. Well, there was nothing to do but leave. When we got outside I found that I had left a valuable Patchen book in there. I rang the doorbell and let Cornelia do the talking. The rich lady answered the door.

"We left a valuable Patchen book in there," Cornelia said.

The rich lady was angry. We walked in and got the valuable Patchen book. Then we were out again. We had parked at the top of the driveway and it was a long walk up. There were sagebrush and grass and rock all about. It was a long climb upward and several times we stumbled.

"I'm through hustling for Patchen," I said. "That's it."

Cornelia threw herself down on the grassy edge, spread her arms and her legs.

"Come on," she said, "let's fuck."

"No," I said, "not here, my god."

"Look, Bukowski, we've got the stars and the moon and the earth, let's fuck."

I helped her up. We walked a few yards more then Cornelia threw herself down again.

"Come on, Bukowski, let's fuck. Let me have it. Put that hook to me, daddy, lemme see that hunk of bologna . . ."

I got her up again. She threw herself down once or twice again and then we were at her car. Cornelia drove. I didn't remember the ride home but I remembered getting into bed and then Cornelia was upon me . . .

"This Patchen thing," I said, "it's getting monotonous. I can't stand it anymore."

"Kiss me," she said, "kiss me HARD!"

"After all, Patchen does live in Palo Alto."

"Kiss me . . . Kiss me or I'll SCREAM!"

I kissed her. Up there, and then down lower and lower. It got better. Then I was upon her and I was in, thinking of her walking about in her red pajamas and her long dark hair and those deep brown eyes that looked and looked and looked . . . I forgot all about Kenneth Patchen. I even forgot the professor's terrible play. I even forgot that I was a poet. Then it was over and I was on my back, listening to the crickets, the sweat on my chest and forehead. We'd saved a bad night. The rich could keep their whiskey and Kenneth would get mailed that dollar 32 cents that was dropped in the hat.

THE L.A. SCENE

THE POETS, THE MADMEN; THE IMPOVERISHED

AND THE RICH OF SOUL; THE BLAND, THE

BASTARDS, THE DRUNKS AND THE DAMNED . . .

I was born in Andernach, Germany, August 16th, 1920, the bastard son of an American soldier with the American Army of Occupation. At the age of two I was brought to the U.S. and after a couple of months stay in Baltimore I was brought to Los Angeles, and after maturity (?) I bummed the country at random, back and forth, up and down, in and out, but I always returned to Los Angeles and here I am today living in a falling down front court just off the poor man's Sunset Strip. If anybody is an authority on the scene I ought to be, though granted, the scene has filtered down through days and nights of wine and beer and whiskey, and perhaps a desperation that has twisted my perspective a bit, but I was here, am here, and speak of it . . .

The Alvarado street scene, alone, is worth retelling, even though my material dates from 15 years ago. I imagine there have been changes but that the changes have not been rapid. Or have they? It was just a week ago I was sitting in a nudie bar on Sunset with girls grinding their boxes at me. But that area between 3rd Street and 8th Street on Alvarado and the bars running up and down those streets have hardly changed as much. It is the poor man's area, there across from the park where they sit waiting on luck, waiting on death. It is the 2nd skidrow of L.A.

I opened those bars and closed them, fought in them, met women in them, made the old Lincoln Heights jail a dozen times. There is a whole section of people down there who live on air and hope and empty returnable bottles and the grace of their brothers and sisters. They live in small rooms, always behind in the rent, dreaming of the next bottle of wine, the next free drink in the bar. They starve, go mad, are murdered and mutilated.

Until you live and drink among these you will never know the abandoned people of America. They are abandoned and they have abandoned themselves. I joined them. And among all these, there are women, most of them harpies, but here and there, women of body and mind, alcoholic, mad. I lived off and on with one of them for 7 years; with others for shorter periods. The sex was good; they were not prostitutes; but something had fallen out of them, something in life had made them incapable of love or of caring. Police raids on our unpaid for rooms were not uncommon. I became as violent and could curse as well as any of those ladies on the wine. Some of them I buried, some of them I hated, some of them I loved but they all gave me more wild action, albeit it was mostly bad, than could fill the lives of 20 men. Those ladies from hell finally put me in the L.A. County General Hospital, all the way to the critical list, and coming out, I retired from Alvarado Street, but if you'd like to try some, I imagine the same breed nourishes the death wish down there . . .

After a bad marriage I decided, well, hell, I might as well be a writer, that seems easiest, you say anything you want to and they say, hey, that's good, you're a genius. Why not be a genius? There are so many half-assed geniuses. So I became another half-assed genius.

My first thought was to stay away from writers, artists, creators, feeling that they could take one off the path with the misdirection of their ambitions. After all, a good writer need only do two things well: Live and write, and the job is done. In Los Angeles it is possible to live in total isolation until they find you, and they will find you. And drink with you for days and nights, and talk for days and nights. And when they are gone, others will come along. One doesn't mind the women, of course, but the others are definitely consumers of the soul.

One of the first to find me was M.J., the well-known beat poet of the '50s, mostly out of New York City, well, Brooklyn. M. just came beating on the door. He was no longer a young man and he had been writing a long time. I was even older and I had just begun writing. Well, that was fair. I had a hangover.

"Bukowski, you got wheels?"

"Yeah, but let me get a beer first. Want one?"

"No, I'm on the wagon."

"What's the matter?"

"Listen, I got beat up two nights in a row. I got beat up in Frisco and the next night I'm down at *Barney's Beanery* and I get into another fight. This guy's a pro. He beats me so bad I shit myself. I had to wipe off with a newspaper. No place to sleep . . . I want you to drive me to Venice . . ."

"Sure."

"This guy's good for a twenty."

On the way down M. told me how they "owed" it to us. We'd paid our dues, he said. Yeah, Henry Miller used to tap these rich guys when he started. All artists had a right.

I thought it would be nice if all artists had a right to survival but my thoughts were that everybody had, and if the artist didn't make it monetarily he was in the same shape as anybody else who didn't. But I didn't argue with M. He was no longer young but he was still a powerful poet. But somehow in the poetic circles he had become locked out. There were politics in art as well as anywhere else. It was sad. But M. had gone to too many literary parties, he had fallen for too many suck plays, he had crept around too many Names simply because they were Names; he'd made too many demands at the wrong time and in the wrong way. As we drove along he pulled out a little red notebook of "taps." All those names were good for a tap.

We made Venice and I got out with M. and we went up to a two-story house. M. knocked. A kid came out.

"Jimmy, I need a 20."

Jimmy left, came back with the 20, closed the door. We got back in the car, drove back, drank all afternoon and night as M. talked the poetic scene. He had forgotten he was on the wagon. The next morning it was beer for breakfast and out to the Hollywood Hills. Another two-story house. M. had to beat on the windows. A house full of cats and kittens, the smell of catshit dominated. M. got another 20 and we drove back. And drank a bit more.

I saw M. off and on. Now and then he gave a poetry reading in town here. But they were ill-attended. He read well and the poetry was good, but the hex was on. M. was marked. The taps were running out. Then he found a girl who took him in. I was happy for M. But M. was like any other poet: he fell in love with his women, perhaps too much so. He was soon on the street again, sometimes sleeping on my couch, bitching against the fates. Since nobody would publish his books any more he began to mimeo his own copies. I have one here now: *All American Poets Are In Prison*. He inscribed it for me:

> L.A.
> Feb. 1970
> For Charlie:
> By the Grace of the Gods
> Sometimes we can still raise it.
> Show it to me he yelled. Show it
> to me. Man I'm trying to find it.
> Take it easy. Here man here it
> is. On the palm of his hand was
> a speck of white seed. I don't
> come as often as youse do he
> said. Here man you want to see
> my cock. Here it is standing like
> a tree naked in the asparagus
> Sun.
> Love,
> M.

Then M. began writing songs. I have a book of his songs somewhere. "I'm going up to see Janis Joplin and show her my songs," he said.

I felt it wouldn't work but I couldn't tell M. He was such a Romantic, he had such hopes. He came back.

"She wouldn't see me," he said.

Now Janis is dead and M., last I heard, was swinging a mop in Brooklyn, working at last—for his brother. I hope M. comes back, all the way back. For all his Name hang-ups and panhandling, there are worse poets on top right now. Maybe all American poets are in prison. Most of them, anyhow . . .

Then there was N.H. of the Paris Beat scene, the Tangiers scene, Greece and Switzerland, the Burroughs gang . . . N. appeared along with myself and another poet in a recent *Penguin Modern Poets* series. Suddenly he was down at Venice Beach, rotting on the shore, no longer writing; complaining of a decaying liver and being looked over by an aged mother he kept well-hidden. Often when I went to see N., young men would come knocking at his door. Although his liver was decaying it was evident that his pecker was well in order. N. was supposed to go both ways but I never saw any women about.

"Bukowski, I can't write anymore. Burroughs wouldn't talk to me anymore, nobody wants to see me. I've been put down. I'm on the shit list. I'm finished. I've got six books ready and nobody wants to touch them."

N. later claimed that I had axed him with Black Sparrow Press, a publisher of most modern American poetry. It was untrue but this was N's mindstate. Every visit to him consisted of listening to his bitching about how he had been blackmailed out of the scene. Actually I had asked Black Sparrow to publish him, feeling that he deserved it.

"You've never done anything for me, Bukowski."

One would like to think that creation does its own work, but N. had forgotten that I had written a foreword praising him for his work in a special *Ole* magazine edition of his poetry. N.'s persecution mania became so bad that once after N.C. and I paid him an hour's visit we had to run to the elevator and once the door was closed we began rolling on the floor in laughter. We were afraid to go out the front way for fear he would hear us and his feelings would be hurt so we ran it down to the basement and rolled on the floor there, laughing for five minutes among the boilers and spiderwebs and dankness.

N.H. was still a damned good poet. But it was sad the way they could go, ranting. I suppose we'll all go, ranting. The poetry, the prose climbing the walls like snakes; our suicide mirrors showing grey hairs and grey ways and grey talents. N. had lost his European backer. Things were not so well. The poets would visit him once, then stop. *The Free Press* offered him a job of writing reviews but N. didn't follow it up. Educated, talented, knowledgable, he was rotting. He admitted it. I told him he could find it again.

Once another poet and I visited him and suggested a round of drinking but N. said he had been invited to a party, a special invitation. Would we like to come? Why not? we asked. He had the address. When we got there it was a benefit for somebody, admission one dollar. We got in the back way and stood around listening to the band. I found a gallon jug of wine and began drinking it. I talked to a couple of women, kissed one, walked around.

Then the poet I was with asked me, "Do you think anybody knows you're Charles Bukowski?" It was an interesting thought. I forgot all about N. and my desire for him to begin creating again. I walked up to a girl. "Listen, you know I'm Charles Bukowski?" "Charles who?" she asked. The poet with me laughed. I asked several people if they knew I was Charles Bukowski. "Never heard of him. Who's that?" "Charles Bukowski. Is that Tiny Tim's dishrag?"

I drank the rest of the wine and when the benefit was over I ran down to the bottom of the stairway and blocked the exit. *"Now you people, this is to let you know that I am Charles Bukowski. Now before I let you out I want you to say, 'I know you. Charles Bukowski!' Now say it!"*

"Come on, man, let us out of here!"

"Bullshit, man, let us out of here!"

"Come on, Charles, don't be an asshole," said N.

"All right, say it!" I screamed. *"Say that I am Charles Bukowski and that you know me! Now say it!"*

I had 150 people blocked on that stairway and inside. Then the poet next to me said, "Bukowski, the police are coming!"

I was gone fast, running down the streets of Venice West, N. and the poet running behind me. Yes, N. and I were both having bad days and nights.

But last I heard he was making a nice comeback, going to Frisco and putting out a magazine, and I've lost the flyer but I believe he's printing Ginsberg, Ferlinghetti, McClure, Burroughs, all of them. He'd finally gotten away from Rose Ave., down there around the parking lot, the soulless hippies sitting on the cement benches, starving, bumming, trying to steal from that Jewish grocery store and waiting for Tim Leary to tell them — Drop out, to what? But Leary isn't there. Just the seagulls and the waiting and no creation . . .

. . . ah, then there was Mad Jack the painter. A woman was taking care of him, a young woman with a fairly large house. Jack had the whole basement to himself, his paintings spread on the cement down there. I think they were rather good, done with India ink scratches in black and toned up in these blobs of yellow applied with a brush. There were hundreds of them and almost all of them looked alike.

Jack always had a bottle of wine in his pocket, port, and he was always drunk or getting drunk. He seldom bathed and the mucous ran from his nose and dried in black designs above the lip and mouth. Even his beard was dirty and he screamed when he talked, always something melodramatic and just a bit stupid. I had to drink to bear up with him. As I said, though, the paintings were good and I forgave a lot for that. I suppose his girl thought the same way and he probably ate her up pretty good too. Or so he told me.

I'd go over there and get drunk all night, smoking a bit too, and some pills. I don't know what the pills were, we threw it together, and there was a piano there and I don't know how to play the piano but I played it. I played it like a drum, for hours, getting these strange sounds that I don't think anybody ever got off a piano before.

One night we all went out for drinks and we were screaming back and forth at each other on the streets and in the liquor store, his girl was along, and this guy came back with us, he thought we were interesting, but the guy started bragging how he'd killed guys in the war, and I told him that didn't take any special merit, that was sanctified, and that it was much more of a thing to kill a guy out of the war.

"You don't like me much, do you?" he asked.

"Not at all," I said.

He left. When he came back he had a gun belt and holster on. He walked over to me. He pulled the gun and put it to my belly.

"I'm going to kill you," he said.

"I've got this suicide complex," I said. "Go ahead."

"You're scared."

"A little. Death isn't easy. Shoot. I don't think you've got the guts, killer."

He put the gun back in the holster. We never saw him again. . .

Mad Jack was always coming around to my place for the touch, 15 cents, 10 cents. Enough to round out a bottle of wine. He finally became a bit boring—in spite of his paintings. A certain type of genius can be awfully dull. In fact, most genius is dull most of the time until they are ready to explode into their art. The vocally brilliant ones are always the fakes. Anyhow, I got to avoiding Jack. Then I heard he had an exhibition and sold some of his paintings for $6,000. He flew to Canada and drank it all up in the same bar within a week. Then he was back at my door, begging pennies. Last I heard his girl threw him out and he's living with his mother.

Some day he'll be rich on his paintings but he'll still be walking around with dried snot under his nose and a bottle of wine in his pocket, and all those screaming little dull melodramatic things he does will be looked upon as ultimate and precious brilliancies . . .

Then there's big T.J. up in Echo Park. I don't think he's written a new poem in ten years, he always read the same ones over and over at poetry readings. T.J. has a problem . . . Anyhow, he's a huge man, a sort of myth . . . he used to hang out at Venice West when it was going strong, you know, the naked girls in bathtubs, the Holy Barbarians, in a sense the whole sick scene that had to fade because it was based more on a play of creation than real creation, but it all counts, like gas stations and weenies and Sunday picnics, so let's not get bitter; anyhow, T.J. used to sweep in from the walk into one of those places and with one swing of his arm knock five guys off their stools. Then he'd look for a table to put his chess set up on and brush those guys to the floor too. Then calmly sit down, light his pipe, and begin his game with his partner.

You can see T.J. now up in Echo Park scrounging around in trashcans looking for his special junk. T. is a great junk collector. His place is full of junk, you can't sit down. A tape is usually playing. Among the junk sit thousands of books, some of which he has read. He is a special expert on Adolf Hitler. His walls are covered with photos and clippings and sayings and nudes and paintings. It is a crass confusion and T.J. sits in the middle of it.

"If I ain't happy," he says, "life ain't worth living." His work of ten years ago is some of the best work done in our time. It is classical and erudite and it moves easily and contains knowledge and explosions. T.J. doesn't work. T.J. doesn't do anything. How does he make it? Ask her. Ask L.

The strange ones keep coming around. They all want to drink with me. I can't live with them all or be nice to them all or even find them all interesting. But the types are all alike in one aspect—they are disgusted with our present way of life and living, and they talk about it, some of them almost violently, but it is refreshing that all of America hasn't swallowed the common bait.

Not all that come by are artists (thank the purple liverwurst Christ), but some are simply strange. L.W. He's been a bum for five or six years, lived in the flophouses, missions, rode the freights, and had some interesting stories of the Road.

He came by. And he was a good actor. He acted out his past experiences, playing the parts of different characters. He was intense and serious but quite humorous because the truth itself is more often funny than serious. L.W. would come at four in the afternoon and stay until midnight. Once we talked for 13 hours and had breakfast at *Norms* at 5:00 a.m. in the morning.

L.W. was an artist who had no outlet for his art except a vocal expulsion of it. I got some stories out of L.W. which I used to my own advantage. Not too many. One or two. But he got on the repeat kick, especially when other people were around. I'd have to listen to the same stories twice over, thrice over. The others laughed as I did the first time. They thought L.W. was great.

What got me was that L.W. told the same stories word for word, never altering. Well, we all do it, don't we? I began to weary of L.W. and felt it. I haven't seen him in some time. I doubt that I will. We have served each other. . . .

There are others. They keep coming. All with their special brand of talk or living. I've drawn some good ones, these Los Angeles characters, and I suppose they'll keep coming. I don't know why people bring me themselves. I never go anywhere. Those few who arrive are dull, I dispose of them quickly enough. I'd only be unkind to myself if I did otherwise. My theory is that if you are kind to yourself you will be truthful and kind with others, in that certain way

Los Angeles is full of very odd people, believe me. There are many out there who have never been on a 7:30 a.m. freeway or punched a timeclock or even had a job and don't intend to, can't, won't, will die first rather than live the common way. In a sense, each of them is a genius in his or her way, fighting against the obvious, swimming upstream, going mad, getting on pot, wine, whiskey, art, suicide, anything but the common equation. It will be some time before they even us out and make us say quits.

When you see that city hall downtown and all those proper precious people, don't get melancholy. There is a whole tide, a whole race of mad people, starving, drunk, goofy, and miraculous. I have seen many of them. I am one of them. There will be more. This city has not yet been taken. Death before death is sickening.

The strange ones will hold, the war will continue. Thank you.

NOTES ON THE LIFE

OF AN AGED POET

After 100 jobs and years on the bum I looked up and found I had been on the same job for eleven years. I began to notice when I could no longer lift my hands higher than my waist after a day's work. Nerves gone. They had me. I tried many types of cures, many doctors. Nothing worked. I was the only thing that worked—8 hours, 10 hours, 12 hours a day. On this job I didn't have a choice. Overtime was mandatory and they called the hours off one by one. You never knew when your day was over.

The job was killing me. For ten years I had endured it, only being spiritually indignant at being forced to do rote, dull work. Then in the eleventh year the body began to die. I decided that I'd rather stand down on skidrow barefoot than die in security. A man could get security in a jail or in a madhouse. At the age of 50, with a child support problem, I quit. Strangely, this angered most of the fellow workers; they preferred that I die with them rather than alone.

I had, since the age of 35, been writing poems and stories. I decided to die on my own battlefield. I sat down to my typewriter and I said, now I am a professional writer. Of course, it wasn't simply that easy. When a man works for years at the same occupation his time is another man's time. I mean, even with an 8-hour day, that day is taken. Add travel time to and from work, plus work, plus eating, sleeping, bathing, buying clothes, automobiles, tires, batteries, paying taxes, copulating, having visitors, getting sick, having accidents, having insomnia, having to worry about laundry and theft and weather and all the other unmentionables, there isn't ANY TIME left to the man for himself. And, when overtime is called often some of these necessaries must be left out, even sleep, and, more often, copulation. What the fuck? And there are even 5-and-one-half-day weeks, 6-day weeks, and on Sunday one is expected to go to church or visit the relatives, or both. The man who said, "The average man lives a life of quiet desperation," said something partly true. But the job also soothes men, it gives them something to *do*. And it stops most of them from thinking. Men—and women—don't like to think. For them the job is the perfect haven. They are told what to do and how to do it and when to do it. 98 percent of Americans over the age of 21 are working, walking dead. My body and my mind told me that within 3 months I would be one of them. I demurred.

I had a typewriter and no trade. I decided to write a novel. I wrote it in 20 nights, drinking a pint of whiskey a night. Black Sparrow Press accepted the novel, *Post Office*. I also sold 2 or 3 chapters to the magazines as short stories. A strange new life was forming.

My first mistake was in imagining that I could write many hours a day every day. One *can* write this way but it will be diluted and forced material.

Other writers began to arrive, to knock on the door, bringing in their six-packs. I never visited them but they did arrive. I drank with them and talked but they brought me very little and had a way of arriving at the wrong time. The ladies arrived too but they usually brought along something more useful than literary chitchat. Bad writers have a proclivity to talk about writing; good writers will talk about anything else but that. Very few good writers arrived.

I received some feelers for poetry readings and I accepted. I disliked reading poetry, it was a most terrible hour, but it was survival and it was a quick manner of paying for survival, say something like robbing a liquor store. I felt that the audience was not interested in poetry; it was interested in personality. What did the poet look like? How did he speak? What happened after the reading? Does he look like his poems? What do you think of him? How do you think he'd do in bed?

Once after reading at a Patchen benefit in a rich home in Hollywood Hills, a girl cornered me at the bar when I was pouring 2 drinks. She was beautiful and built and young and she put these very large brown eyes upon me while blocking my path and said, "Bukowski, your poems, your reading was so much better than the rest of them. I want to fuck you. Let me fuck you!" Dear old K. Patchen, god rest him, we both might have benefited that night, but I pushed past the girl, informing her that I had arrived with another lady, and, even if I hadn't, I wasn't one to fuck at the drop of a poem . . .

Most poets read badly. They are either too vain or too stupid. They read too low or too loud. And, of course, most of their poetry is bad. But the audience hardly notices. They are personality gazing. And they laugh at the wrong time and like the wrong poems for the wrong reasons. But bad poets create bad audiences; death brings more death. I had to give most of my early readings while quite intoxicated. Fear was there, of course, fear of reading to *them*, but the disgust was stronger. At some universities I simply broke out the pint and drank as I read. It seemed to work—the applause was fair enough and I felt little pain from the reading, but, it seemed I was not invited back. The only 2nd invites I have received have been at places where I didn't drink at the reading. So much for their measurements of poetry. Now and then, though, a poet does fall upon a magic audience where everything is right. I can't explain how this works. It is very strange—it is as if the poet were the audience and the audience were the poet. It all flows.

Of course, parties after readings can lead to many joys and/or disasters. I remember after one reading that the only room available to me was in the woman's dorm, so we partied there, the profs and a few of the students and after they were gone I still had a bit of whiskey left and a bit of life left and I looked up at the ceiling and drank. Then I realized that, after all, I *was* THE DIRTY OLD MAN so I left my room and walked around knocking on doors and demanding entrance. I wasn't very lucky. The girls were nice enough, they laughed. I walked all about knocking on the doors and demanding entrance. Soon I was lost and I couldn't find my room. Panic. Lost in a girl's dorm! It took me what seemed several hours to find my room again. I believe the adventures that come with the readings are what might make them possibly more than survival goals.

Once my ride in from the airport arrived drunk. I wasn't entirely sober. On the way in I read him a dirty poem a lady had written me. It was snow-ing and the roads were slick. When I reached this particularly erotic line my friend said, "Oh, my god!" and he lost control of the car and we spun and spun and spun, and I told him as we were spinning, "This is it, Andre, we're not going to make it!" and I lifted my bottle and there we tumbled into a ditch, unable to get out. Andre got out and thumbed; I pleaded old age and sat in the car sucking at my bottle. And who picked us up? *Another* drunk. We had six-packs all over the floor and a 5th of whiskey. That turned out to be some reading.

At another reading, someplace in Michigan, I put down my poems and asked if anybody wanted to arm wrestle. Then while 400 students circled around us I got down on the floor with this student and we began. I beat him and then we all went out and got drunk (after I got my check). I doubt I will ever repeat that performance.

Of course, there are times when you awaken in a young lady's house in bed with her and you realize that you have taken advantage of your poetry or that your poetry has been taken advantage of. I don't believe a poet has any more right to a special young body than a garage mechanic, if as much. This is what spoils the poet: special treatment or his own idea that he *is* special. Of course, I *am* special but I don't believe this applies to many of the others . . .

For over a year I made it as a writer. Beer, smokes, rent, child support, food . . . survival. Arise at noon, go to bed at 4 a.m. 4 nights a week my landlord and landlady came down and got me and I sat in their place and drank gallons of free beer while telling stories and listening to stories and singing old songs and smoking and laughing. I took out the garbage and brought it back to help pay the rent. Some royalties came in. The sex mags liked my dirty and immortal stories. Then the recession hit. The sex mags more than halved their rates and slowed payment until some time after publication. Meanwhile prices rose and the nights got longer. The women's lib arrived in the offices of the editors and there was no longer such an animal as a rotten woman, just as there couldn't be such an animal as a rotten black man or anything wrong with the revolution or rock or the American Indian. Not that I said there was, but it became a restrictive time for free creation and I felt it, and the editors were nervous and the publishers worse. The stocks fell and the mailbox wavered empty. Nothing to do but get drunker than hell and keep writing. If a writer can hold long enough and if he has anything at all, he will break through. Of course, in hard times a writer must act as his own collection agency. This is a time-consumer but if you don't have this touch, or the touch of asking for $10 or $20 for something that usually goes for free, you're going to end up swinging a mop. The sex mags are easy enough — you simply exert a gentle and decent pressure — just enough to let them know that you realize that they are selling magazines and making a profit with your stories in them, and *if* they want more *good* stories they'll simply have to pay. The European translation markets are more difficult. It usually takes a threat of murder to get that advance as per contract for that book of short stories or that novel. I have experienced some bad times with the Germans. The distance alone makes them feel safe, damn the contract.

I had a very difficult time with one outfit that brought out a book of translated short stories. I had heard that the book had gotten a good review in one of Germany's largest newspapers and the translator, a fairly good friend, had told me that the book was moving well. All I wanted was the $500 advance stipulated in the contract. I must have written 4 or 5 letters without response. They even sent me ten copies of the book, 8 soft cover, 2 hard cover. A fine job of printing but no dollars. I remembered how other writers had bitched about publishers and how I had once thought that was petty; better writers than I — Céline for instance. Now I understood Céline, both as an artist and a bitching machine and a collection agency. I got drunk and wrote an immortal 10-page letter. I explained my position as a human being and a writer — I shit, ate, drank, smoked, fucked, tore sheets with my toenails, drove a car 11 years old, took out the garbage cans, fondled the landlady's tits, masturbated, was a coward and an alcoholic, detested tv, hated baseball, football, basketball, was not homosexual, didn't particularly admire Hemingway, realized that I was almost immortal but not immortal, liked symphony music, had never seen an ice hockey game, and had once met the great editor Whit Burnett, the discoverer of Saroyan and Bukowski, I had once met this great editor on a New York street, so forth, so forth . . . then as I went on I began to get slowly violent, I moved slowly toward violence, being from Germany and Hollywood and Los Angeles, it came easy to me, until I was raving, until I was threatening to get on that plane for Germany and CONFRONT—FACE TO FACE!—yes, yes, YOU SEE? FACE TO FACE!—you hideous snail-sniveling cowards. SPACE COULDN'T SAVE YOU FROM THE BUKOWSKI!!! I would either collect or take a life. It was as simple as that. Honor. I was a German. Born in Andernach. I had it. Try me. Sirs, I will give you 3 weeks to respond with real true cash. Then that will be it. Protect yourself as you may. So forth, so forth. Sincerely yours, Charles Bukowski . . .

The check arrived within a week. I don't see how they did it so quickly. They must have believed that all my short stories were true. They are only 3/4 true. Invention mixed with truth equals Art. Anyhow, they paid . . .

And the professors are difficult. The professors will come knocking. They are a better breed than the professors of old but they do lack a certain tact. Opening you a beer from the six-pack, they'll say, "I'm teaching you to my class in modern American Lit. It creates quite a stir."

What is a writer supposed to say to that? Especially a writer whose best book has perhaps only sold 6,000 copies in an underground press? Mailer wouldn't even bother to spit in my face, even though I am the better writer. So you open the beer and say nothing, drink it, and think, here goes, I might feel better after a couple. Blue sails in the Sunset.

Then there are always the detractors, those non-creative people whose only wish is to see you fall, who almost demand that you fall, ahead of time, to make them feel good. They, too, arrive uninvited with their little precious six-packs and measure your breath symbols and talk about your funeral, who will give the speech, *who* will say *what*, who will hold the left handle, what they will really think of you. And the women, oh my god, the women, they are *really* going to expose one . . . no soul, beats me every night, flogged my ass with a barbed whip, wouldn't let me talk at parties, a *terribly* jealous man, petty, fearful, stingy, masturbated every morning before breakfast, tortured frogs . . .

The greatest detractors can't write at all. You give them strength with the total force of your writing and they admire that, but the very fact that you've given them light also gives them the pleasure of your fall. An instant death would be too easy. They'd rather slowly see you turn into an imbecile drooling spit down his chin and chest . . . Your darkest night will be their greatest birth. But I'm sure we're all familiar with these rhymers, these snails, these pettifogging bloodsuckers who draw light and then scream in pleasure and joy when the only light they've ever seen fails in life as life or finally goes into death even as they must . . .

Reading back over these pages now I realize that I might have been a little too precious but I realize now that this is an article mostly for writers and that we are a spoiled, thin-skinned, and over-exaggerating lot, but I feel that over-exaggeration creates Art, somehow. We scream when we are supposed to yawn. That's the point. There's simply not enough. We want a new contract. Born to die. What the shit is that?

Well, it's difficult for all of us. Will Rogers used to say, "I never met a man I didn't like." I say, I have yet to meet a man I truly liked. Will Rogers made a lot of money; I am going to die broke. But like I like to think: we all die broke, if not broken.

Writing is, finally, the only way for me, and if they burn me at the stake I won't consider myself a saint. I will only have believed that it was the only way. It's just a matter of doing what you want to do: not one man in a thousand is doing what he wants to do. My defeat will be my victory. There is no rejection. I am all I can possibly be at this moment. Now then, fuck this talking about writing. That's for hacks. I've let myself slip over here just to make you feel good. Forget it. Who's going to win the 4th race at Turf Paradise Wednesday afternoon?

UPON THE MATHEMATICS OF

THE BREATH AND THE WAY

I was going to begin this with a little rundown on the female but since the smoke on the local battlefront has cleared a bit I will relent, but there are 50,000 men in this nation who must sleep on their bellies for fear of losing their parts to women with wild-glazed eyes and knives. Brothers and sisters, I am 52 and there is a trail of females behind me, enough for 5 men's lives. Some of the ladies have claimed that I have betrayed them for drink; well, I'd like to see any man stick his pecker into a fifth of whiskey. Of course, you can get your tongue in there but the bottle doesn't respond. Well, ha ha among the trumpets, let's get back to the word.

The word. I'm on my way to the track, opening day at Hollywood Park, but I'll tell you about the word. To get the word down proper, that takes courage, seeing the form, living the life, and getting it into the line. Hemingway takes his critical blows now from people who can't write. There are hundreds of thousands of people who *think* they can write. They are the critics, the bellyachers, and the mockers. To point to a good writer and call him a hunk of shit helps satisfy their loss as creators, and the better a man gets the more he is envied and, in turn, hated. You ought to hear them razz and demean Pincay and Shoemaker, two of the greatest jocks ever to steer a horse. There's a little man outside our local tracks who sells newspapers and he says, "Get your paper, get your info on Shoemaker the Faker." Here he is calling a man who has ridden more winners than any other jock alive (and he's still riding and riding well) and here's this newspaper guy selling papers for a dime and calling the Shoe a fraud. The Shoe is a millionaire, not that that's important, but he did get it with his talent and he could buy this guy's newspapers, all of them, for the rest of this guy's life and into a half dozen eternities. Hemingway, too, gets the sneers from the newspaper boys and girls of writing. They didn't like his exit. I thought his exit was quite fine. He created his own mercy killing. And he created some writing. Some of it depended too much on style but it was a style he broke through with; a style that ruined thousands of writers who attempted to use any portion of it. Once a style is evolved it is thought of as a simple thing, but style not only evolves through a method, it evolves through feeling, it is like laying a brush to canvas in a certain way and if you're not living along the path of power and flow, style vanishes. Hemingway's style did tend to vanish toward the end, progressively, but that's because he let down his guard and let people do things to him. But he gave us more than plenty. There is a minor poet I know who came over the other night. He is a learned man, and clever, he lets the ladies support him so you know he's good at something. He is a very powerful figure of a man growing soft around the edges, looks quite literary and carries these black notebooks around with him and he reads to you from them. This boy told me the other night, "Bukowski, I can write like you but you can't write like me." I didn't answer him because he needs his self-glory, but really, he only *thinks* he can write like me. Genius could be the ability to say a profound thing in a simple way, or even to say a simple thing in a simpler way. Oh, by the way, if you want to get one angle on a minor writer, it is one who throws a party or gets one thrown for him when his book comes out.

Hemingway studied the bullfights for form and meaning and courage and failure and the way. I go to boxing matches and attend horse races for the same reason. There is a feeling at the wrists and the shoulders and the temples. There is a manner of watching and recording that grows into the line and the form and the act and the fact and the flower, and the dog walking and the dirty panties under the bed, and the sound of the typewriter as you're sitting there, that's the big sound, the biggest sound in the world, when you're getting it down in your way, the right way, and no beautiful woman counts before it and nothing that you could paint or sculpt counts before it; it is the final art, this writing down of the word, and the reason for valor is all there, it is the finest gamble ever arranged and not many win.

Somebody asked me, "Bukowski, if you taught a course in writing what would you ask them to do?" I answered, "I'd send them all to the racetrack and force them to bet $5 on each race." This ass thought I was joking. The human race is very good at treachery and cheating and modifying a position. What people who want to be writers need is to be put in an area that they cannot maneuver out of by weak and dirty play. This is why groups of people at parties are so disgusting: all their envy and smallness and trickery surfaces. If you want to find out who your friends are you can do two things: invite them to a party or go to jail. You will soon find that you don't have any friends.

If you think I am wandering here, hold your tits or your balls or hold somebody else's. Everything fits here.

And since I must presume (I haven't seen any of it) that I am being honored and criticized in this issue I should say something about the little magazines, although I might have said some of it elsewhere? — at least over a row of beer bottles. Little magazines are useless perpetuators of useless talent. Back in the '20s and '30s there was not an abundance of littles. A little magazine was an event, not a calamity. One could trace the names from the littles and up through literary history; I mean, they began there and they went *up*, they became. They became books, novels, things. Now most little magazine people begin little and remain little. There are always exceptions. For instance, I remember first reading Truman Capote in a little named *Decade*, and I thought here is a man with some briskness, style, and fairly original energy. But basically, like it or not, the large slick magazines print a much higher level of work than the littles — and most especially in *prose*. Every jackass in America pumps out countless and ineffectual poems. And a large number of them are published in the littles. Tra la la, another edition. Give us a grant, see what we are doing! I receive countless little magazines through the mail, unsolicited, un-asked for. I flip through them. Arid vast nothingness. I think that the miracle of our times is that so many people can write down so many words that mean absolutely nothing. Try it sometime. It's almost impossible to write down words that mean absolutely nothing, but they can do it, and they do it continually and relentlessly. I put out 3 issues of a little, *Laugh Literary and Man the Humping Guns*. The material received was so totally inept that the other editor and myself were forced to write most of the poems. He'd write the first half of one poem, then I'd finish it. Then I'd do the first half of another and he'd finish it. Then we'd sit around and get to the names: "Let's see, whatta we gonna call this cocksucker?"

And with the discovery of the mimeo machine everybody became an editor, all with great flair, very little expense, and no results at all. *Ole* was an early exception and I might grant you one or two other exceptions if you corner me with the facts. As per the better printed (non-mimeo) mags one must grant *The Wormwood Review* (one-half-hundred issues now) as the outstanding work of our time in that area. Quietly and without weeping or ranting or bitching or quitting or pausing, or without writing braggadocio letters (as most do) about being arrested for driving drunk on a bicycle in Pacific Palisades or corn-holing one of the National Endowment for the Arts editors in a Portland hotel room, Malone has simply gone on and on and compiled an exact and lively talent, issue after issue after issue. Malone lets his issues speak for themselves and remains invisible. You won't find him beating on your door one night with a huge jug of cheap port wine saying, "Hey, I'm Marvin Malone, I printed your poem *Catshit in a Bird's Nest* in my last issue. I think I'm gonna kick me some ass. Ya got anything for me to fuck around here?"

A vast grinding lonely hearts club of no-talents, that's what the littles have evolved to, with the editors a worse breed than the writers. If you are a writer seriously interested in creating art instead of a foolishness, then there are, at any moment, a few littles to submit to, where the editing is professional instead of personal. I haven't read the mag that this piece is submitted to but I would suggest, along with *Wormwood*, as decent arenas: *The New York Quarterly*, *Event*, *Second Aeon*, *Joe Dimaggio*, *Second Coming*, *The Little Magazine*, and *Hearse*.

"You're supposed to be a writer," she says, "if you put all the energy into writing that you put into the racetack you'd be great." I think of something

Wallace Stevens once said, "Success as a result of industry is a peasant's ideal." Or if he didn't say that he said something close to that. The writing arrives when it wants to. There is nothing you can do about it. You can't squeeze more writing out of the living than is there. Any attempt to do so creates a panic in the soul, diffuses and jars the line. There are stories that Hemingway would get up early in the morning and have all his work done at noon, but though I never met him personally I feel as if Hemingway were an alcoholic who wanted to get his work out of the way so he could get drunk.

What I have seen evolve in the littles with most new and fresh talent is an interesting first splash. I think, ah, here's finally one. Maybe we have something now. But the same mechanism begins over and over again. The fresh new talent, having splashed, begins to appear everywhere. He sleeps and bathes with the goddamned typewriter and it's running all the time. His name is in every mimeo from Maine to Mexico and the work grows weaker and weaker and weaker and continues to appear. Somebody gets a book out for him (or her) and then they are reading at your local university. They read the 6 or 7 good early poems and all the bad ones. Then you have another little magazine "name." But what has happened is that instead of trying to create the poem they try for as many little mag appearances in as many little magazines as possible. It becomes a contest of publication rather than creation. This diffusion of talent usually occurs among writers in their twenties who don't have enough experience, who don't have enough meat to pick off the bone. You can't write without living and writing all the time is not living. Nor does drinking create a writer or brawling create a writer, and although I've done plenty of both, it's merely a fallacy and a sick romanticism to assume that these actions will make a better writer of one. Of course, there are times when you have to fight and times when you have to drink, but these times are really anti-creative and there's nothing you can do about them.

Writing, finally, even becomes *work* especially if you are trying to pay the rent and child support with it. But it is the finest work and the only work, and it's a work that boosts your ability to live and your ability to live pays you back with your ability to create. One feeds the other; it is all very magic. I quit a very dull job at the age of 50 (twas said I had security for life, ah!) and I sat down in front of the typewriter. There's no better way. There are moments of total flaming hell when you feel as if you're going mad; there are moments, days, weeks of no word, no sound, as if it had all vanished. Then it arrives and you sit smoking, pounding, pounding, it rolls and roars. You can get up at noon, you can work until 3 a.m. Some people will bother you. They will not understand what you are trying to do. They will knock on your door and sit in a chair and eat up your hours while giving you nothing. When too many nothing people arrive and keep arriving you must be cruel to them for they are being cruel to you. You must run their asses out on the street. There are some people who pay their way, they bring their own energy and their own light but most of the others are useless both to you and to themselves. It is not being humane to tolerate the dead, it only increases their deadness and they always leave plenty of it with you after they are gone.

And then, of course, there are the ladies. The ladies would rather go to bed with a poet than anything, even a German police dog, though I knew one lady who took very much delight in claiming she had fucked one President Kennedy. I had no way of knowing. So, if you're a good poet, I'd suggest you learn to be a good lover too, this is a creative act in itself, being a good lover, so learn how, learn how to do it very well because if you're a good poet you're going to get many opportunities, and though it's not like being a rock star, it will come along, so don't waste it like rock stars waste it by going at it rote and half-assed. Let the ladies know that you are really there. Then, of course, they will keep buying your books.

And let this be enough advice for a little while. Oh yes, I won $180 opening day, dropped $80 yesterday, so today is the day that counts. It's ten minutes to eleven. First post 2 p.m. I must start lining up my horse genes. There was a guy out there yesterday with a heart machine attached to himself and he was sitting in a wheelchair. He was making bets. Put him in a rest home and he'll be dead overnight. Saw another guy out there, blind. He must have had a better day than I did yesterday. I've got to phone Quagliano and tell him I've finished this article. Now there's a very strange son of a bitch. I don't know how he makes it and he won't tell me. I see him at the boxing matches sitting there with a beer and looking very relaxed. I wonder what he's got going. He's got me worried . . .

NOTES OF A DIRTY OLD MAN

L. A. Free Press, DECEMBER 28, 1973

1.

"Will you call me tomorrow?" she asked. "Of course," he said, then hung up. She had told him they had this new instrument down at the club that allowed a woman to look into her vagina. Women had walked around for centuries without really knowing what their vaginas looked like. A man could just look at his thing, it was all out in front there. If a woman could relate to her vagina, much of the mental hazard would be over. She was really a very intelligent woman. While she related to her vagina he undressed and went to bed alone.

2.

I just ate a baby octopus with melted butter, but looking into the mirror afterwards my eyes are still as mad and demented as August rain. Maybe one shouldn't eat an octopus with butter, not while listening to Rachmaninoff. Maybe there is a special sauce. As an American citizen I should stick to hamburgers and rock music. Thinking is more dangerous than fucking and good American citizens do very little thinking.

Maybe the butter was stale. The little arms tasted like mop strings. And me still in love with Zsa Zsa Gabor.

3.

We're laying on the bed together. "I've got to pee," she says. "All right," I say, and let go of her. She sits down to the sewing machine. ZRRRRRR! ZRRRRRR! ZRRRRRR! "O, goddamn it!" She drops the scissors. ZRRRRRR!

ZRRRRRR! I hear her cutting cloth with the scissors. It's Thursday night tonight, cold outside, it's December. Well, it's supposed to be cold. ZRRRRRR! ZRRRR! ZRRRRRRR! She's been working 20 minutes. She has on an orange sweater and green pants. I've known her about three years. We live together most of the time. ZRRR! ZRRRR! ZRRRRRR! She has various pieces of cloth, blue with yellow flowers, green with red flowers. She appears to be making little blouses. Kissinger is in Syria, sweet-talking with one hand, threatening with the other. The dog is asleep on a red coat on the floor. She's been working about 30 minutes now. ZRRRR! ZRRRRR! ZRRRRR! I wonder when she's going to pee?

4.

Horses' asses in this German bar off Glendale Boulevard, Friday night, lousy Germans these are, they couldn't be dog piss under a dead Nazi's boot. American Germans from Glendale and Burbank playing out the movie version . . . with belching and gross voices, these warehouse attendants, these Sears-Roebuck bargain-basement salesmen.

My girl orders a sandwich for $2.10 and the dark beer is 50 cents a mug. Me, I make less than $3,000 a year—which ain't bad for getting up at noon.

This bar, these yellow German faces of a Friday night of worn-out people, the jukebox playing like at a high school lunchroom. The men spoil the waitresses but there is nothing else for the men to do. They sit around in this place without women. I have been in the same way but I have never begged like that and I won't. I get the tab: $7.10. I leave a dollar tip as if I were a worthy citizen and we make the parking lot. Tomorrow's closing day. Pincay's been set down, Tejerica's on the highweights, Valdez hasn't gotten over his spill, and Rudy Campas belongs up at Bay Meadows. And me $40 out. Belmonte let himself get trapped on the rail, rode it in like a sackful of wet shit, reading three under a morning line of 12. Belmonte, you had the horse, but I thought you'd have the natural given godliness to stay near a crippled first quarter and a beer and tomato juice half.

Well, $40 isn't everything, the philosophers and bullfighters have gone wrong, too, and Diamond Jim Brady had unspeakable visions. I flick my headlights on and we drive out of the lot. Endurance is sometimes more important than truth.

5.

The idea that suffering only belongs to the gifted and the noble and the intelligent, the sensitive and the daring and the inventive—that is the tallest stack of shit of them all. They raided the bars last night, had a Supreme Court order in their back pockets; backed by the highest court in the land they swept the girls off the bartops like dead flies, like dirty napkins, all those poor lovelies screaming, their immense tits flopping in panic, their huge voluptuous rears twisted in surprise, they swept them off and away half-dressed into vans and automobiles to be booked, fingerprinted, photographed, and jailed. Such a waste. Such a waste of Grade-A goods. Speak about indecency—the cops were the most indecent thing about that night. A poor girl can't make an honest buck anymore. All they were doing was bringing a horny night to lonely men. I've just got to believe Supreme Court boys can't get it up anymore.

6.

I have created the eternal drunk image somewhere in my work and there is a minor reality behind it. Yet, I feel that my work has said other things. But only the eternal drunk seems to come through. I get phone calls, usually about 3:30 a.m. in the morning:

"Bukowski?"

"Yeah."

"Charles Bukowski?"

"Yeah."

"Hey, man, I just wanted to talk to you!"

"You're drunk, baby."

"So a rabbit shits, too. So what?"

"Listen, I don't know who you are but you don't just go phoning people at 3 a.m. in the morning when you're drunk, especially strangers. It's just not done."

"Really?"

"Really."

"Not even to Bukowski?"

"Especially not even." I hung up.

Those boys think they have a soulmate, just because I get drunk and phone people at 3 a.m. in the morning. They have to be more original than I. I remember once I got so fucked-up and ran off so many women that I dialed the time operator and listened to her voice for five or ten minutes: "It is now 3:30 and twenty seconds, it is now 3:30 and thirty seconds. . . ." And you know what a voice *she* has. Next time you think about phoning me, phone the time and, if possible, beat off.

7.

I had a friend come by the other day who just gotten out after doing 19 years and he said that most of the guys were in there for sex offenses instead of monetary rip-offs against the republic. He claimed to be a writer. At least he did much writing in prison. He wrote to me through my publisher and I got these letters from prison. And I answered them and he was a flattering soul, he kept telling me that my books of dirty stories were passing from cell to cell and that the boys were getting their nuts—except for one guy who maintained that I had no idea of the proper use of the English language, and I wrote back, you tell that guy that he is right and that is the best thing about me. Other cons started writing me, and I found out two things—there were very many men in jail and most of them were writers. My friend, the con, said he also had letters from William Saroyan (*also* a great human) and that my letters and books were still fluttering around in stir, including my columns in the underground newspapers, my god, I was great.

He came by with his old lady and another con who had just gotten out and his old lady. He was working as a carpenter for $15.75 an hour and they had come in from the north to see Disneyland, and me. They had four cans of warm beer and he said, "My god, you *are* as ugly as your photos." I knew that but I didn't know that a good man could keep a hard-on for an hour and ride a woman three times a day. He never mentioned anything about the tongue. Anyway, he claimed most crimes were sex crimes, he had the letters from William Saroyan and he kept leaning against the fireplace and zipping and unzipping his fly as he looked at my girlfriend. He seemed an authority.

8.

I saw Katherine H. in the *Glass M.* the other night. I wonder if we will ever grow enough to know that this type of actress is a very bad actress and that this type of play is a very bad play? Snobbishness and preciousness in both acting and writing is the one thing that has kept it away—the two things that have kept it away from the masses. The devil knows that I have no love for the masses having lived very much among them, granted, under the worst conditions. But still they are small of soul and of movement but no smaller and perhaps less small and kinder and more real than Katherine H. and T. Williams and the *Glass M.*

It's a coin with two heads—or two tails, but since they are attached to each other they can't quite get away from each other. The masses dislike K.H. for the proper reason: she's a bad actress, a very phony phony who has gotten away with the mutilation and the exaggeration of all things real. But since their noses are ground into shit every day and they are very tired they have no alternative but to imagine her the grand lady of soul and *elsewhereness*, and since the critics are frightened of intellectual pompoms and garlands and ghostly shadows (without Joe Namath shaves), of G. K. Chesterton and George Bernard Shaw and old Tolstoy and Gogol and Shakespeare and Proust, they fear to tread against the sickening and obvious because if they admitted that this was trash then the trickery and the malfunction would be over and they, too, would be going to Knotts Berry Farms on a Sunday afternoon with the masses, or concerned about the Super Bowl or the toilet bowl or sweat (that stinks) under the armpits.

It will take centuries to get the Hepburns and the critics out of the way, and that's what makes it sad, more than sad: each of our lives is hardly made up of centuries, and what has killed us is not the Nixons and the Hitlers but the intellectuals, the poets, the scholars, the philosophers, the professors, the liberals, all our friends—or, more properly, your friends.

I have always much more enjoyed the conversations of men in jail than I have enjoyed the conversations of men in universities; I've found men on railroad track gangs with more guts and light and less boredom than those who get $400,000 a week for a four-week stand in Vegas. Why is this? I don't know. I don't think God can solve it. I only know that we've been tricked for centuries, it goes way back, even Christ smells bad, Plato smells bad, and I don't mean under the armpits.

I guess all we can do is take our small snapshots, wait, and get out.

NOTES OF A DIRTY OLD MAN

L. A. Free Press, FEBRUARY 22–MARCH 1 1974

About this time every night, the little man below me comes home from work and he whistles happily. He can't go into his own apartment and whistle, he has to stand out there in the courtyard and he whistles and all the birds chirp. If there's anything I can't stand it's the happiness of an idiot, an unfounded happiness.

This whole court is full of idiots. I can't leave this apartment without being accosted by one of them. Why this morning I wanted to get into my car in back here and there was the maintenance man. "I'm washing my car," he told me, and sure enough he was washing his car. "I use hot water," he went on, "it gets the dirt off better." He has a round English face and a round English accent. And if you want to know what a round English face is, you come see my maintenance man.

And the manager and his wife are always prowling about, scrubbing and sweeping, trimming, cleaning, primping. They never get drunk, never go to the races, never scream at each other. He *does* go into his apartment but she's always outside prowling, peeking, probing. "It looks like a lovely day," she says to me most of the time. Other times it's, "Well, I guess the sun isn't coming out today."

"No," I answer, "I guess it isn't."

I've had a very bad week. I've spent most of it in Safeway and Von's parking lots waiting for women to get out of their cars so I can see up their legs. It's been a very bad week. More and more women are wearing slacks. You know, I'll be sitting there reading my newpaper and I'll see a woman drive up. I'll be in perfect position, on the door side where she is going to get out, my view is unfettered. I'll see that she is fairly young and frustrated, careless, something on her mind—the price of bacon, or should she buy tan-

141

gerines. I figure I'm going to see some leg, the skirt pulled back as she exits from the car, a look at some knee, some nylon, some petticoat, some flank. I wait. The car door opens and she gets out, she's wearing slacks. It's been going on all week. Women have stopped wearing dresses.

I come home and I can't write. The poems have stopped, the stories have stopped. I go to the racetrack and lose. I walk up and down the rug. The guy below me plays an accordion. There is a letter in the mail.

". . . I have been nibbling at last night's dream. Of course you figured prominently and before the urge to write you leaves forever I will tell it to you. There were three of us, you, me, and my sister. You said you would lay with her—she wore a red straw hat on her coal black hair—No, I said: you looked at me and took her hand. She was silent and superior. Hell, I said I'll watch them . . . No one objected so I perched on the side of the bed to look. There was no carnal embrace (i.e. you did not fuck) but a long beautiful possessive kiss. I turned my head. Scene shifts. Now we are three in my bedroom and I am lying on a narrow, NARROW—cot—room for one only—you have just come from the tailor's and are wearing a new suit not quite finished cause there are large stitches along the seams. You also have an Irish hat on your head and fling it grandly, smiling, to the floor. I feel like a patient ready for surgery—sister stands there draped in a towel showing thighs heavily veined in blue.

"You will both leave presently for her double bed with goose down silk quilt, but in the meantime, you lean over—you are three times larger than life, a Laird Cregar . . . if you remember him—and plant a kiss full on my mouth and put some coins in my hand—"Leave off with those pennies," I say, my heart breaking at what is to come—"Ah, me lovely! (can't help that, I just am reading Donleavy) you say, "those are no pennies, the horses have been going good, look again," and indeed the coins all have signs on them showing they are 10 and 20 dollar pieces. There was more but it's fuzzy."

I throw the letter away and piss, come out and stretch out on the green couch. My girl was a taxi dancer, my girlfriend that is not the one in the letter. That's over. Now my girlfriend is no longer a taxi dancer, she is a lady bartender just off Alvarado street and she will meet glamorous alcoholics and I will be alone again. I look at the ceiling. I am supposed to be a writer. I can no longer write. This is what they have been waiting for. Bukowski the tough boy come to ineptness and defeat and quavering. My god, they'll march through the streets with trumpets and banners. I won't get any more hate letters in the mail.

Well, men change, and change doesn't always work. Tolstoy moved toward God at the end and flattened. Gorky, after the revolution, had nothing to write about. Dos Passos became a capitalist with a face like a barber and died in the hills above me here. Céline became a crank and forgot how to laugh. Shostakovich never changed, wrote his fifth symphony and then wrote it over and over again in all the symphonies that followed. Mailer became an intelligent journalist, as did Capote. Pound just got darker and darker and pissed out. Spender quit, Auden quit, Olson begged to the crowd. Creeley got angry and tightened. Abraham Lincoln hated blacks and Faulkner wore a corset. Ginsberg sucked to the sound of himself and was overcome. And old Henry Miller long done, fucking beautiful Japanese girls under the shower.

And I get up because the coffee water is boiling and I pour a cup of coffee. (My girlfriend has a large house and I am over there much of the time. I watch TV with her 12-year-old boy. He watches much more TV than I do but I hang in there pretty good. "How many commercials you seen today, kid? A hundred?" "Oh," he answers, "more than that." We watch movie after movie. "Now," I say, "the brother will come in with a knife." The brother comes in with a knife. "Now the casket will be empty," says the kid. The casket is empty. After you've seen one movie, you've seen them all. It's the same thing over and over again. My girlfriend sits in the other room writing dozens of new poems.)

I drink the coffee, then take a bath. "Some day I will tell them about you," says my girlfriend. "I will tell them that you are afraid of the dark, that you take five baths a day but don't use soap, that you keep a knife taped to your door." I'm afraid that nobody will be interested.

I towel off and get dressed. I'm out of toilet paper. I have to go back to Von's. I go down the stairway. There's a broom going.

It's her, the manager, sweeping. She's dressed in white, she's always dressed in white. "It gets chilly early in the evenings now, doesn't it?" she asks me. "Oh yes," I say.

I can walk to Von's. Right up Oxford and then a left to Western. I am living in apartment house row. A special breed. They vacuum their rugs every day and never go to sleep with the dishes unwashed. They deodorize the air and listen to three newscasts a night. None of them have children or dogs or insomnia and when they drink they drink very quietly and sneak their bottles into the trash. At 10 p.m. every night everything becomes absolutely silent. I pass a downstairs apartment with a large glass window facing the street. I call it the apartment of the Dolly Sisters. The Dolly Sisters sit in that large window all day talking and drinking tea and eating tiny cookies. They are heavily rouged with stupid, hard faces and their grey hair is dyed red and they wear four-inch false fingernails; their lips are very heavily caked with magenta lipstick. They look at me as I walk by and I nod like a country gentleman. They think I am a retired circus barker. They have no idea that I'm a once-immortal writer gone to seed. All three of them view me and one of them gives me a big smile, it's like a leper's kiss of death. The moment the sun goes down, a huge purple curtain is pulled across the glass window. The Dolly Sisters are afraid of being raped.

Von's is fairly empty, the workers haven't arrived from their jobs yet. I get a cart, decide to get a few other things as long as I need toilet paper. I push around the corner and there she is: high heels, short skirt, white blouse, all her hair is piled on top of her head. The skirt is not only short and tight but has a slit on each side, running up. The pantyhose are decorated with a false top, a darker shade, as if they were an old-fashioned pair of nylons like women used to wear when they were women. But they are actually pantyhose. The darker section can be seen near the top of the slit cut into the skirt. She is 38, of rather ugly and simple face, two pearl earrings dangling down from long thick chains, cheeks sagged in, mouth small and flat and dumb, but she is tall and her body moves and the slits show things and she bends and picks up a can of soup and for a moment I see the edge of her panties. She straightens. She knows that I am watching her but gives no indication. I follow her about, trying not to be too obvious. Her skirt is white with pink stripes. The colors slide into my brain. Why does she have those slits in her skirt? I ask myself. I can't answer the question. In the meat section I am next to her. She is over the lamb chops, staring at the lamb chops.

"Pardon me," I say.

She looks at me but makes no effort to speak. Her eyes are bland, drained.

"Pardon me," I repeat.

"Yes," she says.

"Aren't you Henry Miller's secretary?"

"Henry Miller?"

"Yes, he's a writer."

"No, I'm not his secretary."

She turns and looks back at the lamb chops. It is as if my hand were not attached to my will. I feel it moving toward the buttock nearest me and I can't stop it. The hand falls lightly upon the buttock under that pink-striped skirt and the fingers pinch gently, then let off. I roll my shopping cart away. Five aisles up I stop and look back. She is still over the lambchops but her face is a bright burning red. I look no more. I wheel up to the counter and get checked out. I have my toilet paper and a can of corned beef hash. The line isn't long. I am soon outside and I buy an L.A. *Times*. I need to check the race results. I turn east toward Oxford and walk back to my place. The Dolly Sisters are in the act of pulling their purple curtain. It's getting toward night. I manage to get back to my apartment without speaking to anybody. I hang up the toilet paper and stretch out on my green couch. There is nothing but the ceiling up there. The life of a writer is unbearable.

One time I was at a party, she told me, and I was fucked out. And I was asleep and this guy came in with his girlfriend and he came in with a bottle of turtle oil. And the two of them picked me up off the floor and put me on the bed, face down, and she was holding the turtle oil and he was holding his cock, plus they were both putting me on the bed, and I'm going uuur, you know . . . I was asleep.

And so she spread one leg out one way and he spread one leg out the other way, and he gets this turtle oil and he puts it all over my cunt. And this wakes me up a little bit, and I went uuur, I'm tired, I'm asleep . . . and he doesn't listen to me, so he puts his cock in me and he starts fucking me but he keeps going soft . . . because he hasn't fucked anybody all night. He was the first person to take his clothes off but all he does is get drunk and get in fights. And so he goes to these fuck parties, he gets drunk and gets in fights with everybody, he doesn't fuck anybody so he decides he's going to fuck me because I'm asleep.

So he puts this turtle oil over my cunt and he starts fucking me, and he says to his girlfriend, "Give me some more turtle oil, she needs some more turtle oil," and she says, "Honey, you've got enough." And he says, "No, give me some more," and he puts some more on me and he starts fucking me again. And he gets soft again and he says, "Give me some more turtle oil," and she says, "Honey, you've got enough," and he gets it away from her and he puts some more on and he starts fucking me some more and he keeps getting soft and they keep going through this routine.

Finally, he's just like pumping away with his soft cock. And you can't tell anything anymore . . . by this time I have awakened and you can't tell anything from the turtle oil . . . I mean, he's just slidin', you know. And I'm just going uh uh uh and he's going ummm ummm ummm and she's saying, "Honey, that's enough turtle oil," and so . . . finally . . . Brad was on the floor . . . Brad's my boyfriend . . . and she goes over to Brad and shakes him and says, "Brad, Brad, it's time to go . . ." because we'd driven with them and Brad went, "Arr, yeah, all right, all right . . ." and then he goes back to sleep and this guy's going UH UH UH and I'm going oh and he's saying "Give me some more turtle oil," and she says, "Honey, you've had enough turtle oil," and she walks out the door and slams it so he takes a whole bottle of turtle oil and he pours it all over me.

She's supposedly going out to fuck somebody but she doesn't fuck anybody else either. She just walks around the party nude and instigates these arguments that he gets in. So they get in a fight and she fights with him and he fights with other people. So finally we are just bathed in turtle oil and I'm wide awake and this guy falls asleep on top of me and he weighs like 200 pounds. This turtle oil was $25 a bottle and he's asleep on top of me. And his cock gets soft and it starts rising up between the crack in my ass because like it's getting small and it's soft, you know, and it's really terrible because the stuff is dripping all down my sides, down my things, it's dripping all over me, and he's got it in my hair and he's snoring in my ear ... he's going CSHEWWWW ... and Brad's on the floor, and *he's* snoring, only he's snoring louder.

So finally she comes back in the room and she says, "Brad, get up, we're going to go," and Brad says, "Yeah, yeah, all right," and he finally gets up and he finds everything but his socks, somebody has stolen his socks, and finally he gets this guy off of me and we get dressed and we get into the car and they get into the front and we get into the back and right away Brad goes to sleep in my lap and the sun is coming up and we have to drive home from Orange County and these two ... they start fighting ... and pretty soon I start laughing, and she falls asleep and all the way home this guy talks about being a hustler in Fort Lauderdale, Florida, and I've been to parties three times and this guy has never gotten a hard on. I sucked him off one time. I sucked his cock for 20 minutes and this guy did not get hard until he came. He gets hard, and just like that, he came. And he came so little that I swallowed it with ease. Absolute ease, it didn't even drip out of the corners of my mouth, didn't come out through my nose, it didn't even make me cry.

This guy is a poor excuse ... ha, ha ... he's got a little dick, ha, ha, ha, ha, ha, ha ... and that's a true story, and now he's growing a beard, and he comes into the bank where I work, he won't talk to me now. . .Why doesn't he? Do you think they're mad at us? Ha, ha, ha, ha ... his little dick.

NOTES OF A DIRTY OLD MAN

L. A. Free Press, MARCH 22, 1974

You really like shit, don't you? I've noticed that over the few years, that you're really fond of the word "shit" and shitting . . .

No, no, no. I'm not fond of the word "shit," it kind of puts me off. I don't like people who say "SHIT!" I seldom use that word.

No, but I mean the very function of shitting is somehow pleasurable to you.

To me only?

Well, I don't know. You seem to enjoy it more than most people; they never seem to mention it as much as you do.

They don't admit it as much as I do.

Admit it?

I mean, you run in there and say, "Give me some newspaper," that's so you can enjoy it. I mean you're reading something and a turd drops out and you're reading . . .

But I'm not nearly as aware of my turds dropping out as you are. To me, they just drop out there.

You mean you don't look at them and admire them afterwards?

No.

Oh, there's this great sense of *loss*. You're going to flush those turds away and you'll *never* see them again. You'll never see those *same* turds ever again.

I don't feel any loss at all when I flush them away . . . I think, oh, it stinks . . .

I try to memorize every pattern of turds I've ever left. Because each pattern is different, it's like a painting. The shit never comes out the same. How many times does the average person shit in a lifetime? Countless times, no doubt. But each shit is infinitely different from any other shit you've ever taken. Each turd is different, the sizes are different, the number of them, the way you feel, the places you shit, the temperature, the weather, who you're living with or not living with, whether you're unemployed or employed, there are so many innuendoes mixed in. And then even you have the extra thing: you reach for the toilet paper and it can be different colors, it can be green, it can be blue, it can be yellow, purple, so forth. And then you reach up and wipe your ass and you look at the paper and you think, oh oh, I'm still dirty. I better wipe with some more, somebody might be able to smell my shit. And while you're wiping your ass you think, maybe some people don't wipe their asses as well as I do. Or maybe I don't wipe my ass well enough. Listen, I'm going to let you talk in a while but I'm not into the shit thing. Wait, wait, wait, wait, wait . . . I was in the supermarket prowling, you know, like I do, and I came into the toilet paper row and there was an old woman about 92 years old and she's looking for the best bargain in toilet paper.

But *everybody* does that.

But I mean, when you're 92 you might die tomorrow morning so why save three cents? I mean it's just marvelous to be able to shit at 92 so why not buy the most expensive and kind of celebrate? Waste three cents. O.K., I'm getting carried away.

See, you get carried away with shit. I told you you loved it. You're definitely in love with it. I've noticed that. What do you think of the idea that psychologists put out about shit freaks . . . you know, when you're a kid and your parents are demanding things of you, the shit was the thing that you could hold onto, that was yours.

I don't know if one could hold onto it.

And no matter what they had you could go in there and this hunk of shit belonged to you and it was something that was definitely and beautifully yours.

Well, let me tell you this, the psychiatrists and psychologists never had parents like mine. Because when I shit I thought, this shit belongs to my mother and my father because they told me how much they had sacrificed to feed me, how much they sacrificed to put clothes on my back, and how it hurt them to raise me, so whenever I took my shit I realized it was their shit, not mine.

Should we get off shit?

All right, it's difficult but we'll get off shit except I've got to say that I did read something interesting. You know New York City has been dumping their shit into the ocean for quite some time now and I read in this article that this shit had formed into this huge glob and that the glob was slowly approaching New York City at something like five miles an hour and the experts had no idea of how to hold it back ... they couldn't talk to it, they couldn't bomb it, they couldn't spray it, prayer didn't help. Right now there's this huge glob approaching New York City and there's nothing that can be done about it. When I read this article I wasn't exactly too unhappy because if any city deserved to be drowned in mountains of shit, that city is New York.

I thought we were going to get off shit.

All right, let's get off it. It transfixes one but we can get away.

Are you sure?

It takes courage but we can do it.

Let's talk about sex or go to sleep.

Can we do it?

Shit, yes.

UNPUBLISHED FOREWORD

TO WILLIAM WANTLING'S

7 ON STYLE

I had been corresponding with Bill Wantling since the days of the mimeo revolution, since the days of Blazek and *Ole*, when I noticed his work and some letters became exchanged. I wrote Wantling so many letters that he dumped me into a quicky novel using portions of my correspondence as my speech. I was a washed-up actor who lived in Hollywood and took pills and drank overmuch (actually I live right off of Hollywood Blvd. and Western in the whorehouse district but I've never done much acting.) The years went on, the letters thinned, I lived with different women but Bill stayed on with his wife Ruthie who was his sanity, his love, his survival factor. We both finally had some luck with our writing: I even began to pay the rent with mine; Bill continued to work the miserable jobs when he was straight, and he was very much discovered in England and New Zealand—his writing didn't contain the trickery and the sheen that the larger American poetry audience demands—and things never became easy for him, that's why he continued to write very well.

With Ruthie bailing water, mending the sails, and catching dinner off the port side Bill became universitized. The G.I. Bill helped too. It scared the shit out of me, Wantling going through all that college because he had a hard and natural way of laying down a line across the page and I thought the ivy might diminish him. Not so. Anyhow, he didn't go long enough to acquire a professorship. So there he was this year, suddenly an instructor— one-year tenure, non-renewable. That's how I met him. He put the screws and torches to the English dept. to have me come out to Illinois State and give a reading. He managed to get me $500 and since the horses were running badly, I went.

On that plane it got fearful, I mean thinking what might happen. I had made it a policy to avoid writers as much as possible; they weaken one another, partying together, gossiping together, bitching together. Almost every writer I've met believes that he is immortal and neglected when the fact is that they simply write very badly. Most writers are hardly delicious people, and flying out I thought, well, Christ, here it will happen again, I'll meet him, dislike him, then begin to dislike his poems. Bill always said examine the writer, not the man. But I am emotional and I can't help examining both. Then too, I thought, how about me? I'm a bad dresser. I dislike clothing stores. I had on a coat 15 years old, a pair of cheap pants that didn't fit, shoes down at the heels and my dead father's overcoat, 2 sizes too large. Also my hair doesn't stay combed, I don't get haircuts, hair styles, I just give a woman a scissors now and then and say, go ahead. If there's a woman around.

From out of Chicago I had to take one of those propeller-driven jobs that all the passengers joke about as they ride along. But you can get a drink on them too. And the plane rocks and the stewardness bumps you with hips like promises. That's bad writing, isn't it?

Well, I was the last one off. A wind came from the back and blew all the hair down in front of my face. I hunched on in and there they were standing, Bill and Ruthie. I don't exactly remember the conversation, the openers, but I got a feeling of kindness from both of them. I liked them right off. Bill noted that he'd never quite seen anybody dressed like me but he said it almost as a compliment. We got in and drove off, "Your voice is so soft," said Ruthie. "And you don't chatter," said Bill. Bill had the vibes, the good vibes, you could feel them right off, he was surrounded by them, rays, blessed easy rays. We stopped someplace for beer and went right on into Ruthie's house. They were in a process of divorce. He had written me: "Blew it with Ruthie, finally, she'd been putting up with my shit & vomit & dope for 9 years, couldn't take it any longer."

There was something at 2 p.m. at the university, part of the show. I went over and scratched a few students and then we came back. The reading was at 8. We drank some more beer and I noticed that Bill was a listener, not a talker; so was I. So it was quiet, but not *that* kind of quiet; a comfortable quiet—no push, no shove, no megaphones. We went over to Bill's room on skid row for a while. He had a front upstairs apartment over Bloomington Gun, Main St., Bloomington. There was space and it was light. It would be a good place to write, probably was. Then we went back to the house. More beer, at my insistence. The professor in charge of the reading came over; he was enthusiastic, childish, but likeable; bubbling but sincere. Bill offered me some pills in the hall but I declined, "Bad stomach, kid, that stuff tears me." The professor advised me not to drink too much more, then we went out to dinner. I suggested someplace where we might get beer. All during the talking and the planning I was very conscious of Bill; I felt him there always, the rays coming off, good solid grade-AAA rays, *soul*, if you wish. He had a simple manner of saying things but everything he said lifted the game up out of the muck, made it gently human. There are all manners of ways that men tip off little hatreds, prejudices, petty insanities, jealousies; Bill showed none of these. Don't let me make a god of him; he was simply a very good human being and I liked him, much.

We made the reading, I read, we came back to the house. Some of the crowd followed. Students, a couple of professors, some others, unknown. The drinks came about. The co-eds were lovely, all the traps were there. I am always relieved after a reading; it's a dirty job to me, I sweat it. I began drinking heavily, the relief flowed into me and I began to "chatter." It was expected, part of the proceedings but the easiest part—I already had my check. I mocked the literary scene . . . "Oh, I say, have you read Lawrence? No, not Josephine, not the guy from Arabia, but the guy who milked cows and women . . ." I went on. It saved me from answering questions about myself. Once during the night I reached out and got a handful of Bill's hair: "and this fucking *junky* here, what's he good for?" It got quiet. "You know," I said, "there's one poem Bill wrote that really put the chill bumps on my arms . . . Bill, the one where your girl offers to do some tricks so you can score, and you get mad, cry, and she says—'Don't cry, daddy, it's just another way to burn a sucker.'" Then we got on some of the rest of Bill's stuff and we all felt better . . .

■

In the morning Ruthie had to work, so Bill and I were alone in the house. We were both sick, Bill more so than I. We both managed to get down a warm beer and then I suggested we try some soft-boiled eggs. Bill boiled them too long. After we ate I heard him suddenly run out into the yard, he said, "Bukowski," then vomited. His physical shape was bad. He finally got down some bread soaked in milk. "We'd better go easy, kid," I told him, "my life plan is to live to the year 2000." "Hell, me too," he said, "I had a dream I was going to die in the year 2000." He even had it down to the hour and the minutes of the day. I went in and took a bath; warm baths help me when I'm sick. I finished that, had another beer. Bill still looked bad; it was the pills, the shit. It got darker and darker. Ruthie phoned and said there was a tornado on the way. It looked like midnight and the wind blew, blew. I had another beer and made plane reservations out. Ruthie came by for lunch and Bill said, "Bukowski is resilient, a resilient son of a bitch, he's got the body of a 19-year-old." 2 poets came by for the next night's reading; a young girl and a man in his mid-thirties. They began talking, non-stop talking . . . and the talk was not good. I began to appreciate Bill's easy way more and more. Bill walked out of the bathroom, "Bukowski, did you masturbate when you took a bath?" "No." "Good, I won't have to wash the tub." Ruthie went back to work. The professor came and took the girl poetess off to some function. The guy talked on.

Bill came out of the bathroom. "Listen, man, you haven't stopped talking since you got here. It's been an hour."

"Well, that's better than mumbling. All you do is sit around and mumble."

Me, I thought the mumbling was much better.

Bill had to make class. The professor and the girl poetess came back. Bill strapped this thing on his back. "What the hell's that, Bill?" I asked. "I carry my books and papers in there. I ride my bicycle to class."

"Oh, come on, I'll drive you," said the professor, "there's a tornado coming out there."

"It's all right, I'll make it." He walked over to me. "I don't know how to say goodbye," he said. "Don't then," I answered. There was a light handshake and he was out the door and onto his bike. That was April 3rd. Bill Wantling died at 12:15 p.m. May 2, 1974.

I was sitting typing a poem when the phone rang. Ruthie told me. After she finished I phoned my girl who worked as a lady bartender. "Wantling died," I said, "Ruthie just phoned me. Wantling died." The tears rolled out of me; I shook. "I'm sorry," I said, "I told you how much I liked him." I hung up. It was true. Bill had been one of the few men who had ever come through to me. I was used to death, I knew about death, I wrote about death. I went out and got some booze and got very drunk. The next morning I was all right; it had settled; it was the first rush of it that had confused me.

At the end Bill was concentrating on Style. He knew about style, he was style, he had style. He once asked me in a letter, "What is style?" I didn't answer the question. I had written a poem called "Style" but I guess he felt that the poem didn't answer it entirely, but I still ignored the question. I know what style is now that I met Bill.

Style means no shield at all.

Style means no front at all.

Style means ultimate naturalness.

Style means one man alone with billions of men about.

■

I'll say goodbye now, Bill.

JAGGERNAUT

They opened on the 9th at the Forum and I went to the track the same day.
The track is right across from the Forum and I looked over as I drove in and
thought, well, that's where it's going to be. Last time I had seen them was at
the Santa Monica Civic. It was hot at the track and everybody was sweating
and losing. I was hungover but got off well. A track is some place to go so
you won't stare at the walls and whack off, or swallow ant poison. You walk
around bet and wait and wait and look at the people and when you look at
the people long enough you begin to realize that it's bad because they are
everywhere, but it's bearable because you adjust somewhat, feeling more
like another piece of meat in the tide than if you had stayed home and read
Ezra, or Tom Wolfe, or the financial section.

The tracks aren't what they used to be: full of hollering drunks and cigar
smokers, and girls sitting at the side benches and showing leg all the way up
to the panties. I think times are much harder than the government tells us.
The government owes their balls to the banks and the banks have over-lent
to businessmen who can't pay it back because the people can't buy what
business sells because an egg costs a dollar and they've only got 50 cents.
The whole thing can go overnight and you'll find red flags in the smoke-
stacks and Mao t-shirts walking through Disneyland, or maybe Christ will
come back wheeling a golden bike, front wheel 12-to-one ratio to rear. Anyhow, the people are desperate at the track; it has become the job, the survival, the cross instead of the lucky lark. And unless you know exactly what
you're doing at a racetrack, how to read and play a toteboard, reevaluate the
trackman's morning line, and eliminate the sucker money from the good
money, you aren't going to win, you aren't going to win but one time in ten
trips to the track. People on their last funds, on their last unemployment
check, on borrowed money, stolen money, desperate stinking diminishing
money are getting dismantled forever out there, whole lifetimes pissed
away, but the state gets an almost 7 percent tax cut on each dollar, so it's le-

gal. I am better than most out there because I have put more study into it. The racetrack to me is like the bullfights were to Hemingway—a place to study death and motion and your own character or lack of it. By the 9th race I was $50 ahead, put $40 to win on my horse, and walked to the parking lot. Driving in I heard the result of the last race on the radio—my horse had come in 2nd.

I got on in, took a hot bath, had a joint, had 2 joints (bombers), drank some white wine, Blue Nun, had 7 or 8 bottles of Heineken and wondered about the best way to approach a subject that was holy to a lot of people, the still young people anyhow. I liked the rock beat; I still liked sex; I liked the raising high roll and and roar and reach of rock, yet I got a lot more out of Bee and Mahler and Ives. What rock lacked was the total layers of melody and chance that just didn't have to chase itself after it began, like a dog trying to bite his ass off because he'd eaten hot peppers. Well, I'd try. I finished off the Blue Nun, dressed, had another joint, and drove back on out. I was going to be late.

S.O. And the parking lot was full. I circled around and found the closest street to park in—at least a half-mile away.

I got out and began to walk. Manchester. The street was full of private residents behind iron bars with guards. And funeral homes. Others were walking in. But not too many. It was late. I walked along thinking, shit, it's too far, I ought to turn back. But I kept walking. About halfway down Manchester (on the south side) I found a golf course that had a bar and walked in. There were tables. And golfers, satisfied golfers drinking slowly. There was a daylight golf course but these kitties had been shooting for distance on the straight range under the electric lights. Through the glass back of the bar you could still see a few others out there jerking off golf balls under the moon. I had a girl with me. She ordered a bloody mary and I ordered a screwdriver. When my belly's going bad vodka soothes me and my belly's always going bad. The waitress asked the girl for her I.D. She was 24 and it pleased her. The bartender had a cheating, chalky, dumb face and poured 2 thin drinks. Still it was cool and gentle in there.

"Look," I said, "why don't we just stay in here and get drunk? Fuck the STONES. I mean, I can make up some kind of story: went to see the STONES, got drunk in a golfcourse bar, puked, broke a table, knitted a palm tree towel, caught cancer. Whatcha think?"

"Sounds all right."

When women agree with me I always do the other thing. I paid up and we left. It was still quite a walk. Then we were angling across the parking lot. Security cars drove up and down. Kids leaned against cars smoking joints and drinking cheap wine. Beer cans were about. Some whiskey bottles. The younger generation was no longer pro-dope and anti-alcohol — they had caught up with me: they used it all. When 27 nations would soon know how to use the hydrogen bomb, it hardly made sense to preserve your health. The girl and I, our tickets were for seats that were separated. I got her pointed in the direction of her seat and then walked over to the bar. Prices were reasonable. I had two fast drinks, got my ticket stub out, put it in my hand and walked towards the noise. A large chap drunk on cheap wine ran toward me telling me that his wallet had been stolen. I swifted my elbow gently into his gut and he bent over and began to vomit.

I tried to find my section and my aisle. It was dark and light and blaring. The usher screamed something about where my seat was but I couldn't hear and waved him off. I sat down on the steps and lit a cigarette. Mick was down there in some kind of pajamas with little strings tied around his ankles. Ron Wood was the rhythm guitarist replacing Mick Taylor; Billy Preston was really shooting-off at the keyboard; Keith Richards was on lead guitar and he and Ron were doing some sub-glancing lilting highs against other's edges but Keith held a firmer more natural ground, albeit an easy one which allowed Ron to come in and play back against shots and lobs at his will. Charlie Watts on tempo seemed to have joy but his center was off to the left and falling down. Bill Wyman on bass was the total professional holding it all together over the bloody Thames-Forum.

The piece ended and the usher told me that I was over on the other side, on the other side of row N. Another number began. I walked up and around.

Every seat was taken. I sat down next to row N and watched the Mick work. I sensed a gentility and grace and desperateness in him, and still some of the power: I shall lead you children the shit out of here.

Then a female with big legs came down and brushed her hip against my head. An usher. Grotch, grotch, double luck. I showed her my stub. She moved out the kid on the end seat. I felt guilty and sat down on it. A huge balloon cock rose from the center of the stage, it must have been 70 feet high. The rock rocked, the cock rocked.

This generation loves cocks. The next generation we're going to see huge pussies, guys jumping into them like swimming pools and coming out all red and blue and white and gold and gleaming about 6 miles north of Redondo Beach.

Anyhow, Mick grabbed this cock at the bottom (and the screams really upped) and then Mick began to bend that big cock toward the stage, and then he crawled along it (living that time) and he kept moving toward the head, and then he kept getting nearer and then he grabbed the head.

The response was symphonic and beyond.

The next bit began. The guy next to me started again. This guy rocked and bobbed and rocked and rolled and flickered and rotor-rooted and boggled no matter what was or wasn't. He knew and loved his music. An insect of the inner-beat. Each hit with him was the big hit. Selectivity was non-comp with him. I always drew one of these.

I went to the bar for another drink and after getting this kid out of my $12.50 seat again, there was Mick; he'd put his foot in a stirrup and now he was holding to a rope and he was way out and swinging back and forth over the heads of his audience, and he didn't look too steady up there waving back and forth. I didn't know what he was on, but for the sake of his bisexual ass and the heads he was going to fall upon I was glad when they reeled him back in.

Mick wore down after that, decided to change pajamas and sent out Billy Preston, who tried to cheese and steal the game from the Jag and almost did, he was fresh and full of armpit and job and jog, he wanted to bury and replace the hero, he was nice, he did an Irish jig painted over in black. I even liked him, but you knew he didn't have the final send-off, and you must have guessed that Mick knew it too as he buried wet ice under his armpits and ass and mind backstage. Mick came out and finished with Preston. They almost kissed, wiggling assholes. Somebody threw a brace of firecrackers into the crowd. They exploded just properly. One guy was blinded for life; one girl would have a cataract over the left eye forever; one guy would never hear out of one ear. O.K., that's circus, it's cleaner than Vietnam.

Bouquets fly. One hits Mick in the face. Mick tries to stamp out a big ball balloon that lands on stage. He can't push his foot through it. One saddens. Mick runs over, jumps up, kicks one of his fiddlers in the ass. The fiddler smiles a smile back, gently, full of knowledge: like, the pay is good.

The stage weighs 40 elephants and is shaped like a star. Mick gets out on the edge of the star; he gets each bit of audience alone, that section alone, and then he takes the mike away from his face and he forms his lips into the silent sound: FUCK YOU. They respond.

The edge of the star rises, Mick loses his balance, rolls down to stage center, losing his mike.

There's more. I get the taste for the ending. Will it be "Sympathy for the Devil?" Will it be like at the Santa Monica Civic? Bodies pressing down the aisles and the young football players beating the shit out of the rock tasters? To keep the sanctuary and the body and the soul of the Mick intact? I got trapped down there among ankles and cunt hairs and milk bodies and cotton-candy minds. I didn't want more of that. I got out. I got out when all the lights went on and the holy scene was about to begin and we were to love each other and the music and the Jag and the rock and the knowledge.

I left early. Outside they seemed bored. There were any number of titless young girls in t-shirts and jeans. Their men were nowhere. They sat upon the ends of bumpers, most of the bumpers attached to campers. The titless young blonde things in t-shirts and jeans. They were listless, stoned, unexcited, but not vicious. Little tight-butted girls with pussies and loves and flows.

So I walked on down to the car. The girl was in the back seat asleep. I got in and drove off. She awakened. I was going to have to send her back to New York City. We weren't making it. She sat up.

"I left early. That shit is finally deadening," she said.

"Well, the tickets were free."

"You going to write about it?"

"I don't know. I can't get any reaction. I can't get any reaction at all."

"Let's get something to eat," she said.

"Yeah, well we can do that."

I drove north on Crenshaw looking for a nice place were you could get a drink and where there wasn't any music of any kind. It was O.K. if the waitress was crazy as long as she didn't whistle.

PICKING THE HORSES

HOW TO WIN AT THE TRACK,

OR AT LEAST BREAK EVEN

First, let's begin with some don'ts:

Mental clarity is a must. Don't arrive at the races after fighting last-minute traffic. Either arrive early and settle down easily to your business or arrive around the second or third or fourth races. Get yourself a cup of coffee, sit down and inhale and exhale a few times. Realize that you're at no dreamland, that no money is being given away and that beating the horses is an art and that there are very few artists around.

Don't go to the track with anybody else. If you must be concerned with their welfare and with how their luck is going or whether they want a hot dog or a Coke or a whiskey sour, that is just going to add more weight against your chances of thinking easily and making the proper bets.

Once you are at the track don't sit near the loudmouths and the advisors. These people are poison. They know nothing and they are lonely hearts. They want to talk. Their idea is that we are all good guys in this thing together and we can beat the track. There's no truth to it. The people bet against each other. There is roughly a 16 percent take on the dollar; half goes to the track, the other half to the state of California. The toteboard coughs up the remainder of the money in prices paid to the winning ticket holders.

Don't go to the track with tight money or borrowed money or rent money or food money. Try to arrive with windfall money, an income tax refund, something of that order. Have money that you can *afford* to lose, then you might possibly win. The racetrack is no place to go to try to solve your problems. The game is a mean game, a vicious game. Look around at the faces after the third or fourth race.

Don't bet exactas or daily doubles or any kind of gimmick bets where you are offered a lot for a little. It only adds to an obvious pressure and gets you into the hole very fast; and when people get into the hole, they panic and make wild and impossible bets, trying to solve one impossible dream with another. They lose all conception of what money is.

They'll bet from $20 to $50 on exacta tickets; but when they go into a supermarket they won't pay $1.75 for a decent steak—they'll buy greasy hamburger instead. They'll buy 50 bucks worth of exacta tickets (an exacta ticket is where you must predict the exact finish of the first two horses) but grind their motor to shit because an oil-change and a filter change might cost 8 bucks.

Now, here's a final don't, and if you listen, it's going to save you much money. Beware the big closer. That's a horse who in his last race or in many of his previous races closed many lengths on the winner. This is a favorite horse with most horseplayers and his price is beat down to a sliver of his chances. The pros call this type of horse the Sucker horse or the Leadass. He looks good charging down the stretch, closing lengths, but he seldom wins.

If you go down the *Form* you can see his losing races at 8/5, 5/2, 4/5, 6/5 and on and on. They'll keep sucking, thinking surely he'll make it this time. To make it he needs all the luck: a burning, fast early pace and a lane of open traffic through all the other horses.

The next biggest sucker bet to that one is the lightweight horse—one in with 109 pounds or 105 pounds. Weight off doesn't make a horse run faster, not to any noticeable degree . . .

All right, now you're at the track. You've got a program and a *Racing Form* and the toteboard churns. All right. The first thing you must do is evaluate the horses. You get that Pasadena newspaper; it has the master consensus of the 17 leading handicappers. You give five points for win, two points for place, one point for show. Add them up. Then next to your morning line you write down the evaluation. (The morning line is the track handicapper's evaluation of the horse's chance of winning). All right, next to the morning line you write down the consensus evaluation.

Let's take the fourth race, April 15, for maiden fillies, three years old, bred in California.

HORSE	C	M
1) Count the Take · · · · · · · · · · · · · · ·	1	3
2) Cathy Charmer · · · · · · · · · · · · · ·	2	2
3) Queeki · · · · · · · · · · · · · · · · · · ·	7	30
4) Tonga Rhythm· · · · · · · · · · · · · · ·	3	10
5) Miss Pung Jeun · · · · · · · · · · · · · ·	8	30
6) Enyo· ·	6	8
7) Centuries Cherub· · · · · · · · · · · · ·	9	30
8) Lucky Coloullar · · · · · · · · · · · · ·	4	4
9) Jane Young· · · · · · · · · · · · · · · · ·	6	6

C: CONSENSUS   M: MORNING LINE

The crowd jumped on Lucy Coloullar. He opened at 2/1 on the first flash of the board, rose up to 7/2 during the betting, then came back down to 2/1. In other words, the crowd was sending off the fourth consensus choice as the favorite. Cathy Charmer with Shoemaker opened at 9/2 on the first flash of the board and through the betting finally came down to her morning line as a slight second favorite in the betting. Count the Take opened at 4 and came down to 7/2 over a morning line of 3 and won easily.

Lucky Coloullar, the horse bet out of context, finished up the field. It's only a matter of reasonableness. The moment the crowd lands on something, it dies. The crowd is always wrong; that's why most of the cars in the track parking lots are over four years old.

In the fifth race the crowd sucked on Dorset Cay, sending the sixth consensus choice in a field of nine horses off at 4/1. The horse never got a call. *Whenever a horse's odds are below his consensus rating, he is a bad bet that seldom ever wins.* And there is almost always one of these horses in every race.

If you just cut this one horse out of every race, your percentages of winning are increased by whatever that horse's odds are. That is your edge in the betting. The winner of this race was Approval, carrying 121 pounds and going off at 7/2 on a morning line of 7/2 as second choice in the consensus.

Let's take the seventh race, basically a two-horse race, all the others going off at high odds. O.K, here's the scam: Messenger of Song, the consensus choice of the 17 leading handicappers, is given a morning line of 2 by the track handicapper. The second consensus choice, Fly American, is given a morning line of 8/5. On the first flash of the board Messenger of Song opens at 8/5 and Fly American opens at 2/1. By the time the betting is finished, Fly American the second consensus choice, is reading *even* money and Messenger goes off at 9/5. Fly American, being the only horse going off below its consensus choice is your sucker bet at even money! He finishes a distant second to Messenger at 9/5. Logic. Basic logic.

I know one old-timer who makes it at the track who does nothing but buy a program. No *Form*, no newspapers, nothing else. All he does is buy the one or two horses that are going off near their odds. Nothing out of context to the eye. No big underlays, no big overlays, just worth per worth's sake. He does all right.

There are no bargains at the track. Horses reading 6 on the line and going off at 10/1 or 12/1 or 13/1 do not win. Horses reading 10 or 12 on the morning line and going off at 5 or 9/2 or 4 or 7/2 do not win either. *The betting money must agree with the odds* (a very slight underlay is preferred) *and the horses's consensus rating.* All the other out-of-context pigs finish up the track.

Of course, any kind of horse *can* win and sometimes does, but what we go on is what happens most of the time and what continues to happen. I've seen thousands of horse races, and what you go on is the overall results of all of those races. What kills people off is the 30-minute wait between races and the memory of the last race. The last race is what appears to them to be the truth because it happened most recently, and if it is a freak race and a freak result, it still seems to them to be the truth.

Betting horses properly takes ultimate character. I have a saying: A man who can beat the races can do anything he makes his mind up to do. A guy like Hemingway found moments of truth at the bullfights and in wars. I find moments of truth and follow through and style at the racetrack and at the boxing matches. It's all determined upon what sets the picture up for you.

I find great holes in my character at the racetrack. Sometimes I get to thinking that I'm pretty good and I go out there and find out that I don't have total follow-thorough. And knowledge without follow-through hurts more than not having any knowledge at all.

Oh, I must put this in because it's important, and if you set up your betting as I've urged you to, there is a certain type of race that works in reverse. And it's a race for two-year-old-maidens who have never run a race. In this type of race the horse that goes off below its morning line and below its con-sensus-rating is the winner. These types win 95 percent of their races but you seldom see one on the card when you go to the track. But beware when you do.

The reason I don't mind giving away these secrets is that I know human nature. You won't assimilate what I've told you, you'll think it a con. Each man or woman has to get burned in their own way. Nothing I tell you can save you. You'll still go out and shit all over yourself. And sometimes there will be races that won't make sense or a whole *day* of racing that won't make sense.

There's a friend of mine who once took his wife out to the track. He stayed up all night getting set up. He knew all the traps, he had all the experience but this *one* day, this only day he ever took his wife to the track, it was a freak day. She caught a 22/1 shot in the first race because that horse had the same name as her Aunt Edna's dog. She missed the second but she got the third because the horse's name was like the song her brother used to sing when he got drunk. It paid $62.80. She missed a couple more and then near the end she caught one that paid $78.40 because "that was the name of my first lover."

Then on the walk to the parking lot she turned to him and said, "You and all your fucking numbers and figures. They don't mean nothing!" And, of course, that day she was right. They have since become divorced.

It would really take many more pages than this to help you get down to a real sensible reality of horseplaying. But do try to remember some of the things I have told you: near the morning line, *slightly* underlaid if possible, and in line with the master consensus. Then you might be standing out there and all the other horses will be out of context except two and you'll wonder — which one? (By the way, when I speak of betting I speak of betting to *win*. Betting to place or to show is just a deathly grind-down. You might as well stay home and switch your money from one pocket to another and then tear up a $5 bill. It's the same thing.)

O.K., if your two horses have odds high enough bet them both. But say you have a 9/5 versus an 8/5, you might as well get the right one. So, in order of importance, you separate them like this: you take the horse that ran in front or off the pace in his last race and *fell back a bit* in the stretch. Take the horse carrying the *most* weight. Take the horse with the lower speed-rating off the last race. Take the horse that seems to have the worst jockey. Those are four points. If you can score on three of these four points, you have a probable winner. If you can score on all four, you have a waltz-in.

If it breaks even, 2 on 2, select the horse who has the worst post position at the distance. If the post positions are about equal, then listen to the loudmouths — they are always available. Listen to the horse they are touting, then bet the other.

And don't go to the track day after day. It's like working a factory; you'll get jaded and dull and stupid. And remember, any damn fool can pay his way into a racetrack just like any damn fool can sit on a barstool and pretend that he's (she's) living.

Oh, yes, before I leave you, there is one more bit I might add. Horses usually win when they come down from the odds they ran at in their last race. A horse coming down, say, from 12/1 to 6/1 is a much better bet than a horse that was 2/1 in his last race and is now going off at 6. In fact, a horse coming down from all his odds showing on the *Form* is usually a good bet, a very good bet, if he goes off anywhere near his morning line.

My best advice about racetracks is—don't go. But if you do go, at least realize that simple reasoning against the prejudices and concepts of the crowd is your only chance. And, luck, my friends.

WORKOUT

Nina and I were basically on the rift. She was 32 years younger than I, and there were other inconsistencies, but we saw each other two or three times a week. We had very little physical contact—an occasional bit of kissing and a far less occasional fallback into sex—so it was a pleasant rift, much less cruel than most. Nina was a pillhead and I was an alcoholic, but I took her pills and she drank my booze; we were not prejudiced that way.

Nina was 24, small, but with a near-perfect body and long hair that was the purest of reds. She had gone the route: borne a child at 16, then had two abortions, a marriage, a slight run at prostitution. Barmaid jobs, shackjobs, benefactors, unemployment insurance, and food stamps had held her together. But she had a great deal left: that body, humor, madness, and cruelty. And she walked around and sat around and fucked around under that long red hair. All that long red hair. Nina was a rifleshot into the brain of the psyche; she could kill any man she wanted to. She had almost killed me. But so had some others.

The first time I met Karyn was when I drove to her place with Nina. They were friends, and Karyn had some pills. Nina had three or four doctors who wrote her prescriptions, but she consumed her pills quickly. Karyn had a $350-a-month apartment in Los Angeles. Nina pressed the intercom button and announced us; something buzzed and the door opened. We took the elevator to the sixth floor. Karyn let us in. She was 22, smaller than Nina, who was quite small—in height, that is—(both girls were big where they were supposed to be big and small where they were supposed to be small). It seemed as if they had been sculpted directly by a hand that wanted to drive men mad. They both looked like children who had suddenly become women, yet who had remained children somehow. It was a dirty trick against men, and a dirty trick of nature too, because for each one that nature had molded in that fashion, 5,000 others were created ugly or deformed or awkward or bent or blind or with curvature of the spine or hands too big or no breasts and so on and so forth. It wasn't fair, but when you looked at them you didn't think of fairness, you thought of sex and love, and laughing with them and fighting with them and eating in cafes with them and walking along sidewalks with them at high noon or at 3 A.M. or at anytime.

Karyn had long black hair, blue eyes that almost looked kind, and lips that made you think of kissing, kissing and almost nothing else. Just to kiss would seem to be enough, but of course it wouldn't be. If she had a fault it seemed to be that her snub nose was too short and rounded, just as Nina's nose seemed to be too sharp and too long. Yet, with each of them, the eyes finally settled on the nose and stayed there. One's body became excited as if within all that beauty the flaw was the glory—as if without the flaw the beauty would not be so beautiful.

So there I was at the age of 56 sitting in West L.A. at 3:45 p.m. with two of the most handsome women in all of America—or anywhere else for that matter. And with two of the most ridiculously hard women in the world; they were caught in their own forms and how others responded to those forms, and it was difficult for them to remain human with everything going that way. Yet they both had the inner glow and gamble; they had not entirely succumbed to appearance. It was confusing and deathly and wonderful.

Not much happened that first time; Nina got up the $20 for the pills—uppers—and it was a definite overcharge, but then I really got up the $20; it came out of my wallet, so it wasn't an overcharge—for Nina. She got the pills, only mild "mind modifiers," and we each took one. Karyn had her tv on—50-inch, cable, color. They talked about things. Modeling mostly. Karyn had a $50-an-hour gig. She brought out some of the milder photos. They were O.K. We looked them over. I chose my favorite, waved it around in the air, kissed it, returned it. Then Nina spoke of her modeling experience. Most of it was all right. But how she hated split-beaver—Christ, how she hated it. She didn't have a cunt like most of them; her cunt was really cute. Christ, some of them looked like they had hair-covered wallets hanging out of their asses. God-awful. Nina's cunt was O.K. I nodded: yes, yes. Only one day, Nina went on, her mother had gotten into her purse and found these *photos*, and the photos were really all right but her mother didn't understand. It had something to do with the era—that mother just didn't know. Mother had really objected to one; Nina naked, hair thrown back, wild and red, head looking at the ceiling, arms spread and she was pissing on the floor. Quite sexy really; really really sexy. Mother howled. Nina was forced to hit her. It was terrible. But the old lady had no right to be prowling in her purse. Right?

Then Karyn walked out and came back with a mass of blouses and more or less asked, do these fit you, darling? And Nina stood up and tried them on. She stood up and tried them on, and she didn't have a brassiere on. And Karyn and I sat there and watched her try them on, now and then showing us those milky white breasts of a 200-pound pregnant woman, seemingly welded to the body of a child. *Jesus.* She stood in front of the mirror buttoning and unbuttoning. "Which one do you like, Hank?"

"Oh," I said, "all of them."

"No, really, Hank, which one?"

"I think I like the purple best," I said, "the purple—the one with little strings that dangle, those leather strings."

Anyway, she took eight or ten blouses and we left. . . .

■

I don't remember the days or the weeks. The rift between Nina and me was getting bigger, and I was glad. It always feels good to know that you can live without a person that you thought you could never live without. But I had found other girlfriends, none as beautiful, but each, basically, kinder. My new girlfriends were both self-sustaining businesswomen, and some of the hardness of the business world had rubbed off on them, but it was not as bad as the hardness that can be dealt off upon a woman with an overcompelling beauty. So then Nina phoned again.

"Hello," I said.

And she said, "Hank, I want you to drive me to Karyn's."

And I said, "Sure, be right there. . . ."

■

It happened quickly. As we got into the door of Karyn's apartment, Nina screamed, "Oh, no, you bitch!"

She had been standing in front of me in the hallway leading from the door to the inner apartment when she turned and ran toward me. I heard Karyn scream, "Grab her, Hank!" Being drunk and on uppers, I reacted. I grabbed Nina. It felt good. She fought against me; it was nearly sexual. It *was* sexual. She had on tight blue jeans and a thin blouse, worn, shredded, a see-through. I held her and we struggled. Then Karyn, who was 15 pounds lighter and one inch or more shorter, ran up and grabbed Nina by those pounds and pounds of roaring red, red hair, strangling strands of every-thing, ripping moss and sadness, and rampant sunrise and yowling red hair, rich and long—Karyn grabbed it all in her hands and yanked Nina away from me and down onto the floor.

Karyn fell on top of Nina, still pulling at her hair. Then they rolled and Nina was momentarily on top. She had her fingers on Karyn's throat but the grip was not strong, or it was misplaced, awry. Then Karyn, yanking at her hair, spun Nina underneath again and got her arms pinned with each of her knees. Then she pulled Nina's head up by the hair with one hand and started slapping her rapidly across her face, saying, "Bitch, bitch, rotten bitch! Whore! Cunt! Redheaded shit! Bitch, bitch, bitch!" Then she dropped both of her legs back and grabbed Nina behind the head and put her mouth upon Nina's, kissing her savagely, moving her mouth around and around Nina's. Then she pulled her mouth away and kissed again, pulled her mouth away and kissed again. I hardened and watched. It was the most magical and powerful thing I had ever seen. They were both such beautiful women—not a touch of lesbianism in either of them. Nina pushed against Karyn but couldn't hold her off. Nina's face was wet with tears and she was sobbing. Karyn kept kissing and cursing Nina. Then she let off the kissing and pulled Nina's hair again with one hand and slapped her with the other, quite hard, again and again. Then she grabbed Nina's head with both hands and kissed her cruelly and relentlessly. They were on the kitchen floor and the light was bright and Karyn's long black hair mixed with Nina's longer and fuller red hair, as they kissed. They were both in tight blue jeans, and their bodies rolled and struggled against each other as they fought. And there was Karyn's snub nose dug under Nina's large and fascinating nose, as they fought and kissed. I rubbed myself and groaned.

Then Karyn leaped up and pulled Nina up by the hair. Nina screamed. Karyn began ripping Nina's blouse off. The breasts came through. She slapped Nina again, three or four more times, brutally. Nina seemed dizzied and could hardly fight back. Karyn grabbed her upright, both hands on the cheeks of Nina's tight blue jean ass. Then she kissed her again. Their heads rocked back and forth as they staggered about the kitchen. Then Karyn let go and began slapping Nina viciously, harder than ever, with both hands. Nina rocked back against the sink, her red hair flying, all sprayed out. The electric light shone against her hair as it flew and bounced. Her hair seemed redder than ever, longer, fuller, more glorious. Then Karyn grabbed her and kissed her again, bending her over the sink, the mirror showing both of them.

Karyn stepped back, undid her own blouse, took it off, and there were her breasts, punching out, flesh flouncing. Then she slid down her blue jeans, taking them off over her high-heeled shoes. She was pantyless. Her ass was just as miraculous as the rest of her. Then she slapped Nina again with a hard right. She undid Nina's belt, unzipped her blue jeans, and slid them down.

She tore off the remainder of Nina's blouse, then slipped her panties down and off. Nina seemed dazed. They were both in their high-heeled shoes, looking at each other. I don't know who had the best body—Nina perhaps. The breasts were larger and there was more haunch and where there was supposed to be haunch, and the hips went in a bit more. Both had very white skin. The contrast was Nina's red long hair and Karyn's long black hair. I unzipped and began rubbing my cock out in the open.

Suddenly Karyn grabbed Nina by the hair and dragged her toward the bedroom. It must have hurt, but Nina seemed to have lost the ability to fight. She screamed and was pulled backwards by the mass and mesh of red hair. I followed them. Karyn was pulling her with one hand. When she got Nina into the bedroom she put both of her hands into Nina's hair and yanked her backward, violently. Nina was thrown to the floor. She landed flat on her back on the rug near the bed. Karyn leaped upon her, body upon body, writhing; she grabbed Nina's head with both hands and kissed her harder still, smashing Nina's lips back, getting inside her mouth, sucking at her teeth while tonguing. Once again the black and the red hair intermixed; it was gross and beautiful beyond conception. God, or whoever had built these machines of flesh, must have meant it to be that way. I thought of cathedrals and murders and miracles. I was blessed with the sight of it.

Then Karyn got off of Nina and pulled her onto the bed. I thought perhaps that Karyn would go down on Nina, but she didn't. Once again she fell full upon her and began kissing harder and harder, each kiss harder, somehow, than the preceding. Then Karyn let off, bent back, pulled Nina's head up by the hair and slapped Nina's face rapidly with her free hand, saying, "Lift your legs! LIFT YOUR LEGS, WHORE, BEFORE I KILL YOU!" Then she let Nina go. Nina's legs lifted and Karyn began kissing her again, pulling at her hair, kissing, kissing, and at the same time she rubbed her cunt against Nina's cunt, rubbing, rubbing, black hair against red, breasts rubbing upon breasts. It was total glory and total heat. I couldn't believe it. Now and then Karyn would let off kissing and slap Nina with one hand while pulling her hair with the other, screaming things at her. Then she would kiss Nina again and gyrate her cunt against Nina's. Nina kept her legs up. I stood near them, masturbating. I only have a medium-sized cock but it seemed enormous, I think, because the unbelievability of the circumstances excited me so. Then Karyn began to moan. She was near climax. I reacted to the moans, watching the cunts grind together: Nina's legs up with her high-heeled shoes on, all that hair tangled top and bottom, all that body tangled, everything tangled. Karyn moaned, nearing closer and closer to climax. I began whimpering, playing with my cock, totally in pace with Karyn's near-climax. As Karyn began to climax, I climaxed, pointing my cock at them, somehow wanting to drop sperm upon them—their bodies, their faces any part of them. But as I moved toward them, it spurted out and dripped on the rug. It took Karyn longer. I'm not sure if Nina climaxed, but her body began to writhe more and more, as if in response to Karyn's. Nina's legs dropped and Karyn stayed there on top of her. I went into the bathroom, got some toilet paper, and wiped up my come from the rug.

■

Several weeks passed. I didn't see Nina. I stayed with a businesswoman who lived in Marina Del Rey. I stayed there much of the time. She was a good soul—clean, but a bit crazed like anybody in our society—and inventive enough, hardly dull, and basically pissed at men and what men had done to her—the old story. But she had a fine apartment and an excellent body; her eyes were best—defeated but still hopeful—a large brown, glowing as fine as any flower, as fine as anything. Time gets in the way and eight-to-fives and yard sales and friends (of hers). I didn't have any friends. But damn all this—what I'm trying to say is that several weeks passed and then Nina phoned. Nina had a way of phoning—slow withdrawn voice. It made you see her hair, her body again, her mind again, everything that pulled her together, and made me feel things that other women could not ever quite make me feel.

"Hank," she said, "what are you doing?"

"Nothing. Nothing at all."

"I need a favor."

"O.K."

"I want a ride to Karyn's."

"All right."

"She's got these mind modifiers. They're not much good, but they're all right, and I've run out of pharmacies I can go to."

"I'll be right over."

"Give me 15 minutes."

"All right."

"One thing," she said.

"What?" I asked.

"We get the shit and we split. I don't want anything like that last time. It was horrifying."

"All right.

I hung up.

■

When I got to her place, Nina was dressed in blue jeans and blouse, but no shoes. She often went barefoot. Whether she didn't like the shoes or hardly knew what she was doing, I never asked. But the strange thing about Nina was that no matter whether she was in high heels or barefoot, her haunches were wonderous. Most women looked better from the rear in high heels. Not Nina. But it didn't matter. Not with haunches like that. And it didn't matter if she gained weight—the haunches looked better—or if she lost weight—the haunches looked better. Every day they looked better.

When I arrived she was immensely and perfectly there, with a blue ribbon knotted somewhere in the mass of her long red hair. And her hair blazed RED; it kept making you look at it. Under it all she seemed cool, almost indifferent—the most maddening woman on earth, and yet she wasn't in the movies, or even on Broadway. She wasn't driving millionaires to floating her parts in U.S. $$$$.

In a way she knew, but at the same time she didn't know: she was the world's sexiest woman. I was mostly glad that she didn't mostly know, or I wouldn't have been around. Anyhow, we got into the car and I moved it toward West L.A.

"All right, fucker," she said, "remember what I told you."

"What?"

"I don't want a trip like that last trip. We get the pills. We go."

·

The sun was full and we drove along with the wind pulling at the fire in her hair. Living miracles occur and most often they occur quietly. So to change that, I turned on the radio and she got her feet up on the dashboard and began snapping her fingers to the music. Then she began to sing along with the words. Her voice was high and lilting, one pitch above the tonality, a voice joyous and full of humor.

Then she pulled a wooden match out of her blouse pocket, scratched it against the ball of one of her feet, and lit the cigarette that was in her mouth. She smoked half a cigarette, tossed it out, and put some gum into her mouth. She worked on the gum. Then she turned her head and looked at me. And out of her mouth came this stretching ball of purple bubble gum and it got larger and larger and I looked at it and I looked into her eyes and the gum went:

"SPLOTTTT...."

·

The elevator took us on up. Karyn opened the door.

"I'm just coming for the shit, Karyn," said Nina. "Then we're splitting."

They walked a little ways inside. Karyn turned around and said, "You'll get the shit, whore, but before you get the shit you're going to get something else, whore, whore, whore ... cunt with the same color as your hair on your head, *whore!*"

Nina turned and ran toward me, ran toward the door.

"Hank!" Karyn screamed. "Grab her!"

I grabbed Nina and wouldn't let her go by me. I had both of my arms around her, holding both of her arms to her sides. Karyn came up and slapped her while I held her. The slaps were light but they cut.

"Shit-whore, you're not getting away from me!"

Then Karyn grabbed Nina by the hair and kissed her rapidly five or six times. My cock hardened as I watched this, and I slid down and let it ram into the back of Nina's blue-jeaned haunches. Karyn slapped her again, this time a bit harder, and put her mouth on Nina's mouth and moved it around. I pulled back, unzipped my fly and let my naked cock dig into the back of Nina's blue jeans, into that ass.

Then Karyn leaped back saying, "Strip her down, Hank!" and she began to undress herself. I worked at the belt on Nina's blue jeans, then worked at the zipper. She was fighting me and it was hard work. I got pissed, reached up and grabbed both of her breasts, and squeezed them hard. Nina screamed. I reached down and slid her blue jeans off. By then Karyn was nude and she closed in on Nina. I felt my cock slip into Nina's bare ass, just at the beginning of the crevice. I remembered all my starings at that ass in the afternoons, in the mornings, at midnights—it slid in: victory and glory. Karyn smashed her across the face with a closed fist. I heard Nina moan. My cock slid further in. I didn't move it. I just let it slide and grow. Karyn had both of her hands pulling back on Nina's hair, kissing her wildly on the mouth, spreading Nina's small mouth open, sucking relentlessly at her soul. Nina's hair fell back into my face, my mouth. I began moving my cock in and out of her ass. A radio was playing somewhere, loudly. Then I heard a siren, an ambulance. It went by. Nina's hair across my face felt much rougher than it looked. I began smashing my cock into her ass. It was the moment of my lifetime, the moment of all moments. Then my cock slipped from the ass and into the cunt. I was home and I ripped. Her cunt was wet and it was ready. I was inside of Nina, slipping up and down, rudely, with prayer and yet with total wonderment. Nina was squeezed between Karyn and me. As I was about to climax I reached around and grabbed Karyn's ass and spread it wide. Then I reached over Nina's shoulder, found Karyn's face, her mouth, and I kissed her, spreading her ass wide as I pumped semen into Nina's cunt. I finished coming, let off, and walked away. Karyn and Nina continued.

■

Karyn carried Nina into the bedroom and put her on the bed. Then she spread Nina's legs and began eating her cunt. . . .

■

Later, everybody got dressed. We sat in the kitchen and drank a few beers and smoked some Colombian. The pill transaction took place and I was out another $20. Karyn showed us some more recent porn photos, and then we left. We got down to my '67 Volkswagen, I did a U-turn, got it straightened back toward the section of town where the poor good folks lived — east Hollywood. We had some Shermans, and Nina lit one for each of us.

We drove along, and finally we were running along Fountain. I turned the radio on. Nina put her feet on the dashboard and improved each hit song. Then there was a long commercial; no, it was a series of short commercials. I tried another station, another, still another. Nothing but commercials. I turned the radio off. We passed a gas station. It was still afternoon. Then Nina started to sing:

> *Redhead,*
> *Everybody loves a redhead.*
> *I'll tell the world that she's my*
> *best gal.*
> *Everybody loves a redhead.*
> *I'll tell the world that she's my*
> *best gal.*
> *That's a redhead, and she's my*
> *best gal. . . .*

We drove along Fountain to Western, then I took a right down Western, past the motels, past the taco stand and the Pioneer Takeout, past Hollywood Boulevard, then a left at Carlton. Hard parking as usual, but I backed it in and got out.

Nina sat there looking at me. "Hey," she said, "*Fuck* this! I don't want to go to *your* place. What makes you think I want to go in there?"

"Where to, then?"

"I want to go to Elbert's. Drive me to Elbert's."

■

Elbert was a four-foot, eleven-inch Puerto Rican with a ten-inch cock who pretended he came from Argentinean royal heritage. He had just graduated from dental school and made false teeth. His apartment was full of false teeth and his walls were covered with cheap paintings and insipid mottos and sayings. (Nina had shown me around one night while Elbert was watching the Lakers play basketball—a macho out-with-the-boys night). Elbert was very close to being subnormal but Nina told me he was "a great fuck." She also mentioned all the gold that was in some of those false teeth.

I drove her to Elbert's and she got out of the car. She came around to my side, leaned through the window, and gave me a most tiny kiss, moist, with just the right touch of tongue.

"Goodbye, pops," she said.

Then I watched her walk across the street toward Elbert's apartment, that long red hair waterfalling down her back and stopping just above that ass—those haunches that went up-down, down-up, up-down, down-up.

Nature would always be better than art. It was truly hell to be old, and I ached in what was left of my soul.

Then Nina was gone up the stairway that led to the second floor and Elbert's apartment.

I loved her. But there was nothing I could do. Yes, there was: I started the car and drove away.

At the corner of Franklin and Vermont there was a crazy old news vendor. He leaped into the street in front of my car and waved a newspaper at me. I hit the brakes, just missing him. He stood there and we looked at each other through the windshield. That news vendor: His face was impassive; he looked like Van Gogh, sunflowers, chairs, the potato eaters. He got out of the way and I drove on toward my place where I was going to get very drunk, very soon, as Elbert sent the big ten home.

THE WAY IT HAPPENED

It was raining outside but you couldn't hear the rain; the Interrogation Room was soundproof. Sanderson sat under the white hot light. It was like a scene from a movie. There were two agents. One was fat, badly dressed, scuffed shoes, dirty shirt, wrinkled pants—he was Eddie. The other agent was thin, neatly dressed, his shoes reflected pools of light, his pants were pressed, his shirt crisp and new—he was Mike. Sanderson sat in his undershirt, a pair of old jeans, and worn tennis shoes.

Eddie walked up and down the cement. Mike sat in a chair. He stared at Sanderson. Sanderson sat in front of the interrogation table. The tape recorder was on.

Eddie stopped walking, stood in front of Sanderson.

"Why did you write those letters to the president?"

Sanderson shook his head wearily. "I told you: this country is in danger, the whole earth is in danger."

Eddie inhaled, you could see his whole big gut suck in a half-inch. Then he exhaled and it came out a half-inch, maybe more.

"Is it true that you were twice convicted of child molestation?"

"One Harold L. Sanderson was."

"Don't be cute! Twice, right?"

"Twice."

Mike leaned forward in his chair. The left side of his face twitched once. Then stopped.

"You *care* about the future of the earth, eh, Sanderson? You want those little girls around, don't you?"

"I'm fond of children—"

Mike half rose in his chair. You *slime*, don't *joke* about this!"

Eddie pushed Mike back down in his chair. "Take it easy. We're trying to get at something else."

"I just hate to deal with these freaks. That's all he is, a freak, a nut."

"So was Oswald. And in his way, John Wilkes Booth. We've got orders to check this one out thoroughly."

"I'm not trying to kill the president. I'm trying to save him."

"Shut up!" said Mike. "The only time you'll speak is when we ask you a question."

"You know what the cons call these guys?" Eddie asked Mike. "They call them 'Short Eyes,' and they have their own way of dealing with them."

"Listen," asked Sanderson, "can I have a cigarette?"

Eddie took one out of his pack and almost jammed it into Sanderson's mouth. Then Eddie threw his cigarette lighter on the table.

"Light your own."

Sanderson's hands trembled as he lit his cigarette.

Eddie walked south down the cement, spun, then walked back in front of Sanderson again.

"O.K.," he said, "let's go over it again. Just for the record."

Sanderson sucked on his cigarette.

"Well, the world has been invaded."

"Invaded by what?" asked Eddie. "Roaches? Fleas? Hookers?"

"Space creatures."

"Space creatures?"

"Yes, they're everywhere, they're just waiting."

"O.K., Short Eyes," asked Mike, "where are they waiting?"

"Well, they've taken over the bodies of the animals, the fowl, the fish, even the insects, and they are hiding there."

Mike grinned from his chair, looked up at Eddie. "Hey, you got a dog, Eddie. You realize he's a space creature?"

"If he is, the son of a bitch sure likes to chomp on dog food!"

"Have you noticed," Sanderson continued, "have you noticed that your dog has stopped chasing cats? Have you noticed that cats have stopped catching birds? Have you noticed that spiders no longer eat flies?"

"I haven't noticed," said Mike.

"Me neither," said Eddie.

"Have you noticed that the hawk no longer dives for the hare?"

"Listen, Short Eyes," said Mike, "*we'll* ask the questions here. I told you *before* not to speak unless you were asked."

Sanderson looked down at the floor.

"You kept one of those little girls in your camper for three days," said Mike. "I feel like beating the shit out of you—"

"All right, Mike," said Eddie, "our job is something else right now." Then he looked at Sanderson.

"So the spiders have stopped eating the flies? Why?"

"Because each is a hidden space creature. Unlike earthlings, space creatures don't destroy each other. And space creatures don't need food. They have inner survival capabilities independent of outside sources."

"Oh," said Mike, "like a zoo where you don't have to feed the animals?"

"If you'll check with *your* zoo you'll find that the boa constrictor no longer eats the mice and the rats."

"We'll check them in the morning," said Eddie. "Meanwhile, tell me how come my dog chomps up his dog food? If he's a space creature?"

"That's a front to lull you into security until it's time to strike."

Eddie took another walk south along the cement. Mike rocked in his chair once, then settled back. Then Eddie was back in front of Sanderson.

"How about human bodies?" he asked.

"What about them?" asked Sanderson.

"Have they been invaded?"

"Just a few. You know these people who call themselves Breatharians? Who claim they can live on air? Well, they are space creatures."

Mike leaned back in his chair and sighed, "Well, we've got a real nut right here—"

"Yeah," said Eddie, "this sure seems more of a job for a shrink. I'll have to recommend that. But meanwhile, for the record, we'll continue this interrogation."

Eddie took his little run south along the cement, came back.

"Now, tell me, Sanderson, if what you say is true, how come *you* know all of this?"

"I don't know. I don't understand it."

Mike leaned forward, stared at Sanderson.

"Has a space creature invaded *your* body?"

"All I know is that we trust the Source."

Mike reached out and grabbed Sanderson's shirt just below the collar.

"Don't give me elusive talk! Has a space creature invaded your body, Short Eyes?"

"I don't know—"

"All of a sudden we're getting a hell of a lot of 'I don't knows' out of you!"

"Let go of him, Mike! You sound like you're beginning to *believe* his line."

Mike let go. "I just want to get somewhere or another with this nut."

Eddie tried a run north along the cement for a change. When he got back Sanderson asked him, "Can I have another cigarette?"

Eddie stuck another cigarette into Sanderson's mouth.

"So space creatures smoke cigarettes?"

"I don't know."

"All right," said Eddie, "all right now. If this invasion of the space creatures is due, when is it? And *don't* tell me you don't know or I'm going to remember those little girls and I'm going to bust you one!"

"But I *do* know."

"You *know?*"

"Yeah."

"When?"

"Within this hour."

"*Holy shit!*" said Eddie in feigned horror. He laughed. Mike laughed. Then they stopped.

Eddie bent his huge bulk near Sanderson.

"How do you *know* this, Sanderson?"

"I don't know. I trust the Source."

"Hey," said Mike, "now we're back on the 'I don't know' merry-go-round again."

"I think this fucker has seen too many science-fiction movies," Eddie said. "He's a *Star Wars, Star Trek, E.T.* freak, that's all."

"Yeah," said Mike, "and a *Short Eyes* on top of it all."

"Listen, man," he continued, poking his finger hard, in the middle of Sanderson's chest, "what makes a man molest little girls, anyhow? Tell me, what makes you do that?"

"That wasn't me," Sanderson answered.

Mike drew his right hand back and backhanded Sanderson across the face with great force. Sanderson's cigarette flew out of his mouth as his head rocked with the blow.

"And *that* wasn't me," said Mike.

Eddie offered Sanderson another cigarette. Then he turned to Mike.

"Listen, Mike, this isn't a top-priority thing, but I don't think we're handling this quite in a professional manner. It's all on tape, you know."

"You mean like the Nixon tapes?"

"Not *quite*. We probably won't lose *our* jobs. But let's try to be a bit more professional about what we're doing."

"O.K. It's just that I hate those fuckers."

"O.K., O.K. Just take it easy."

Eddie tried to run south along the cement. Then he was back in front of Sanderson.

"All right, let's *say* you're a space creature. In that case, why would you try to warn the world against an impending invasion?"

"First of all, I trust the Source. I feel I'm doing what I have to do."

"Talk sense."

"All right, perhaps I somehow got cut out of contact, rather like a short circuit of some sort, and although I have some of the knowledge of the space creatures, I am also, at the same time, grounded in human relationships and therefore sympathetic."

"Now we're *really* getting somewhere . . ."

The tape machine clicked.

Mike reached over, shut the machine off, put in a new tape, then started it again.

Eddie cleared his throat. "As I was saying, now we're *really* getting somewhere. So, now, *if* all this is true, don't you think your fellow space creatures are rather pissed at you for divulging all this?"

"Well, there's the Source. And then *they* realize that I'm short-circuited and that the fault isn't mine. Error still exists, even in *their* world."

Eddie rubbed his fingers over the huge soiled expanse of his dirty shirt.

"Well, Sanderson, the interrogation is over. I'm recommending you for a psychiatric examination."

Eddie nodded toward Mike. Mike shut off the tape machine, leaned over the table, and pressed a button.

The door opened and a guard entered.

"Take this man back to his cell, O'Conner," said Eddie.

O'Conner was damned near as fat as Eddie. He had a young daughter who was studying ballet and who also sculpted very well. O'Conner pulled his gun from the holster, clicked off the safety catch, pulled the trigger, and fired a bullet between Eddie's eyes. Eddie stood a moment, then fell straight forward. The next two bullets shattered Mike's skull.

Sanderson stood up.

"O'Conner, why do we have to kill some of them? Why can't we just take over their bodies?"

"I don't know," O'Conner answered. "The Source knows."

O'Conner walked out of the room and down the corridor and Sanderson followed him."

"Snyxikolivsks," said O'Conner.

"Previxcloslovckkkov," Sanderson answered.

At that moment the president of the UNITED STATES OF AMERICA bent over to pet his dog. The dog's name was Clyde. Clyde was an old mongrel but he was clever: he could fetch the *New York Times* or piss upon the imposing leg of an imposing congressman within 15 seconds of a given signal. He was a great old dog. He was allowed in the Oval Office. Clyde and the president were in there alone together with Security just beyond.

The president bent over to pet Clyde. Clyde wagged his tail and waited. As the president bent close, Clyde leaped upward, snarling; he snapped at the jugular vein, missed, but ripped off the left ear instead. The president fell back upon the rug, holding the left side of his head with his hand.

It had stopped raining outside.

Clyde snarled again, leaped upon the president, found the jugular, ripped it, and the purple pump of stinking blood began. The president rose. Grasping his throat with one hand he staggered toward his desk and with his free hand slid open the secret panel, and as Clyde watched, sitting in a northeast corner of the Oval Room, the president pushed the button, the red button that released the warheads.

Why he did it, he didn't know. Perhaps the Source knew.

The president of the UNITED STATES OF AMERICA fell forward across his desk as all across the earth the creatures of space returned to space, and the spiders began to snare flies and suck their blood, and the cats began to catch birds, and the dogs began to chase cats, and the boa constrictors began to eat mice and rats, and the hawks dove for the hares—for a while, for a very short while.

JUST PASSING TIME

... When I got back to the bar there was almost a whole new gang there, except for Monk, who was sitting there with his sleeves rolled up, showing off his biceps. There was something wrong with those biceps, they didn't look healthy; they were big but they looked sick somehow.

I looked around. It was a fling, a sputtering, dismal fling for all of us on those bar stools. It was the best we could do. And it was a fine bar because it was the only bar for us. We just wouldn't look right anywhere else.

I sat down on my stool and ordered a whiskey with a beer chaser. That was the action, the meaning, the fruit on the tree, the flower on the stem. It was victory. And after one victory you needed another.

Well, I wasn't bored in that place, but I wasn't bored anywhere. And I wasn't lonely. I got depressed, suicidal, but that wasn't the same as being lonely. Being lonely meant you needed somebody. I didn't. All I needed was for them not to suffocate me. What was I doing with them in a bar? I was watching them. They were a bad movie but it was the only one playing and as an actor *my* bit part was shoddy stuff indeed.

Monk grinned down at me from his rolled-up sleeves.

"Hey, Hank, how about a drink?"

"Wait'll I get a haircut."

"Hey, I'm not gonna live that long!"

Some of the patrons laughed.

"Give him a drink," I said to Jim.

Then three or four others started hollering, "Hey, how about me?"

I looked at Jim: "Take care of them."

A cheer rattled the dirty walls.

It was a place to be. It wore you down so you could accept whatever there was to accept. It made you less, but who needed more? When you felt like you needed more, then that's where the trouble began: thinking of those things to do between shitting and dying.

I bought some more rounds. Time began to waver. Time began to wag-gle. Butterflies' wings.

Jim left, and the night bartender, Eddie, came on. A few women entered, old, insane, or both. Yet it changed the atmosphere. They *were* women. It made it more carnival. *Caimans*, gavials, chuckwallas, geckos, molochs, skinks, and tuataras now sat on the stools. We watched their heavily painted mouths as they stuck cigarettes into them or laughed or poured the drinks down. Their voices were way off the edge, as if their vocal cords had been burned out, and their frazzled hair came down and sometimes—oh, at such rare times, in a moment of neon haze—as they turned their head they al-most seemed young and beautiful again, and then we all felt better and laughed and said almost inventive things. The dream was just around the corner. And if not, it had been.

Some moments were sometimes like that. And we all felt good, you could feel it reaching all around: we were there, finally, everybody was beautiful and grand and entertaining, and each moment glowed, bright and unwasted. You could really feel it.

Then—it stopped. Just like that.

We seemed to feel it all altogether. All conversation ended. Like that. At once. We felt each other sitting there, uselessly. Quiet. Nothing wrong with quiet. But not that kind. It was is if we had been cheated. Out of energy. Out of luck. Stuck there—bare.

It lasted some time. It lasted too long. It was embarrassing.

"Well, shit," somebody finally said, "who's going to brown this turd?"

Which always started the motion and the action over again. New ciga-rettes lit. Lipsticks applied. Trips to the pisser. Old jokes with new endings. Lies. Minor threats. The flies awakening and spinning through the blue gray air.

I don't know how it came about, but it appeared to me that Monk just kept on staring at me, looking down at me, and it got to me. I figured he should have something better to do. I think he was only trying to be friendly and funny but he really didn't know how to do either, and although I knew it wasn't his fault, I still reacted out of some stupid peevish ignorance that just jumped up and took me over:

"Monk, you're wearing thin. Why don't you turn those mucous blandishments you call eyes upon somebody else?"

"Well, kiss my ass!" he said. "Look whose leanin' out of his loony bin!"

"You're nothing but a big batch of subnormal flub."

"What's that?"

"I'm saying that all your muscle is fake. It's like you took an air hose and blew yourself up. There's no reality of texture. In your head or in your body."

Monk got off his stool, puffed himself up.

"You wanna care to back up your mouth?"

"I don't want to hurt you, Monk."

The whole bar laughed. I think even some of the flies laughed.

That was it. Monk walked toward the rear entrance. I followed him. And the bar followed us out to the alley.

It was a beautiful night. Other places, people were fucking or eating or bathing or sleeping or reading newspapers or screaming at their children or doing other sensible things.

Monk and I squared off in the moonlight, and then I got the thought, *I'd rather be watching a couple of guys do this than being one of those in the do.*

But I didn't feel any fear, I was too drunk for that. All I felt was a general sense of weariness, like here we go again and what does it mean? Something to do, I suppose, like spreading peanut butter on a sandwich.

Monk and I began circling. Now and then he flapped his arms and hit his sides with his open palms. Very effective. The bar folk stood about holding their drinks. I walked up to one guy, grabbed his beer bottle, and drained it. Then I held onto the bottle. Monk and I circled. I swung back to the end of the building, knocked the bottle against the bricks. The bottle broke but it didn't break right. I was left just holding this tiny bottle neck and I had cut my hand. I threw the nub away and Monk charged in. My hand was bleeding badly. I thought, *Maybe if I can get some blood in his eyes I might blind him.*

I sidestepped as he cruised by, tried to kick him in the ass, and missed. He turned and faced me again.

"I don't want to hurt you, Hank, but I'm going to have to!"

I think he meant it. This time when Monk charged I couldn't seem to move. I don't know why. My feet just stayed there. There was a flash of darkness, a feeling of gravel and rocks biting into my body. I felt a searing in one of my ears and almost a feeling, in spite of all that, of peace. Peace in our time. All troops kiss. I was down in the alley, my palms skinned, and there on my belly I saw Monk rolling over and over and he finally crashed into a row of tall garbage cans.

We both got up.

I was a coward and I wasn't a coward. That was my problem: I couldn't make up my mind. Monk didn't have to bother with analysis; he just came charging in again.

I stopped him with a straight left jab. A spear in the nose. He blinked and swung.

Monk threw sidewinders. I could see them coming. I blocked some, ducked under others. Jabbed him. Caught him with a right to the ear. Box the fucker. Make him look bad. He was full of eggs and doughnuts. Probably loved his mother and his country. No backbone.

I moved in and caught him with a combo. Then I stepped back.

"Had enough, fart bag?"

Monk puffed himself up.

"I'm gonna kill you!"

He charged again. He came like something on rails. All he knew was a straight line. I moved to the left and cracked him with a right as he went by. He was so easy that it was shameful. And he didn't take a good shot. He shook his head, appeared to be dizzy. As he turned I threw a left hook. I caught him on the elbow and really hurt my hand. Then he caught me with a right. The moon had been behind him and it came out of there like a rocket. My head sang and I tasted blood in my mouth. Red, white, and blue sparks whirled before my eyes. I heard Monk charging in again. I ducked behind a guy in the crowd, shoved him out at Monk. As Monk shoved the guy off, I moved in and give him a rabbit punch and a kidney shot.

"Shit," Monk said.

He was slowed again. I slammed a right, hard into his gut. He bent over, and as he did, I locked both of my hands together, raised them over my head and brought them down against the back of his neck.

Monk dropped. It was a splendid sight. He needed that. Flashing his biceps day and night. Sitting on his stool like he did, killing the dead air. Some dull stack. A zero with hairs in his nostrils. The fucking barber hadn't snipped them out.

"Jesus, Hank, I didn't think you could take him," said some guy in the crowd.

I looked over. It was Red-Eye Williams.

"You got bad judgment, Red-Eye, just pay off your bet."

"At three to one, that hurts. I don't understand. You lost your last two."

"That's because I was betting on the other guys."

The crowd laughed.

Monk was up on his knees, shaking his head.

I walked over.

"Hey, look! Now he wants to give me a blow job!"

Monk shook his head again, looked up at me.

"What do you charge for head, Monk? Five bucks?"

Monk grabbed one of my legs, lifted. I fell back on my ass. He leaped at me and I caught him with a foot in the face as he came in. He caved down again, shaking his head some more. I could have landed on his back with both my feet but I really didn't hate him. He just disgusted me.

"Come on, I'll buy you a drink. There isn't a man in the world who wins them all."

I reached my hand down to help him up. He grabbed it and pulled me down. Then we were wrestling, rolling over and over. Next think I knew he had me in a neck-lock. He had me good. What a hell of a thing. What a dirty, dirty trick. Men didn't fight that way. I couldn't breathe. I couldn't speak. I reached to grab his balls. There was nothing there! I grabbed and grabbed. Nothing at all! *I was fighting a goddamned eunuch!*

I couldn't break the neck-lock. I was getting weaker and weaker. I couldn't breathe, I couldn't move. It was ugly, indecent, unfair. I was going to die.

Why doesn't somebody stop this? I thought.

Why didn't I drink alone in my room tonight, the way I had thought of doing?

Then my thinking processes stopped.

■

When I came around I was in the alley, alone. They had left me there. It was still dark. I could hear music from the jukebox bar.

They had left me there, they had left me there.

That one cut sharp. I mean, I didn't expect much from them. But not this. I mean, I was surprised. They had left me like a hunk of meat. No concern. No ambulance. No word. No sound. It wasn't even a good joke.

All those free drinks I had poured down them. What did it mean? They just took me as the ultimate fool.

I still couldn't believe it. At any moment I expected them to come rushing out with drinks and laughter and wet, soothing towels.

It was difficult to consume their indifference. I had scored them low, but never that low.

All I was to them was a freak, a sacrificial freak.

I thought they understood that I was just joking. That I was passing time in a world that never became what it should have been.

They didn't even hate me. They didn't even think of me.

Then I heard a woman laughing in the bar. It was a long high laugh but it wasn't a good laugh; it was fake and forced, quite unpleasant, like the stage laugh of a bad actress in a bad play before an audience with sheared-off sensibilities. Holy shit, where was I? I was a pygmy in a land of dwarfs.

I'd get up and tell them. I'd get up and walk in there and tell them what they were.

I tried to raise up. As I did, my head began to roar and throb, a pain shot from the center of my skull and ran down my backbone. It was like a line of fire, I could feel my eyeballs rolling back into my skull, and that was it . . .

When I regained consciousness the sun was up and I was next to a bright new garbage can, and the light from the sun reflected off it and upon me and it was hot, and when I looked at the can I saw the lines along the sides and it was dumb and unreal but true.

For it all, I only had a slight headache. If I hadn't been drunk the whole thing would have killed me. Like everything else. The worst thing was my left hand. It was puffed up almost double size.

I pulled myself up by the garbage can, stood there.

I knew the next move and I feared it.

It had happened so many times before while drinking. After nights with the ladies of the streets. After any number of nights, any number of times, without any ladies of the streets at all.

I stood a while before trying it.

Please, just this *once*, let it be there. I mean, I'm tired, and as you can see, not in very good shape. All I want, you know, is five or six dollars; to me that's like ten thousand dollars to anybody else. Let the wallet be there. It's always so warm, so personal, it shapes and fondles the right rear buttock, it gives slight hope in the bad dream. I don't ask much, just a little.

I reached.

The wallet was gone.

And that wasn't a surprise. The surprise would have been the other. The miracle. The love for humanity.

Then, anyhow, I looked in my other pockets, in my shirt, everywhere, knowing as I did so that I was just going through dumb rote maneuvers to forestall the obvious.

I had been rolled again.

The good guy rolled. Decency pissed upon once more. Oh boy.

Sometimes, knowing the sharks were there, I often hid my wallet.

I lifted the lid of the garbage can and looked in. It was full and it stank. A waft of stench rose upward and I couldn't handle it. I was very sensitive to smell. I just vomited right into the garbage can. Then I straightened up.

I was a clever fellow. I often hid my wallet very well. Once I had hidden one behind the mirror upon the inside of a bathroom door. I had unscrewed the whole mirror while drunk, put the wallet behind there and screwed the mirror back on—to make sure that the lady of the street waiting upon my bed wouldn't get it. Two weeks later I had found it sitting upon the crapper and noting a slight bulge in the mirror.

I began pulling all the garbage out of the can, stopping once to vomit again. I pulled everything out: coffee grounds, grapefruit rinds, and the various and sundry, including something that looked like a human head. I spread it all around.

No wallet.

"Hey, poor white trash, yo *that* hungry, I'll give yo' something to chew on!"

"No, no, ma'am, I'm all right."

"Yeah? Yo all right? Well, if yo is all right then yo pick up that there shit and put it back where yo found it, hear?"

"O.K."

I began picking up the garbage and putting it back into the can. Some of the papers sacks broke through the bottoms and I had to pick the stuff up with my hands and scoop it into the can. I puked once more, mildly.

I put the lid back on and then bowed to the lady who was standing behind her screen door watching me.

"O.K.," she said, "now yo get the fuck out of here, yo hear?"

Then, remembering my cleverness, I lifted the can and looked underneath. No wallet.

"Now what the fuck yo doin'?"

"Nothing, ma'am."

I walked down through the alley and out into the street. It must have still been around seven or eight in the morning, cars were rushing by both ways, driven by wafts of people who hated their jobs and feared losing them. I didn't have to worry about that. I walked toward the room; I still had my room, and there weren't any roaches because there were mice. I didn't like that but I accepted it. It was better than there weren't any mice because there were rats.

I never slept well in flophouses and missions.

I moved toward my room, feeling almost victorious.

DISTRACTIONS IN

THE LITERARY LIFE

It's a hot summer night, a very hot summer night, and I'm sitting in the kitchen, typer on the breakfast-nook table, only there's no breakfast-nook and we are always too sick to eat breakfast. Anyhow, I am trying to type up some kind of story, well, not some type, rather a dirty story for one of the mags (Jesus, writing's hard: wasn't there an easier way to say that?). Meanwhile, one of the table legs keeps slipping out from under and I have to stop typing as the whole table begins to tilt and it's a matter of trying to grab the typer, the bottle, *and* the table leg, trying to hold my whole world together like that: some drunk has kicked the table leg out one night and I try glue, hammer, nails, all that, but the wood is split and won't hold, but, anyhow, I try to push the table leg under there again. It holds a little while like that and I take a drink, light my cigar stub, begin typing, hoping to get in a short paragraph before the table begins to tilt again.

The phone rings in the other room and I put the typer and bottle on the floor and get up to answer, and as I walk into the other room Sandra has the phone. Sandra of the long red hair that looks good from a distance but when you get close and touch it, it's like her, unaccountably hard, unlike her big ass and breasts. I can put her big ass and breasts in a story but they'll never believe them, those black Jewish fag editors have trouble believing. Once I sent in this story telling about how I fuck these three different women in one day, I really don't want to but circumstance forces me, and this editor sends back this raging letter: "Chinaski, this is *sick*! *Nobody* gets this type of action! *Especially* an old *bum*, an old *fuck* like *you*! Get back to *reality*! Blah, blah, blah . . ." he goes on and on . . .

Anyway, Sandra hands me the phone; she's drinking sake (cold) and smoking one of my cigars. She puts down the cigar. As I say "Hello?" she unzips me and begins sucking on my string.

"Listen," I say, "will you leave me the fuck alone?"

"What?" asks the guy on the phone.

"Not you," I say.

I am in my undershirt and I take it and stretch it over Sandra's head so I can talk less hindered.

It's my dealer who lives in one of the courts up front, a much larger and nicer court than mine, and he tells me he just got in some coke. I sit in his place sometimes as he redilutes the stuff and measures it out in these little Ziploc bags on his little scale while his beautiful class-broad struts about on her immense heels. I never see her in the same dress or the same pair of shoes. We fuck once with the dealer watching. He uses the good stuff, nothing bothers him. Or maybe he likes to watch.

I still hold the phone.

"How much?" I ask.

"Well, for you, since we're friends, one hundred bucks."

"You know I'm broke."

"I thought you said you were the world's greatest writer."

"It's just that the editors don't know it."

"All right," he says, "for you: fifty bucks."

"What do you cut the stuff with?" I ask.

"Secrets of the trade—"

"Come on, tell me," I insist.

"Dried come—"

"Whose? Yours?"

"I'll be down in thirty minutes," he hangs up.

Sandra has finished me off. She pulls her head out from under my undershirt. She puts the cigar back into her mouth, puts a lighter to it, sucks it back to life. I zip up, walk back to the kitchen, check the table leg, put the bottle and typer back on the table, begin to type some more. Updike never had to write under such conditions. Or Cheever either. I get them mixed up. But I know that one is dead and the other can't write. Writers. Shit. Met Ginsberg once after a mass reading of him, his buddies, and me. What a groaning, moaning night that was in that soft turd city of Santa Cruz. At the party afterward he and his buddies just lean against a wall and try to look learned as I do a drunken dance. "I don't know how to talk to Chinaski," Ginsberg tells one of his buddies.

Just as well.

I type away . . . In my story I have this guy trying to fuck a baby elephant up the trunk—he's a zoo keeper and he's tired of his wife . . . The keeper has stuck his string into the elephant's trunk and is working it around when suddenly the elephant snuffles the zookeeper's balls in there too, just sucks them in, and it feels all right, really does, *too* great—the guy climaxes and makes ready to withdraw but the elephant holds, won't let go. No, no, no, some living hell. It's a joke. *Leggo!!* The guy takes both thumbs and sticks them into the elephant's eyes. No good. The elephant only sucks harder. Holy Mary. The keeper tries everything. Relaxing. Pretending to be asleep. Talking: "Just let go. I promise never, never to fuck another animal." Now it's 3 A.M. and the elephant has gripped him for an hour and a half . . . Never trouble like that with his wife, she had no grip at all . . . The elephant only holds him. Then the keeper gets brilliant, takes out his cigarette lighter, flicks it to flame, places it under the trunk. The grip begins to loosen, then the lighter goes out. The keeper flicks the lighter again. No good. He flicks it and flicks it. Out of fluid. Out of luck. Fifteen years' seniority and they'll find them like that in the morning and he'll lose his job, or worse . . .

"Hey, Jack Off!" Sandra hollers from the other room, "you writin' some good shit?"

"Yeah, but I don't know how to end it."

"Have them drop the fucking bomb."

"Hey, *great*! I'll do it! Nobody, *nobody* has written a story like this!"

Just then the table leg gives way and I only have time to grab the bottle as the typer crashes to the floor. Never happened to Mailer or Tolstoy. I take a slug from the bottle, then go over to the old typer. Don't die on me, m.f., in any way at all . . . It *has* landed upright. I sit down on my ass, reach out, and tap at the keys. I type: DON'T DIE ON MY INFINITY. It types me right back, like that. It's tough, like me. I take a drink of joyful celebration for the both of us. Then I get bright: I decide to type on the m.f. floor, I will finish typing the m.f. story on the m.f. floor. Céline would dig that.

■

Just then an outrageous screaming from the sky plus exploding sounds and also a sense of undeclared war as shards of fulsome, flailing, furious, fucking glass rip into walls and windows, sundry things. No chance in Dixie. No chance anywhere. Bing Crosby shakes and rattles in his grave. It's war. It's war in East Hollywood, just off of Hollywood and Western boulevards, near those all-night take-out stands, near me, near us, they've been trying to clean up the district for years but it just gets worse.

(Forgive me, but let me tell you about the best time I can think of, I mean when the candle was burning tall and life was, finally, good: this pimp rented out a whole block, southside on Hollywood Boulevard. Well, it wasn't an *entire* block, but it was most of the block between the outlet store and the killer nudey bar, and he had the girls sitting in the windows in homelike circumstances: chair, tv, rug, sometimes a cat or dog, drapes, and the girls just used to sit there in the windows, almost glasslike, waxlike, and if not always beautiful, I thought very brave or at least slightly gallant, all this so that the patrons could make a leisurely and proper choice . . . Here was the pimp with the ultimate style, but evidently he couldn't make the ultimate payoff: one night after 18 nights they were there, the next night they were gone.)

But, meanwhile, I step out on the porch with Sandra behind me, resting her udders upon my back. The explosions abound as zips, flicks, daggers of glass shoot and fly about. I slip into my shades to protect my eyes. So, over on Western is the large old hotel, it's 8 or 10 stories high, filled with druggies, prosties, pimps, criminals, madmen, madwomen, imbeciles, and saints.

There is this naked black guy up on the roof of the hotel and we can see that he's naked and black because the police helicopter which is always buzzing Hollywood and Western is shining their lights upon him. We can see him. Nicely. But the copters don't send in the squad cars. No need for that. Not as long as we are destroying each other. We are nothing to protect. We don't matter, because between the 3,000 of us estimated to be bunched up in that area, we can't show a total, say, of two grand on hand between all of us at that moment. And we have no home to leave and an American Express Card without. So, as far as the law is concerned, we can murder each other until our blood runs, hell no, *walks, seeps,* like a thick, dumb, stinking red malt in the streets . . .

We look up as the naked black hurls more empty wine bottles. Under the helicopter's blaring lights he is shining like a hot piece of coal. He looks good, mean, what a hell of a stage. We all need release and we so seldom get it. We fuck and drink and smoke and poke and snort, and it all flattens. He is getting his. Now.

He screams: "*Death to Whitey! A black death to Whitey! Fuck you, Whitey! All your mothers are whores! All you brothers are fags! All your sisters fuck dogs and suck black dick! Death to Whitey! God is black and I am God!*"

We hate each other so much, it does give us something to do.

Now his bottles roar down again, most break against the walls, the tops of the courts, but some bounce like crazy things, don't break, or only partially break and then crash through some of our windows, and that's a bit sad because we are poor; it might be better if we could throw those bottles all the way through some of those windows in Beverly Hills.

Then I see Big Sam step out of his rear court. He's on ATD and he walks out into the courtyard and stands in the middle of the flying and breaking bottles and he looks up at the naked black. Big Sam is carrying a shotgun. Then he sees me. Somehow he thinks I am the only friend he has. He might be right. I never saw him as crazy.

He walks over to me.

"Hank, I think I should shoot him. What do you think?"

"The best rule in any given situation is to do what you want to do."

I can't see a shotgun doing much at that distance. Sam reads me.

"I got a rifle too—"

"I wouldn't shoot him, Sam."

"Why not?"

"Hell, I don't know."

"You let me know when you know."

He puts the gun to his shoulder and marches back into his court.

The wine bottles keep coming but somehow it's just not as interesting anymore. Some of the people go back into their courts. The lights come on, gradually. Finally, even the helicopter flies off. There are a few more crashes of bottles, then it's quiet.

Inside, I switch from wine to whiskey. It's hard typing there while on my ass on the floor, but I don't worry now about the table leg, and the whiskey puts tiny little roars into the sentences and I am into it and about to drop the bomb when there's a knock on the door. It's got to be the dealer, and when I walk out Sandra has him in the doorway, she has her hand around his balls, and he smiles at me and says, "Sandra always makes me feel welcome."

"Well, hell, we don't have a 'Welcome' doormat so we do the best we can around here."

Sandra unleashes the dealer and he says, "I got a couple of lines here." And I bring out the glass and the razor and we sit down and he sets it up, and then we have three lines and Sandra takes hers and the dealer takes his, then I suck mine in and wait. I know that if he has cut it with too much speed I will react accordingly. On speed I get vicious. Not toward people except vocally. But I break things: mirrors, chairs, lamps, toilets; I take rugs, turn them over. Not much else. I never break dishes.

I wait. It's all right, he hasn't cut it with too much speed.

"Where's Deeva?" I ask. Deeva is his old lady. The one of the many dresses and shoes.

"She's doing the dishes," says the dealer.

She was some rare woman. She wore dresses and high heels *and* did the dishes.

I hand him two twenties and a ten, and he hands me the Ziploc.

"I still get a better high on booze," I tell him. "With this stuff there's no arrival point; it drops away and you have to boost yourself again."

"When you get the real shit," he says, "you'll stop drinking."

"Like seeing Christ, eh? Bring it around sometime."

"Better than Christ. No thorns, no hell. Just a gentle nothingness."

He walks to the door, his tiny little ass too tight in his pants. At the door he turns, grins.

"What was all that noise down here a while back?"

"Some black. Mad at his skin. And mine."

The dealer leaves.

Sandra is working on a couple of lines. If she's like me: chopping it seems more pleasurable than snorting it. I knew in the morning I'd have a suicide head. That the walls would be dark blue and that every meaning would be meaningless. It's like subtract from subtract. Cats with faces like dogs. Onions with spider legs. An American victory like a curtain of vomit. A bathroom with one tit, one ball. A toilet bowl that looks at you with the true blank face of a true dead mother.

But you only work on the morning when you get there.

I shout at Sandra: *I'll* set up the next lines! You fucked me over last trip, *yours* was double thick!!"

We are at the same old thing: arguing about lines.

Then, something else begins—there is this terrible deathly scream of a woman in fear of her life, and another woman screaming also:

"You whore, you whore, I'll kill you, you whore!"

We walk outside again. It is from the same hotel. One woman hangs out of a ninth-floor window verily by an arm and a leg, most of her body dangling as if to drop. The other woman is leaning out over her from above and beating at her with some object. It goes on and on, the sound of it is more painful to one than any imagined ugliness one might ever conceive of being in.

The helicopter is back. It flashes and fondles its light upon the agony of these bodies. The helicopter floats and circles, beaming its great light upon the ladies. Who continue as per se.

Sam marches out again with shotgun, looks at me.

I say, "Sam, go ahead, shoot those whores, they make too much noise!"

Sam lifts the gun, aims, fires. He blows away somebody's TV antenna. It falls in a whirl of arm and wire, that ever-fruitless tree diving into its deserved darkness.

Sam lowers his gun, walks back inside his court.

Sandra and I enter ours. I walk into the kitchen, look at the typer down there on the floor. It's a dirty floor. It's a dirty typer that types dirty stories.

Outside, the screaming continues, unresolved.

I remember the whiskey, pour myself one. Have it.

This is why I became a writer. This is why I fought my way out of the factories. This is the meaning and the way.

I walk back into the other room.

"I don't think I'll finish that story tonight," I say to Sandra.

"Who gives a fuck?" she asks.

"You have the soul of a centipede," I say.

There's nothing else as pleasant as being unpleasant when there's nothing else to do, and there's usually nothing else to do, and I take Sandra's wrist, twist it, take the razor, and say, "I told you I was going to set up the next lines."

I lean forward and, with some dexterity, do that.

I MEET THE MASTER

When I was a very young man I was a starving writer. The fact that I was starving to death didn't bother me very much for life wasn't very interesting to me, and dying didn't seem to be too bad a prospect—perhaps a new shuffle of the deck? I worked, at times, as a common laborer, but not for long. A paycheck or two and then as much time off as possible. All I needed was the rent and money for something to drink, and the stamps and the envelopes and the typing paper. I wrote from two to six short stories a week and they all came back from the *Atlantic Monthly, Harper's,* and the *New Yorker.* It was difficult for me to understand because the stories I read in those magazines were carefully-written, *crafted* might be the word. But essentially the stories were bloodless and boring, and worst of all: humorless. It were as if everything were a lie and the more craftily you lied the more you were accepted.

I wrote and drank at night. During the day I hung around the L.A. Public Library and read all the writers and it was *hard* reading; the writers used long paragraphs and pages of description, building the plot and developing character, but their characters were quite uninteresting and what the stories finally said wasn't very much. Little was said of the wasted lives of almost all the people, the sadness, all the sadness, the madness, the laughter through pain. Most of the writers wrote about the experiences of upper middle-class life. I needed to read something that would get me through the day, across the street, something to hang to. I needed to get drunk on words, instead I had to go to the bottle. I felt, I suppose, as every failed writer does, that I really could write and that the situations and the ins and the politics were against me. Sometimes they are; other times you just think you can write and you really can't.

I starved and wrote. I came down from 190 pounds to 137. My teeth loosened in my mouth. I could push my front teeth back and forth in my mouth with my fingers. They were loose in the gums. One night, playing around,

I felt something give and I had a tooth in my hand. There it was in my hand: right side upper. I placed it on the table and had a drink to it.

And, of course, when you're buying time on a part-time laborer's salary there are things you give up besides food. They are young women and the automobile. You walk, and you find yourself an occasional whore. Also, you wear your shoes so long that the soles become holes and you stuff them with cardboard; also, the nails finally come through so badly that it's impossible to walk in the shoes anymore. And there's hardly a Sunday suit and no free Thanksgiving or Christmas dinners. Starving writers live worse than skid row bums. And that's because there are two things they need: four walls, and to be alone.

. . . But one noon in the L.A. Public Library something happened. Talk about being well-read, I was stuffed, to the extreme: D. H. Lawrence, all the Russian writers, Huxley, Thurber, Chesterton, Dante, Shakespeare, Villon, all the Shaws, O'Neill, Blake, Dos Passos, Hem, why go on? Hundreds of known writers and hundreds of unknown . . . And they all hurt me because they were all good at times but only in shots and spurts, then they lapsed back into a heavy literary dullness. This was more than discouraging be-cause it meant that centuries, CENTURIES of literature and writers had failed me. At least, they had failed to give me what I needed in the written word.

But, as I was saying, this one noon I was killing my usual day pulling down books, flipping them open, reading a page or two, putting them back. Well, I pulled down another. *Sporting Times? Yeah?* By one John Bante. I opened to a page expecting the usual and the words, yes, they leaped at me, like that. They came right off the paper and drilled me. The words were sim-ple, concise, and they spoke of something happening right there! Even the type on the page seemed different. The words were readable. There were gaps of space and then words. The words were almost like a voice in the room. I took the book to a table and sat down. Each page had the power. I couldn't believe it. I felt as if the pages would leap from the book and just start walking around or flying around. They had a remarkable force, a total reality. Why had this man never been mentioned anywhere? I was also into reading critical literature, Winters, all those bastards, all the *Kenyon Review* and *Sewanee Review* darlings and they had *never* mentioned this man. Nor had he ever come up in my half-ass two-year sleep at L.A. City College.

I looked up from my table. Well, it wasn't mine, it belonged to the city, the tax payers, and I didn't pay very much tax. But I had the book by John Bante before me and I looked at the people at the other tables, at the people walking about or just sitting around, many of them bums like me and none of them knew about John Bante . . . or they would have started glowing, they would have started feeling better, they wouldn't have minded so much being whatever they were or had to be.

I had a library card and I got John Bante out of there. I took him back to my room and started at the first page. He was even funny at times but it was a strange, calm type of humor, like a man being burned to death yet winking at the man who had first lit the fire or At The Man Up There. Bante had a religious bent even if it rang with a strange smile. I didn't have that, but coming from him I liked it. And he was writing about a starving writer who hung around the L.A. Public Library and the Grand Central Market, which is what I did. Holy Christ. But it wasn't the similarity of lives so much as the easy way he expressed the dumb occurrences of living. I noted that he lived on oranges from the Grand Central. My diet differed: potatoes, cucumbers, and tomatoes. When I could afford them. Potatoes first. Inch for inch I found the potato cheaper and more filling. But Bante had come from Colorado. Being Californian, I had seen oranges forever almost like fleas upon a cat's fur. That's bad writing. Bante never wrote badly: each word was where it belonged and each word spoke perfectly.

He had been discovered by the great editor, L. H. Renkin, who ran the magazine the *American Calamity*. Renkin also edited for one of the New York publishing houses and wasn't a bad writer himself. I was to go back to the library and get all of John Bante's books. There were 3 others but I still liked *Sporting Times? Yeah?* best.

I had memorized all the descriptions of the neighborhood in *Sporting*

Times. I lived in a screen shack behind a roominghouse for $2 a week. The neighborhood was called Bunker Hill. And I set out to see where Bante had lived. I walked down *Angel's Flight* and found the exact hotel he had described and I stood there outside of the hotel looking in. I felt one of the strongest feelings of my life run through me. I was, yes, transfixed. It *was* the hotel. That was the window his strange girlfriend, Carmen, had crawled through. Strange and tragic Carmen.

I stood there and looked at the window. It was early afternoon and dark in the room. The shade was halfway down and there was a slight breeze and the shade moved just a little. That's where Bante had written *Sporting Times.* It had all come out of that room, a room I had passed for months on my way to the Grand Central Market or my favorite green bar, or just to go downtown to walk around. I stood there wondering who was in that room then. Maybe Bante was still in there! Maybe I should go around and knock on the door?

Hello, Mr. Bante? I write too. Not nearly as well as you do. I just want to say how much your words jump around inside me and that I was lucky enough to read you. Now, I'm going. Goodbye . . .

But I knew that I could never disturb a god. Gods had things to do. Even when they slept they slept in a different way. Besides I knew that Bante wasn't in there. In his last book of short stories he had mentioned in one of the stories that he was in a room in Hollywood, that rent was $7 a week and the landlady was getting ready to kick him out and he was praying to Holy Mary.

I was not a hero-worshipper. Bante was my first. It was the words, the simple clarity of them. They made me want to weep yet they made me feel like walking through walls.

I decided I wanted to see the room anyhow, the room where it had been done. I grabbed the railing to the walkway, kicked my legs over the side and dropped down to the walkway next to the hotel. I walked around to the front of the hotel and entered. There was the lobby just as he had described it. And there was the little table in the center where he had placed several copies of the *American Calamity* with his first published short story in it,

The Little Dog Laughed Hard And True. I walked down the hallway, took a left, and stood next to the room that had the window looking out over *Angel's Flight*.

Room #3. I raised my hand to knock, paused, then did it. Three short gentle knocks. I waited. Nothing. I knocked again, louder, three loud knocks, but, still knocks of reverence. I heard some sound within the room. Then the door opened. There was a blast of heat—it was Dante's *Inferno*. It was a warm June afternoon but there was a gas furnace blasting full-on. An old woman stood there wrapped in a blanket. She was quite small and almost bald but she had several long white hairs still growing out of her head and the hairs were long, quite, and came down over her ears and around her chin.

"Yes," she said.

"Pardon me, but I'm looking for a friend of mine who used to live here, one John Bante . . . ?"

"No," said the old woman.

She had unbelievably beautiful eyes, as if all that had remained of her had gone to the eyes and just waited there for the end.

"He was a writer . . ."

The old woman just looked at me. We stood there like that, for a moment.

Then she said, "Shit on you!" and slammed the door . . .

■

I continued my starving writer ways for some years. My typewriter was in and out of hock, and finally I got so fucked up that I couldn't get it out. I sold my pawn ticket for money for drink on one night in a bar and after that I handprinted my stories, often with illustrations. I bummed around the country and went on with my hand-printed stories. Finally, one of the most prestigious literary magazines of that moment accepted and published my first story. The pay was lousy but I got letters from other magazines, including *Esquire*, which said they'd like to see my work. And letters from people who said they'd like to be my agent, if I didn't have one. Hell, I didn't have an agent *or* a typewriter. Something about crashing through like that finally deflated me instead of boosting me. I decided that I could write well enough but that I had nothing to write about. I stopped writing for ten years and concentrated solely upon drinking. I ended up in the charity ward of the L.A. County Hospital with some priest leaning over me trying to give me Last Rites. I ran him out of there and got a job driving a delivery truck for a light fixture house. I got lucky, found a nice court on Kingsley Drive, got a type-writer, and I came home each night, but instead of dinner I had two or more six-packs of beer each night and found myself writing something very strange: poetry.

To keep it concise: a marriage came and went. I had hundreds of little magazines with my poetry within but so did everybody else, like wiping their asses or replacing a washer in a leaking faucet. The wars and the years went on, and the insane girlfriends and the insane, useless jobs. How does one recount 2 or 3 decades of waste? In a tick. It's easy. The years are meant to be wasted.

Because of my boozing mad ways I rather became the town freak. A pro-fessor invited me over to his place and after a nice dinner with wine followed by more wine the discussion got around to art and poetry which are two things I generally dislike and got up and smashed his China closet and, somehow, this was credited to me as an act of genius. This stupidity got me a job writing a column for an underground newspaper. And it was as if I had forgotten John Bante. But I really hadn't. I had misplaced him.

Right here, skip some wasted years . . . I got into a night job at the post office, clerk, and after eleven and one-half years the job, as jobs will do, was killing me. I became one nerve. My body was taut, a freeze of agony. I couldn't turn my neck. If somebody bumped into me, shots of pain would roar through my body. I had dizzy spells where I would bite my tongue to keep from passing out. None of the other clerks were aware of this. I was the glad fellow, the clown, I jive-assed with the most vicious jive-asses night after night and I generally held vocal sway, but it was a useless act, a shield: I was dying.

This night I was driving home after the usual three and one-half hours overtime. I had run a series of traffic tickets and had gotten a warning from the DMV that they were considering suspending my license. The cops had me spooked. Then I had to make a left turn. I had no blinkers in my old car. I moved my left arm, with some difficulty, toward the window in order to signal a left turn. The pain jumped through me as if it had been turned loose from spigots. And I found that as far as I could move my arm was to place just a portion of my hand out of the left window. Just the hand, not an arm at all. And I watched myself doing this as if I were two people — one watching the other. I lifted one finger of that hand out into the night, one tiny useless finger, and with the other hand I turned the wheel to make the left turn. And then I began laughing; it was all so stupid, I was letting them murder me. But the laughter was good, though, a total release. And then as I drove along I knew I had to get out. I knew that any skid-row bum sleeping in an alley had a better life than mine, that I was one of the biggest fools ever placed upon the earth. It was a night to remember. And even though this is the story of John Bante, I don't think there's any way to tell it without working some of this in. Now, add a couple of days or weeks and some curious luck arrived: a strange balding man, one J. K. Larkin, who was later to become my editor-publisher, offered me a sum of money each year for *life* no matter if I ever wrote anything else if I would just quit the post office. I accepted and got the fuck out of there . . . It had been such a long time since I had knocked on Bante's door and the old woman in the blanket had told me where to take it . . .

∎

I had the window facing the street and I wrote my first novel in 19 days. I was able to drink my ass off and not report to any job but my own. There I was, age 50, a professional writer, maybe. I gave poetry readings at various universities, I gave them drunk, and I jive-assed with the audience. My bullshit training with the bad-ass boys in the P.O. was paying off. I was almost impossible to insult and I counterpunched with immense efficiency. The Arts were a candy cream, no problem.

Throw out some more years. I got on. The women arrived; I jumped in and out of bed with them, fought with them. It was terrible and unusual for me and they were more clever than I; they knew how to work angles, trap me, corner me but I was still able to type. What fame I had was mostly in Europe through translation. In the U.S. stories went about that I beat my women, hated homosexuals, and was a vicious and terrible person. The university dandies had it in for me. A student came by one night and over some beers he told me, "My prof says you're a Nazi and you'd sell your own mother out for a nickel."

"That's not true," I told him. "My mother is dead."

Let all that be. I still kept typing and had some luck. Now, we're getting closer. My editor, Larkin, read an interview I gave somewhere where I mentioned my influences: Céline, Turgenev, and John Bante.

"Bante?" he phoned me, "I've heard you mention the name before in your writings but I thought you just made it up, you know, as a joke."

"No, he's there."

"Where?"

"He might still be in the library. I don't know. I hope so. There are just his early books. He seems to have stopped. Maybe he's dead."

"Is he that good?"

"He's the best."

"Why is he never mentioned?"

"You tell me. If you find his books begin with *Sporting Times?* Yeah?"

Some time went by. A woman attempted to murder me. She failed. So this night, the phone rang, she loved telephone dramatics, and I picked up the phone and said, "Look, I want you to stay the FUCK out of my life!"

"This is Larkin," I heard.

"Oh . . ."

"Listen, I read *Sporting Times*. It's really powerful! I'm going to republish it!"

"Great. Great . . ."

"The original book only sold 632 copies. Bante is still alive and living in Malibu . . ."

"Malibu? Oh, oh . . ."

"He went into the movie industry . . ."

"Damn it . . ."

"It was the depression; he had to survive. You know how it was. You have to forgive him."

"Sure. You can't write if you're dead."

"And most of us can't write the other way. Anyway, I'm going to re-run the book and I thought you might like to do a foreword."

"I'll have it in the mail tomorrow."

"Great!"

There it was: one of the greatest novels of our time to be pulled out of the nowhere darkness almost 40 years after I pulled it from that shelf on that very lucky day. I moved toward the typer to pronounce the miracle of the age, to want to feel good about goodness coming forth in spite of everything.

The phone rang again.

"Hello," I answered.

The voice came in an even monotone, each word measured without rise or drop. It was like a recording: there was no passion, just this certain finality: "I tried to kill you but I'm not certain that I won't try it again."

"But we agreed that if I didn't go to the police that you would stop that sort of thing."

"I can't be certain of anything," she said. "Don't you understand that?"

She hung up.

Sporting Times? Yeah?

I moved off from the typer, circled back toward the kitchen, and poured a tall one . . .

■

I wrote the foreword for *Sporting Times*. It rolled out easy. Then I read it. I realized that admitting John Bante had been such a great influence on my writing might detract from my own work, as if part of me were a carbon copy, but I didn't give a damn. It's when you hide things that you choke on them. I mailed the foreword off to Larkin who lived in Santa Barbara. Larkin was one of those who got into things. There he was on the phone.

"The foreword's fine. You know, I've been in touch with Mary Bante, John's wife. She says John wants to see you."

"Holy Christ!"

"There are complications. He has advanced diabetes. He's blind and an amputee; they've had to cut away a great portion of his legs."

"I didn't realize that happened with diabetes . . ."

It was all I could say. There was John Bante, probably the world's best writer, laying there chopped up and blind!

"It doesn't happen so much anymore. It got to him before these modern techniques set in."

"Son of a bitch . . ."

I then remembered the short story Bante had written where his father had the same thing, had ignored all medical advice, and drank himself to death.

"The doctors say he doesn't have long. Mary says he loved your foreword. He's starting a new novel . . ."

"Wait, how . . ."

"He dictates it to Mary . . ."

"Son of a bitch . . ."

"Anyhow, they want to see you. I have their phone number here. . ."

The term "see you" didn't quite fit. But I had the phone number. I gave them a call. Mary answered and told me what a lift having *Sporting Times* republished had given John.

"But he has to go back to the hospital. If you want to see him you'll have to see him there."

"Of course I want to see him. I wanted to see him 40 years ago."

We set up a date and time and I got the instructions on how to get there. I was one of those people without a sense of direction, I could get lost going to the supermarket. Luckily, I was living with a good woman, Alta.

I showed her the instructions. "Alta, baby, do you think you could help me find this place?"

"Sure."

"You don't mind going?"

"No, not at all. I'd like to meet John."

She had heard plenty about Bante during my drunks. About how the world was so stupid not to know his writings were there. How the world was so stupid to honor guys like Mailer and Capote and Bellow and Cheever and Updike when one simple paragraph by John Bante could say more with an astonishing simplicity.

The best did not *always* rise to the top either in writing, music, painting, acting, politics, or whatever the hell else. That wasn't anything new in the centuries of Humanity.

"Good," I said to Alta, "we'll go."

■

It was the Motion Picture Hospital, an odd name. When movies had begun they had thought of them as pictures in motion. The hospital was a place for actors, directors, writers, cameramen, anybody who had worked for the movies for any length of time. Hollywood, they used to call it, only Hollywood was no longer there. Hollywood was now skidrow.

Anyhow, I parked and Alta and I got out. The place was all one level and looked quite peaceful. Most of the rooms contained just one person. Which was great. I had done most of my hospital time in large dark rooms packed with beds, the whole thing looking more like a quick set-up in a church basement after an aerial bombardment.

We got directions to the room and found our way outside there when a woman stepped out. She was thin, graceful, sad.

"Chinaski?" she asked.

"Yes, Mary," I said. "This is Alta."

"He's sleeping," said Mary.

"Let's not wake him," Alta said.

We walked to the dining room or the commissary or whatever it was and had some coffee.

"The doctors give him 6 weeks at the most. He'd rather be home but they have to operate. They have to cut more away. The legs."

Jesus, I thought, how far can they cut? To gain him 6 weeks?

"I've read him some of your things and he likes them," Mary said.

"Thank you."

A patient came walking in; he whirled about talking to himself. He picked up an empty coffee cup and started talking into it.

"God wears green stockings," he said. "God has nine heads and no sexual organs. His favorite game is basketball . . ."

Then he put the coffee cup down and walked out.

"That's the former famous actor V.M . . . He's harmless."

V.M. ? That was V.M. ? The handsome slave boy who had shaken down the very temples upon the heathens after he had killed the lions?

"Maybe John's awake now," Mary suggested.

"We could come at another time," said Alta.

"Let's try," Mary said.

We walked back to the room. Mary sensed that he was awake.

"John, you have visitors . . ."

Here was this little guy under his sheet. There wasn't much left of the legs. They had left the arms, the hands. His hands looked very pale. But he had a great face, he had a little bulldog's face. There was much tenacity there. A kinder word is "courage."

I took his hand. "Hello, John, I'm Chinaski. And I'm with Alta."

Alta took his hand. "Hello, John, we're glad to see you. If there's anything we can possibly do, let us know."

Mary bunched the pillow under his head.

"Listen," he asked, "can anybody open a window just a bit? It's very hot in here."

Alta got up and opened a window a bit.

"I've been looking for you a long time, John, 40 years. I used to hang around Bunker Hill and starve just like you did."

"Your voice is soft," he said, "but I'll bet you can be real tough if you want to."

"You guessed it," said Alta.

I went on to tell Bante how I had located the hotel and had gone to his room and knocked on the door. I told him where I had leaped over the railing and what the hotel had looked like.

He smiled. "You had the wrong place."

"What?"

Bante gave a little laugh. "I lived in the hotel one notch up."

"Well, I've found you now . . ."

"Yes, you have . . ."

"You got away from me for a while . . ."

"Yes, my disastrous Hollywood career."

"I'm sure you wrote some good crap. A man's got to live . . ."

"Yeah," he smiled.

"Can we give you some water or anything?" Alta asked.

Alta had better common sense than I had.

"Yes, could somebody light my cigarette?"

Mary took a cigarette out of the pack and put it in John's hand. He lifted the smoke to his mouth and Mary struck a match to it.

John inhaled. "Thank you."

"How was all that Hollywood, John?"

"It was just like it was. Each writer had his own separated studio. We were on salary. We didn't do much. 'We'll let you know when we need you,' they said. Months went by. Faulkner was there for a while. He just went into his studio and started drinking. He drank every day. He never missed. At the end of each day we had to pull him out of there and put him into a cab. We drew salaries for doing nothing, for just being there. It was like they had cut our balls off and put us out to pasture. It was like being paid for sitting in hell."

"You still wrote those books, John; nobody else could have done that."

"I didn't do enough," he said, "I quit."

"It was enough."

"You should hear Hank talk about you," said Alta.

(I was Hank. Sitting there.)

There was some silence then. Alta reached out and held his hand.

"You're a good girl," he said. "Hank's lucky."

"Yeah," I said.

Then John spoke again. "There's this young buck doctor. He comes in here and looks me over, then he says, 'Well, well, I guess it's time. We're just going to have to *lop* off some more of you, old boy!' That's the way he said it: '*lop* off' You know, just like, '*lop* off.' And that's it. I'm not fond of him."

"Son of a bitch," I said. "I'll kick his ass!"

He exhaled a blast of smoke. "It's all right, Hank, forget it . . ."

Then Bante held the cigarette down by his side. His hand stayed there. It was quiet for all of us. The cigarette began to burn toward his fingers. Mary reached out, took the cigarette.

"He's sleeping again. You'd better go. I'm going to stay a while. You don't know how much this meant to him, your coming like this."

"We'll be back, Mary . . ."

We got back on the freeway with the after-work traffic. It didn't seem to matter. Alta and I didn't speak much. It was obvious: what happened to people, good people, bad people, even terrible people, hardly seemed fair. But "fair" was just a dictionary word. We drove on in among the metal machines of a trapped life in a trapped world . . .

■

John Bante made it through the operation, another operation. They had started the whole procedure by cutting off one foot, then the other. And they had just kept on chopping away. I suppose he might have died without it but the other choice hardly seemed much better.

Mary phoned me that he was back home and that they'd like to have us over for dinner. "We'll even have some wine," she told me. A date was set.

When we arrived Bante was sitting at the table. He was in his wheelchair. It seemed much more pleasant than with him stretched under a sheet. His son, Harry, and his wife, Nana, were there. Mary introduced us. We sat down and Mary poured the wine.

"I'm going to have a glass of wine with you, Chinaski," John said.

"I'm honored . . ."

We lifted them.

"You like the taste, Chinaski?"

"It's just fine, Bante."

"Harry and Nana have been reading your books. Now, they're hooked."

"I was taught by the master, one John Bante."

"You would have come through, anyhow."

"I borrowed some of the style. But, hell, on content we're different, John. You write like a good soul; I've got more bastard in me."

"You're right. Have some more wine. Mary, make sure Hank gets some more wine."

Then Mary brought in the dinner and Nana helped. Nana had cooked the meal. The food was nicely done. We ate quietly, making small comments. Then we were finished and there was more wine.

"I'm going to have another glass of wine with you, Chinaski! This is my big night!"

"One more and that's all," said Mary.

"I hear you hang around *Musso's*," John said.

"We used to go there about once a week when we lived out there," said Alta. "Now that we're in San Pedro we don't go so often."

"You ought to try *Chasen's*," Bante said.

"Too fancy for me," I admitted.

John was into his second wine. He was coming around. I loved it. I could feel the life returning to him.

"I went to *Musso's* often myself. I was sitting at a table one day when my favorite writer walked in. Big Red. You know who Big Red was?"

"No . . ."

"Sinclair Lewis."

"Holy Christ!" But I didn't say anymore than that. Sinclair Lewis had not been one of mine.

"Hey, what's that you're smoking? It sure smells odd!"

"It's a cigarette that comes from India. No nicotine but it goes great with wine."

"Can I have one?"

I looked at Mary. She nodded "yes." I lit one and placed it in his hand. Alta came around with an ashtray.

"The ashtray is right here, John. Feel it?"

"Yes, thank you. Anyhow, I was sitting there and Big Red walked in. I mean, it was like seeing God, you know?"

"Yes, I know," I answered.

"Anyhow, he sat down at a table with these two women and they ordered. I was just a kid, you know, and here I was . . . sitting in the same room with Sinclair Lewis . . . They brought him a bottle of wine and he and the ladies had their drinks. There he was, sitting there, Big Red. It seemed totally impossible. I didn't want to bother him. I tried to hold back but I couldn't. I was alone there. I had a notebook with me and was making as if I were working on this movie script. But I hated it. So I had many blank pages. I tore out one of the pages and walked over to Sinclair Lewis. I stood at his table. He was talking to one of the women . . . I think this Indian cigarette has gone out . . ."

Alta got up and re-lit his smoke with her lighter. "They keep going out, no chemicals, you know."

"Thank you, Alta . . . Anyhow, I stood there and then I said, 'Pardon me,

Mr. Lewis . . .' He looked up. His ladies also looked at me. 'I'm a writer. My name is John Bante. You've long been my favorite writer. I really don't want to bother you, but here I am. I wonder if you would autograph this piece of paper?'"

There was a pause. John drained the last of his wine. It was as if he were back at *Musso's* again standing at Big Red's table. Then, he continued.

"Sinclair Lewis acted as if I weren't there. He ignored the piece of paper I held out and he began talking to one of the women again."

"That son of a bitch," I said.

"I went back to my table and thought about the whole thing. The more I thought about it the worse I felt. Big Red had cut me cold. I got the waiter over and paid my bill. Then I walked back to Lewis' table. He looked up at me. 'Listen, you bastard, I am published by the same publishing house as you are. Maybe L. H. Renkin would like to know what a prick you are!' Then I walked off toward the exit. I peeked back and saw him rising from the table to follow me. I went out the back and jumped into my car and hid. I saw him run out the back and look around. He looked terrified. But he couldn't find me. He stood there some time, then walked back in. I had scared the hell out him!"

■

Frankly, I didn't like the story; it just seemed like a clash of vanities. But I could see Bante's let-down with his hero, and it was also good to see Bante forgetting his blindness and what they had done to his legs.

"That's a funny story," I said. "Did you ever tell L. H. Renkin?"

"No . . . no, of course not . . ."

The Indian cigarette had burned out and I took it from his hand.

"Pour Hank some more wine," he said. "I know Hank loves his wine. Mary has read me his books . . ."

"I'm all right, John, I'm fine . . ."

"You like the wine?"

"Yes, it's great. Don't worry about me. I'm very glad to be here."

"And I am too," said Alta.

"Alta, you take care of him, eh? He needs help . . ."

"I'll take care of him, John . . ."

Bante sat there a while. His little bulldog face seemed to sag a bit.

"I'm tired now . . . Will you please excuse me?"

"Of course, John . . ."

Mary came around and got behind the wheelchair and moved him away from the table, preparing to take him to his bedroom.

"Goodnight, John . . ." each of us said.

"Goodnight," he said.

Mary pushed him back to the bedroom. She stayed some time, then came out.

"You don't know what this had meant to him, getting his books rediscovered, having some people care again. Everybody has seemed to have dropped away since this thing has happened to him. People we have known for years have simply dropped away. It's like he were out of the contest and nobody is any longer interested."

"This is when people should be interested," said Alta.

"It doesn't work that way," said Harry.

"It's been like some kind of spiritual blockade," said Nana, "as if they had buried him already. . ."

Mary poured some more wine. She looked at me. "You wrote him one letter. Sometimes he asks me to read it to him again . . ."

"Oh, hell," I said, "I'm a hell of a guy . . ."

"No, Hank, it has really helped."

"There was no pity involved. I only said what was true."

"He's really into his new novel. I'd say about 60 pages, and it's funny and it's good . . ."

"John can write," I said, "much better than Big Red."

"Do you like the wine? John found out your brand. He insisted."

"I thought it tasted familiar."

Then there was a howl from the back bedroom. It was not the howl of a human. It was the howl of a wolf wounded and dying in the snow, in the darkness of nowhere without anybody around. Mary jumped from her chair and ran to the back room.

We waited. Harry refilled our glasses. There was nothing to say. We drank quietly for some minutes, then Mary returned.

"Listen," I said, "it's been a good night. But we better go. There he is back there. He can hear us talking, drinking, maybe laughing. He's not here. It's not fair . . ."

"I think he wants to hear you being here," Mary said.

"You think so?"

"Yes."

Mary waved to the walls. "We purchased this place years ago when John first went to Hollywood. It was cheap then. The years went by and we looked around and we were surrounded by millionaires."

"That's no sin," I said. "Inherited wealth is the sickness; it takes away from character because you never have to use it."

"What are you writing now, Hank?"

"It doesn't matter. It will never match what John did."

"Even so, you should continue to do it."

"I guess so. I don't know what else to do . . ."

Then the howl came again from the back bedroom. Mary leaped from her chair and ran back.

"Poor Mom," said Harry, "it's been hell on her too. Since this, she's been his eyes, his legs, everything. She loves him completely. If only she didn't it would be easier . . ."

After some minutes Mary came out again. She looked totally tired, I mean as if she had seen something that could never be solved . . . neither by love, patience, or miracle. It was the ultimate humiliation against goodness, against reason. It was what happened many times in separate places and nothing worked. It was the total impossibility of constant agony.

"It's been good," I said, "but we've got to go."

"All right," Mary said.

"Tell John we were happy to see him," said Alta.

■

Alta drove back. I had a recent drunk driving rap. We drove up the coast toward Santa Monica. There was the ocean out there and the dark sand. There was the moon. There were the fish. Headlights going past us. We followed bright red tail lights. Hell stood straight up and down in the sky and waved its arms. Not many saw it but they would.

I listened to the motor, trying to get some salvation out of sound. Toward Santa Monica the tall palm trees started to appear up and over high to the right. Those palm trees that John Bante, the kid from Colorado, had so often mentioned in his writings. Being weak, I uncorked a bottle of wine, passed it to Alta. She took a hit like a pro, steering straight forward, then passed it back . . .

Bante actually finished the novel. I mean, he got out of the hospital after the operation and he dictated it off to Mary who typed it off. Maybe John was watching the clock. I got a copy of the typescript and it read well. It wasn't *Sporting Times* but for a blind man without legs it was a fine work. Even for a man with all his parts it would have been a fine work. I was happy when Larkin told me he was going to publish it. And also some of Bante's other early works. Bante had risen out of nowhere. *Sporting Times* had sold well and the reviews had been great. The critics were astonished that this man had remained hidden for all those decades. *Sporting Times* was being translated to be published in Germany. And Bante was even mulling over the possibility of *another* novel in his mind.

Perhaps another week or so went by, no, it was more like three weeks, pardon me. Anyway, I got a phone call from Mary on a hungover morning.

"He's back at the hospital, Hank . . ."

"Another operation?"

"Yes . . ."

Goddamn it, I thought, how much more can they slice away? What's left?

I got his room number and Alta and I drove out . . .

When we got there Bante was alone in his room. He appeared to be asleep. I could see him breathing. We went off for a coffee.

When we got back there was a nurse in there, one of those cheerful ones who had seen so much of the dead and the dying that it had almost become a joke. She grinned at us over her shoulder: "Just a minute, baby's getting his shot!"

We stood outside and waited. Then she came out, still grinning. "Okey doke, he's all yours!"

We walked in. "Hello, John, it's Hank and Alta."

"I hate that nurse," he said, "she's got the sensitivity of a Japanese beetle."

"We brought you some flowers," said Alta. "Maybe you can't see them but you can smell them. Here . . ."

"Yes, they smell good . . . I'm glad you two have come . . ."

"There isn't a vase here," said Alta, "I'm going to see if I can get a vase." She left.

"Well, Hank, how's it going?"

"I was going to ask you the same but I was afraid of the answer."

"Well, you know, Dr. Lop is sharpening his knife again."

I sat down. "You need any water, cigarettes? Bed pan emptied?"

"No, everything's all right . . ."

"Like hell."

"I wish I were home. I can't do any work here."

"I know. Listen, I was wondering about something . . ."

"What?"

"Whatever happened to the lovely Carmen in *Sporting Times*? Did she really vanish into the desert?"

"No, she came back. She turned out to be a goddamned lesbian!" he laughed.

"Holy shit!"

∎

Alta came back with the flowers in a vase. "What kind of a hospital is this? I could hardly find a vase."

"It's a circus," said Bante. "This morning we had a guy who used to play Tarzan; he was running up and down the halls giving his jungle call. They finally got him back to his room. He's harmless. But I think he made us feel better. It took us all back to the past when we were in the action . . ."

"Did he ever come in here?"

"Yeah, I bared my fangs and he ran off . . . Maybe it's best that I'm here. At home Mary has to sit with a shotgun so the trashmen don't carry me off . . ."

"Don't talk that way," Alta said.

"What bothers me most is my eyes. I'm not crying about anything but the tears keep coming. They tell me that the only way to stop it is to take the eyes out. What do you think, Hank?"

"I'm no M.D. But if it were me I'd say 'no.'"

"Why?"

"I always believe in the possibility of the miracle."

"I thought you were the tough realist?"

"I'm also a gambler. You going to go another book?"

John's face had been a brown grey. Light began to enter as he roughly told us his plot idea. He finished.

"It sounds very good," Alta said.

"You oughta do it," I said.

There was silence then. The talking had helped but it had made him tired. They had told us it was all right for him to talk. What did they know?

Some minutes went by. Then Bante spoke again. "It's strange how they all dropped away, all the people I used to know. Pals, good friends . . . People I'd known for years, many many years. . . . When this happened to me, I heard from them a little, at first, then they just dropped away. They're into their world and I no longer fit. I never would have guessed it would be this way . . ."

"We're here, John . . ."

"I know. It's good . . . Tell me, Alta, about Hank . . . Is he really as tough as he writes?"

"No, he's butter. He's 220 pounds of melting butter."

"I thought so."

"Listen, John, that's a good plot idea for your next novel. But why don't you write about what's happening now? How all your great friends have left you and run around the corner?"

And I wanted to add, leaving you there stretched under that sheet for hours, legless, blind, nobody around, leaving you just laying there like that. As they went about chasing money or women or men, or holding bright conversations at parties. Or watching widescreen tv. Or whatever those people did, those Hollywood people who just produced crap and crap and more crap but they really believed it was something else, just like their public.

"No, no, I don't want to do that."

John Bante, the good guy to the last.

"The one thing I've seen so much in so many people is bitterness. It's a terrible thing, how almost everybody turns bitter. It's sad, it's so terribly sad . . ."

"You're right, John," Alta said.

"I'm tired now. You better go . . ."

"Goodbye, John . . ."

"Goodbye . . ."

I got into my own writing which I felt was going all right—with the help of Céline, Turgenev, and John Bante. But writing is an odd thing: you never arrive anywhere; you can get close but you never arrive. That's why most of us have to keep going: we're tricked but we can't quit. Foolishness is often its own reward.

I heard from Larkin that Mary was about to lose the home in Malibu. The Movie Hospital finally only was willing to cover so much in expenses. The Dr. Lops had to be paid. Operations were costly and they didn't want to drive the old Mercedes too many years . . . Procedures were under way to claim the Malibu home. Not dying was very costly. Hospitals, which were supposed to be Houses of Mercy, were houses of business, big fucking business.

Before we could get back for another trip, and I waited too long, I'm sure I wasn't much better than John's friends who had dropped away, before we could get back for another trip the phone rang. It was Mary.

"John's dead," she said.

I don't recall what I said. I don't think it was very good. I came up blank. I think I said something like, he's better out of it. Are you all right?

Dumb, dumb.

I got the place of the funeral, place and time.

Live, die, get buried. Those who remain get oil changes, lube jobs. Fuck maybe. Sleep. Ask for their eggs scrambled, straight up, or over easy . . .

It was a hot day; we found the church, almost late. Pacific Coast Highway had been blocked off and they circled us into a massive traffic jam and the only way I found the church was that I followed a hearse and it turned out to be the right one.

The family was there and a few friends. I had been asked to do the eulogy but had declined knowing that I would have gone to tears and made everybody feel bad. I saw Ben Pheasants there. Ben had given Bante great backing in articles, one of which appeared in the L.A. *Times*. We had once been buddies. But I had burned him in a poem.

Most of us began walking toward our automobiles. Alta held my hand. Mary remained in her chair. As we moved away I saw John's son, Harry. "Go get 'em Hank!" he said.

"O.K., Harry . . ."

Then, after saying that, I felt very selfish but it was too late. I knew what he meant, though, in a sense, *maybe* I knew what he had meant: his father, John Bante, had lent me a touch of the way it was to be done . . .

And that was it, that was all there was.

I had met my idol. Very few people ever do that.

CHARLES BUKOWSKI'S

LOS ANGELES FOR LI PO

Well, with Li Po I'd take him to *Musso & Frank's* and we'd go to the bar while we waited for a table. I'd put in a request for a table in "the old room," with Jean as the waiter, if possible. I never mind waiting at the bar except on a Saturday or Friday night, when the tourists bevy up to the wood. I prefer to partake of vodka-7s and Li Po, a good red wine. Upon getting our table we'd order a bottle of Beaujolais and look over the menu. I'd tell Li Po that Hemingway, Faulkner, and F. Scott used to get stinko at *Musso's* and that I did too, mostly in the mid-afternoon, ordering bottle after bottle at the table while checking out the menu, and then most of the time not eating at all.

After *Musso's*, we'd simply go to my place and drink some more, probably more red wine, and we'd smoke Sher bidis from India. I'd talk and he'd listen, and then I'd listen while he talked. There would be some good laughter, and then that would be the night. Unless he wanted to write some poems, burn them, and float them in the L.A. Harbor.

In any town, good taste and good sense are not so much what you see and do, but more what you don't see and do. What is outside of us is hardly as important as what is inside of us, though granted, we must also live with what is outside of us. Li Po would know this, and so, slowly drinking away the night would be the finest thing for both of us. Oh yes, yes, yes.

LOOKING BACK AT A BIG ONE

The longer a man is dead the more we are apt to distort his strengths and weaknesses; his lack of response lends bravery to our judgments. And Pound has been chewed upon for some time now, and in his wake has left Poundian schools and scholars, and these scholars are better equipped to tell you about E.P. than I. I can only tell you what I sense and feel from a viewpoint which could lack proper depth. Having wasted most of my life as a common laborer, about the best study I ever made was of myself. Anyhow, let's get going . . .

First off, let me say that at least one school that Pound left behind did shape the progress of a certain section of our poesy, only this school was better at bitch-snobbery and petty clannishness than it was at leaving any lasting monument of work. And one of the things Ez insisted upon was: "Do your WORK!" These boys *talked* more about how poetry should be, and wrote critical articles on how poetry should be. This ate up most of their time and, finally, it ate them up. Being careful of the path and the way of the Word can be worthwhile if these theories do not lead to constipation and restrictiveness. Many of the inbred dictums, the little turnabout word-phrases about What was What and What Wasn't, were mostly just so much incest bullshit of some not-so-really clever men. We can blame Pound for some things but not for leaving . . . these . . . behind him.

So? Well? During the heights of a ten-year drunk when I wrote almost nothing, read almost nothing, and starved proficiently, I had a rather standing joke with a lady. You might say that she was a lady of the streets I was shacked up with for a couple of years. I would enter our room after that rather long walk from the downtown library—and there I'd be packing it again, that big heavy book, and she'd always ask me, "You got that goddamned book again?" And I'd answer, "Yes, baby, it's the *Cantos*." And her response would always be the same: "But you never *read* it!"

I suppose that answered a great deal. But I *was* able to read certain portions of the *Cantos*, and although I wasn't always sure of what I was reading, I had to admire how, in some fashion, he made those lines ride the paper in a high and fine style. Pound was to poetry what Hemingway was to prose: they each had a way of inciting and exciting when there really wasn't much of that about. Some of us may tend to downgrade them, but there's hardly a way not to talk about them at all. Pound left his *indent*. And one of the best things he did was to send fresh blood, fresh troops to a magazine then called *Poetry: A Magazine of Verse*. And, of course, he wrote *more* than the *Cantos*.

Whether Pound was an anti-semite or a fascist or whether he had the right to be either is another kind of debate. The radio speeches that I read sounded more like the imbecile gibberish of a high school boy who thought he was bright—rather than the ramblings of a madman. Also, in many creative minds, there is the natural urge to see the other side. And a desire to sometimes stand with the other side just for the hell of it. Because the first side has been there so long, so steady, and seems so worn. Céline, Hamsun, others were caught, at times, doing this. And they were not forgiven. In an attempt to get beyond Good and Evil (if such do exist), the balance sometimes wavers and one goes to Evil (saying it might be there) because it seems more interesting—especially when your own countrymen just blithely accept to follow what they are told is Good (and never doubting it). Generally, there is a tendency in intelligent men not to believe what most of the masses believe, and most of the time this puts them right near target; other times it gets their asses burned, especially in the political arena where the winners dictate which side is right.

Pound got burned, and to save his soul-ass we put him in with the loonies and said that he couldn't help it. Yet, if the fascists, the Nazis had won, I think Pound would have been one of the first to turn against them, damn the price. He just got caught with a Loser and a Loser has never won a War-Crimes Tribunal yet.

Also, in America since the end of World War I, the so-called intelligentsia, the universities, have leaned to the Left (with an especially giant surge from 1931–1947). And for an artist to lean to the Left, even to the extreme Left, has not only been seen as forgivable but also as a high form of creative bravery.

Pound did not fit within their spiritual picture frame.

So, where does this leave us? The Poundian disciples claim that an entire work is to be judged as that, and minor political eccentricities are to be put aside. Non-producers claim that the total man must be judged. (Which means, judged by their standards. If I am right, you're wrong. Right?)

Is the history of Man (Wo-Man) formed by some possible ultimate interior goodness of Man, or by the Greed and Need of Power to assert itself? Or by an admixture? I don't know. I am one of those shameful ones who has no politics. I don't know that little or that much.

All I know of Pound is what I have been able to read of his works. I think that as an artist he has an excellent sense of the Word: where to place it and how. And how, and how. He was also a trickster and he often laughed below his palms at how he was putting it over on us. I felt that he knew that much of his stuff was con and sham, yet the fine style in which he duped us was another art form in itself.

Wasn't it Nietzsche, who, when asked about the Poets, said: "The Poets? The Poets lie too much."

Pound improved upon the Lie; he put it within the context of a high and involuted entertainment. Sometimes even he didn't know. His sometimes great writing could lift one high; other times it was just cold fish.

Few men can run the straight, hard line. If, at worst, Pound is the Ultimate Fake, then who would you replace him with? Robert Lowell?

Poets, of course, aren't the only ones to suffer in our world, they just talk more about it. And the critics, my friend, the critics, what a rotten lobster flesh they are. Forgive me this, it's all that I know in my pitiable way. Basically, all I have to say is: Ezra, yes.

Yes, yes, yes, yes, yes, yes, yes, yes, yes, yes, and yes.

out in the '40s, edited by Caresse Crosby, Black Sun Press, widow of Harry Crosby who kept writing about suicide and the Black Sun until he did it one night along with a prostitute in a hotel in Paris, anyhow at age twenty-four I submitted to *Portfolio* and got accepted.

Pass a year or two, I am totally mad and trying to be a writer, I am in a tar paper shack for $1.25 a week in Atlanta, no water, no heat, no light.

I feel worse than Kafka and maybe lousier than Turgenev; I am starving everything gone, disowned by parents who didn't have anything anyhow, I'm out of coin, don't even have a penny, but I do have stamps and envelopes and the old *Portfolio* address and the address of Kay Boyle. I write them both 5- or 6-page letters explaining what's left of my soul and my flesh—both of them rapidly dwindling, and I mail the letters and wait, I wait and I wait; I try to steal an apple at a fruit stand and I am caught, I am shamed. I had never tried to steal before, and I waited and I waited and my $1.25 rent got overdue but I was allowed to slide because the owner of the place was dying, just like I was, lots of Christs on lots of crosses, and so anyhow, Kay Boyle never answered, that great liberal, that great feeler for the oppressed; I never liked her writing style anyhow, too slick, no edges. I had asked for $10, I had promised repayment; I would have, I am that way.

Anyhow, here came a letter from Caresse Crosby; *Portfolio* was dead but she remembered my story, great story, she now lived in a castle in Italy and her life was dedicated to helping the poor. There were many poor in the village below her and it had been good to hear from me.

There was no money in with the letter; I shook the pages again and again in my dark shack, it was freezing outside and inside, and I sat in my thin California shirt and pants and then I ripped the envelope open and looked in all the crevices—nothing. Were the Italian poor more worthy than the American; did their bellies feel hunger more?

I got out of Atlanta by signing on with a railroad track gang going west and I had to fight off a whole gang of guys because I didn't laugh at their dirty and dull and obvious jokes. "There's something wrong with you, man!" "Yeah . . . I know it . . . just stay the fuck away from me!" . . . as the old passenger car with the dusty and mud-caked windows took me from one hell to another.

THE OTHER

I was stretched out on my bed when I noticed it for the first time. The bathroom door was slightly open and there, standing in front of the mirror—or so it seemed—was a man, and this man looked very much like I. "HEY!" I yelled. I leaped from the bed and ran toward the bathroom. When I got there, it was empty—that is, of another being. Being badly hungover, I went back to bed. The clock radio read 1:32 p.m. I thought about what I had seen, or imagined I had. Then I forced the thought from my mind. There was still time to catch a few races at the track. I began to get dressed. . . .

I got there for the third race. It was a Wednesday afternoon and not too crowded. I bet the third race, lost, then walked over and got a sandwich and coffee.

I began to feel better. The racetrack was where I unwound. Maybe it was a stupid place, but I couldn't think of any other place to go to unwind. Without the racetrack and a few drinks now and then, life could get pretty dark and senseless.

I finished eating, then walked over toward a water fountain. It was at the far northwest corner, under the grandstand. As I walked along, I heard footsteps behind me. I didn't like people walking behind me. I changed the route of my path, but I still heard footsteps behind me. Then I felt somebody tapping me on the shoulder as I walked along.

"Pardon me, sir . . ."

I stopped and turned. The man asked, "Can you tell me where the men's room is?"

"Go back past the betting windows. There's a stairway at the end of them, to the right. Take it on down."

"Thank you," the man said, then turned and walked off.

I stood in disbelief. The man had looked exactly like I. I should have engaged him in conversation more than I had. I should have kept him about, found out more. He was almost at the stairway to the men's room. Then I saw him walk down. I set off after him.

I pushed open the door to the men's room and walked in. He wasn't at the sinks. I walked around the corner and checked the urinals. He wasn't there. Had to be in one of the stalls. Only three of the stalls were occupied; I could see the legs underneath the doors.

I would wait. I leaned against a far wall and pretended to be reading the *Racing Form*. In a few moments, a man came out of one of the stalls. He was a short black man in a blue jumpsuit. He saw me looking at him over the *Form*. He was friendly.

"Got a hot one in this race?" he asked.

"Naw, nothing," I answered.

He walked over to a sink to wash up.

Another stall door opened. An old man came out. The poor fellow was terribly bent over. He could hardly walk. But he needed the racetrack. He was hooked. He made it over to a sink and began washing his hands.

That left one stall. I was going to confront the guy when he came out. Surely he must have noticed the exact similarities between us? What was he up to? Why hadn't he mentioned anything? When he looked at me, it must have been like looking into a mirror.

I saw the last stall door begin to open. I moved toward it. A man walked out. He was an Oriental. I was a white, a tired-looking California white.

"Listen," I started to say to him.

"Yes, what is it?" he asked.

"Nothing," I said.

"THE HORSES ARE AT THE GATE!" I heard the announcer call.

I jumped into a betting line. In front of me was another tired California white and in from of him was a tired Central American. The tired Central American was having trouble with the language. Then he finished his transaction. Then the tired California white asked for a two-dollar show ticket on the favorite. Jackoffs like that clutter the lines every day. Then he moved off.

I was at the window. I slammed down a twenty.

"TWENTY TO WIN ON THE 9!" I yelled.

"What?" the clerk asked me.

It was deliberate. He was a sadist. One-third of the mutual clerks were sadists.

"TWENTY TO WIN ON THE 9!"

He started to punch out the ticket. The bell rang and the machine shut off and the horses busted out of the gate.

I picked up my twenty and went to watch the race. It was a mile race. By the time I got the field into view, the 9 had a length-and-a-half lead on the backstretch and he was running easy. At the last curve, he opened up three lengths. At midstretch, he had four lengths. Then he began to tire a bit. Four or five horses rushed down at him. The jock laid the whip home hard, and the 9 still had a length at the wire.

I went to get a coffee. By the time I got back to my seat, the price was up. The 9 had paid $18.70. That fucking sadist had cost me $167.

I stayed at the track. I walked about looking for the man. I didn't see him anywhere. I saw many ugly people, a few jerkoffs, a murderer or two, but I didn't see *him* again. I left after the eighth race and drove on home . . .

■

I parked my car and walked toward my court. I unlocked the door and walked inside. There was my girlfriend, Carine. Dear Carine with the innocent brown eyes, those thin hips, those fat calves. She was sitting on the couch watching TV. She had a key to the place. She looked up.

"I thought you left for vodka. Where's the vodka?"

"What the hell are you talking about?"

"You said you were going to get vodka when you left."

"Left what?

"Left here. About twenty minutes ago."

"I wasn't here twenty minutes ago. I've been at the track all day."

"Are you trying to be funny?" Carine asked. "Don't you remember that great love we made?"

"What love?"

"Earlier this afternoon, big boy. You were good, you were really good for a change."

I went into the kitchen and poured half a glass of whiskey, took a hit of that, opened a bottle of beer and came out, sat down with the beer and whiskey. I sat in a chair across from Carine.

"So I really made good love, eh?"

"And how! I really don't know what got into you."

"Now, Carine, listen, look at me. Was I dressed this way when you last saw me?"

"No, come to think of it . . . When you left for the vodka, you were dressed in a white shirt, dark blue pants, and black shoes. Now you're dressed in a yellow shirt, tan pants, brown shoes. That's strange . . . Did you change clothes somewhere?"

"No."

"What did you do, then?"

"I didn't do anything. That guy you went to bed with wasn't me."

"Oh, come on!" Carine laughed. "If that wasn't you, who was it supposed to be?"

"I don't know."

I finished my whiskey and had a hit of the beer.

Carine stood up. "I'm getting out of here. I don't like the way you're acting. When you finally come to your senses, phone me."

"All right, Carine."

Then she was gone, out the door.

Maybe I *was* going crazy. But I *had* been at the racetrack that afternoon. I *couldn't* have been home. Maybe I had split in half? Maybe I could be in two places at once? And could only remember one of them?

I needed help. But I didn't know where to go. Nobody would believe me.

I went to the only place I could go: to the kitchen for another drink.

As I did, I remembered how the man at the track had been dressed: white shirt, dark blue pants, black shoes . . .

■

Several weeks passed and there were no further occurrences. I even started seeing Carine again.

Life went on in its usual dull and dreary way. About the recent past, I figured I had just gone momentarily mad and had imagined everything. I began to drink and gamble more heavily to relieve myself of as many thought processes as possible. The two main things in life, after all, are to avoid pain and to sleep well nights. Right?

Things plodded along until this particular day. It was another Wednesday—no, it was a Thursday and I had had a fair day at the track. I was headed back on the freeway when I noticed this guy in a pale-green late-model car; he was tailgating me pretty close. I caught him in the rearview. He was pretty damned close to my bumper. I hit the pedal for more speed, but he moved with me, staying right on my bumper. Well, people are full of various hatreds; their lives don't turn out like their expectations, and the freeway is one of the places where they release their angers.

I cut over a lane to get this guy off my ass but he cut right with me and was on my bumper again. I had drawn some kind of goddamned nut.

I switched lanes again, punched my radio in, and lucked it onto Mahler. That might change my luck. I checked the rearview again. The son of a bitch had swung over and latched onto my bumper again.

I tapped my brakes. He tapped his. There was a slight bump against my bumper. He had hit me, ever so lightly. I felt a warm rush of blood; it ran up the back of my neck and circled my ears. I was getting pissed. It took a lot to piss me off, but I was getting pissed. I don't like to get pissed, because when I get pissed I stay pissed for a long time. I never much cared for people, but if they left me alone, I'd leave them alone. Now I was getting pissed.

I checked my right mirror and the rearview, then made a swift change to the right. I locked myself between a pick-up and a Caddy. I had the bastard off my bumper. But I was still pissed. He was driving a little ahead of me and to the left. I saw my chance and swung left, hooked myself upon *his* bumper. Now I had the fucker. I saw his license plate: 6DVL666.

He made another lane change to my right. I stayed right on him.

Then he shot off the next freeway exit. I was right after him, glued there.

I saw his eyes checking his rearview. The eyes looked frightened. They should be. When I got pissed, I was a fucking tiger. More than a few guys had found that out.

He took a right at the boulevard and I followed him, bumper to bumper. He breezed toward a signal; there were no cars in front of him. The light turned red, and he hit the throttle. I went right with him. Some guy on the other side jumped the signal. His car came at me as we went by. He hit his brakes but hit the back of my car. I went into a half spin, straightened it again, then went after my friend. He was trying to pull away. Somehow my car had more guts, and I was again on his bumper.

I would follow that bastard to hell. I would put him in hell. I'd had too many bad marriages, too many bad jobs, too much bad everything to take shit from a guy like that.

The next light was red. He stopped and waited. My bumper was right on his. For a moment I thought of leaping out of my car and trying to get him. But he had the windows rolled up and, no doubt, locked. I'd find a way.

The signal changed and I followed him. He cut to the inner lane. I followed him. I was like death. His death.

Suddenly he cut into an alley. I followed, right on him. Then he made a mistake: He took a cut-off from the alley and it was a dead end. I had him.

He pulled up to a loading dock in front of a closed warehouse. The front of his car touched the loading dock. I pulled up behind him, pressed my bumper to his. He was locked in.

He sat in his car. He still had the windows up. He was very still. Evidently he didn't have a car phone to call for help.

I sat in my car thinking about what to do.

I could let the air out of his fucking tires. I could bust up his car—his windows, the car body. But I wanted him. I wanted to bust *him* up.

Mahler was still playing on my radio. When the symphony ended, I'd get out and do something; I had time. Plenty of time. No hot babes waiting for me to return to my place.

We both sat there. I wondered what he was thinking. He'd surely never ride anybody's bumper again.

Mahler played on and we both waited. Then, just before the Mahler ended, he swung open his door and stepped out of his car.

The unexpected. It shook me a bit. He was accepting my challenge. He was showing some guts. He was calling my card. Good. Good. Good fucking good.

I got out of my car. Then I saw him clearly. It was *him*, of course.

I moved toward him.

He didn't back up. He had 6 or 8 feet behind him, but he didn't back up.

I walked to about 3 feet in front of him, then stopped.

"Okay, fucker, let's hear it."

"Hear what?"

"Why are you playing with me? What do you want? Who are you?"

"That's my business."

"You talk pretty cool for a guy who is about to get his ass kicked from here to Honolulu."

"That's to be seen."

"Yeah?"

"Yeah."

"You went too far when you fucked my girl."

"Nice girl," he grinned. "Nice tight pussy."

I rushed forward, swung a right. He ducked under, straightened.

"You'll have to do better than that."

"I will. I'll take your ass."

"Try me."

I moved in, feinted a right, and caught him a left behind his right ear. He shook his head, acted stunned, then blasted me with a right that flashed against my forehead with great force. He wasn't bad. But I sensed that I had him. I rushed forward throwing both fists, street fashion. He swung back. I caught some good ones. But I felt myself beginning to dominate and as his punches lessened, I could see better and targeted in. I left-hooked him to the gut, then gave him the right uppercut. He dropped and rolled over. I didn't kick him. I stood back and waited for him to get up. I was going to give him an old-fashioned slow and easy and brutal beating that he would not only remember in his waking hours but also in his sleep.

He got up, shook his head, wandered back toward his car.

"No good, baby," I told him, "I'm going to finish you off."

He was in the front seat. Then he came out.

He was holding a neat-looking little black pistol, and not so little at that. I had faced a gun before and let me tell you a secret. The first thing you notice about about a gun is the hole in the end of the barrel. It is a fascinating hole. That's where it's going to come out. The hole is like the eye of a snake upon a bird, a rabbit, whatever the prey. All too ultimate.

"All right, buddy," he said, "get into your car, back it out of here, and I'm gone."

"I'm not backing my car."

"You want to die?"

"No."

"Then back your car."

"I want to know why you're fucking with me. What is it getting you? What does it mean? Why do you look more like me than I do?"

"You're not in a position to ask questions."

"Pull the trigger, asshole; I'm coming for you."

I moved on in . . .

∎

When I came to he was gone. My car was there. I felt the gash on my head. He had clubbed me with the gun. There was a cut on the top of my head. The blood trickled down. I got out my handkerchief. I held it there for a while. I walked to my car. It had been moved. He had gotten my keys out of my pocket. I opened the car door. The key was still in the dash. I got in, backed out of there, got back onto the freeway.

I punched in the radio. I got Mozart's "Requiem in D minor." Appropriate. . . .

■

When I got back to my place, Carine was sitting on the couch watching TV. She said, "What is this? I thought you just left for vodka. Where's the vodka?"

"Holy goddamned shit," I said.

"Oh, you're drunk again," said Carine. "I'm leaving."

■

I sat at the back table of the Chinese café and waited. My contact was ten minutes late. Maybe he wouldn't show. He'd been selected for me by a reliable source.

I got the waiter over for another beer.

"And I'll also have an order of chow mein. Shrimp chow mein."

He left and was back with the beer soon. I took a good pull. I never drank from a glass. It tasted better out of the bottle.

The far door opened and a man walked in. He was rather pleasant looking. Somehow I expected a harder-looking type. But maybe it wasn't him? He moved toward me. There was another man at a middle table. He walked on by toward mine, pulled up a chair, sat down.

"Good evening," he said.

"Yeah," I said, "how did you know it was me?"

"We know," he answered.

The waiter arrived.

"Hot tea," he told the waiter. The waiter left.

I leaned a bit forward.

"What is this going to cost me?" I asked in a low voice.

He answered in a low voice. "What do you have in your bank account?"

"Ten thousand."

"Twenty thousand."

"How did you know?"

"We know."

"It's a lot of money."

"That's the price, You want it or not?"

"I want it. You'll have a cashier's check when it's finished."

"Cash only. All in hundreds. Unmarked."

"That'll be hard."

"Do it."

"How will I get it to you?"

"We'll let you know."

"You don't want an advance?"

"No, we'll take it all—afterwards. Meanwhile, withdraw it from the bank tomorrow, for sure. Got it?"

"Yes."

The waiter came with his tea.

"Thank you," he said to the waiter, "but please bring me some lemon." The waiter left.

"How do you know I'll pay you?" I asked.

"You'll pay, and when we tell you."

There was silence then. He just sat looking at me.

We had spoken in low tones throughout. Somehow I felt as if I were in a movie, a cheap one.

"I like lemon with my tea," he said, "don't you?"

"No. Listen, all I have is his license plate number. How are you going to find him?"

"We'll find him. Write the number on that paper napkin and slide it toward me."

I had a pen. I wrote the number and slid it over.

"Thank you," he said.

The waiter arrived with his lemon.

"Thank you," he said to the waiter.

As the waiter walked off, I spoke.

"You know, this guy looks just like me."

"We know."

"How do I know you won't hit me instead of him?"

"We don't like the word 'hit.'"

"What word do you want me to use? What term?"

"Use nothing."

"Are you afraid I'm bugged?"

"We're not afraid. And we know you're not bugged."

He squeezed his lemon into his tea, then took a sip. He put his cup down and then looked at me again. I wondered if he were a man with a family.

"How long will this take?" I asked.

"Everything will be completed within five days."

The waiter arrived with my chow mein, then left.

"The food isn't good in this place," the man said.

"I don't have food on my mind right now. Listen, how will I know when you're done? And that you've really done it."

"You'll receive evidence. We are reputable."

"I don't see how you can find this guy with what you have. This is a pretty damned large city. Maybe he isn't even around anymore."

"We'll find him. Everything will be finalized within five days."

"Doesn't anybody ever talk?"

"Talk?"

"I mean, the client."

"The client never talks."

I looked down at my chow mein.

"I don't know if I want this done."

"That's all right with us. If you don't, it costs you five thousand. If you do, twenty."

There was silence then. A good three minutes.

The man spoke.

"You want it done or not? Tell me now."

"All right, do it."

"All right," said the man, "you'll hear from us."

He stood up. He looked down at me.

"Damn, you know, I don't think it's rained in six or seven months. It must be the greenhouse effect, don't you think?"

"Yes, I believe they've fucked up the stratosphere for us."

"Bastards," the man said. Then he turned, walked to the door, opened it, and was gone without looking back.

The chow mein didn't look good. I finished the beer, nodded the waiter over. I asked for the check.

I decided not to come back to that place. It didn't seem to be a nice place.

Four days later, around 7 p.m., I found an envelope under my door. I opened it. There were photographs. Photographs of him. Dead. He was leaning over in a stuffed chair. He was upright but leaning a bit to the right. A bit of tongue was hanging out of his mouth. And there was a large hole in his forehead. I began to feel dizzy. I inhaled deeply and my head cleared. There were eight or nine photos taken from different angles. Then there was a note. It was composed of print cut from a newspaper and pasted to the paper.

Burn these photos. Now. And this note. Do it.

Now.

I walked to the fireplace and held the stuff out, lit it all with my lighter. I dropped it in there and watched it burn. It made a stink. The photos, probably.

Ashes to ashes.

He was dead.

I walked to the bedroom and sat on the edge of the bed.

The phone rang.

"Hello?" I asked.

"Do you have the money there?" came through the receiver.

"Yes. How will I get it to you?"

"Don't worry about that. Just sit still until you hear from us."

He hung up.

I put the phone back in the cradle and stretched out on the bed.

I began to feel as if I were entirely covered with moss or slime or something. My tongue was dry and I felt weird.

I shouldn't have done it. I could have lived with it. Now this seems worse. And I'd never know what the other meant, what had caused it.

The bathroom door was slightly open and the light was on in there. Then I saw it. Or did I? It looked like me standing there looking into the mirror.

I jumped up and ran into the bathroom. There was nobody there. There was nothing there.

Then I heard a knock at my front door. I turned around and walked toward it.

BASIC TRAINING

On the "language" bit you asked for, I gave it a shot. It was an excuse. My wife is having company downstairs. They are all right. Maybe. Anyhow, I just walked up here and began typing. I am the writer, you see. If I have to drink, I prefer it at the typer.

—Buk

The language of a man's writing comes from where he lives and how. I was a bum and a common laborer most of my life. The conversations I heard were hardly erudite. And the years I lived were hardly laced with upper class relationships. I was down in the dung pits. I was a bit mad but it was an odd madness because I nurtured it. I allowed my mind to circle about, to bite its own ass. I goaded my instincts, fed my prejudices. Solitude was my ace card. I needed it to puff up my reality. I truly valued leisure; it was my fix. Being alone with myself was the sanctuary. In one city I found an abandoned graveyard and I slept there in the high noons with my hangovers. In another city I sat for hours looking at a dirty stinking canal, not really thinking at all. I needed hours, days, weeks, years of my own. I found small rooms where I starved. I had the ability to make a little money last a long time. I sacrificed everything for time. And to stay out of the mainstream. A candy bar a day was my meal, generally. My largest expense was a cheap bottle of wine. I rolled my cigarettes and I wrote hundreds of short stories, handprinting most of them in ink. The typewriter was in hock more than out. For my observations of humanity I sat on a bar stool bumming drinks. At six feet tall I could often check in at 135 pounds, soaking drunk. I was the original Thin Man with bats in his Belfry.

I wasn't in misery. I almost delighted in my poverty. Starvation is only difficult for the first 2 or 3 days. After that you get into a strange high. You float down stairways; sunlight becomes very bright and sounds very loud.

Perceptions enhanced rather than dimmed. Holidays and world events were meaningless. I wasn't quite sure of what I was about but for it all, I was in fair health. There was no problem with loneliness. The main problem was my teeth. I was attacked by enormous toothaches. I swished the wine about in my mouth and walked rapidly about the room. My teeth became loose, I could wiggle them with my fingers. Sometimes a tooth came out in my hand. A very curious thing.

In the libraries I read the literary magazines (among sundry other things) and I was perplexed as to what was accepted as top writing. The pages were preponderate with a surface slickness and a sludgy inner dullness. There was no gamble, there was no light, there was no joy. I read the classics, the works of the past famous, and it seemed to me, at least, that these of centuries past—with rare exceptions—seemed full of lies, preening, prancing, and trickery.

I didn't know what I was doing yet I did. I became more fixated with where I was heading. I hurled myself toward my personal god: SIMPLICITY. The tighter and smaller you got it the less chance there was of error and the lie. Genius could be the ability to say a profound thing in a simple way. Words were bullets, words were sunbeams, words cracked through doom and damnation. I played with words. I tried to write paragraphs that read the same across as down. I was playing. Time to play is important.

I played for decades. And with very little acceptance. The editors most probably thought I was crazy, especially when they received those long handprinted manuscripts. I remember one fellow writing back, "WHAT THE FUCK IS THIS?" And he might have been right.

And I was crazy, in my way. Often I pulled down all the shades and stayed in bed for a week. And once I overheard: "Helen, you know that man in 3? There's nothing but wine bottles in his trash. And he just sits in the dark listening to music. I'm going to have to get rid of him."

Such things as women, automobiles, etc., and later—tv sets—were only odd externals to me. There were occasional women, very occasional, hardly top grade.

"You're the first man I ever met without a tv set!"

"Come on, baby, cut the crap, show me some leg!"

■

Finally, after decades of small rooms, park benches, the worst of jobs, the worst of women, some of my writing began to seep through, mostly in the little magazines and the porno journals. I found the porno journals to be a great outlet: you could say anything you wanted and the more direct, the better. Simplicity and freedom at last, between the slick photos of beaver shots.

In time I began to seep through more, even into some of the more respectable publications. I even had some books published. But, I think that I held onto my style, my method. I liked jagged rocks in my sentences, crooked laughter, belches, farts. I still offend people but I don't write to offend people. That's too easy . . .

My wife's mother, who is only ten years older than I, came to visit last year. I came in from the track one evening and there she was reading one of my books.

"I gave it to her," said my wife.

"What for?" I asked.

My mother-in-law likes to play Scrabble, work crossword puzzles, and her favorite tv program is *Murder, She Wrote.*

Some days went by.

We drove her to the airport.

Pass a week.

I asked my wife, "How did your mother like my book?"

My wife is a good actor. She inflected her voice with a hissing indignity: "*Why* does he have to *use* language like *that*?"

Most probably she meant the dialogue but I'm sure she was also upset by the sentences between: stiff, cracked, wobbling, Stygial. Hardly Shakespearean.

I had worked faithfully in the dank caverns to get it that way. I felt vindicated that she found it distasteful. To have had her embrace the work would have been fearful to me, a sign that I had softened, gone the way of the practitioners.

I had had a long motherfucking apprenticeship.

I wanted to endure through the traps, to die at the typer with the wine bottle to my left and the radio playing, say, Mozart, to my right.

SOURCES

"Aftermath of a Lengthy Rejection Slip," *Story*, 1944, reprinted with the permission of Black Sparrow Press. "20 Tanks from Kasseldown," *Portfolio*, 1946. "Hard Without Music," *Matrix*, vol. 11, nos. 1–2, Double Issue, Spring–Summer 1948. "Trace: Editors Write," *Trace*, no. 30, February–March 1959. "Portions from a Wine-Stained Notebook," *Simbolica* 19, 1960. "A Rambling Essay on Poetics and the Bleeding Life Written While Drinking a Six-Pack (Tall)," *Ole*, no. 2, March 1965. "In Defense of a Certain Type of Poetry, a Certain Type of Life, a Certain Type of Blood-Filled Creature Who Will Someday Day," *Earth*, no. 2, 1966. "Artaud Anthology," *L.A. Free Press*, April 22, 1966. "An Old Drunk Who Ran Out of Luck," *Open City*, vol. 2, no. 1, 5–11, May 1967. "Notes of a Dirty Old Man," *Open City*, vol. 2, no. 2, May 12–18 1967. Untitled Essay in *A Tribute to Jim Lowell*, ed. T. L. Kryss, Cleveland: Ghost Press, 1967. "Notes of a Dirty Old Man," May 15, 1968, *National Underground Review*. "Should We Burn Uncle Sam's Ass?" *Notes from Underground*, no. 3, 1970. "The Silver Christ of Santa Fe," *Nola Express*, no. 75, 1971. "Dirty Old Man Confesses," *Adam*, vol. 15, no. 9, October 1971. "Reading and Breeding for Kenneth," *Adam Bedside Reader*, no. 49, vol. 1, February 1972. "Notes of a Dirty Old Man" [MS title: "The L.A. Scene"], *L.A. Free Press*, May 19, 1972. "Notes on the Life of an Aged Poet," *San Francisco Book Review*, vol. 22, June 1972. "Upon the Mathematics of the Breath and the Way," *Small Press Review*, vol. 4, no. 4, 1973. "Notes of a Dirty Old Man," *L.A. Free Press*, December 28, 1973. "Notes of a Dirty Old Man," *L.A. Free Press*, Feb. 22, 1974. "Notes of a Dirty Old Man," *L.A. Free Press*, March 1, 1974. "Notes of a Dirty Old Man," *L.A. Free Press*, March 22, 1974. "Jaggernaut: Wild Horse on a Plastic Phallus," *Creem*, vol 7, no. 5, October 1975. "Picking the Horses: How to Win at the Track, or at Least Break Even," *L.A. Free Press*, May 9–15, 1975. "Workout," *Hustler*, July 1977, reprinted courtesy of *Hustler* Magazine. "The Way It Happened," *High Times*, October 1983, reprinted courtesy of *High Times*. "Just Passing Time," *High Times*, March 1984, reprinted courtesy of *High Times*. "Distractions of the Literary Life," *High Times*, June 1984, reprinted courtesy of *High Times*. "I Meet the Master," Parts One and Two, *Oui*, December 1984/January 1985. "Looking Back at a Big One," *What Thou Lovest Well Remains: 100 Years of Ezra Pound*, ed. Richard Ardinger, Boise, ID: Limberlost Press, 1986. "Charles Bukowski's Li Po," June 1986, *California Magazine*. "Another Portfolio," *Portfolio* 1990, appears courtesy of David Bridson and David Andreone, *Portfolio* Magazine. "The Other," *Arete*, vol. 2, issue 5, 1990 appears courtesy of David Bridson and David Andreone, *Arete* Magazine. "Basic Training," *Portfolio*, January 1991, appears courtesy of David Bridson and David Andreone, *Portfolio* Magazine.

Charles Bukowski was born in Andernach, Germany in 1920 and brought to California at age three. Although Bukowski spent two years at Los Angeles City College, he was largely self-educated as a writer. He spent much time in his youth in the Los Angeles Public Library, where he encountered some of the writers whose work would influence his own: Dostoevsky, Turgenev, Nietzsche, D. H. Lawrence, Céline, e.e. cummings, Pound, Fante, and Saroyan. He was a prolific poet and prose writer, publishing more than fifty volumes. City Lights has published several Bukowski titles including *Tales of Ordinary Madness*, *Notes of a Dirty Old Man*, and *The Most Beautiful Woman in Town*. Charles Bukowski died in San Pedro, California on March 9, 1994.

David Stephen Calonne is the author of *William Saroyan: My Real Work Is Being*, *The Colossus of Armenia: G. I. Gurdjieff and Henry Miller*, and *Charles Bukowski: Sunlight Here I Am/Interviews & Encounters 1963–1993*. He has lectured in Paris and at many universities including UCLA, the University of Chicago, the University of Pennsylvania, Columbia University, UC Berkeley, the European University Institute in Florence, the University of London, Harvard, and Oxford. He has taught at the University of Texas at Austin, the University of Michigan, and presently teaches at Eastern Michigan University.

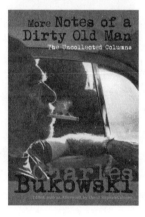
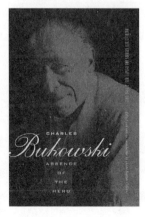